ON
THE EDGE
OF THE SEA

ON
THE EDGE
OF THE SEA

F · L · GREEN

READERS UNION / MICHAEL JOSEPH

This volume is produced in 1946 in complete conformity with the authorized economy standards. First published in 1944 by Michael Joseph Ltd., it has been set in 9 on 10 point Times New Roman and reprinted at the Peach Hall Works, Tonbridge, by Tonbridge Printers Ltd. It is one of the books produced for sale to its members only by Readers Union Ltd. of 38 William IV Street, London, and of Letchworth, Hertfordshire. Particulars of Readers Union are obtainable from either of these addresses

Part One

Because his temperament was nervous and impatient, and also because the weather was so abnormally hot that he had been unable to sleep last night, Foss had been irritable all day. The other partners in the firm of Foss, Brighart and Molloy, Export Agents, were on holiday; consequently, the entire responsibility of management fell upon him moment by moment with increasing pressure. He sustained it at first from habit, and later by a conscious effort which sapped his nervous energy and tired his mind. He lost his patience, which was always thin. Then the whole of his raw, anxious sensibility was exposed.

Upon it, the heat poured implacably. He could not remember a time when the weather had been so relentlessly warm. Yesterday, after the usual summer alternations of rain, sunlight, cloud and temperate breezes, the sky had opened wide from horizon to horizon. The breeze had subsided. The motionless air became full of the sounds of summer: the hum of insects; the languid impact of echo upon echo from the city's traffic; the throb of some indescribable pulse which the heat created in the earth. In the city, the pavements and roadways and the great walls of the buildings absorbed the heat and diffused it in a quivering haze.

Foss panted in his room. The air was sultry. He bore it until his nerves revolted. Then ringing for his assistant, he got up from the desk and padded into the corridor. He was a small, plump figure without a jacket and with his shirt-sleeves rolled back to his elbows.

" Kelpey! Kelpey! "

A slim, handsome youth of twenty-five, fair and pleasantly self-confident, appeared from an adjoining room.

" Yes, sir ? "

" The windows . . . the fans . . ."

Foss gesticulated and frowned. " Just see about them," he added.

" I have, sir! All of them," Kelpey said. " I went over the whole building an hour ago. All the windows are wide open. . . ."

" But the place is awful," Foss murmured, hurrying off along the corridor. " No air. . . ."

5

" It's the same everywhere in the city, sir."

Foss sped about the passages. Typewriters were crackling like the sound of little drums. Listless glances met his hot, stiff gaze as he stood at the doors of rooms and pointed to the windows.

" Keep them wide open! "

On the ground floor, he and Kelpey found a sere, elderly employee engrossed in stock sheets in a room whose windows were shut and whose canvas blinds were drawn.

" The windows! " Foss exclaimed, turning to Kelpey. " Didn't you tell me . . ."

" Yes, Mr. Foss. But Horsby says . . ."

Horsby explained : " When I was out East, sir, we used to close the shutters, and in that way . . ."

" This isn't the East! This is England! Open. . . ."

" . . . kept out the heat, sir! I assure you."

" I want air, a draught! " Foss shouted, waving an arm.

He sped out. " I thought you told me . . ." he grumbled to Kelpey. " You see, I have to do everything myself! I can't even trust you to see to a little thing like that! "

At that instant, he saw such a look of genuine distress and anxiety on Kelpey's face that he felt as though he had discovered him in a shameful misdemeanour. He trusted Kelpey. He liked him because of the merits of his ingenuous character and his unspoiled nature. He had advanced him because he wanted to train him for an important executive position. He admitted him to his confidence. But there was one important secret which he had not confided to him because he dared not commit it to this young, inexperienced mind. He had divulged it only to his partners. And because they were on holidays, he felt its weight upon him, and knew that his nervous temperament was almost overborne by it and thrust into these fits of irritability.

" All right, Kelpey," he said, kindly. " I'm not complaining about your work. I'm only saying . . ."

He broke off and added quickly : " We're not accustomed to this sort of weather. We haven't the devices to counteract it. Fans, and proper sunblinds, and the sort of food and drink. . . ."

He panted loudly. He stood at the top of the stairs where on most days draughts blew whenever the heavy street doors were opened, but where on this torrid afternoon thick surges of heat poured around his body. Crossing to the open window, he tried to breathe the dry air which the fans agitated. He tried to convince himself that a cool merciful gust was beginning.

Going along the corridor, he saw the empty rooms of his partners.

" They're very lucky," he murmured, pausing at the doors and remembering that Brighart and Molloy were in Norway.

He saw the sombre fiords below hundreds of feet of forest slopes, and the dark, placid waters in whose depths those slopes were mirrored.

" . . . wearing our overcoats yesterday! " Brighart had written to him.

He moved on quickly and halted at the foot of a narrow, bare flight of stairs. The attics above them were rented by a man of sombre repute named Collis, who called himself an accountant and earned a good livelihood by writing up tradesmen's books and preparing their accounts.

" And up here ? "

The question seemed to throw Kelpey into confusion. He stammered. His glance slid away from Foss like a guilty thing.

" Collis's place . . ." he said.

" It smells hot," Foss said. " Why isn't it ventilated ? Run up and tell him I should like it if he would . . ."

" He's out, sir. The doors are shut."

" Well, open them! That's where the heat boils. No wonder we're so warm down here! "

" The roof windows are open, Mr. Foss. You can see . . ."

" I do wish," Foss snapped, " I do wish you wouldn't be so obtuse, Kelpey! I say that if the doors were open . . ."

" But he has to lock the doors when he goes out, sir! "

" Oh, very well, very well! But tell him when he returns."

Foss passed on to the big window overlooking the city. He could see an extensive tide of roofs stretching far away to the east where it was merged in the heat haze, with steeples and towers and proud giants of buildings riding above the tremulous expanse. Doming all was a naked sky in which the blue was drained by the stiff white light of the sun. The whole scene was submitted to the enormous pressure of the heat. The heat penetrated to the shadiest streets, invaded the parks and gardens and glared in blinding reflections from the glass roofs and the fountains, as well as from the walls and pavements. It burned into the stones and held them in a rigid, sultry grip. It possessed the air and muffled the roar of the traffic. Along the River, it lay over the waters and levelled the surface into a glutinous mass upon which the tiny corrugations made by the ascent or descent of the gulls was quickly erased. It robbed the wharves of their lusty echoes and sat in a vast shimmering veil over the hot decks of the vessels moored alongside the quays. Triumphant, it was upon the loftiest tower and the meanest cobblestone, encompassing all things, invading shop, office, warehouse, factory, restaurant, hotel, bar, subtracting energy and leaving only inertia. Last night, it had robbed thousands of their sleep. To-day, it stole into the mind and retarded the will. It was everywhere, unquenchable, invincible.

Foss returned to his room and flopped down in his chair.

" Shall I send out for anything for you ? " Kelpey said.

The fan stirred the air and lightly lifted the ends of his silk tie. Foss shook his head and smiled ruefully.

" No . . . no, thanks."

He glanced at his wristwatch ; and Kelpey, who knew what he was going to say next, felt a hot, hard little thread of terror stream through his body.

" Well, now . . . this Herr Rennenberg," Foss said, turning over the papers on his desk.

" I shall want all the Berlin accounts. Tell . . ."

" I've got them ready for you, sir."

" Good! Let me have them at once."

Kelpey went to bring them.

" Oh, and look! "

Coming back, Kelpey waited.

" And all the correspondence as well."

" Yes, sir."

Kelpey turned to go.

" Oh, and . . . and . . . Kelpey, I wish you wouldn't keep running away! What's the matter with you ? Can't you stand still ? I'm speaking to you! "

" I'm sorry, sir."

" Bring me . . . what was it ? I can't remember. You keep interrupting me. However . . . the accounts—the Berlin agency accounts, and all the correspondence. That's all."

When Kelpey was gone, Foss rested his hands on the warm edge of the desk and sat back against the upholstery of the chair. He tried to compose his thoughts about the subject which Herr Rennenberg was sure to discuss with him. He had waited several days for this important visitor. Waiting was the worst feature of the whole affair. It fretted his nerves. It bared his tense, nervous sensibilities, and thereby gave his conscience an opportunity to upbraid him. He sat at his desk and braced his shoulders as though by giving his body a semblance of composure he might attain mental ease as well.

But because he had never before met Herr Rennenberg who had been admitted to Von Pless's confidence rather late in the plot, and also because he believed that Rennenberg was coming to give him some final instructions prior to the closure of all discussion and the beginning of action, he was reduced to abject anxiety. He discovered what fear was, and how profoundly it bored into the mind and subjugated the body.

He was trembling, and his pulse was increasing at such a rate that his throat was constricted by the swollen arteries of his neck.

" I'll be all right. . . . I shall feel better when he arrives," he thought.

It was a few minutes before four of the twenty-first of June. An important date which he had anticipated for many weeks. He drew letters and accounts towards him when the messenger brought them from Kelpey. He tried to concentrate his mind upon them. His thoughts began to break free and plunge fearfully to and fro about another subject. He kept glancing at his wristwatch.

Six minutes to four.

He anticipated the end of all the preliminary arrangements. Rennenberg would certainly inform him that all was settled : the lodgings for Jey reserved ; the route of the procession confirmed ; the names of confederates who would meet Jey with a prearranged signal which he would answer with another sign ; the plan of the house in which Jey was to lodge and from which he was to fire the shot. And thus the beginning of action after months of careful plotting.

" I'll feel better when he comes," Foss thought.

Again, he examined his watch.

" Everything is ready. Jey is waiting for the signal from me."

★

II

★

But his conscience clamoured at him, insisting that he was planning murder. No matter how he vindicated the purpose of the plot, it persisted in presenting itself to him in stark terms. Murder. The taking of human life. Assassination. That, and nothing more. He extinguished the idea, but it flared again in another direction. It had sidled towards him when he had sat talking with honest people. It encompassed his life and horrified him. Why had he listened to Von Pless ? Why had he agreed to participate ? Why had he agreed to accept that enormous fee ? And why had he contacted George Jey, when all the time his conscience declared that no matter how far he himself would stand from Jey when the shot was fired, he would be as much an assassin as Jey ?

But he was deeply and irretrievably involved, not so much in the physical sense as in all the mental processes which had conceived and propelled the project across life. He had encouraged it. Why ? Because of an inherent weakness in his character which had yielded to all Von Pless's persuasions ?

He remembered the day in February when his Berlin sub-agent—the sedate, reputable Kuno Von Pless—had taken him to an inner room of his suite. Four other men were there. Two were seated. The others awaited him with folded arms as they stood leaning against the big table. Von Pless introduced them to him, whereupon all four regarded him intently and gathered about him at the table as though he had some kind of gift for them, or salvation to offer them, or a secret to divulge to them.

He was flattered by their attention. What was the meeting for ? Why did these four strangers show such interest in him ? Even while Von Pless was speaking to him, their eyes clung to him.

" These are four of my comrades," Von Pless said.

" Comrades ? " thought Foss.

The word had a military flavour which he found vaguely distasteful because it implied the Nazi creed.

" The five of us are the leaders. Associated with us, there are seventy-five others. Men and women," Von Pless continued.

" Something to do with National Socialism," Foss thought. " Some association formed to put over some kind of propaganda."

" And," added Von Pless, lowering his voice to a whisper, " we are opposed to the National Socialist State."

Foss knew then that he was on the fringe of a conspiracy. He was startled. His sense of personal danger discomfited him. His horror of danger compelled him to remain silent. But silence almost suffocated him when he thought of this small, secret group amidst the noise and pomp and power of the Nazi State.

" You are risking your lives ! " he exclaimed.

At once, all five began to pour out explanations. He heard hatred, rancour, loathing and distress in their words.

" They're under a steel heel," he thought. " They want to destroy the cruelty and the terror. They want to be free."

They went into long accounts of recent history. He had only a sketchy idea of what had happened inside Germany prior to the advent of the Nazis. Names : Hindenburg, the Weimar National Assembly, the Junkers, the figures of the Nazi Party. But with the rise of the Nazis, he had read much of current affairs in Germany. He read of how the Nazis had taken and consolidated their power, and of how they had extinguished opposition.

Yet here, in the living bodies of these men, was Opposition ! It frightened him, for the five voices became more expressive of the ideas which, if overheard or suspected, would be punished with death or imprisonment in the dreaded camps of concentration.

" Yes, it's hard for you, here, in Germany. Very hard," he murmured ; and he hoped that they would all become quiet and bring the conversation to an end rapidly so that he could depart. But they began to gesticulate. He read frustration and anger in their eyes. Words tumbled swiftly from their lips. They all spoke at the same time, adding their remarks to one another, urging the conversation forward.

He knew that they were trying to convince him of the horror and despair of their lives.

" Can you conceive the kind of life we live here ? " Von Pless said. " Don't you realize the way things are going ? "

He wanted to say yes, yes, he understood, but they interrupted him with lengthy accounts of the crimes and misdeeds of the Nazi Party.

" . . . and it will mean war, a ghastly war! " Von Pless declared at last.

" Deplorable! " Foss said.

" We have no desire to fight anyone," Von Pless continued. " There are thousands of us, and we do not feel the desire to go to war. We desire peace. We have vowed to one another to do all we can to avert warfare."

" Yes, of course," Foss said. , " Naturally——"

He supposed that they were trying to convince him of the truth regarding the attitude of German men and women to Britain.

" You could help us," Von Pless said, resting a hand on his arm.

The others were silent. They sat watching Foss as though the question of war or no war depended upon him.

" I can assure you," he said, " My friends and neighbours at home have no feeling of enmity to——"

One of the men nudged Von Pless and said : " Tell him."

Foss waited nervously for what was coming. He became afraid again. He saw Von Pless point to the wall where a portrait of Hitler hung above a vase of dead flowers.

" We are determined to kill him,". he whispered ; and he was no longer the sedate gentleman but a trembling vessel of fury and determination. The others implemented that simple statement with expressions which cracked across Foss's sense of hearing and bewildered him.

" Yes, but, please . . . what has . . . what has it all to do with me ? " he exclaimed.

" Help us! " Von Pless said. " You could, if you wished."

Foss got up from the table. He wanted to say no, no, I don't want to become involved in this affair ; but he found himself making instead a ridiculous little speech.

" I should prefer not to participate in anything of such a nature. Not that I condemn you for your desire to rid yourselves of a man whose actions are, to say the least of them, highly . . . highly . . . But don't think, please, that I misjudge you. You have my sympathy. The fact remains, however, that I could not permit myself to meddle in such affairs. And after all, there is no gainsaying the fact that it is murder."

Von Pless smiled the whole time.

" So much for the ethics of it, eh, Mr. Foss ? Now let us discuss business, shall we ? "

Foss shook his head. " If you don't mind . . ."

" We are organized, Mr. Foss. We have funds . . ."

" As I said before . . ."

" We are prepared to pay most generously for services. We ask you to help us."

" But look here! What could I possibly do? I live in England. . . ."

" So much the better! "

" But I'm a British subject. And I'm a partner in a large firm, and I assure you that never in my life have I thought of becoming a confederate in a plot to assassinate anyone! "

" All we want you to do is to find a man for us."

" A man to . . . you mean a man to . . ." he said to Von Pless.

Von Pless nodded slowly. One of the men said in a plaintive whisper : " We are watched all the time here. What can we do ? "

" And for your services, and his," said Von Pless, " we are willing to offer a fee of fifteen thousand pounds."

Foss repeated softly : " Fifteen thousand . . ."

Then his thoughts poured out over territories into which they had never previously wandered. He heard Von Pless and the others urging him, enticing him ; and although he continued to erect little barriers of refusal which the Germans negotiated as easily and as rapidly as he fashioned them, he knew that he was committed to a part in this plot. And from that fact his imagination took flight so that he found the man Von Pless required. And into that man's hand plans were put, and into his ears words were whispered. Vows were made. Rewards were determined. Then after this swift, imaginative flight a single condition gave reality to all the conversation. Fifteen thousand pounds.

Foss sat down again. " What must he do ? " he asked.

" Fire a shot," one of the men said.

" But before that ? "

Von Pless whispered : " He must come to Germany by a certain date. He must go to a certain city, to a house where he will be lodged. A Party Conference is due to take place at a certain date in that city, along a certain route. He will be given a plan of the house, so that he will be able to make his own arrangements. But he must fire the shot."

" I really don't know," Foss murmured. " It's all so . . . really so . . ."

" Listen," Von Pless continued. " There is a Jewish merchant in Prague—a dealer in china and glass. He has been ordered to dispose of his business to an Aryan. I have been approached in the matter, but I am holding off for a while. We could say that you were interested in the purchase of his stock, amounting in your currency to almost a quarter of a million pounds. Your commission on the sale of this

12

stock to a suitable purchaser would be fifteen thousand pounds. And your agent will be coming to Germany later in the year to examine this stock, and so on and so forth, eh ? "

Foss made some criticism. " But I don't import! My partners and I are purely in the export . . ."

" On the side," Von Pless said.

" It's really . . . really . . . I don't know."

" And on the day when your man arrives and takes lodgings in the house, a bank in Geneva will make the agreed transfer to your bankers in London."

They anticipated all his criticisms and even his thoughts. They brushed paths for his thoughts to travel unimpeded. In that secluded room, shuttered and barred, with the five figures in such proximity to him, he was deluged by the idea of the plot. Their plans were sound and feasible. And he saw determination in their eyes and heard it in their words and recognized it in their attitudes. The stuffy atmosphere of the room held it, and he breathed it.

" I should like time in which to think it over," he said.

He rose and stood with his hands joined. " I really don't know . . . even if I found someone—and I couldn't be sure—I don't really know . . ."

" We have trusted you, Mr. Foss," Von Pless said. " We have explained the outline of our plans."

" Yes, oh, yes, they seem quite . . . quite applicable. What I'm worried about is . . . I mean, the possible discovery of this . . . project."

Von Pless tapped his own skull. " It is here. It is concealed here," he whispered.

Foss said : " Well, let us leave it like this ; let me consider it. Then later on, soon, I'll let you know."

He had a violent headache and a sickness in his stomach. He shook hands with the men and went to the door with Von Pless.

" My dear Foss, we beg your aid," Von Pless whispered.

Foss went out into the cold evening along Kurfürstendamm. The lights and the traffic and the crowds of pedestrians bewildered him. Here was the hard, active world of the Nazis. Here was audible incessantly the name of the man against whom the plot was directed. Foss remembered great snatches of the conversation in the room, as well as the urgent faces and words and the air of positive resolve of those five conspirators. To assassinate . . .

His mind reeled. His glance fell before the high, proud gaze of young Guards, stout Storm Troopers, and ordinary pedestrians. The knowledge which was concealed in his mind would surely communicate itself to them, striking merely by its significance some receptive sense in them. Death to their idol! Death to one to whom the great ones

13

of the earth were still bowing! While he, Foss, an export agent, had listened, had promised to consider, had heard details. . . .

What he had been told was rendered terrible and fantastic by the impact which the great city around him made upon it. It was so secret a fact as yet, like a seed struggling against the resistant soil which so much power and allegiance to authority had made about it.

Foss entered a chemist's shop and bought some tablets to cure his headache and sickness. He returned to his hotel and rested on his bed. He could think of nothing but what Von Pless and the others had told him. It gave him a heavy sense of guilt and foreboding, and when later he went down to dinner he felt that his knowledge was written all over him.

His appetite was poor. He tasted a little of the courses and drank much wine. That night, his headache became worse, and his gastritis threatened him with a bad attack which would prevent him from travelling home for a few days. Next morning, he got up and went to see Von Pless about the agency affairs.

Neither of them mentioned the previous day's meeting. But at parting Von Pless whispered : " We hope," and he looked significantly at him with his large eyes.

Foss said in the same tone : " I won't promise. I shall see what can be done, and I'll let you know on my next visit."

As soon as he arrived in England, he felt better. His appetite returned. His headaches ceased. His gastritis was cured by the comforting, familiar scene. He hastened to his partners. They were in Brighart's room when he entered and closed the door quickly behind him and went towards them with a solemn air.

" Hullo, Foss! Had a good trip ? "

Molloy, who said that, was a dark, impulsive man, forthright and assured.

Foss sat down slowly and put his hands on his knees.

" What's wrong ? " Brighart said.

Brighart was tall and fair and taciturn. A solid man of forty-eight. Foss glanced up at him and then at Molloy and did not know how to disclose his secret to them.

" I heard a most extraordinary piece of information," he began.

His partners were waiting. Their eyes encouraged him.

" Von Pless and some of his friends are the leaders of a plot to assassinate Hitler," he said.

Brighart was silent. Molloy burst out laughing.

" What ? To——"

Foss made an abrupt sign with his hand.

" Sh! "

There was silence in the room except for the sounds which penetrated

14

from outside. A bell rang in one of the offices. A door slammed. A voice shouted incoherently.

Foss continued : " The day after I arrived, Von Pless took me to a little room in his suite of offices. There were four other men there, and they led up to the subject quite quickly and asked me to help them."

" And what did you say ? " Molloy exclaimed.

" Well, what could I say ? No, of course. But . . ."

" Quite right," Brighart said.

" But Von Pless was so insistent, and he told me their preliminary plans. He wants me to find somebody on this side who'll . . ."

" You couldn't possibly take a hand in it," Brighart said.

Molloy said : " Go on, Foss."

" He asked me to find somebody who'll go over to a certain city during a Nazi Party Conference. He told me what course the man would have to take once he arrived in Germany. It was all quite cut and dried. And he explained how I could help him in this matter by pretending that I was arranging to import some china and glass—the whole stock-in-trade of a Jewish merchant in Prague. . . ."

" Wait a bit," Brighart interrupted. " Explain that, will you ? "

" And you said ? " Molloy asked.

Foss explained the method whereby the man from England would enter the plot under the guise of an agent in trade going to Germany to inspect china and glass.

" And on the day he arrives in Germany, a sum of fifteen thousand pounds will be transferred from a bank in Geneva to our bankers."

Brighart and Molloy glanced at each other. Their eyes were full of thought and surprise.

" And what did you say when Von Pless said that ? " Molloy asked.

" We must have been in that room for two hours. I had an awful headache, and I felt quite sick. It frightened me to hear what they said, because in Germany even a breath of criticism is sufficient to get you into trouble, let alone a fully fledged plot of this kind. . . ."

" Did you agree to help them ? " Brighart said.

" I said I would consider it all before saying yes or no."

Brighart shook his head and frowned.

" Very dangerous. We have to think of our German connections. If Von Pless were arrested, where would we be ? "

" Of course, I didn't commit myself."

" No. But the Gestapo in Germany is pretty thorough. I should say it knows everything. I'm willing to bet that it suspects Von Pless already."

" But Brig ! I didn't commit myself ! "

Molloy walked to the window.

" Fifteen thousand ! " he said.

Turning towards Foss, he said : " Did you think of anybody who'd be likely to undertake a job of that sort ? "

Foss rubbed his hands together slowly and said : " I thought of George Jey."

Molloy smiled. " Oh, Jey! Yes, he's a likely one."

Brighart nodded. " Possibly."

" I thought he'd agree to undertake the job for say three or four thousand," Foss said.

Brighart stirred angrily. Frowning, he said : " But think of it! It's dirty! It isn't the sort of thing we care to be mixed up in, surely! Oh, it's . . ."

" Von Pless said that he and his friends want to avert a war," Foss said quickly.

Brighart laughed crisply. " You know very well that you aren't an altruist, Foss! "

" A war," said Molloy, " would close the whole of our Continental connection in five minutes. It would almost finish us. Von Pless knows that."

" That's why I said I would consider their proposal," Foss said.

" For fifteen thousand pounds," Brighart retorted.

He glared angrily at Foss and lit a cigarette.

" The whole thing is fantastic. It will end in exposure and disgrace for us." He was emphatic. " I grant that a war is inevitable. But if we are found to be implicated in this plot, our name will be under a cloud with our own Government for the rest of our lives. I don't like it at all."

" Then you think . . ." Foss began.

Molloy interjected : " Our name need not be in it at all."

Brighart smiled sardonically. " These plots give out something intangible but obvious. Men are seen coming and going to a certain house. It's all obvious to people like Gestapo agents. And our own agents over there are just as quick to scent things like that. And another thing : if Jey fired that shot, he'd be shot to pieces by guards or else tortured until he confessed everything. Think of the row in Berlin and London! We'd bring the world about our ears in no time! It happened before, in 1914. They shot an Archduke or somebody, and the war broke out a month or two later. It would precipitate a war, and not avert it! "

" This would be different," Molloy said.

" Well, if you think like that about it," Foss said to Brighart, " I'll tell Von Pless. I'll say no."

" Fifteen thousand," Molloy murmured.

There was silence. Brighart flicked the ash from his cigarette and dusted his knee. Molloy looked out of the window. Presently, Foss said : " I'd take the utmost care to keep our name out of it."

16

Brighart retorted : "It's your business. I take no part in it. Go ahead, since you seem so set upon it."

"But I haven't said yes or no yet!" Foss protested.

Brighart smiled. "You are in it already, old man."

"You think, then . . ." Foss began.

"I've told you what I think," Brighart said, rising. "I have an appointment," he added. "I must go."

When he was gone, Foss said to Molloy : "What would you do, if you were me ?"

"You don't want me to tell you!" Molloy said, laughing.

He came and stood over Foss and went on : "You know damn well you've made up your mind already."

Foss was silent. He realized that he was committed to the plot. It was rooted in his mind and he could not eject it.

"Yes, I suppose so," he said, pensively.

"Then you had better be very careful. Look out for yourself when you see Von Pless again, and be careful what you say to Jey, when you see him."

Foss felt afraid. When Molloy spoke like that, he felt as though curious forces had compelled him against his better judgment to take a share in the plot. He got up and went back to his room. His conscience gibbered at him. Murder! Assassination! International crisis! Disgrace! Ruin! Fifteen thousand pounds! Blood money!

Behind the phrases others sounded, and he had an ear for them because from early manhood his spirit had been attentive to such enticements.

"Fifteen thousand pounds to be transferred to your credit. . . ."

His hands twined together. They were like his thoughts that were entangled hopelessly around a hard little core which reason and morality could not melt. Fifteen thousand pounds.

He went home and pondered the whole episode at ease without reaching the kind of resolve or conclusion which he desired. He knew that he was an accomplice already and that soon he would look for Jey. And in his uneasy spirit he was not satisfied with his position. Nor was there any solace for him in the contemplation of the refusal of that large reward.

The subject slept beside him in his bed and sat beside him at meals. It was an invisible presence, and he was afraid that his young wife, Tilly, would detect it.

"Roland, dear, what's the matter with you ?" she said. "You don't sleep well, and your appetite is feeble. Is it your tummy again?"

He was sick for a week.

"I'll have to go to Paris soon," he told her one day. He seemed forlorn and anxious. "Business is difficult," he said, making a grimace of dejection.

He said Paris, but that was a lie. He was going to Berlin. When-ever he thought of it, his mind expanded with horrible visions ; and he almost decided to renounce the trip. Nevertheless, he went. He travelled by 'plane.

Throughout the journey, his active imagination made dreadful visions which affrighted him so that he could not eat or sleep. In Berlin, he met Von Pless again as well as several people who were important in the plot ; and he made plans with them and said yes to everything ; yes, yes, he could find someone to climb to the summit, alone, an intrepid man who would go step by step to that solitude while they watched him ; yes, he would find the man who would aim a revolver at a certain figure in a car and squeeze the trigger and not miss the target. He said that, then he returned to his hotel near the Central Station and tried to compose his mind by sleeping for an hour. It was impossible. His mind pulsated incessantly under a single fact which recurred with an increasing pressure. He got up and dressed and went and bought some soda mints from a chemist. He kept telling himself that he was in Berlin to meet his agent, Herr Kuno Von Pless, who represented several agencies for the firm of Foss, Brighart and Molloy. He walked along the bright avenues and told himself that he and Von Pless had examined several agency accounts and had arranged a new account for cotton goods. So far, his visit was obvious only as one connected with commerce between England and Germany, yet no matter how he reminded himself of the fact that he was a director of a reputable firm of agents, he could not clothe his conscience in innocence.

He dreaded the State police, believing all the stories which he had heard and read of them. He feared arrest, exposure, the failure of his business, poverty, the loss of Tilly's love under the circumstances of that poverty. His mind was brimming with fear. Yet he went forward. He swallowed soda mints to cure his indigestion. He drank fruit salts, and dabbed his throbbing forehead with frozen eau-de-Cologne. At last, he returned to England by 'plane.

" Did you have a nice time, darling ? " Tilly said. " You didn't write! You didn't 'phone, either! Where did you stay ? "

" Oh, I stayed at . . ."

He was about to confess that he had gone to Berlin. Better not. Better say that he had gone to Paris.

" . . . to a place where I got this," he said.

He took from his suitcase the present which he had bought her. A platinum ring with diamonds. A little trumpery which kept her amused until she forgot that he had gone away for five days without writing to her the whole time.

He was enticed forward by the thought of the fifteen thousand pounds. It seemed to him to be so easy to gain that reward. After all, what had he to do ? Only to find Jey and win him to the idea, and then instruct him and notify Von Pless ; and, when everything was agreed upon, coach Jey in the details of the alibi. But his conscience would not rest. It spoke to him of murder, of the horror of assassination. It swept aside all the details of the plot and lifted a terrible curtain which revealed all the consequences. Then he saw the whole machinery of crisis, and felt its ponderous rhythms in him. Telegrams. Headlines. Consternation in the Embassies. Summoning of parliaments. Ultimatums. And war.

His body trembled. His heart pounded, and merely to allay his fears he went to Brighart's office where Molloy joined them in discussion.

" I told you," Brighart said, " it's a dirty business."

" Might avert a war," Molloy said.

" It's more likely to start one! " retorted Brighart.

Molloy said : " Well, I don't know so much. I've thought about it, and I believe that if that man were removed the whole structure of Nazi Germany would come crashing down. . . ."

Brighart looked at him and laughed. " I thought you had more sense! " he interjected.

" Isn't the whole edifice built around him ? " Molloy asked, angrily. " Isn't he the absolute head ? "

" Nonsense! Nonsense! " Brighart declared. " That's a stunt! A piece of showmanship. He is the head of the Nazi Party. But there is the German military set, and the German industrial set. If his plans didn't coincide with theirs, he wouldn't have power for a day longer! And you can be sure that whatever he has done so far has met with their approval. And his plans for the future are probably made already and already approved by the German Military High Command. If he went, somebody would take his place and the plans would still go through."

" I don't believe it," Molloy said. " Look! One man. One damned torturer who has killed thousands, and who'll kill millions more before he is finished. Everybody knows . . . everybody all over the world knows that there is going to be war because he wants a war and because his Party wants a war. How many people will that war kill and ruin ? How much trade will go down the sink ? If somebody has the courage to kill him, it will deter Germany from war. The German people will not be ready to give allegiance to another leader. They'll begin to revolt against oppression. And the German army and the industrialists won't feel ready to trust themselves to a fight, as long as their home front is unstable. I say the plot is worth trusting. I believe it is a good thing. Now I must go. I'll be back in an hour."

The door slammed behind him.

" He doesn't understand," Brighart said.

" In a way, I believe he's right," Foss said.

He wanted the money. although he would not confess that much. Everything of the project began for him from the fact that he had been offered that substantial reward. But he wanted to be sure that the rest was feasible, was good, would not torture his conscience if Jey were successful.

Brighart said : " Their State police are clever. They're ubiquitous, Foss. They know everything."

" Tell me frankly, Brig," Foss said. " Am I wise to go into this affair ? I mean, even if the whole matter is likely to succeed. . . ."

" It won't succeed."

" Never mind that. I want your opinion about . . ."

" I've told you already."

" No, but looking at it from other points of view . . ."

" There is only one way to look at it," Brighart said.

He was a substantial, suave personality. Upon every circumstance of his existence he turned the same bland stare : upon love, hatred, ambition, hope. As though he had no particular heat for anything, but wanted only the just proportion of all things in their place.

Foss walked about the room with his gaze downcast.

" Yes. . . . I suppose so."

" You ought to know what to do," Brighart said. Then he added : " It's the cash you are thinking about, isn't it ? "

Foss stopped at the window and was silent.

" In the way of legitimate business, I'd encourage you," Brighart remarked. " But it's nothing to do with commerce at all. It's your personal affair. I can't tell you what to do. You must decide for yourself."

" It would make history! " Foss said.

Brighart smiled. " You let your imagination run too freely! "

Foss returned to his own room. All his hours were impressed by the thoughts which flowed in his mind. All his sleep was influenced by peculiar dreams. Sometimes, he was depressed ; sometimes he was happy. The year emerged from winter into spring, and spring bloomed and blossomed into summer. In June, his partners went for holidays. And Von Pless wrote from Berlin to say that he was sending a new senior assistant—Herr Kurt Rennenberg—to discuss urgent details of the agency accounts.

By then, Foss had found George Jey and had made a proposal to him which Jey had accepted. After that, Foss informed him of many important details. Now Jey was waiting in the city for the word " go." Everything was ready. The springs were wound tautly. Fear had been overcome. But suddenly there was this new personality. Herr Kurt Rennenberg. A change of plan ? Evidence of hesitation on the part of Von Pless and his friends ? Indication of a setback, a fracture through which light would gleam to a world of watchful eyes ? The first signs of imminent disaster ?

Foss became nervous. His gastritis afflicted him. On the nineteenth of June he stayed at home in bed.

★

III

★

A message scrawled on a piece of paper by the Commissionaire was left on Miss Dewlash's desk that morning.

June 19th, 1939.

For Mr. Foss's Secretary

> *Mr. Foss telephones to say he is indisposed. Please send out by messenger all urgent correspondence.*
>
> K. Smith

Four members of staff who had arrived early and gone to Dewlash's room saw that note and read it. They loitered in the room, and left it only to wander into other rooms where, instead of the usual brisk pace which the presence of Foss, Brighart and Molloy imposed on the staff, there was an easier atmosphere decided by individual temperaments. Thus, responsibility became a pleasant garment which could be worn to taste and not according to rules. Characteristic habits expressed themselves more freely. In a little while, it was evident to the least observant member of staff that Foss was away, for voices were raised in conversation and laughter, cigarettes and pipes were still alight, hats had not been removed, newspapers were spread wide open upon desks, the senior member of staff had retired to his room and was indulging in an access of authority, and discord rattled across the life of the firm like badly conducted music.

Then began the scramble for correspondence. Custom had decided that all letters should be opened and distributed by the senior assistants in the Secretary's office. The firm's cashier directed this work. But instead of sorting the letters for delivery to all the departments, he grouped them into five large baskets and sent them round for further distribution.

It was done to save time. Everybody understood that and appeared to approve it. Now, with the absence of Foss, the trifling, unrelenting jealousies between departments flared and became eloquent.

" My letters. . . ."

Jealousy, vanity, trivial notions of authority, were audible in those words. Heads of departments invaded other offices to collect at the source what they regarded as being their personal property. Hands snatched stacks of letters and turned them over. Eyes read what was

21

addressed to Foss, to Brighart, Molloy, Appleton the Secretary, other chiefs. Curiosity had an opportunity granted it which it could not renounce. And Kelpey, like the others who feared that a slender authority might be stolen, disregarded, insulted, was as impulsive as the rest.

A brimming basket of letters had been left on Dewlash's desk by a messenger. When Dewlash arrived promptly at nine, five colleagues were gathered around her desk. They were smoking pipes and cigarettes. Their hats were on her desk and her chair. One of the men gave her the note from the Commissionaire. She read it quickly, and without removing her hat and gloves, she went down to the Cashier's office.

" Mr. Long, shouldn't the whole of the mail be sorted by your staff ? " she began, after the usual greetings.

" In theory, yes," he said.

He was one of those amiable, humorous personalities whose temperaments conceal a considerable strength in the guise of wit and pleasantness. Forty, bald, very efficient, his invariable expression was one of lugubrious humour. It was almost impossible not to laugh at him.

" I hate to complain," Dewlash said. " But my room is like a bear garden. Couldn't you apply a little theory ? "

He smiled at her. " Everybody is so zealous," he said. " Everybody wants to begin work right away. They just can't wait."

" I wish you'd come up and drive them out of my room," she said.

" You do it," he said. " Take a stick to them. Use your personality. Tell them Appleton has arrived. Ring some bells and make 'em jump! "

He thrust a bundle of letters at her.

" For you."

She went back to her room. Only Kelpey remained there.

" I've sorted them," he said, indicating the neat piles of correspondence arranged along the desk.

She gave him a sharp, resentful glance and turned aside without a word to remove her hat and gloves.

Then her anger expressed itself. She came back quickly and ran a hot hand above the letters.

" These are mine," Kelpey said, taking up a little sheaf.

She took them from him with a quick, adroit movement, and rested her hands on them as she put them on the desk.

" You've been through everything! " she exclaimed. " You've turned everything over and done my work for me! You've interfered! "

They were two young, attractive people who, morning after morning, sat together at her desk and sorted the correspondence. What was his responsibility as Foss's assistant, and what was her province as Foss's secretary had never been precisely determined. There was a line of demarcation which existed only in the terms of good sense and understanding. And for two years, ever since Kelpey had first sat at the desk beside her, good sense, civility, duty, had been confused by an antagonism which had its source so deeply in their natures that neither of them understood it or could escape it. Sharp conflicts of a trivial kind grew between them for no sound reason. They flared into outbursts of curious spite which seemed inimical to his pleasant character and her grace and dignity. Both of them suffered hurt. They momentarily hated each other with an intensity which appalled them later and compelled them to seek each other and repair and renew a goodwill which was often difficult to sustain. This goodwill was something which each longed for after they had hurt each other ; yet when it was established again, neither of them was at ease in it. They feared it. They could not give it progress. They were afraid to submit themselves to it. They hesitated to trust themselves to each other. And all this had happened because they were two youthful people unable to appreciate that they loved each other and were unwilling to confess it either to themselves or to each other.

" You come in here," she exclaimed. " And you interfere . . ."

Anger possessed her body. She was trembling.

" I wish . . . oh, I wish you would keep out! "

It was the expression more of something intensely personal to her than of this trivial matter of correspondence.

He did not realize it at first. His own angry retort came quickly : " I have to come in here, haven't I ? I don't want to! I never wanted to! I hate sitting there. . ."

Everything yielded in him to this devouring anger. He faced her as furiously as she faced him. It was an ultimate emotion, and they expressed it candidly, speaking from the significant mood which each always struck from the other.

He had gone close to her in an involuntary movement. He did not realize how close was his proximity to her until she lifted a hand to shield herself from what she imagined would be a blow from his hand. Then her hand touched him, resting impulsively on his shoulder, perhaps to silence him, perhaps to appease him or to engage what was now so obvious in the sullen depths of his words.

He saw then what was expressed in her behaviour, and it appalled him. It was as if he had evoked this secret distress, this frank declaration from her. And it was the frankness of it, and the profundity of it which touched him. It was an emotion which could only have been expressed to himself, from faith in him, from understanding, with an appeal to him to release her from it. Suddenly, his hand caught hers, at first to wrench it away, but then to engage her, to appease her anger, to calm her distress.

It was the first physical contact between them. It was a fusion, the end of anger and havoc and frustration and reticence. It became quickly an instant of tenderness. And in that instant during which everything was declared at last by them, they began to retreat shyly.

He turned away. Lying on the top of one of the stacks of letters was one from Berlin. It was for Foss. It would go to the Translations Department and be returned to Dewlash who would pass it together with the translation to Foss. It was in German, and Kelpey was curious and jealous about it. He wanted to be the first to read it in translation, because for some months there had been much correspondence with Von Pless, and Foss had made several journeys to Berlin, and Kelpey's naturally inquisitive spirit sought to penetrate letters and journeys to discover something which, perhaps, Foss had not confided in him.

He snatched up this letter and left all the others.

" You can see them . . ." he murmured, hurrying out.

He went to his own room and closed the door and sat down at his desk. Folding the letter and pocketing it, he pondered what had happened. So close to her . . . more in an intimacy of emotion than physically. The release from a sense of conflict, and the exciting commencement of something tender, secret, which they shared in silence, which had as yet no words but which would bloom from words into actions, into all the conditions of love.

His thoughts were touched by a pervasive contentment ; but although he felt that he would be happier were he to keep silent to her, he felt a compelling desire to continue from this moment and to pursue her. And at the thought of all that lay before him, a sense of defeat began in him, telling him that he had lost something singular, necessary to his personal life. It was as if the conflict had been resolved and he had suffered a humiliating defeat. And to recover himself he must see her again, and then again, and again, and must seek her and merge her life with his.

He sat for a long time with his hands empty and resting on his desk.

He foresaw his future in this love which had opened in his life ; and it seemed to him that although it had taken only an instant of time in which to move from its cloudy shyness into fact, months, perhaps years, must elapse before that indefinable sense of defeat and anxiety were resolved.

IV

At last, he remembered the letter. He brought it from his pocket and examined it again. His knowledge of the German language was limited to a few facts of syntax and vocabulary which he remembered from a year's study of German when he had been a boy of fifteen. Only half a dozen words of the letter were intelligible to him. The rest eluded him. He went over the sentences word by word, but their sense did not emerge for him.

He put the letter aside and completed several matters. Then he saw it again, and once more his impulsive curiosity prompted him. After a few minutes, he folded the letter and pocketed it and got up. He went upstairs to the attics occupied by Collis and tapped on the door and went in.

" Collis, could you translate this for me ? " he said.

Collis was a thick, middle-aged man in an untidy blue suit. His head was massive, with its round brow bulging over his spectacles and his thin hair brushed back over the earthy skin of his skull. Below, his face was compressed between brow and chin so that the nose was splayed and his eyes were almost buried under puckers of flesh whose ripples seemed to flow all ways over his countenance and to make little bulges and hollows through which innumerable expressions flowed in all the mobility of his active thoughts.

" What is it ? " he said, reaching for the letter.

" I know you won't say anything about it to anyone," Kelpey said, giving him the letter. " I know I can trust you."

Collis said nothing. He spread the letter flat on his table and held his large hirsute hands over its margins.

" It says . . ." he began, then he relapsed into silence.

" I want to know what it says before our Translations Department sees it," Kelpey explained.

Collis glanced up at him and then resumed his study of the letter. It was a short letter, and Kelpey could not understand why Collis took so long to translate it.

" What does it say ? "

" This," said Collis. " It says : ' We regret to have to inform you that our Herr Kurt Rennenberg whom you have not previously met and who was to have arrived at your office on the twenty-first of this month, has had to postpone his departure indefinitely. We hope that this will not inconvenience you in any way, and we hasten to assure you that we shall do our best to arrange another date for his visit to you, although at the moment it seems unlikely that he will be able to travel for several weeks yet.' "

" Oh," Kelpey said. " Not coming! "

He held out his hand for the letter.

" Thanks very much, old man."

Collis kept his hands spread upon the sheet of paper.

" Any of your people below seen this ? " he said.

" Only the messengers."

" Who is this fellow Rennenberg ? "

" Somebody at our Berlin agency, I suppose."

Collis returned the letter to Kelpey and took up his pen and blotting-paper and resumed his work. He had before him a massive ledger with grimy pages, and a cash book. With the blotting-paper held by the third and fourth fingers against the palm of his left hand, he deftly turned the heavy folios of the ledger and put neat violet ticks against the entries in the accounts and blotted them at once. It was a mechanical process of his hands into which he admitted a rhythm. Suddenly, he stopped. Kelpey had just finished scribbling the translation.

" So this fellow Rennenberg won't be coming on the twenty-first, and Foss doesn't know ? " Collis said.

" Foss is away ill," Kelpey said.

Collis began to snigger. Little flutters of breath gusted from his nose, reminding Kelpey of a tiny engine beginning to puff out of a station.

" What are you laughing at ? " Kelpey said.

" Shall I tell you ? "

Kelpey put away the letter and the translation in his pocket. Collis leaned back and began to fill his pipe.

" Shall I tell you, Kelpey ? " he repeated.

" What ? "

" I know somebody from Berlin. He's been here about a week."

" Who is he ? "

Collis looked up at Kelpey and smiled. " We could call him Herr Kurt Rennenberg."

" What for ? What are you talking about ? Who is this fellow ? Is he a German ? "

" Yes, he's a German," Collis said.

" Why do you want to call him Herr Kurt Rennenberg ? What's it all about ? Who is he ? "

" And if he came to see your Mr. Foss on the twenty-first—the day after to-morrow—he could say he was Herr Rennenberg from Berlin, and nobody would know that he isn't, except you and me. Providing, that is, that you keep hold of that letter, And you and I could give him a few facts regarding your agency in Berlin and there you are! "

Collis applied a match to his pipe while Kelpey stood over him frowning.

" Look here! " Kelpey exclaimed. " What are you talking about ? This letter is important. I only asked you to translate it for me as a favour. You mustn't say anything about it outside the firm."

Collis puffed at his pipe and regarded Kelpey with a detached, pensive air.

" You could give him a few details to carry him through any discussion with Foss," he said, from his quick thoughts.

" I can't make out what you're driving at! " Kelpey said.

Collis grinned at him and seemed to come alive. He sat upright and his body seemed to fill with an eagerness which excited Kelpey's curiosity.

" I haven't told you, have I! " he said. " Well, I'll explain. Some friends of mine introduced me to this German a few days ago. He seemed a pretty good sort. I didn't ask what line he was in, because the conversation didn't turn that way. I didn't need to, actually. As a matter of fact, he told me himself that he was over here on a bit of a holiday and was doing a little private business. He asked me if I knew of anyone who would care to look at a diamond pendant, a nice little thing. I didn't ask any questions. I got the idea he had this thing and didn't want to show it round, but was anxious to get in touch with somebody who would buy it privately. He wanted to get into touch with somebody with cash to burn on a thing like that. Somebody in some smart set who would take it and have it altered a little and pay a good enough price for it. I said, I told him straight, no I'm afraid I don't know any of the smart set, and moreover I said, I wouldn't care to touch anything hot like this pendant or necklace or whatever it is. It is hot, I suppose, I asked him, and he grins and says well, it is rather, that's why I don't want to go to a dealer or anybody except someone who'll give me a fair price for it and ask no questions. I thought he was one of those chaps on the Hamburg-New York Line, very classy and full of confidence, but not on the level at all. International naughty boy, playing at crook, you know. Then he asked me a funny thing. He says, do you know a smart lady called Tilly Foss, and I told him I didn't but that I rented a suite of offices from her husband. Oh, he said, I've heard of him. He's very close and keeps an eye on Tilly because he knows she's an extravagant sort. Then he said he must get an introduction to her, and could I manage it somehow for him. I told him, I didn't move in that set at all, but that if he wanted to meet Tilly it wouldn't be difficult because she mixes in a big crowd of all sorts of people, and some of them are quite approachable and would easily arrange it for him. No, he says, I must come from irreproachable sources with my offer. And what do you think he said then ? He said that—but first of all he showed me what he had for sale : lovely thing, little necklace and pendant, platinum and diamonds. He said that if I could work an introduction for him to Foss, he'd give me a commission of four hundred pounds. He said that the necklace and pendant were worth a couple of thousand and that he was prepared to pay a good commission to anyone who could get him where he wanted. I had to tell him that as far as introductions went, it was out of the question, simply because Foss and I weren't anything but landlord and tenant, and that I didn't know Foss socially or his wife either."

He stopped and chuckled. He nudged Kelpey.

27

" But now you come and show me this letter, Kelpey, and I believe the two of us have a chance to make a couple of hundred each. I'm willing to split, fifty-fifty, if you'll keep that letter out of the files downstairs and just turn a blind eye. . . ."

" Good lord, no! " Kelpey declared emphatically. "What do you take me for ? "

" Two hundred for you. Two hundred for me. Easy! "

" I said no. I wouldn't dream of it! "

" All you have to do is to keep that letter in your pocket and let this German come here the day after to-morrow—the twenty-first of June."

" Not under any circumstances! Not for a million pounds! Do you think I'd do a thing like that ? Do you ? "

" No harm in it! Foss expects Rennenberg. Let him believe he's talking to him! "

" I couldn't, Collis. It's a bad thing. I wouldn't do it."

" Nothing in it. . . ."

" I wouldn't discuss the firm's affairs with an outsider."

" You don't need to."

" You said just now . . ."

Collis shrugged his shoulders. " Oh, just a few broad facts for our Rennenberg to go on. No harm in that! "

" As if," Kelpey said, scornfully, " as if Foss wouldn't realize in five minutes that the fellow was a fraud! "

" That's up to our Rennenberg himself. Let him take the risk. I'll just tell him that Foss is expecting somebody called Kurt Rennenberg from Berlin, but I won't tell him about the letter you've just showed me."

" I don't want to talk about it any more. I'm not going to listen, Collis."

" It's harmless, Kelpey. You know I don't indulge in any criminal business."

" This is criminal! You want me to deceive Foss! "

" It's simple. For two hundred. And you know what Foss does when your foreign agents come over. He always invites them to stay a couple of days with him. It's such a good chance for our Rennenberg! Think of it, Kelpey! "

Kelpey shook his head. " No! Not me! I don't want to discuss it or think about it."

Collis sighed. " Throwing away two hundred pounds! "

" It's a dishonest business ! You know it is ! "

" All right," Collis said, applying a match to his pipe. " We'll say no more about it. We'll forget it."

Kelpey sat on the edge of the big, stained desk.

" You weren't serious, were you ? You wouldn't really try a dishonest thing like that, would you, Collis ? "

Collis blew a little cloud of smoke.

" Lots of things look dishonest on the face of them, but they're quite innocent in the end," he said. He added : " When was your Rennenberg due to call on Foss ? "

" At four on the afternoon of the twenty-first," Kelpey said.

" Would you like to see my Rennenberg ? " Collis said, grinning.

" Not much."

" Come and meet him. He's a pleasant chap."

" He's a crook," Kelpey said, shaking his head.

Collis took his pipe from his lips and thumbed down the tobacco in the pungent bowl.

" Oh, quite! But it's interesting to meet fellows like this one. It's an education," he said. Then he looked at Kelpey and continued : " You ought to meet men like our Rennenberg! You ought to be able to recognize chaps like that. It's all experience, you know. Broadens the mind. Teaches you a lot about human beings. Teaches you how to rub shoulders with all sorts, and how to mix and hold your own. All very useful for when you get out in the world. The more people of different types you meet, the more experienced you become. Look at you, for instance. Just for example : look at the way you live at present. You only meet the same crowd night after night. Nice, respectable bunch of youngsters, articled pupils and young chaps in their fathers' businesses. Very nice boys, but all inexperienced. Won't really help you to develop your personality. Now suppose your firm sent you abroad. Quite likely. Quite on the cards, isn't it ? Smart young chap like you. Strong, good appearance, clever at your work. Almost certain, in a year or two, providing there isn't a war and I don't think there will be one. But you'd find it hard, very hard. You'd be out of your depth. And why ? Because you've never learned how to mix without showing your inexperience. You ought to meet this fellow, if only to recognize the type and learn something from it."

Collis put down his pipe and took a match. He pared it with his penknife until the end was pointed. Then tossing aside the knife, he began to pick his teeth with the match.

" Where ? Where does he live ? " Kelpey said.

" The ' Carlton Court.' "

" Is he staying there ? "

" No. I meet him sometimes in the lounge there," Collis said, and he continued to dig the point of the match slowly over his teeth while Kelpey watched him and felt a sudden urge to enter that wider world of which Collis had spoken.

" You ought to come, Kelpey," Collis said, glancing at Kelpey with an inviting look of encouragement. " You ought to be in the crowd there! After all, you're not a junior clerk, or an articled pupil.

You'll be a director before you're thirty, if you go on as you are going! You should mix with important men. Be one of them! Be in the swim! Come and meet this chap, just for fun! "

He threw away the match and relit his pipe and settled quickly again to his ledgers and journals and cash books.

" Well, yes, all right. When ? What time ? " Kelpey said.

" At the ' Carlton Court,' of course," Collis said, glancing up at him with a grimace of light contempt. " You don't want me to take you in by the hand, do you ? Just go in. You'll see me there, about eight or so. If I don't happen to be there just then, sit down and wait. Order a drink for yourself and wait."

He laughed softly. " What a babe you are, Kelpey! What a lot you've got to learn about yourself and the ways of the world! "

" Shut up! " Kelpey grumbled, smiling. He stood up and went to the door.

" About eight," he said, going out.

★

V

★

He was there at twenty minutes past eight. He arrived late because he did not wish to wait there alone amongst strangers. The place was almost full. He saw the big, brassy, bull-necked figures of city life in all its less reputable standards congregated there with swarms of friends, acquaintances, victims, and accomplices. And at the far side, beyond those assorted characters, he espied Collis sitting with three men at a table. Shabby as ever, yet assured in a characteristic, insolent fashion, which seemed to be expressed as much by his unpolished boots and his worn suit and bedraggled collar and tie as by his loose air, Collis had a glass of whisky before him and was smoking his pipe.

" Hullo! " Kelpey said, standing at his elbow. " Am I late ? "

Collis stared up at him as though he could not understand such a greeting. Then, much to Kelpey's surprise, he turned his glance away and finished what he was saying to the others, leaving Kelpey to seat himself amongst them with as much nonchalance as he could muster from his discomfiture.

When Kelpey was seated, Collis stared at him as though he barely noticed him ; then in an offhand way he said :

" This is Mr. Kelpey. Mr. Smith. Mr. Lane. And this is Herr Kurt Rennenberg."

Kelpey nodded to Smith and Lane, and turning finally to Rennenberg he smiled as he said : " Oh, Herr Rennenberg, eh ? "

The German was a big, fair man. Size made him. Size of body, of spirit, character and purpose. A big person in all ways.

" Call me that," he said to Kelpey, offering him his hand.

" Well . . ." Kelpey murmured, clasping the hand.

" And what will you drink, Mr. Kelpey ? Come, please! Have . . . what will you have ? Whisky ? Sherry ? Vermouth ? "

He was like a huge wave that bore down towards Kelpey only to surge gently beneath his spirit and uplift him in a thrilling ascent.

" Oh, sherry, thanks! "

" Sherry."

He beckoned the waiter and gave the order, naming a special sherry from his own wide knowledge of wines and spirits. He had met Kelpey before, not in the flesh, not in this body, but certainly in this particular inflection of the type, in many counterparts of the type, in all the degrees of its temperate, modest expressions and in all the shades of its ingenuous spirit. He understood him at once. Everything of Kelpey's character and personality was predictable to him. He knew its depths, and the length and breadth of it ; and it constituted no obstacle to him. Within a few minutes, he had encompassed it all, and in the process he had enchanted Kelpey.

" Foss, isn't it ? " he was saying, his voice descending to an intimate murmur. " You're with Foss, Brighart and Molloy, aren't you ? "

" Foss's personal assistant," Kelpey said.

The German noted the tiny streak of pride and the simple fashion in which this youth was content to allow his character to submit itself. He swept on.

" Oh, Foss ? I know him! I met him in Berlin."

He said it as though it meant little and was not intended to convey anything important. But Kelpey believed him and was interested in that fact.

" Do you ? Do you, really ? Collis said . . ."

" Oh, yes! We've met." With a slight flourish of his right hand and a condescending pout, the German added : " I know him quite well. Herr Kuno Von Pless introduced us to each other."

Kelpey was delighted. " Oh, you know our agent, Von Pless, as well ? "

" Of course! Von Pless is very well known in Berlin."

He stabbed a little finger at Kelpey and continued : " So is your Mr. Foss. Oh, we all know one another ! We are all pretty well acquainted. I know most of the important foreign agents."

He broke off and sipped his drink, while Kelpey struggled with a sudden tangle of thoughts. " If he knows Foss, as he says he does," he was thinking, " why doesn't he go to him and visit Mrs. Foss, as he wants to, instead of asking Collis to work it all ? "

" When I say we know one another," the German said, as though he had divined Kelpey's thoughts, " I mean in a general way. Like you and me here. One meets many people. There are big bars, big lounges in the hotels. The Eden Bar : I met your Mr. Foss there. One meets many Englishmen. But . . . if we came face to face, we should not recognize each other." He looked full at Kelpey, and his hard, grey eyes challenged every suspicion in Kelpey's mind and dispersed them all.

" You know Berlin, of course ? You have met Von Pless ? " He did not wait for an answer, but continued : " Charming chap, he is, as you know. I saw him not long ago."

" I haven't met him," Kelpey said.

" Not ? "

" I've never been to Berlin."

" No ? "

" No, my job is with Foss. I was going last year, but he asked me to stay in England as his personal assistant, and I didn't like to refuse."

It was a lie, and the German knew it. His eyes played over Kelpey's face as the eyes of a sculptor might examine a plastic mass before his hands began to mould it into shape.

" No ? " he said, charmingly. " Well, Von Pless is a grand chap. And you know he has made a remarkable success of his agency for your firm. Not so much with the cottons and silks, as you know, because there is a considerable rivalry for those goods. The cheap products from the Polish factories. Heavily subsidised by the Polish Government, of course. But with other imports, yes, oh! a fine success. He was showing me the figures only a fortnight ago."

" Is that so ? "

Kelpey was puzzled. Who was this German, with his apparently intimate knowledge of the agency affairs ? His words showered little confidential details as he continued.

" Yes, a total of twelve thousand pounds for the month of May! Excellent, isn't it ? "

" Yes, that's right! I know that. I saw the accounts myself, not long ago! " Kelpey exclaimed.

" Of course. And Von Pless told me . . ."

" But listen," Kelpey said, and he felt as though he were talking to a colleague and not to a crook. " Listen! Are you an associate of his ? "

The other laughed softly and at length. " But of course! How else would I be able to mention such matters as these to you ? Not . . . you understand ? . . . not in partnership. But associated, yes. My firm is in that way of business, and my friend, Von Pless, often has considerable business with us. I represent . . ."

He reeled off names. He showed fine engraved business cards, and produced letters with well-known headings, and took them from

Kelpey's hands only to produce others which he removed in the same forceful fashion before Kelpey had time to scrutinize them. He was quick, vital, dominant. Obviously, his world was the large one of many affairs, of success and enterprise and many acquaintances. A large, ringing place from which he had travelled.

He related amusing anecdotes which proved his charm and good humour and courtesy. He ordered more drinks. He spoke about his work, and let Kelpey understand that he was the foreign representative of two large fashion houses. In a cursory way, he spoke about furs and gowns. He tipped down his drinks easily and gracefully, and invited Kelpey to take more when his own glasses became empty. Then at last he was silent. He sighed softly, and gazing at Kelpey in a curious rather intimate way, he smiled. He put his big hand on the table and indicated it by a nod of his head. When Kelpey looked down, the German lifted his hand. A jewel case was left lying on the table. The German smiled and quickly opened it.

Kelpey saw a little choice necklet of diamonds with a pendant, a little pure thing scintillating with its own sheer loveliness.

" I am going to offer it for sale to Mrs. Foss," the German said in a whisper. " I am going to call on your Mr. Foss, the day after to-morrow. And since I am Herr Rennenberg, he'll invite me to stay at his place. Good enough, eh ? "

He closed the case and returned it swiftly to his pocket.

" Well, I don't know," Kelpey murmured.

The sherry had fumed into his brain. He could not think coherently. The presence of this German was more exciting than ever with its surging conversations and moods and sudden confidences. He and Rennenberg, as he insisted on being addressed, spoke together, leaving the others outside their conversation. The German was quick, nimble, always a little distance ahead of Kelpey, enticing him, then waiting for him with a charming, attentive air which flattered and encouraged him as he sat there with his mind fogged and all his defences melted and confused by the German's massive personality which, although destructive, remained like a point of stability for all Kelpey's irresolute perceptions to fasten upon.

Kelpey smiled. " I don't know . . ."

" The day after to-morrow," the other whispered, resting a persuasive hand on his arm.

" No," said Kelpey. " I don't think I could be a party to that sort of thing."

Something assembled itself around those words. Although Kelpey was impressed by this big man and his positive personality, honesty and all its attendant virtues remained steadfast in him and found courage as soon as he had spoken.

" No," he added. " I couldn't agree to it. Mr. Foss has been very kind to me. He's promoted me and given me this job, and I'm not going to do anything to deceive him. I'm not going to do anything dishonest. I mean, I don't suggest for a moment that you are . . ."

A look of consternation had come into the German's eyes. They were fastened upon Kelpey in such a way as to express an extreme distaste for the mere mention of the word dishonesty. Insult seemed to declare itself.

" Don't misunderstand me, will you ? " Kelpey explained. " I'm only looking at it from my point of view. I don't mean to infer that you were . . . that you are sort of trying . . ."

He hesitated. The repetition of the word dishonesty seemed to him to betray his opinion of the German. Perhaps it was an erroneous opinion. Perhaps he had insulted him. Dishonesty, crime, wickedness, seemed inimical to this large, reputable person who was obviously acquainted with Von Pless who was a man of irreproachable character. Nevertheless, the purpose which the German was pursuing had a positive taint of evil.

Kelpey stared at him with tipsy boldness. Around them, the crowded lounge echoed with the laughter and conversation from the noisy groups at the tables. Collis and the two dark men were laughing softly over something which one of them had remarked. But for Kelpey there was only the persuasive yet baffling presence of the German. And as he watched him, he began to feel that no matter whether he agreed to his proposal or not, the German would make the venture and assume Rennenberg's name.

" No, look here," he added, in an attempt to make clearer his own attitude, " I don't want to listen to anything like that. It's not . . . not quite . . . see ? "

He smiled pleasantly. " No bad feelings . . ." he murmured. And he imagined that he had stated his point very forcibly.

But had he ? Had he not listened and been persuaded ? Had not his protest been ineffectual ? Was not his weak, good-natured response something over which the other had stepped easily ? And was not the whole point of the conversation merely to test the strength of his opposition to the project ?

It was at that moment that the German puckered his lips and whispered, smiling : " Two hundred for you, my dear chap! A little commission, eh ? "

Kelpey heard him and was silent. His brain was more thickly fumed than before, but a core of reason remained unimpaired in it, and from that source words came. He knew that it was time to make a resolute protest, to refuse the bribe, to tell the German that he intended to disclose the matter to Foss, to rise and take leave of this party.

" No! " he said, shaking his head. " No. I don't want to listen! "
He put his hands on the edge of the table and attempted to rise.

" Not going ? " the other exclaimed softly.

Kelpey flopped back in his chair. His limbs were flabby and weak.
And when he spoke, his words were incoherent on his tongue. They
made only a confused tangle of sound which he heard with a feeling
of shame and exasperation.

" I'm drunk," he told himself.

He was silent after that, not daring to trust himself to speak. He
listened to the German. He felt callow, weak, foolish. Only a
veneer of sobriety remained on him, and he floundered behind it like
someone hopelessly bewildered. His thoughts flowed of their own
volition. He had lost track of time. He wondered how many
sherries he had swallowed. He heard the German talking to him,
and he listened and watched and said yes, yes, yes, impatiently and
sometimes truculently.

" Yes," he burst out furiously at last, " yes, look here, listen!
Doesn't make any difference what I say, does it ? Does it ? You've
made up your mind . . ."

He was shrill. Flushed with anger for an instant, he stared at the
German and tried to rise ; but again he flopped back, grinning and
falling back too into a gush of intemperate gaiety which was quenched
very quickly by the imperative gaze which the German turned on him.

" Anyway," he said, " go on, say so! If I said I'd tell Foss, it
wouldn't make any difference to you, would it, Mr. —— whatever you
call yourself."

" My name is Rennenberg," the other said, sharply. " Kurt
Rennenberg."

He showed Kelpey his passport, running a demonstrative finger
along the line on which his name was written. Kurt Rennenberg,
Kelpey read.

" But you won't say no to me," the German said, putting away the
passport. " And you won't say a word to anyone. I shall call on
Mr. Foss the day after to-morrow—the twenty-first—and then . . ."

Kelpey threw himself back in his chair and looked first at the bogus
Rennenberg then at the numerous glasses on the table. He lifted his
head quickly.

" I might! " he declared. " You never know . . . I might! "

His tipsy, vaunting threat! His weak protest at last! He smiled.
He taunted the German with a grin of mockery, and set him at a little
distance which the other made haste to cover. Kelpey saw his clenched
fist come up a little way and strike the table several times, very quickly,
with hard little blows which made the glasses tremble and rattle.

" Oh, no! You won't do any such thing, Kelpey! " he said, leaning
forward and speaking incisively. " You won't do anything of the

sort! You wouldn't be such a fool as to stand in our way now! Von Pless wants me to see Foss. And we are all quite determined to go ahead, and we don't propose to allow anything or anybody to prevent us. Understand? So don't be a fool! Take your commission, and think no more about it. You have nothing to do, except to make sure that nobody prevents me from seeing Foss. You will watch the correspondence and ensure that no letters from Germany get through to Foss. Now! Have a drink?"

It was like a command. It had been preceded by those aggressive thumps on the table. Kelpey was stung to resentment.

"I don't want a drink!" he retorted. "And if I did, I'd buy it myself. And another thing . . ."

Rennenberg took no notice of him. He turned and spoke to Collis who had been talking very earnestly with Smith and Lane.

"What?" Collis said, and he turned to Kelpey.

"What's the matter with him?" he added.

Smith and Lane lifted their heads and smiled when they saw Kelpey.

"He's tight," Smith said softly.

"He'll be all right," Lane remarked.

Kelpey frowned. "I'm not tight!" he declared. But he was surprised by the tone and volume of his voice. It was loud and assertive, as though something were released in him for the first time in his life.

"I'm sober!" he said. "And another thing . . ."

He addressed Rennenberg, tapping him on the arm.

"Another thing . . . I'm not used to being told what I must do! No, old man! Not by my friends. . . ."

"No?" said Rennenberg, as though he were listening to an interesting exposition.

"I said, I wasn't . . ."

"Oh, what's the matter with you, Kelpey?" Collis said.

"I'm not talking to you, Collis!" Kelpey said. "I'm telling Rennenberg or whatever . . ."

"Don't be so damned disagreeable!" Collis retorted.

"He's tight," Smith said again. And again Lane said pleasantly in a precise, clipped tone: "He'll be all right."

Collis was frowning at Kelpey.

"Are you drunk, Kelpey?"

"Oh, yes," said Smith. "He's quite drunk."

"I'm not," Kelpey asserted.

They all laughed quickly and continued to stare at him.

"Yes, he's . . ."

"Not very much," Rennenberg said, chuckling.

"Funny, the way he bowled over so quickly and got so disagreeable," Collis said.

36

" Isn't he usually disagreeable ? " Smith asked.

" No, no! " Collis said. " Nice, quiet sort o' lad."

" Yes, of course. It is obvious," Lane said.

Kelpey lifted his head and looked at Lane.

" Are you a German, too ? " he said.

They all laughed quickly.

" Oh, no! Mr. Lane is from Holland. Aren't you, Lane ? "

Before Lane could speak, Kelpey said : " Is that a fact, Lane ? "

" Yes, it is a fact," Lane said, smiling.

Kelpey looked at Rennenberg. Wherever he looked, he saw smiles.

" What are you all grinning at ? " he shouted.

Rennenberg said to Collis : " Hadn't we better take him home now ? "

" Oh, not yet," Collis said. " Give him another sherry. Have another sherry, Kelpey, my boy! Have a drink, and shut up."

" I don't want another drink! And look here . . ."

Kelpey nudged Rennenberg who took no notice of him, but turned to Collis to ask : " Where does he live ? Shall we take him home and then come back ? "

" Sheraton Road. He has apartments there," Collis said.

" Is it far from here ? " Smith said.

" Ten minutes on the 'bus," Collis said. " But we needn't go yet."

" Stop staring at me! " Kelpey said. " Stop talking about me! "

" Is he often like this ? " Smith said.

" I told you . . ." Collis growled.

" He's very drunk," Smith said.

" But he has only had a few, four or five," Lane said. " He isn't drunk. No! " And he whispered something to the others.

" No, of course not, are you ? " Rennenberg said, nudging Kelpey gently.

Kelpey was slightly pleased by their solicitude for him. He closed his eyes and relaxed. It seemed to him that their voices came from a great distance and that between himself and them there was an immense gulf. Then he envied them. They were sober, but he was drunk.

" Yes," he murmured, " drunk, drunk . . ."

Rennenberg said : " Come on, Kelpey! Here's a sherry for you! "

" Don't press it on him," Collis said.

" Do you think he'll make a nuisance of himself ? " Rennenberg said.

" Oh, no! " Collis said. He laughed. " He'd be afraid to."

" You know what I mean ? " Rennenberg said softly.

" Yes. But he's . . . he won't say anything."

Kelpey lifted his head and opened his eyes.

" You think I'm drunk, don't you ? "

"Of course not," Rennenberg said. "You're sober. You hear us, and you understand us, don't you? You are one of us. You're going to help us. You will keep a lookout on all the letters that come in."

Kelpey drew back and frowned. "Stop ordering me about, will you? I told you . . ."

Rennenberg put his elbows on the table and joined his hands under his chin. He stabbed a long forefinger at Kelpey's sherry.

"Drink your sherry, and don't lose your temper," he said, curtly.

"Yes, don't spoil the party," Collis said.

"I'm not spoiling anything," Kelpey exclaimed. "I only said . . ."

He began to thump the table as Rennenberg had done a few minutes previously.

"I'm not taking orders . . . and what's more I don't like this business. And another thing, Rennenberg. Another thing . . ."

He broke off and looked at Collis and began to laugh loudly and significantly.

"Oh, come on, come on, Kelpey!" Collis said, quickly. "Stop that! Relax and let's enjoy ourselves. Drink your sherry."

Smith said: "He's going to be troublesome, I think."

"Yes, I am!" Kelpey said. "Aren't I, Collis, eh?"

They all laughed quickly. Then Rennenberg put his right hand warmly on Kelpey's, saying; "Oh, he's a good chap! He's a very decent young fellow, and it isn't fair to bully him. We have all been bullying him ever since he came in. It isn't fair at all."

Kelpey opened his eyes and looked at Rennenberg and wanted to say that he liked him. But it seemed to him that the German's face had grown to huge dimensions.

"What a big face!" he exclaimed. "Big, big, face you've got!"

They all burst into laughter, making sounds which roared in Kelpey's ears and frightened him. Then he saw that the others, too, had big faces, and he put his hands over his eyes. As soon as he did that, he seemed to float off into a thunderous yet drowsy world in which voices from the distance were louder than those from his neighbours at the table. And yet all the voices were clear and typical, so that he was able to recognize the character which each of them expressed.

"He's passed out," Collis said. "Well, let him stay like that."

Smith said: "Yes, he's out . . ."

"Are you sure?" Lane whispered. "You don't know. Be careful!"

"Is he, really?" Rennenberg whispered.

Then all the voices and all the sounds of laughter were mingled in a pleasant rumble. Kelpey relapsed into himself. He withdrew into darkness and detachment and curled the remnants of sobriety in abandonment in the deep veils of intoxication. He was immeasurably contented. Outside, all his personal problems, all the bonds which dictated his life, were sundered from him. He was happy.

A long time later, Collis and the others shook him briskly to wakefulness. He got unsteadily to his feet.

" Can he walk ? " Smith said.

" I don't know," Collis said. " Kelpey! Come on! Walk! "

Rennenberg muttered something in an angry undertone because Kelpey had suddenly fallen back again into his chair.

" I'll get a taxi," Collis said.

Kelpey made an effort and stood up. Then with his arms linked with Collis's and those of Rennenberg, and with Smith and Lane walking close behind, he walked through the lounge and out into the street. Once there, he closed his eyes and lapsed into sleep.

He heard voices about him. The traffic startled him. He felt sick. No sooner had Collis hailed a taxi and led him towards it than they all remembered that he had left his hat in the lounge.

" I shall go back for it," Lane said.

Kelpey opened his eyes on the swinging, noisy world.

" Good old Dutchy! " he shouted.

" Really," Rennenberg said quietly, " he is in a bad way."

After a little while, someone clapped his hat on his head and the taxi sped off. Kelpey heard the others talking and laughing.

" Our friend will help us," Rennenberg was saying. " I know his sort. Have no anxiety about that."

" I leave it to you," Collis murmured. " It's for you to say."

" Oh, he won't stand in our way at all," Rennenberg said.

" Do you think so ? "

" To-morrow, he'll be afraid to do anything! "

" Well," said Collis, " it's up to you now, Rennenberg. I've done my best. Your namesake was due at four o'clock on the twenty-first. You must get there first."

" I shall! Keep an eye on our young friend," the other said.

Kelpey understood vaguely that Rennenberg referred to him. Somehow, it no longer irritated or troubled him. It was all a part of something criminal and foolhardy which Collis and the German had planned but which he believed they would not dare to enact.

The taxi stopped. Hands took hold of Kelpey's arms. He was nudged and lightly shaken. Opening his eyes, he saw in the dusk the familiar outlines of houses.

" That's right, wake up! " Collis was saying. " You're nearly home, old man! Out you get, quickly! You've had a wonderful time, haven't you ? "

The taxi had halted at a short distance from the house. Rennenberg lightly patted Kelpey's arm.

" We shall meet again, Kelpey! " he said.

Smith and Lane had walked away, leaving Collis to take Kelpey home and Rennenberg to pay the fare.

"Now then!" Collis said. "Best foot foremost! One at a time!"

"I'm all right," Kelpey said.

"Of course you are! But just keep hold of me for safety's sake."

They walked rapidly towards the house. At the door, Collis said sharply :

"Give's the key."

"Listen!" he continued, when Kelpey handed it to him. "Go straight to bed. Never mind about cleaning your teeth or anything. Just tumble into bed and sleep. Now another thing to remember : you keep hold of that letter you showed me! Don't file it or let anybody see it. And don't tell Rennenberg about it, if you see him. Now, in you go!"

He unlocked the door and pushed Kelpey into the hall and closed the door behind him. For an instant, Kelpey stood unsteadily there, then he walked towards the stairs and went up as quickly as his ungainly limbs would permit him.

He felt better when he entered his room and closed the door. Crossing to the window, he opened it and lifted his gaze to the wide, sapphire sky. The early stars wheeled in a great curve. The floor of the room swayed as he turned away from the window. Everything was in motion, lifting at the moment his feet stepped forward or his hands stretched out, heaving, swaying, eluding his feet and his hands, twirling upon spiteful axes to which he adjusted himself painfully. He threw down his hat and stumbled into his bedroom.

The bed rose as he swayed with outstretched hands towards it. The soft edge of it received him, and the floor danced as he dropped his shoes and garments. But the pillows and sheets were cool and tender as his hot body cuddled in one swift motion into them.

He slept swiftly and profoundly and awoke at dawn. Then his thoughts found cohesion, and all the facts which were impressed upon them resumed their pattern. It was like the vast volume and substance of reality insidiously urging him to wakefulness and to the consideration of his existence. His conscience stirred with shame and dread, and he turned to hide himself drowsily in the few remaining veils of sleep before the new day could hammer the cry of his remorse.

Later, when he rose to dress, he remembered with a dull sense of fear and anxiety what had happened the night before. He knew that Rennenberg, as he called himself, had stepped adroitly around him and encompassed him with all the influence and threat of his robust, intrepid personality. He had left upon him a morbid fear which he could not analyse or escape. He felt snared by it. He recalled what Rennenberg had said :

"You wouldn't be such a fool as to stop us, would you ?"

His fears mounted. He knew that Rennenberg and Collis had moved past him. The sheer daring and momentum of their plan had carried them beyond him. They would fling back at him his share of the bribe and leave him to his weak, unavailing conscience. He realized then that his simple virtues had failed him. He traced their defeat from the moment when his curiosity had driven him to a foolish, wilful act ; and he saw then that his virtues were untried, weak, and that he was defeated because of their weakness.

That morning, he was late for work. Already, he had lost touch with the pleasant routine of his days and the sweet essence which lay at the heart of his work. When he arrived, he discovered that Dewlash had already sorted the correspondence and passed him his letters. He saw her for a moment. She was wearing a different costume. Plain, but finely tailored, it clothed her figure in simple, effective grace. A summer tweed of mauve shade, with a blouse to match. Her neck fell sweetly into the shadows of neck and shoulders, and was encircled by a small necklace.

He remembered what had happened yesterday morning. She represented a whole world of grace and beauty, friendship and love, which had opened to his vision. Now it was lost to him beyond an ugly episode which his stupidity and weakness had permitted.

He saw himself very clearly then. An aspiring youth who owed money to tailors, garage proprietor, to a hire-purchase agency for the last four instalments on his car, to high-class outfitters. A young man to whom two hundred pounds represented release from these debts. A youth on the first stage of a good career and promoted and trusted by Foss. But he no longer had faith in himself. He believed that he had failed, that he was unworthy, weak, and that he had allowed Collis and Rennenberg to get past him and hold him down with threats.

He went through his work on that summer day as though he were doing penance for his misdeeds. He was diligent and energetic. He tried to absolve his sin by extraordinary feats of work. He was patient when others were irritable. He wanted to rehabilitate himself in his own simple self-esteem. But he avoided Dewlash, and could hardly face Foss when he saw him.

At last, in the middle of the afternoon, he went up to see Collis.

★

VI

★

" Well," said Collis, looking up at him and grinning, " how is the head ? "

He was in shirt-sleeves. His dark forearm seemed to express as

41

much of him as his eyes and other features as he sat inert in his chair. Dropping his pen and blotting-paper, he began to fill his pipe.

" You owe me three shillings for that taxi last night," he added.

Kelpey sat down on the edge of the table.

" About this business with Rennenberg . . ." he said, sullenly.

" What about it ? "

Very emphatically, Kelpey said : " I'm not having anything to do with it. That's all."

Collis applied a match to his pipe. " As far . . ." he said, drawing quickly, " as I can see . . . there's no need . . . for you . . . to have anything more to do with it."

He dropped the spent match into the ash-tray and added : " Everything is nicely fixed now. Thanks to you."

" I'm not going to stand for it! " Kelpey said. " If that German comes here . . . I'm telling you straight, Collis! . . . I'll let Foss know what he's up to! "

" The silly things you say! " Collis murmured.

" I'm warning you! "

" What for ? "

" Because of what I say. It's to stop! Understand ? "

" It can't stop," Collis said, quietly.

Kelpey hit the table with his fist. " It's got to! And it's going to! I'm not going to stand by and see it done! "

" Too late to talk like that now," Collis said, taking his pen and blotting-paper and resuming work on the ledger.

" I shall warn Foss! "

" Will you ? "

" I'm determined to."

Collis looked up at him. " What will you say ? "

" I shall tell him that this German is a fraud."

Collis laughed. " Will you tell him that you came up here yesterday morning and asked me to translate a letter from Berlin ? "

Kelpey said : " I shall warn him."

" And will you tell him that it was because of that letter that everything started ? " Collis went on. Then he laughed scornfully. " Why, you'll only get yourself dismissed, and you know it! If Foss knew that you had shown me a letter addressed to him, you wouldn't stay five minutes longer in your present job! "

Kelpey was silent.

" Would you ? " Collis insisted.

" I shall tell him the truth," Kelpey said.

" All right," Collis retorted. " Do so! Go and tell him and then come back to me and tell me what he says."

" I'm warning you! " Kelpey said.

" Don't be so silly! "

"Look here," Kelpey went on. "Since that German knows so much about our affairs, why doesn't he come in on his own bat, instead of creeping round with you and waiting for this chance? Why didn't he come straight away? He doesn't need any introduction or any business with you. He understands all about our Berlin agency. Therefore, why doesn't he come in and see Foss and stand on his own?"

Collis looked at Kelpey and shook his head. "What a simpleton you are! Don't you realize that he wasn't certain when the real Rennenberg was due to arrive?"

"The real Rennenberg isn't coming!"

"That," said Collis, turning away, "needn't concern our Rennenberg. As long as you don't let anyone see that letter."

"I shall show it to Foss!"

Collis waved him away. "Don't be tiresome!"

Kelpey stood up and went to the door. Looking back, he saw Collis working as though he were alone.

"Collis, I mean it," he said.

Collis did not trouble to answer him.

Kelpey returned to his room. He wanted to believe that his threat would deter Collis and Rennenberg. For the rest of the day he tried to sustain that belief against all the visions of the German and Collis. He refused to imagine that Rennenberg would plunge into such a project as he had mentioned. He tried to convince himself that no man in his right senses would act so madly and attempt such a daring imposture.

But recollections of that impressive personality were sufficient to present him with fears that Rennenberg was determined to do what he had said. He saw the German as the embodiment of certain qualities : resolve, courage, self-assurance. Rennenberg's fine body expressed all these things, and Kelpey knew that nothing could prevent that redoubtable man from attaining his goal.

He trembled. He had an impulse to pass the letter surreptitiously to Foss and thus allow him to discover for himself, before it was too late, what Von Pless had written. He hesitated ; and he knew why he did so.

It was because he was intimidated by Rennenberg and Collis. Also, he was afraid of Foss. He knew that were he to confess that he had shown Collis one of the firm's letters he would lose in an instant the whole trust which Foss reposed in him. He put the idea from his mind.

He tried again to convince himself that Rennenberg would not come. He considered the project from Rennenberg's situation. That evening, he went home with a fragile conviction that all would end well. And he sustained it sedulously for the rest of the day. But in his pocket he held still Von Pless's letter to Foss.

That evening he stayed at home until ten. He had two good rooms in this quiet house where he had resided for a little more than a year during which time he had made some attempt to create the illusion of permanency by purchasing some small pieces of furniture which he admired. He bought things which he might regard as his and which he imagined expressed his tastes. In his sitting-room, there was a little desk which he had furnished with an inkstand, pens, a perpetual calendar. In the drawers were his stationery and his personal papers. He had purchased two good chairs and a bookcase as well. He liked to believe that he had style and lived comfortably.

But although he had intended to spend the entire evening quietly in his apartments, reading, or writing to his father in Oxfordshire, he went out at ten. He was restless. He felt the inevitability of Rennenberg's visit to Foss. And it was imperative that he should hasten to Foss and prevent the German from deceiving him. He would have to confess everything to Foss. And then ?

His thoughts huddled away from the consequences. In his sitting-room, the air was warm. And the furniture no longer afforded him any feeling of well-being or sense of possession. He saw his desk and the chairs, and his prints of " Shamrock leading " and " Wind and Cloud in the Channel," but they did not ease his miserable thoughts. Nor when he saw his books—the Seventy Famous Classics of Literature—did he feel the former sense of pride in them. They represented a life which had gone awry. They were his, things of a life which up to last night had been normal and good and which had promised much to him. Now he was on a different path. He was in the intolerable position of having to await the outcome of events before he could amend his error.

He walked into town through the warm dusk and had an iced drink in a soda-fountain. The streets were crowded. Nobody seemed anxious to go home. At the corners, around the doors of cafés and milk bars and dance halls, little groups were congregated. Under the neon lights and the glowing street lamps above which the night sky softly leaned, the crowds passed. In the west, the sky held the distant light of departed day : not the hot noon or the torrid afternoon, but all the suggestive colour of summer day. It was there, like an enchanting prospect, above the western horizon, giving a cool aspect to the night.

He saw men in flannels, women in thin, colourful frocks. The lights and the colours made a subtle difference to the scene. It was like a holiday. It was as though the city itself were enjoying some mood which it insisted on these people. The trams and buses went by almost empty. Nobody wanted to go home on this warm night, for there was a pulse in the air and in the laughter and chatter which sounded in the air. Walking aimlessly with the crowd, Kelpey became a part of it, and he forgot for a time his own heavy problem and his predicament. Until he saw a newspaper placard.

" HORE BELISHA'S SPEECH. NEW MOVES IN GERMANY."

He began to wonder why Foss had gone so frequently to Berlin. Then he remembered the letter in his pocket, and again his predicament tore at his thoughts, until he revolted.

" I've been over it all already," he told himself. " I'm afraid to tell Foss. I'm afraid he'll dismiss me, and I'm afraid that if Rennenberg knew I'd told Foss he'd . . . he'd take his revenge on me somehow."

He had supper in a noisy, crowded café. Afterwards, he walked slowly home. All the windows in all the houses were wide open. The night was abnormally warm, and again he felt a curious pulse, as of the beginning of some extraordinary phase of the weather of human affairs.

That night, as he undressed for bed, he tried to calculate how many hours must elapse before to-morrow came and the German arrived. Fifteen ? Sixteen ?

He slept fitfully. The heat was everywhere. It was in the air, in the sheets and pillows of the bed. It penetrated the body and the mind. He awoke after an hour and tried unsuccessfully to sleep again. Absurd dreams had streamed through his mind in sleep, leaving their odour and their hue like dire things which he could not elude. He drank water from the carafe. That wakened him completely, and after that he knew there would be no more sleep for him that night.

Once again he began to muse about the German and Collis.

★

VII

★

As soon as he heard Foss arrive at the office on the following morning, he got up from his desk, adjusted his tie, hesitated for a moment, and then went nervously towards his room and tapped on the door which was standing open. He went in.

Foss was sitting low down in his big chair. He had the telephone in his hand and was speaking.

Kelpey turned back and went away to his own room. The impulse to confess dwindled from his mind, and he felt like a penitent come too late to find absolution. Remorse and self-pity broke like a single wave in him, and he felt very lonely.

Passing the open doorway of Dewlash's room, he saw her at work. She glanced up and called to him.

" Mr. Kelpey! Your post! "

It was the voice of a friend, and he heard in it what he imagined was a new and intimate tone. He went in and took the letters. He forced himself to speak to her.

" Warm, isn't it ? "

She smiled at him.

" Look . . ." he began, lamely.

Slowly, she put her elbows on the edge of the desk and joined her hands under her chin.

" I'm looking," she whispered. But he imagined that she was mocking him and that the grave mood which was so characteristic of her and which showed her in such an attractive way was transformed. Her eyes reflected only her secret, amused thoughts, and there was nothing in them to engage his own mood which sought hers only to invoke her assistance.

" It's . . ." he began again. He lowered his gaze and pretended to examine the letters.

" What is it ? " she said, quietly. But when his eyes sped to hers, he saw only the same frivolous expression as before.

" Oh, it's nothing," he said, despondently.

She ceased to smile. " Are you sure ? " she said. And she settled her chin once more on her joined hands.

" Perhaps it is not nothing but something," she suggested.

She smiled again. He saw it only as a mocking taunt. Going towards the door, he said : " It's only about a letter."

He went back to his own room. Later, after another attempt to summon his courage, he went again to Foss's room. Before he could speak, Foss asked irritably :

" Are all the windows open ? And the fans . . ."

All over the building the air was stifling. Foss got up nervously and went through the premises with Kelpey beside him.

" I can't tell him," Kelpey was thinking. Then it seemed unlikely that the German would come. Recalling what had been said, he imagined it to be nothing but effervescent talk over glasses of wine and spirit, nothing but an enterprise which sobriety would qualify and present in an altogether different degree which would deter Rennenberg.

Nevertheless, as soon as the afternoon came, Kelpey sat at his desk listening intently to all the sounds which rose from the stairs leading to the street. Whenever he heard the big swing doors open and steps sound in the hall and on the stairs, he hurried anxiously to the landing. Each time, he experienced a tormenting apprehension which vanished when he saw that the visitor was a colleague or messenger. Twice during the afternoon, Foss sent for him, and once more the two of them toured the building.

At four o'clock, it happened. Kelpey heard voices in the hall. Hastening to the stairs, he peered down and saw the German.

" Mr. Foss," the visitor was saying loudly and precisely to the Commissionaire. " I wish to see Mr. Foss."

" And the name, sir ? "

" Rennenberg."

Kelpey ran down. " Mr. Foss is out," he said, addressing the Commissionaire and ignoring Rennenberg.

" You sure, Mr. Kelpey ? "

" I said he's out. Engaged. Can't see anybody."

" I have an appointment with him at four," Rennenberg said.

" I saw him come in, Mr. Kelpey, and I know he hasn't gone out," the Commissionaire said. " If this gent has an appointment . . ."

" He can't possibly see anybody this afternoon," Kelpey said.

Rennenberg spoke to the Commissionaire. " I have come from Berlin on business connected with the firm. I have a definite appointment with Mr. Foss this afternoon. Please announce me."

" Mr. Kelpey," said the Commissionaire, " perhaps you'll see about it. Better make sure. If you'll go on up, sir," he went on, turning to Rennenberg.

The German murmured his thanks and strode on up the stairs with Kelpey beside him. At the turn of the stairs, Kelpey said : " I shall tell him! I warn you! "

Rennenberg smiled suavely. " Which way ? Straight ahead along this corridor ? "

He stood there, a large, impressive presence with a fat brief case. Authority, self-confidence, vigour and intrepidity were inscribed all over him. Kelpey clutched at his arm and tried to waylay him. At that moment, Foss came from his room.

" Ah, Herr Rennenberg! "

Kelpey tried to edge past Rennenberg as he advanced to meet Foss.

" Mr. Foss! Sir! Just a minute, please! " he exclaimed, but his words were drowned by Rennenberg's ringing voice, and his movements were screened by that large, striding presence.

" Delighted to meet you, Mr. Foss! How do you do, sir ? "

Foss and the visitor came together and shook hands.

" How are you, Herr Rennenberg ? I hope you had a good trip. Come along in! We're having a heat wave."

They walked side by side towards Foss's room.

" Ah, yes, thanks! " the German said. " A heat wave, eh ? "

He and Foss laughed as they entered the room. Then the door closed for the first time that day. Kelpey stood irresolutely in the corridor for several seconds. He was trembling. He could hardly believe that it had all happened as the German had said it would. It was such a grotesque act of daring, so supremely bland, so calculated, that it seemed to him to have no relation to the criminal purpose, which was so trivial in comparison to this weight of daring, but to be a part of something larger which demanded this proportionate courage and resource.

Returning to his room he sat down and tried to compose his numbed thoughts.

★

VIII

★

It was the last appointment of the day. It had been noted on Dewlash's memorandum pad ₁or some time.

" *June 21st. 4 p.m. Herr R.*"

Now she deleted it with a single stroke of her pencil and felt a great sense of relief, probably because Foss had worried her about Rennenberg's visit and the Berlin agency which Von Pless held. For months, he had been anxious about the agency. She knew that, for he was constantly asking her for the file of correspondence and the Berlin accounts. And he had made several journeys to Berlin. She suspected that something of extraordinary significance attached to those journeys and to his incessant examination of the correspondence with Von Pless.

" War," she thought. " It's because there is going to be a hideous war. And Foss is worried."

When for a few minutes she had the file before her, she turned the letters and read them. They made only the usual impression on her with their phrases relating to the accounts which Von Pless presented each month. But sometimes she believed that she divined in those phrases information which she could not understand but which was suggested by the very obscurity of the passages. She puzzled herself about it all, and concluded that the imminent shadow of warfare lay over these affairs already, making a sombre setting and rendering the words in an especial degree which tantalized her. Once, she asked Foss : " Do you think there will be a war ? "

" I wish I could tell! " he moaned.

" What do you think ? Will there be ? "

His answer surprised her with its violence and vehemence.

" This damned game of diplomacy which they play! " he exclaimed. " Dressing up ambassadors and sending them to him! As if that blasted house-painter cares a pin for those old tricks of prestige! He's going his own way all the time, and he isn't impressed by oblique threats or references to the weight of empires or anything like that! He knows what he wants, and while we dawdle and try to persuade him by threats he has time to complete his plans! "

" So you think . . ."

He sighed. " I wish to heavens somebody would shoot him! "

She was startled by such a statement from him. He continued : " I wonder they have never thought of that way out! The life of one man, a tyrant. Just a spatter of shots and one death, to save the lives of millions of human beings and the chaos and destruction and misery, oh! and everything which results from . . . from . . . Oh, it would save so much that is good and allow us to direct it to good things! "

He broke off and laughed nervously, his eyes glancing strangely at her as he added : " If somebody would only have the courage! "

She pondered what he had said. One shot, and one death. So trifling a sound compared to the protracted thunder of warfare. So trivial a death when compared to the legions scythed by warfare. One stalk, one ugly stem, instead of vast fields of fair, ripe lives.

" But it's . . . somehow, that's a bad principle," she said.

" Is it ? " he retorted, rudely. " So you think it's a bad thing to rid the world of one foul life in order to prevent millions of deaths. Is it unjust to apply to his foul life the very methods which he has commended to his men in their treatment of others ? Is that the way you look at it ? "

She was startled again.

" No, but . . ."

" But what, eh ? " Foss demanded. " Don't raise moral issues, Miss Dewlash! Beware of that! Hasn't he destroyed them ? Hasn't the world this right to apply his own ideas to his own person ? Think of what he promises the world! Have you read his book ? Chapter by chapter, he's making it come about! It isn't an autobiography! It's a prophecy! Some of it is history already! The intellectuals scoff at the grammar and the style. The professors of history say that his grasp of historical facts is unsound. Is that all we have to say about such a book ? If so, let them ask us . . . let the nation come to the merchants and the commercial world, and we could tell them what his book means. Ruin! Warfare! The end of trade, which enriches England! Or if that isn't good enough, let the Foreign Office officials go to the man in the street, the man in the pub, the obscure men who compose half of the nation, and let them ask him. And he'll tell them that he has known for a long time—ever since this filthy tyrant has been in power—that no matter what bribes are offered to the Nazis, the day must come when we shall have to declare war on Germany. But what do we do in the meantime ? Here! Read in the newspaper what we do! Here it is! This. " This morning, our Ambassador in Berlin was instructed to call at the Chancellery and to convey to Herr Hitler . . ." At least once a week! To convey what ? If I and millions of other reasonable men had our way, I'd convey a bullet! I'd convey some justice to Herr Hitler. I'd apply the great laws on which all men try to live! Huh! "

He subsided in his chair, smiled wanly, wiped his wet forehead.

Watching him, she was uneasy about herself, about him, about the firm and all else which composed her life. For years she had believed in the inherent goodness of mankind. Now she appreciated that it lacked faith in itself, and was afraid of tyrants, and even went so far as to attempt to appease a tyrant. And in doing so, it had endangered the stability of human life War was imminent.

It threatened the deep roots of personal security. Hers, and that of others. But she could think only in terms of her own life. She had fashioned so much of her personal life upon her beliefs. Now she discovered that her personal safety, her well-being, even the chance to work, was not ordained by herself despite all her efforts to live reasonably and unselfishly, but by the presence in the world of a wilful maniac named Hitler, whose crimes had horrified the civilized world, whose mind was perverted to evil, but to whom the representatives of great governments and great nations still sent accredited representatives. The hideous falseness and weakness of such a tradition which had permitted that modern tyrant to make the world chaotic! The incredible truth that all human effort towards personal morality was spoiled and broken by the existence of such a man!

What happened to Foss would have effect upon her. What happened to her friends, her colleagues, her neighbours, would make ripples across her life. It was not possible to achieve the complete, inner detachment and calm which her character had formulated and to which her spirit turned. One's life was one's own only to watch it being drawn towards others, into friendships which trespassed upon it, into love.

She had not wanted in an especial, intense way any of those things. She had many friends, but she was never in the community of a circle of friends. Each was distinct and represented something graceful and attractive which she admired and for which she was grateful and to which she responded. And for two years, ever since she had first met Kelpey, she had resisted impulses. Only to be overwhelmed at last by them.

She asked herself why she loved Kelpey. Because he was attractive? Because he loved her? Because she pitied him? She could not tell, could not escape what she felt was a bitter ignominy which, at the moment when she sought to deny it, seemed to her to become transformed and to delight her.

She wondered if he had realized that she loved him. Then she feared to lose him, and could not understand why, after that sudden manifestation of his feelings, he avoided her.

She began to tidy her desk upon which many letters were strewn and awaiting filing. One was a duplicate which had come from Berlin yesterday and which she had not yet shown to Foss because she supposed that he had seen the original. Putting aside that thin sheet of paper, she sorted the rest of the letters and returned at last to the flimsy duplicate. A letter in German which was a language of which she had an inadequate knowledge.

" He must have seen the original," she told herself. " It probably arrived on Monday."

Probably ? But had he ? Had she ? She could not remember. Had Kelpey ?

She felt very tired. The heat over the city was enormous. She yawned and let her hands rest idly on the desk as she remembered all the small tasks which she had neglected. She submitted to the heavy, languorous air, letting her sleepy gaze rest on the duplicate letter.

There were certain verbs and adverbs which she was able to translate, so that from the general obscurity of the letter a thin recognition of the sense increased in her mind. All at once, she stood up. She hurried into Kelpey's office. It was empty.

She tried to recall if she had seen the original. Had Foss ? Had Kelpey ? Had anyone in the Translations Section ? And was not Herr Rennenberg with Foss at this moment, and was this duplicate of no further importance ? Yet did it not remark to the effect that Herr Rennenberg could not come ?

Some suspicions of an abstract, unrelated kind began in her mind. That perhaps a deception . . . that perhaps this Rennenberg who was in Foss's room was bogus . . . was . . . that perhaps . . . A mere little cloud, formless, unsubstantial, too thin to sustain truth, persisted in her mind. She hurried to the Translations Section.

" Petersham," she said, addressing the senior assistant, " this . . ."

" It's a duplicate."

" I know. I can't remember having seen the original. Have you got it here ? "

" It's not here. I haven't seen it," Petersham said.

She referred to the office records.

" It hasn't come through this office," she said. She beckoned one of her staff.

" Roberts, have a look at this, will you ? "

Roberts came and leaned a hand along Dewlash's shoulder.

" This is a duplicate, Dewlash. Where's the original ? "

" I haven't seen it," Dewlash said.

" It says," Roberts said, translating the letter, " it says that Herr Rennenberg won't be able to come."

" But he's here now, with Fossy ! "

" Well, that's what they write. He won't be able to come."

Petersham and Dewlash and Roberts looked at one another. Dewlash said quickly : " Give me the full translation, quickly."

She took pencil and paper and wrote in shorthand while Roberts dictated to her :

"... and who was to have arrived on the twenty-first of this month, has had to postpone his departure indefinitely."

When she had taken it all down, she hurried away to her room and spoke by internal telephone to Foss.

"Mr. Foss, I'm sorry to interrupt you. Could you come into my office for just a moment? Something very important."

His voice rattled back. "What is it? I'm engaged."

"I'll explain if you'll come. It's very urgent. I can't tell you over the 'phone."

"Coming."

He entered quickly a few seconds later and closed the door behind him.

"Yes, what is it?"

Without another word he took the letter which she offered to him.

"It came yesterday morning," she explained. "I didn't pass it to you because I thought you must have seen the original . . ."

He read the translation which she had written for him.

"Original . . . original?" he said, softly, without taking his eyes from the thin sheet.

"Yes, that's only the duplicate. I was going to file it, then it occurred to me that perhaps you had not seen the original."

"Where is it?" he asked rapidly.

"Haven't you seen it?"

"No! I haven't!" He looked down at the letter and its translation. "... had to postpone indefinitely ..." he said.

"Yes, it says ..."

He stared at her, frowning, breathing through his mouth, then back at the letter. His eyes blinked. His tongue slowly licked his upper lip.

"Perhaps it's a mistake," she suggested.

"Mistake? How do you mean?" he said, sharply.

"Perhaps the letter should not have been sent."

His eyes came in a swift gaze to her. "Where's the original?" he said again.

"I haven't seen it, Mr. Foss."

"But it must have arrived! It must have come through the post!"

"It hasn't come to me."

He spoke irritably, tapping the duplicate to emphasize his words.

"But a letter doesn't get lost like that!"

She knew him sufficiently not to engage his irritability. Waiting until he had stopped tapping the sheet and frowning, she said quietly: "I'm sorry. I should have let you have this yesterday."

"I wish you had passed it to me," he said; and in his sudden soft and reproachful tone there was expressed such a weight of distress that it was heavier upon her than the most stormy rebuke.

" I'm so sorry.   It was stupid of me."

He looked at the duplicate and then at the translation.   Shaking his head mournfully, he said again in the same tone as before : " I wish you had . . ."

She felt foolish and troubled.   Standing there, with her face suffused by a blush of confusion and uneasiness, she was silent.   He handed the letter back to her.

" Find the original," he said curtly.   " There must have been a mistake at Von Pless's end.   Herr Rennenberg is with me now.   Find the original, and put it with that duplicate, and . . ."

He hurried towards the door.   " . . . and put them both away. Put them in there."   He pointed to the little safe near the wall.   " Put them in there, and say nothing more about them.   Von Pless made a mistake.   Herr Rennenberg has arrived."

She thought he had been very lenient and good-natured with her.

" Very well, Mr. Foss."

But as soon as the door was closed, she began to wonder why he had instructed her to put both the letters in the safe.   Why not in the file ?   Why in the safe ?   Obviously because he wished to conceal the information from the staff!   But why ?   And why his distress when he had first seen that duplicate ?   For months, there had been this secret thread of tension about the Berlin agency.   Why ?   Why had Foss not told her the purpose of all his visits to Berlin ?

Petersham came in with a typed translation of the duplicate.

" Dew!   Was it all right ?   Have you shown it to him ? "

" Oh, yes!   He wants the original.   It was quite all right.   A mistake, he said."

" Was he angry ? "

" Oh, no!   Von Pless made a mistake.   Rennenberg is here now."

" It's funny," Petersham said, " that the original hasn't come."

" When it comes in, let me have it for filing."

A little later, Kelpey came in.   He gave Dewlash several letters, then he saw the duplicate lying on her desk.   It startled him.   It had a familiar aspect which struck him like a blow.   When he glanced at Dewlash and saw her tranquil, unclouded features his heart lamented his miserable burden of deceit and fear.   He lifted the duplicate and examined it.

" When did this come ? " he said.

" Yesterday."

He blurted the question before he could check the swift terror which drove it to his tongue.

" Has Foss seen it ? "

His manner was so expressive of fear, so full of the indescribable substance of guilt that Dewlash saw him at that moment as though he were a criminal confronted with a clue to his crime.

" Why do you ask me ? " she said.

" Has he ? Has he seen it ? " he persisted.

She held out her hand for the letter.

" Yes, just now . . ."

" What ? Since Rennenberg came ? "

" Yes."

" But it says here . . ." Kelpey stammered. " It says . . . there's something about . . . it says he has had to postpone . . ."

She remembered the instructions which Foss had given her. Without a word more, she took hold of the corner of the letter. At once, Kelpey drew it out of her reach.

" Give it to me, please. I want to file it."

" But it says . . ." he went on.

" Do you mind ? "

Her calm, authoritative gaze was upon him and her hand was outstretched imperatively. " I want to file it," she added.

" But look . . . what did . . . did Foss say anything ? "

There was a pause. She lowered her hand and faced him with a level gaze full of interrogation and surprise.

" Yes," she said, " he did say something."

He glanced at her and waited.

" He wants the original."

He was quite still, silent, his expression frozen on his face with all his guilt and fear and agony of mind concealed behind it and yet somehow perceptible to her.

" If you have it . . ."

His retort came loudly, like a statement breaking into utterance and rushing out to defend him.

" I haven't! "

She was startled. The true character of that denial was instantly obvious to her, and her whole heart filled with genuine distress. Yet, in the next moment, all her suspicions were appeased, for he shook his head and said simply and very naturally : " I haven't seen it! That's what worries me. It says here that Rennenberg isn't coming, but Rennenberg is in with Foss now! "

" Don't worry," she said, taking the letter from him. " It's a mistake, I think. Foss has seen this. You needn't worry."

" He said it's all right ? " he said.

" Yes," she said, pleasantly.

He could not understand it. It baffled him. It was completely inexplicable to him. More than at any other time, he needed advice. He was enmeshed in problems which parted only to plunge him into bewildering mists.

He had turned and gone towards the door. Now he came back and stood opposite Dewlash.

" Will you be home to-night ? " he said. And his features suddenly lost their look of anxiety and became composed in their usual expression. His thoughts, too, were revived by her clear, sympathetic gaze.

" I'll call round . . . shall I ? " he went on. " If you're not going out. I want to see you this evening."

He paused. He waited for her to answer him.

" I want to ask you something," he said.

Of what he had to say to her, she had no accurate surmise. It simply did not occur to her that he wanted her advice, or that the recent episode concerning the letter had relation to his request to visit her. She imagined only that he wished to speak about himself and herself, about their personal lives, about the incident which had occurred yesterday morning. And suddenly her thoughts fled precipitately from it.

" I've promised to see some friends," she said, quickly. ". I don't think I shall be home . . . at least, not . . . not . . . I said I might call . . ."

" Shall I come about eight ? " he said again.

" I don't know . . ."

" At eight ? " he said, and he stood before her and waited for her to answer him.

She did not understand why her answer was not yes or no in her usual precise fashion. She wanted him to come, and yet at the same time she did not want him to come. She could not make a decision. She felt foolish and weak, and suddenly afflicted by a strong pity and tenderness for him which she dared not express.

" I'll call about eight," he said.

Her head was lowered above her work. He went away quickly and noiselessly, and it was only when she heard the door close that she realized he had gone.

She let him go, heedless of what he had said, conscious only of the feeling of pity and tenderness, and of the sudden recollection of the little incident regarding the letter. She took the duplicate and locked it in the safe and thereby hoped that all the issues that swarmed from it towards her and excited her curiosity would be quenched. But the fact that Foss had instructed her to conceal the duplicate would not lapse from her memory, but remained to tantalize her and suggest all manner of ridiculous ideas which the presence of Kelpey only rendered more confusing as she recalled what he had said and the nervous way in which he had acted.

And she could not analyse her strong pity for him. Her thoughts throbbed and revolved with questions. Why had he behaved like that ? Of what did he intend to ask her when he called this evening ? Where was the original letter ? Lost ? Stolen ? And why had she not shown Foss the duplicate when it had come in yesterday ? The

ignominy of having to confess that silly lapse to him! The confusion!
And all the baffling questions . . . and the heat, the headache, the
extraordinary tenderness which she felt for Kelpey . . . and the sense
of shame which came from it!

*

IX

*

Foss had returned to his visitor. The German had risen and was
standing at the wall, lifting the pages of a large calendar.

" Pardon me," Foss murmured, coming in. Then he went on :
" You were saying . . ." and taking his place at the desk opposite
Rennenberg, he fixed his dark eyes on him and tried to pierce his large,
assured manner.

Rennenberg caught the words with a crook of his finger.

" I was talking to Von Pless about transport. In your letter to him
of April 9th, you raised the question of shipments. You were inclined
to think that shipments to Bremen were cleared rather more quickly
than those through Hamburg. Did he give you precise details in
reply ? He mentioned that he intended . . . we had the letters before
us, and he said . . ."

Foss thought : " I'll let him have his head. I'll let him go on until
he's dried up. And then . . ."

He restrained his thoughts, holding out of range the monstrous idea
that Von Pless had been arrested. Yet when he smothered them, and
when he saw his visitor facing him with an air of integrity and knowledge, and when he remembered that a few minutes previously he had
invited this German to be his guest for the next two days, the dread
suspicion dwindled. Reason rejected it. The mind which trusted
itself implicitly on the virtues of mankind refused to believe that this
visitor was an enemy, a member of a State police force, a spy. The
figures of popular fiction in the modern vein were surely the con-
temporary gods who never ventured amongst ordinary mortals!

" You've seen all the correspondence ? " Foss asked.

He watched intently for the sign of hesitation, for the flicker of
revelation, for the tiny betraying fracture in speech and mood.

" Certainly," Rennenberg said.

" Von Pless has discussed . . . everything ? " And here Foss
turned aside with an inconsequent movement and then raised a quick,
incisive look towards the visitor.

" Has mentioned all the points which he expects us to look into ? "
he added.

" Naturally! "

" Good! I'm very glad. He sent several accounts, you were saying ? "

" The more important ones. I have them here."

" I wrote early last week, asking in particular for the silk account. I've not heard. Have you brought it ? "

Rennenberg was ready for that. " You must understand, Mr. Foss, that there are so many little difficulties in the way of bringing out of Germany papers such as . . ."

" But I cabled! Not hearing, I sent a cable to remind him! "

" I know, I know. He gave me instructions . . ."

" But you haven't brought that account ? "

" No."

" But seeing that you left on . . . Tuesday, yesterday, was it ? Seeing . . ."

" As I said, Mr. Foss, there are . . ."

" Quite, quite! But this was important. And I really don't see why it should have been held back."

" So many silly formalities . . ."

Foss could not prevent himself from this pursuit. He had the reins and he felt that he was driving.

" You left on Monday, was it, or yesterday ? "

" Yesterday."

" Well, then, you must have . . ."

Rennenberg closed his eyes and pursed his lips and made an impatient movement of his big body.

" Mr. Foss. I'm sorry, but I haven't brought that account."

Foss let go his hold of the reins. He relaxed.

" Never mind. You say that Von Pless gave you instructions ? "

" But only general ones, to tell you that . . ."

" So he told you nothing precise about that account ? "

" Nothing at all ? "

" And he didn't mention to you that I had written and cabled ? "

" He did. But he said very little more about it."

The German had at that moment the air of a man sustained in himself by authority and by the consciousness of the power which that authority granted him. It was in his body, in the flesh and blood and muscles, as well as in the pose which they afforded him. And watching him, Foss felt assemble about that purposeful body all the ghosts that were needed to complete the scene. They glimmered about him because his pose was that of a man who was proud of his triumph over those ghosts. His cruel expression brought them alive to give substance to him. They were the ghosts of Von Pless and all the other confederates. And they had stood before this redoubtable presence and before other representatives of political and social tyranny, and something of their fear and distress clung to him, in the same way in which love and regard clothed better men.

" . . . in time! " Foss thought, congratulating himself on that piece of good fortune.   " Just in time! "

He smiled at the German and experienced for an instant a delicious freedom from anxiety and guilt.   Despite the heat of the afternoon, his body was cool for a moment, no longer vexed and restless.   His straining, attenuated hopes were rejected, and his life was amended and returned at last to all the reputable habits of a director.   But there was still Von Pless to consider!

Rennenberg detected that change of mood in Foss, and he felt a surge of triumph in himself.   He knew that this dark, energetic little man, this director who loved money and who had been promised fifteen thousand pounds for his active participation in the plot was not so certain of himself at this moment that he could avoid all the questions which clever tactics might put to him.

But of all the ruses and all the questions from them which suggested themselves to the German, and of all the possible answers to them which might leap or dribble in reply, none was more fascinating than the very question which his own presence stated.   It was the most persistent of them all.   And the answer which flashed for an instant in Foss's dark countenance was succeeded by an expression which the visitor, with all his extensive knowledge of the facts, was well able to analyse.

It was a game which Rennenberg loved to play.   He had been trained exclusively for it, and he was noted for his success at it.

" I have with me," he said, " a statement from our friend on the question of shipping clearances.   It is quite explanatory."

He opened his brief bag and extracted the sheets and passed them to Foss who reached eagerly for them to peruse them.

" He completed it over the week-end," he added.

And there upon the top sheet, as well as upon the others, was the date in Von Pless's handwriting.   Proof!   Such undisputable proof that Von Pless had written it!

Then again Rennenberg watched Foss, and again, with his acutely trained powers of observation, he detected in the texture of the face, as well as in the angle of the head and the position of the body, a resurgence of determination about a purpose which the flesh and the fibre of nerves reflected in degrees that, as the German very well understood, were as eloquent and as perceptible as words and gestures. For Foss at that instant was swung like a pendulum to the belief that, after all, this visitor, this associate of Von Pless, was genuine, was not bogus, was here to give the final word that would open the last door for the admittance of Jey to the plot.   Was not the proof of his good faith in the knowledge which he displayed of the agency, and in these accounts that he carried for Von Pless ?   And yet . . . might not these accounts and this neat statement be the very evidence of the pillaging of Von Pless's offices by the State police ?   Might not these accounts and statements in English be the things wrung from Von Pless under duress. And was it not possible that this visitor's extensive knowledge had been gained by one of those prolonged, terrible examinations conducted upon arrested men in Germany ?

But the fantastic absurdity of such suspicions, when it was so plain that the visitor was a man of normal kindness and feelings!

" This is most helpful! " Foss said, glancing up. " I was going to ask you : the usual quarterly transfers are due. However . . ." and here he tossed aside the sheets and turned back his cuff to look at his wrist-watch. " However, we can discuss that later. If you're ready, shall we go ? "

He began to clear his desk. He signed some letters.

" Excuse me, please."

Rennenberg bowed slightly. He crossed his legs and joined his lithe, large hands upon his knees.

" I was correct," he thought, and his body's cruel core sank sadistically upon the belief, " I was correct when I told them that although Von Pless would not confess everything, I could extract the rest from this man Foss. I said that Foss knew everything. And I am right! "

And Foss, signing the letters rapidly, was once more resolved to take his part in the plot. Once again, like a vessel momentarily obscured by storm, the whole enterprise showed clearly.

" Is he well ? " he murmured. " I hope you left him in good form."

" Excellent form," Rennenberg said.

" Good! "

" He sent the best greetings to you, Mr. Foss."

Foss said : " You'll see him when you get back ? "

" I hope so."

They exchanged glances. Foss thought : " Is he ? Could it have happened ? Is he waiting for me to say something . . . to betray Von Pless ? Is he ? Or . . . is he waiting for me to ask him . . . to open the conversation ? "

Rennenberg was thinking : " It is there, in his skull! In that head : everything that Von Pless would not confess to us! If I can gain his confidence, he'll tell me, soon."

And he began to think then, as he had often thought during the years of his brief, interesting career, how remarkable was the substance of the brain when it had the strength to conceal within itself a secret. How profound then were the depths of the mind! Illimitable!

Glancing at him, Foss hesitated again. The pendulum swung back into the region of doubt and suspicion.

" Is he an accomplice ? " he thought, anxiously, " or an enemy, from the Gestapo ? Is he genuine, and did Von Pless make a mistake when he sent that letter ? Or was the letter a warning ? Did somebody manage to get away and type it ? What has happened ? If only I could get word to Von Pless, speak to him . . . find out . . .''

It seemed to Foss at that moment that although the German had an exterior politeness which was intended to create an illusion of civility and confidence and to afford him a place in society, in himself he did not and could not concede anything to others. He was cold, cruel, even monstrous, and for an instant Foss was afraid of him.

★

X

★

In Kelpey's office, the afternoon sunlight streamed in a stiff flame through the open window and fell upon the carpet and the desk. The papers in the trays and on the blotter curled in the heat. The ink oozed from the fountain pen's nib and dribbled to the blotting-paper and dried rapidly. The surface of the desk became very hot. The air, already torpid, became warmer ; and although the little fan on a table near the wall continued to revolve, it made no difference but only agitated the sluggish air. When the sunlight had saturated the furniture, the wood and upholstery emitted an odour of polish and fabric which persisted for a few minutes and became at last a part of the predominant smell of the heat-drenched city. Through the open window, the same heavy odour poured in with the sunlight. The sounds of the city flowed in, too : the incessant muffled clamour of the traffic, from which single sounds lifted for an instant like things rising slowly from a lethargic current and then subsiding. A train's whistle. The sound of a car's horn. A 'bus changing gear as it sped past. The portentous shout of a newsboy. All half smothered by the pervading pall of heat.

Outside the window there was a slated roof upon which the sunlight gleamed in a hard stare. The reflection dazzled Kelpey's sight, and as he sat at his desk he shielded his eyes with his right hand. At once, the hot scene, as well as all the responsibilities which it suggested to him, no longer engaged his mind. What rose then was the single terrifying thought : " Foss knows that he isn't the real Rennenberg! "

He leaned forward and rested his elbows on the desk and remained like that with his eyes closed and his hands covering them for a long time. He heard his own pulse—the subtle beating of life in his body—and from far behind it he heard coming the sounds of the city and the building. Voices drifted through the stiff air. Bells rang. A messenger entered and removed his signed correspondence and left a little sheaf of papers from other departments.

Looking up and yawning and passing a damp hand over his forehead, he fingered the papers, made a pencil note on one of them, half rose to go down to the Chief Accountant, but flopped back again because nothing seemed of importance now except the fact that Rennenberg was with Foss.

He supposed that presently Foss would send for him and demand to know why the original letter had been withheld. Foss, the director he admired and respected, the man he was proud to assist, would question him. Could he sustain that examination? Could he continue to deceive Foss? Would there not be sudden remorse followed by contrition and confession? And then what?

He passed through all the miserable emotions of fear, remorse, and emerged only at the point from which he had started. And there, as before, was the bribe which Collis had promised him. Two hundred pounds.

It represented so much to him that he could not dissociate his mind from all its agreeable persuasions. It was a solid amount of money, far in excess of the monthly thirty pounds which he received as salary. It was the largest sum he had ever had within reach, and as such it was an overwhelming enticement to him. His salary in its twelve instalments was mortgaged, was cut into so many sections that it seldom seemed much to him. It was for his bills, his lodgings, his small liabilities ; and what little was left scarcely sufficed for his lively tastes. There had been a time when half of that sum had been sufficient to extend his life into new and fascinating regions. But now, when he had authority in a good position and when his ambitions were expanding day by day, he discovered that to complete the picture of himself as a man of mark, he needed more than double the amount of his salary. He required money with which to purchase clothes, to live comfortably, to enter a different society, to afford himself new pleasures. He put one foot into a higher plane and stood firmly there only when he had paid his subscriptions to golf clubs, social clubs, and when he had paid hotel bills and the bills from clothiers, garage proprietor, other shopkeepers. And he was over the mark. His bank balance was on the wrong side. Bills fell thickly in his post. He lost money at cards. He spent too much. But he was unable to amend his life, not because he was weak or foolish, but simply because he was drawn day by day too far from the plane whereon he had formerly lived. He could not retreat. He had good looks, good health, and a natural, charming manner which endeared him to his new friends. He could not renounce happiness, for it was deeply woven into his success, his work, his leisure, his simple philosophy and the whole mode of his life. But two hundred pounds would enable him to rehabilitate his threadbare finances, and for that reason it was like a gift from fate.

But coincident with it, there was the threat to his virtues. Honesty admonished him sternly. His aspiring hopes retorted, and his financial difficulties spoke too. He was represented in both statements. He was honest ; but at the same time he was ambitious and weak. And young, too. Experience had not yet moulded his character in a positive form ; and he could not yet apply his natural good sense to the very circumstances that demanded it. He was too much a part of a world which inveigled him into extravagant leisure and which frowned at him when he indulged himself. He had not yet learned that in these personal affairs the individual was entirely responsible for himself, and that society presented the very opportunities which, when taken too greedily, it would roundly condemn in the next moment.

" I've been a fool," he told himself ; and he knew that every fool used that phrase.

He began to clear his desk. Loitering in his office, he waited for Foss to come out so that he could call him aside and warn him. Minute by minute, he heard the rest of the staff leave the building. Typewriters ceased to crackle. An activity began, and it denoted only the long and pleasant hours of summer leisure. An emptiness and staleness grew in the big premises with the silence. He heard Dewlash leave, and his heart experienced dejection and desire.

" At eight, I told her," he thought. " But she's angry because she knows that I have the letter. Does she ? "

Then he heard Foss's voice. He waited an instant ; and when the voice sounded nearer he went to the door of his room and waylaid the director.

" Oh, Mr. Foss! "

Foss gave him a peremptory stare and halted.

" What is it ? A letter ? You sign it."

" There's a message for you."

Rennenberg walked on a few paces and halted with his back to them.

" It's an urgent message for you," Kelpey said, and he beckoned Foss quickly into the room.

" What is it ? Can't you or Miss Dewlash attend to it ? Don't delay me now! "

Foss said that, then he glared at Kelpey with an uncomprehending stare. Kelpey was making signs.

" What ? " said Foss, loudly. " What . . ."

Kelpey gesticulated, put a finger on his own lips and made more rapid signs, and finally pointed in Rennenberg's direction and shook his head. Foss's dark, damp face seemed to assume a thicker look of stupidity and bewilderment.

" What are you trying . . ." he began.

Kelpey interrupted him by leading him to the desk.

" Mr. Foss, this message came for you," he said, loudly. " I didn't want to disturb you before." As he spoke he wrote on a slip of paper in bold, legible letters :

He held it up so that Foss could see it.

" What is it ? " Foss said sharply in a whisper. And although he could see it very well, he fumbled for his spectacles and stared first at the slip of paper and then at Kelpey, still with the empty, stupid expression on his face.

" He isn't Rennenberg! " Kelpey whispered.

Foss stood back from him as though he had been struck in the face. He blinked. He put on his big, horn-rimmed glasses and turned to Kelpey.

" What ? What is this ? " he hissed in a whisper. " Who . . . who said so ? What ? Rubbish . . . I've . . ."

Kelpey was shaking his head vehemently.

" He isn't, he isn't! " he kept whispering.

Foss stared again at the slip of paper. Then he slapped it down on the desk and made an abrupt movement which sent the paper floating to the floor.

" Rubbish! Rubbish! " he whispered.

Suave, stylized, patient, Rennenberg appeared in the doorway. At once, Foss put away his glasses, and turning towards him and giving him a quick smile, he spoke to Kelpey.

" All right. I can't attend to it now. . . ."

" But, sir, they said you would understand. I was to be sure that you understood."

" I haven't time to go into it now," Foss said. He walked to the door. " To-morrow," he said, over his shoulder. " Remind me about it first thing to-morrow. Make a note."

He took Rennenberg by the arm ; and as they passed along the corridor, Kelpey heard him say : " I can't remember a time when we had such heat." Then their voices lapsed into the distance.

Kelpey waited until there was complete silence in the building. He heard a door slam, and heard too the echoes reverberate about the corridors. Somebody shouted a slow good night, and footsteps sounded in a distant passage. Somebody was whistling a popular tune. The sound came loudly for a moment before it was cut by the slamming of a door. Then over the whole premises, silence grew. The fans had ceased. Almost at once, the heat seemed to increase.

Kelpey moved slowly through it, past the open doors of offices from which the fragrant odour of perfume trickled, past others where tobacco smoke hung in static trails. He reached the narrow stairs leading to Collis's rooms and ran up.

The door was locked. " Collis! " he called ; then again, shaking the handle and knocking rapidly, he repeated the name.

" Collis! It's Kelpey! "

And waiting, panting there in the stifling heat, hearing nothing but

63

the pulse of his heart, he turned away at last and went down to his room.

Standing there in the silence, he felt that he possessed the entire building. It was a sensation which, at other times when he had work to complete, he enjoyed. He liked to wander from his room into Foss's, into Brighart's and Molloy's, and sense the character of their occupants in all the appointment of the furniture and the little articles on the desks and tables. He felt invested with a modest power which the silence and emptiness rendered to him from some kind of residue left upon the air by the three partners.

But it was different at this moment. The silence was like an attentive substance which watched him, which purposely reminded him of former days when he had stood thus, and which made the contrast between those pleasant, recent days and this bitter moment when he stood with all his problem throbbing in him. He moved slowly along the corridors and went to Dewlash's room.

There, everything was composed tidily. A small vase of roses stood on the desk which was now empty of everything except the baskets, the blotting-pad, and the covered typewriter. The memorandum pad was turned to show to-morrow's appointments and notes. On the little mantelpiece above the grate, there were some carnations in a slender glass. The whole room bore in a faint yet unmistakable degree the impress of Dewlash's character : neat, pleasantly ordered, reticent. And in the air there remained a faint fragrance.

He moved about the room, aimlessly touching things. He knew her full name, her address, had guessed her age, and had tried to understand her character. But beyond these trivial facts there was a whole life about which he could only make romantic surmises. It seemed to him to be slightly remote from that of others, detached, reserved, gravely and wisely ordered, virtuous, distinctive. He envisaged her in artistic apartments, amongst cultured friends. By comparison, his own pursuits seemed coarse, and he himself seemed rendered dull and commonplace.

But he was committed to the pursuit of her, to the invasion of her life, to the fusion of his life with hers. He loved her, but he was afraid to tell her. He saw her life, and felt a depressing sense of inferiority to her. Moreover, he felt unworthy, stupid, deceitful, with his treachery to Foss, and his debts and his association with Collis.

He went back to his own room. The impulse to find Collis mounted in him. Somewhere in the city—in the " Tower " bar, in Portelli's— Collis would be eating, drinking, sitting at a table and smoking his pipe, perhaps, his eyes full of the reflection of his murky thoughts.

Kelpey rolled down his shirt-sleeves and put on his jacket and hat and went down the stairs.

XI

The heat and noise in the streets dazed him for an instant. The evening exodus from the commercial districts was at its climax : the laden 'buses and trams ; the long lines of vehicles ; the incessant changing of gears, ringing of bells, roaring of horns. And the smell of it all in the pungent fumes of exhausts.

Waiting on the kerb, he let it all thunder past. The heat dripped upon him in a torrent which burned through his clothes and touched his body. He took off his hat and moved back in the shade near the massive wall of a building. Through the ravines of the streets, the traffic swept. He smelt the dust in the air, and the hard, implacable stench of the hot pavements and walls, and the brushing exhalations from perspiring humanity hurrying past to reach suburbs, distant wards, relaxation.

His own way lay diagonally across it, and he hesitated to project himself into that stream. He hung back, the vision of Collis coming to him like something beyond all the distance of fruitless effort. And he knew that it would be fruitless to look for him. He wanted it to be. He clung to the idea of the two hundred pounds which, presently, Collis would pass to him. He knew that the deception had gone too far for him to retard it effectively. So, let it continue! Let it go to its conclusion! A day or two longer. For had he not warned Foss, and had not Foss turned upon him that stupid, irritable expression, and ignored him, told him to mention it again to him to-morrow ? So, let it go on!

Nevertheless, he moved rapidly to the kerb and cut across to the island when the traffic halted. Half-way across. He waited for the next pause in the traffic. He was going the right way. Across the stifling city, to tell Collis, to make a final effort, although he knew what Collis would say.

" Listen, you silly young fool! It's too late to do anything now, much too late. Everything is on the move. So shut up and sit back and say nothing. Now. Have a drink ? "

The traffic stopped. The road opened before Kelpey. He hurried across amongst a swarm of pedestrians. On the pavement, he hesitated. Portelli's was a mile away, in Corby Street. So far, in this heat, through the stench and the hot furnace of the city! And of its own volition, Collis's voice sounded in Kelpey's ears.

" Shut up and sit back and forget it! Have a drink ? "

Men and women collided with his wavering body. The little

current of his conscience with its regrets and admonitions collided
with the echo of Collis's voice. And over the inner vision, he had fair
recollections of Dewlash. Her cool detachment. Her austere life.
The mode and distinction of it far beyond his trivial, ordinary existence.

He turned quickly and travelled with the stream towards Corby
Street.

In Portelli's it was hot. There was a nauseating smell of fat,
vinegar, and tobacco smoke. He sat down and ordered a salad.

" Is Mr. Collis here ? " he asked the waitress. " Has he been in
this afternoon ? "

" Mr. Collis ? I don't know. Not that I know of. I'll see."

She came back and told him : " No, not to-day."

He asked for a city directory and turned to " Private Residents."
There were at least forty residents named Collis. He scanned the list
and found what he thought was the correct address. Duke Square.
He remembered that Collis had once told him the address.

He ate his meal quickly and hurried out to the 'bus stage.

When he arrived at Duke Square, the yellow sunlight of early
evening lay across the haze of heat, and the sky above was like an old
eye, pale, yellow, dulled by years of vision. The haze itself shrouded
the distant vistas so that nothing was visible except the old houses and
the dusty basements with the railings leaning all ways around
them.

Number seventeen had lost a portion of the rails above the basement
area into which paper, dust, and a great piece of sacking had fallen.
Its steps were worn. They sagged in the centre as though from the
accumulated weight of all the feet that had ever passed up and down
them during the course of a century. Above them, the large drab
door was like a glum face. Its knocker hung by one screw, and
Kelpey had difficulty in raising it.

When he knocked, he heard the sound travel through the big house.
A door slammed somewhere in that cavernous interior ; and, after a
pause, several shrill, childish voices were audible in an outburst which
ended when a woman shouted angrily. After that, there was silence
for several seconds. It was followed by the furtive patter of footsteps
in the hall.

Then the flap of the letter-box was raised and two round eyes
showed. After a further pause, the door was opened slowly and a
small girl put her head round the little aperture and stood staring
inquisitively at Kelpey.

" Is your daddy home ? " he said.

The child was an untidy, unmistakable and diminutive counterpart
of Collis. The same round head, squeezed face, sullen expression,
and air of assurance. Perhaps of a similar character, deceitful, wilful,
cunning. Kelpey could not prevent himself from laughing.

" Is he ? " he asked.

The child turned quickly and scampered into the dark interior from which surges of hot, steamy air came.

" There's a man! " she cried, lustily. " Ma! There's a man! "

A woman appeared at the end of the passage leading off the hall, peeping out quickly and disappearing for an instant before advancing apprehensively to the door. A thin, weedy woman of about thirty-seven, obviously once pretty, once with a fragile, deft beauty which had decayed until there was only this timidity over which little layers of mistrust, suspicion and apprehension rippled perceptibly.

" Was it something for Mr. Collis, sir ? "

Her tone was the fawning, timid expression of a sly character.

" Is he in ? " Kelpey said.

" Well, not at the moment."

" Oh! "

There was a pause. She was assessing him to discover his errand. Her darting eyes flickered their gaze over him from his head to his feet. All at once, she seemed to recollect civility.

" Will you step inside ? "

She closed the door behind him. He was in a hall whose linoleum and few mats and massive stand and ridiculous snake-skin nailed on the wall were as ill-assorted as Collis and his secret wealth.

" I wanted to see him about an important matter. Will he be in soon ? " Kelpey said.

" Well, you see, he's on an audit of his. He's away," the woman said ; and as she spoke she kept touching her hair, the neck of her untidy blouse, the belt of her skirt, in futile attempts to furbish her appearance. She made the statement slowly. It was a falsehood, and Kelpey knew this at once ; and in the next moment she tried to amend it. Slyly, she tried to augment what she had said.

" He goes out sometimes, see ? He goes out . . . on the audits and the books . . ."

" Is he out of town ? "

She nodded quickly. " I think so."

And that, too, was a lie.

" For the day, or for a week ? " Kelpey said,

" Well . . . oh, I don't think he'll be away all night. At least, I don't think so, although I couldn't say definitely."

" Just for the day ? "

" Well, see, I couldn't exactly say. Sometimes he does, then other times he comes in late, see ? "

He tried to extract a positive answer from her. He had the impression that she was incapable of trusting herself to a precise, truthful statement. Therefore, he tried another approach.

" He's in the city, isn't he ? "

67

She hesitated. " Yes . . . well, oh, yes! He came home for his dinner. 'bout two," she said.

" And he'll come home some time this evening, won't he ? "

" As far as I know."

The children had crept out from hiding and were clustered about her and peering inquisitively at Kelpey.

" You expect him for dinner, don't you ? "

" Oh, he's 'ad dinner! "

" For tea, I mean."

" Yes, but he's late already. See ? That's what makes me think . . ."

" My name is Kelpey. I know him. His offices are above ours. Is it any use my waiting ? "

Something registered at last in her timid, furtive mind.

" Oh, I see! Oh, you know him! Well, if you'd like to wait in the front room, you're welcome. Perhaps he won't be long."

She opened a door. Kelpey had a glimpse of a bamboo table and a bamboo chair, and innumerable little pieces of china, as well as some gilt-framed photographic enlargements of Collis and this woman, taken many years previously. The room exuded an odour of hot, static air, old furniture, dead years. He could not bring himself to enter it.

" Well . . ."

It was like stepping into the repellent personal life of Collis. His lair. His secret place. The room with its old furniture was soaked by his thoughts, his drab dreams, his tobacco smoke, and the hours of his leisure.

" Look, if you wouldn't mind telling him that I called . . ."

" Yes, all right."

" Just say that Mr. Kelpey called."

" Yes, very well, I'll tell him."

He thanked her and hurried into the Square and drew breath and tried to expel from his mind the vision of that life. The books of account, the suite of attic offices with their year-long crusts of papers, files, dust, and tobacco ash, the red, purple, violet and green inks. The home in which he lived with his wife and children. Such a home! A rancid place! Was that the purpose of his labour, his life, his existence on this world ?

Kelpey hurried from these thoughts as they pursued him through the Square. And he was only free of them when he reached the main road which was thronged with the evening crowds going out to Rainey Park and the cinemas and the shops on the east bank of the River.

Here were the poorer streets with hawkers lining the kerbs with their barrows. A wide, noisy life in a strata which had its own ethics and its own purposes. Perhaps Collis's plane. The noisy pubs with the handles and the sawdust and spittoons, and the rows of glasses shining through the windows. The fish and chip bars, the cheap shops, and the cheap cinemas with films which had taken a month to come down from the classy palaces along the avenues.

He boarded a westbound 'bus. It was cool on top. The swift passage of the vehicle through the streets made a brief illusion of coolness under which he still felt the insidious heat of sunlight. He sat with his hat on his knees and his left arm loose along the back of the seat, and surrendered his body to the motion of the 'bus. The sunlight whose heat subtly touched him beneath the breeze which the vehicle made was like the unyielding argument which his conscience made against his folly and treachery. The seductive ideas which Collis had tried to offer him impacted with that argument but did not overwhelm it. He was pleased. It seemed to him that already he had won the first stage of a struggle. He was midway towards success. The results of his folly still clung to him and retarded him, but he had taken the right course to amend them. And if Foss had been stupid, he himself was not to blame. All that remained now was to find Collis. To-morrow, he thought, to-morrow. . . .

He alighted not far from his apartments and hurried in. He bathed in tepid water and changed into a cool, flannel suit. He left the house at a quarter to nine.

He was unable to decide what to do next. To go to Collis's again, to the stark, broiling streets around that sere Square, to the rancid old house where the destiny of that book-keeper was embodied in the bamboo furniture and the stuffy rooms with their dead air and the swarming children around that canny, wispy woman ? Or to wait until to-morrow and to go instead to Dewlash ?

But already it was past nine, and therefore too late to visit her. And yet . . .

He felt enticed to visit what he imagined was her fastidious, cultured world. An altogether unfamiliar and remote world to him, and so personal, so far removed from his own that he could only make romantic surmises about it. A flat or apartments in an elegant house in that fashionable, residential locality of trees, sandstone pavements, quietude, in which the houses stood behind gravel drives and trim lawns. Number ninety, Grassington Avenue.

He walked slowly and aimlessly towards the garage where he kept his car.

" I'll have a run somewhere," he told himself.

XII

He never quite decided whether or not to go to Dewlash's. He drove slowly into town and then turned west at Nelson Street. He was thinking more of the country beyond the western suburbs. But his way was past the end of Grassington Avenue, and as he approached that locality and saw the name on the wall at the corner, he turned the car and drove slowly, seeing the numbers on the wide gates.

He had never wanted authentic friendship so much as at that moment. He drove even slower, intending to take the by-pass at the far end of the Avenue. And then where to ?

It was a question not only for this moment but for the whole of his life. He knew that he led a normal, healthy existence and that he gave as much to friendship with others as he received from them. Yet it was inadequate. He thought of Dewlash : her sedate life ; her admirable virtues in a character which was constant to itself, rare, as beautiful as her features and her body. He saw her with the eyes of a sentimentalist who imagines that beauty of form ordains beauty of character. And he felt that he might invoke her assistance in his problem.

But that was a weakness, surely ? And courage was what he needed at this moment. He needed her advice, her friendship ; and it was only when he drew up outside the gates of number ninety that he realized for an instant that he possessed a certain degree of courage.

It was impertinent, he imagined. He had told her that he would call at eight, and already it was past nine. Also, he began to imagine that he had come not so much to ask her advice as to venture inquisitively into this quiet, leafy world of hers with its hedges and drives and saplings and its spaciousness and seclusion. Already, as he ventured through the gate and along the gravel drive, he felt that he had come only from curiosity, for each step which he took towards her home was towards an environment which explained her more clearly to him. Even his problem became nothing more than a plausible means to that end as he entered the porch and touched a bell against which her name was engraved on a small brass plate.

He heard the bell ring somewhere in the hush of the house, and he felt a sense of relief and happiness begin in him. Without nervousness, without eagerness, conscious only of his proximity to her, he waited for the imminent moment when her footsteps would sound on the stairs and she would appear.

But after several minutes during which he had touched the bell again without receiving an answer, disappointment came to him. He turned slowly and left the porch. Then it occurred to him that she might be in the garden behind the house. He was undecided what to do. Disappointment drove him to ring the lower bell.

A maid appeared. He asked if Miss Dewlash was at home.

" I don't think she is," the maid said. " I heard her go out, but perhaps she's come back."

" She's expecting me," he said.

" Would you like to go up and see if she's home, sir ? "

He went in. The house was large and airy and well-appointed. When he reached the flat on the first floor, he saw a door standing open a little way and affording a glimpse of a wall against which chairs stood. He tapped and waited. There was no answer. He tapped again and went in.

He opened the door slowly and stood looking about him. In that first rapid glance he saw little except the large and small pieces of furniture and personal possessions which attracted his attention ; but as he ventured into the room after closing the door behind him, its innumerable features crowded his inquisitive vision and he started to examine them all very closely.

There were two large windows facing the garden and the west. He moved towards them and peered down, seeing a large well-tended lawn with borders of many flowers. It was empty except for two deck-chairs in the shade of some sycamores. Books and papers had been left on the chairs, but these were the only signs of habitation about this large comfortable house. Through the branches of the trees, he saw the clear sky and other trees and gardens and houses all standing in the quiet seclusion of the district. His gaze returned to the room.

He left the window and crossed to a small grand piano standing against the opposite wall. Some music was piled on the instrument. He read the titles : Chopin : Nocturnes. Brahms : Waltzes. Debussy : Suite Bergamasque. Schumann : Carnaval Suite. It conveyed nothing precise to him ; but his avid thoughts composed themselves about some delicate, abstract fancy in which his memory of music heard on his radio was mingled with Dewlash's slender fingers and her dark eyes and her presence at this piano.

Above the piano there was a reproduction of Manet's " The Balcony." Who were these people ? And, especially, who was that exotic, proud figure in the foreground whose eyes were like Dewlash's ? What world of fashion and culture had had its day in that woman and her friends ? He imagined for an instant that they were ancestors of Dewlash, and he smiled at this fancy as he turned to examine the photographs on the mantelpiece.

He saw an older Dewlash in the features of an elderly man and woman whose portraits flanked a little clock. Her parents. He saw them as persons of wealth and position ; and his fanciful imagination made scenes in which Dewlash predominated first as a child, then as a young girl, and finally as a young woman returning home during holidays. Between the portraits in their silver frames were an assortment of articles : some cigarettes in a packet ; a box of matches ; an ash-tray ; a needle threaded with blue silk. His gaze loitered on them and turned because his inquisitive nature sought other features of the room that would extend his fancies to an ultimate point where some precise, large reflection of reality would carry them towards truth. He saw the fumed oak furniture, a few simple pieces arranged tastefully about the soft, pink carpet. He saw on the settee some knitting on long needles whose points transfixed a ball of wine-coloured wool. A glossy pattern book lay under the knitting, and beside it was a novel—" Madame Bovary "—with a page marked by an empty envelope addressed to Dewlash.

He opened the book. At once, he felt a swift, mournful jealousy, for the text was in French, a language of which his knowledge was elementary ; and although the book itself helped to extend his idea of Dewlash, it placed her a little way beyond his reach on a plane to which he could not attain.

He read : " On eût dit qu'un artiste habile en corruptions avait disposé sur sa nuque la torsade de ses cheveux . . ."

The sense of the words emerged mistily for him and passed rapidly to melt into new fancies around the delicate image of Dewlash. And after that he saw only with the eyes and breathed and felt only with the senses of one harvesting eagerly to fill his mind with some final feature which would reveal her completely to him.

He wanted now to convert fancy into reality. He wanted to pass from imagination to a precise, accurate vision of her. But what he saw only expanded fancy to further flights. And still she was not verified in all those fancies. He saw a pair of gloves, as well as a crumpled handkerchief, a nail file, and a silken scarf. On a table near the wall to his left there was a row of books between book-ends. There were roses in a vase, and a scatter of petals about the base of the vase. And the air of the room held a perfume which was redolent of Dewlash.

Suddenly, he stopped. He realized that only her presence in the room could satisfy him. These reflections of her presence did not bring her to life for him but only drew his imagination far from the reality of her.

He sat down to await her return. He was happy because he felt in close proximity to what was hers, and also because her advent would afford him a subtle opportunity to renew the shy intimacy which had opened between them. He was patient. He turned the pages of " Vogue " and smoked a cigarette.

An hour passed. There was a new quality in the silence of the room. It seemed to him to resist him, as though his presence there had violated it. He felt more an intruder than a visitor ; and already he began to fear that that was how Dewlash would see him were she to return.

He took out his silver pencil and wrote a hasty note on a scrap of paper, telling her that he had called. Reading what he had written, he felt it to be stupid, unnecessary, perhaps impertinent. And his presence here : was not that foolish and intrusive ?

Footsteps sounded in the hall. Crushing the scrap of paper into his pocket and seizing his hat, he moved to the door and stood listening, like a thief, like a common intruder. Unable to dispel this feeling of intrusion and foolishness and the fear of the humiliation which he would suffer were Dewlash to return and find him here, he stood, rooted there, conscious of his guilty attitude. He tried to think what he would say were someone to discover him here. What excuse would he make for his presence in the room at this time and while Dewlash was absent ? And what answer could he make if he were suspected of a thief's motives ?

He became alarmed. Waiting until the house was silent again, he entered the hall. Then leaving the door open as he had found it, he hurried noiselessly down the stairs and let himself out.

Once in the porch, he felt safer. He put on his hat and walked at a leisurely pace down the drive. It was then that the feeling of disappointment became sharper.

He believed that some delicate, gracious theme of his fate had gone awry. He had missed her, would never truly find her, would flounder and continue to suffer regrets and remorse for his weakness, because this thin thread was not woven into the pattern of his destiny.

Stepping into his car and driving off, he envisaged the kind of evening which Dewlash had spent. He supposed that she had dined with friends in another fashionable part of the city and had remained to listen to music or to play bridge.

He was quite wrong in this surmise. Nothing of the sort had happened.

She had waited for him until almost nine o'clock, after which she had spent the rest of the evening with an elderly friend and her daughter who lived no more than fifty yards from the flat. His silver pencil lying where it had dropped from his knees to the carpet was the first thing she saw when she entered her sitting-room on her return.

She lifted it and recognized it immediately. She was surprised then to discover that there were regrets which this pencil, by its certain evidence of his visit, eased quickly in her.

XIII

Kelpey garaged his car and turned towards home. He had one large resolve fastened firmly in his mind. To see Collis to-morrow, and to tell him . . . to force him to retreat from that deceit . . . to compel him . . . to make Rennenberg retreat likewise.

"I shall tell him that I have told Foss," he said to himself.

He halted abruptly the moment he entered his sitting-room, for Collis was sitting there at the table, hands folded, patient, pensive, like a figure sent by benign fate.

Kelpey was delighted. He closed the door and then stood leaning against it, his features full of confidence, smiling. Then he advanced towards Collis and stood near him, still smiling. And Collis, looking up at him, smiled too.

In his drab, blue suit, with his earthy face lifted in a leer of greeting, Collis's figure seemed to Kelpey to reflect no light, to be detached from the world of colour and movement and to be related only to the murky things of his own evil heart. He was utterly possessed by his own deceitful purposes ; and as he sat there he seemed thicker, sundered from all influences except those born and developed in his wilful, wicked nature.

"I came round . . . soon as my wife told me," he explained. "I didn't get home until an hour ago. I came round here at once."

Kelpey stood back a little and folded his arms.

"Anything wrong ? " Collis asked. "Rennenberg turned up all right, didn't he ? "

"Oh, yes! He came," Kelpey said.

Collis breathed loudly through his open mouth.

"Ah, that's good, that's good! "

"Listen, Collis! " Kelpey said. "Does Rennenberg know that that letter came from Berlin saying that the real Rennenberg can't come ? "

Collis grinned quickly. "Oh, no! Little thing like that . . ." He shrugged his shoulders and added : "I didn't want to let a little thing like that interfere with our plans."

"You know that he wouldn't have gone on with this thing if he had known about the letter ? "

"Why should he know ? You've got the original. You won't say anything to anyone about it. You'll hold it until Rennenberg leaves. So why make him nervous ? That's the way I look at it."

"Yes, but only because you don't want to lose your bribe! " Kelpey said. "You're willing to let him run right into danger. . . ."

" Oh, he . . . he could soon wriggle out of that! "

" Well, he won't! " Kelpey said, sharply.

Collis stopped grinning. His face became heavier in its expression. Something menacing grew in his eyes.

" What d'you mean ? " he said.

" I mean that a duplicate of that letter has arrived."

" What ? "

Collis swung round tensely. " What ? " he gasped.

" And half the staff have seen it," Kelpey said.

Collis was dumbfounded. For several seconds, he sat with his mouth agape and his eyes lifted in a taut stare upon Kelpey. His body was twisted round, and it, too, was taut.

Kelpey went to the window and opened it wider. He stayed there, staring out at the night sky with its early stars. He felt that already he had severed himself from Collis and Rennenberg. His back was towards his visitor, and he hoped that Collis would take the hint and go.

" Well, that's not so good," Collis said, softly. " Not so good at all."

He was talking to himself. He ran his big thumb over the dark stubble on his chin. Kelpey spun round on him.

" Who is this fellow Rennenberg ? I didn't tell this German a word about our agency. He knew almost as much about it as I do! "

Collis paid no attention to the question. He rubbed his chin with his thumb and forefinger. Then he grimaced at Kelpey.

" Puts our Rennenberg in a nasty spot, doesn't it ? "

" You don't care, though, do you ? " Kelpey exclaimed.

Collis burst into a loud, mocking laugh.

" Not much good to care now! " he said. He stopped laughing and continued : " As long as Foss doesn't see the original or that duplicate—and that's where you must help us—there's still a chance that Rennenberg . . ."

" No chance at all," Kelpey said.

" Of course there is! " Collis shouted. " All you've got to do is to get hold of the duplicate and hide it from Foss."

" I'm not going to do anything of the sort! "

Collis got up and gesticulated. " Don't talk silly! The whole thing is in the bag. A day . . . one more day, and it's over, and we get our commission! "

" I told you before," Kelpey said.

" You can't back out now! Not now, when it's all so near! "

Collis came round the table and approached Kelpey and stood before him.

" You can't do it, Kelpey! Don't be a fool! Listen, listen, it's just chucking easy money away! "

" I told you! " Kelpey said, angrily. " Can't you understand when somebody tells you something plainly? Do you think I'm just talking for the sake of talking? "

Collis made an abrupt gesture and turned his back on Kelpey. He walked back to the table and sat down.

" You depress me," he said, taking out his pipe and filling it. " You keep on. But now let me tell you this : if you say one word to anyone about this business, or if you let Foss see those letters, I'll take good care that Foss hears about you showing me that letter in the first place. Now! Now don't say any more about the thing. It's in the bag. It's all over, bar the cash."

" As a matter of fact," Kelpey said, " it's going to fail."

" That's what you think," Collis said, putting away his tobacco pouch.

" I know it is," Kelpey said.

Collis looked up at him apprehensively.

" What d'you mean? "

" Foss has seen the duplicate. To-morrow I'm going to give him the original. Meanwhile, I've told him that the fellow who calls himself Rennenberg isn't the genuine Rennenberg at all."

As soon as Kelpey had said that, Collis got up from the table and stumbled towards him. He seized Kelpey by the arm and held him while he said repeatedly in a thin, rattling tone which quivered with anger, contempt, fear and aggression :

" You didn't! You never said it! You didn't tell him! You wouldn't do a thing like that! "

Kelpey broke away from his grip and stood back.

" I've told you . . ." he said, quietly.

Then Collis stopped whining at him. His face flushed and his full lips pouted, and a great torrent of rage poured from his lips, his features and his gestures.

" You rotten young swine! You swine! Swine! "

The words exploded on his lips and echoed about the room. Into them he put the whole of his contempt and fury, so that the words had a solid, almost tangible force. Others followed furiously : a stream of filthy abuse uttered loudly and wildly. They struck Kelpey like blows. They hit his body.

All at once, Collis lurched towards him. Perhaps to strike him. Perhaps to put his huge, hirsute hands about his throat. Kelpey moved back slightly. He felt the wall behind him. He saw Collis coming at him, shouting obscenities, hands uplifted, face contorted.

He launched out at that threatening figure at the moment when it came within reach. A single hard, lucky blow. It landed fairly and squarely on Collis's chin. Hard, full of impulsive strength, it sent him reeling backwards.

When he recovered his balance, he discovered that all his rage was dead. He took a step towards Kelpey, then he halted. He had no real courage in him, ever. He was a bully. Mostly, rage drove him. Now it was dead in him, like a burden which held his limbs. And seeing that upright, panting, defensive figure before him, he was afraid. His chin hurt.

Only contempt remained. He gave it full expression. Snatching up his hat, he went to the door. There, he halted and faced about. In a thick, sullen outburst, he poured his contempt in words of sodden, indescribable obscenity. And went. And went only because Kelpey was advancing on him.

The door slammed behind him. Kelpey heard him rush heavily downstairs and slam the street door. He opened the door and peered out and saw the landlady in the hall.

She was frowning up at him.

" A nice row, at this time of the night, Mr. Kelpey! "

It was the first time she had ever had to rebuke him. It was the very first occasion on which he had found himself in such a situation.

" I'm sorry, Mrs. Larkin," he said.

" I should think so, too! "

He returned to his room, leaving the door wide open. Within a few minutes, the tobacco smoke had drifted away ; but the air of the room held a faint aroma which persisted and which insidiously permeated the place as well as the little bedroom adjoining it. It was a reminder of Collis's visit and the sombre, evil influence which he had momentarily exerted on Kelpey.

Kelpey imagined that he had amended his folly and broken that influence. He believed that he would be able to sleep to-night in the comforting knowledge that he had acted at last with courage and honesty. Yet, when he went to bed, sleep would not come to him. He turned restlessly for hours in the heat. The recollection of Collis's angry presence recurred constantly to him.

It was the first encounter he had ever had with rage and so much evil. Also, the blow which he had given Collis was the first he had ever given a man. He wondered what Collis would do. What revenge would he seek ? What mean, spiteful satisfaction would he take for himself against that blow and against the defeat of his plans ?

" What will he do ? " Kelpey said, aloud.

And it seemed to him that he had effected nothing useful by his behaviour but had only rendered more difficult what had previously been beyond him to control.

XIV

Jack Collis was thirty-eight. He looked much older than that. He
had always had the appearance of age. Even when he had been a
small boy at school, he had had the manner of a little old man. His
character was compact, independent, formed already by contact with
six other characters : his brothers' and sisters'—in an environment
which gave little to those who were not strong enough to take from it.
And that especial aspect of his character—his power to take—soon
displayed itself. He had a quick mind and a strong body. Nothing
impeded him in the little courses which he set for himself. Already, at
an early age, he saw in the various subjects of the curriculum gifts
which awaited those who aspired to take them.

He became bookish and disinclined to play. He chose his own way
and made his own pace. Often sulky and rebellious, he remained
apart, a solemn, observant boy, insurgent and clever. And in this
way he passed without any appreciable change of temperament from
boyhood to youth and from youth to manhood. He won a scholar-
ship to a good secondary school. A brilliant pupil in his own massive
fashion, he emerged with a flair for mathematics and modern languages.
A year later, he was in business on his own account.

During that year, he had chosen his profession and had taken
employment with a chartered accountant. He went to learn. This
habit of learning was his great virtue. His capacity in that direction
was remarkable. But he learned not only about mankind and work.
For the first time in his life he learned how to play.

It was not in the field of youth at all that he began to indulge himself,
but in the less reputable levels of the commercial world where, upon
the fringes of the exchanges and markets, there loitered slyly all the
disreputable, shifty characters who existed upon crumbs and upon
their own genius for crime. There, he found exciting pleasures, all of
which were open to him. He saw human destinies shaping themselves.
He saw the hunt and the kill, success and failure, tragedy and comedy.
At the end of a year during which he had been an exemplary clerk, he
resigned his position. He borrowed five hundred pounds from a
solicitor who had faith in him, and set up as an unqualified accountant.
His capital was that five hundred pounds ; but his assets were represented also by his knowledge of men and affairs, his power to learn
quickly, and his determination to indulge himself.

He was a realist. He knew what he could take from life and how
much he would have to pay for what he took. He took the large and
small crumbs which were left by the large, old-established firms of

accountants in the city. He gained the confidence of petty tradesmen in the city. Writing up their books and preparing their annual accounts. He had a large clientele, and he worked hard. Yet, from the first, his practice had a sordid, shabby quality which he could not prevent from becoming the target for the contempt of all the sedate, reputable firms of accountants in the city.

Why ? Because he was unqualified ? Because he was successful ? He knew that that was not the reason. It was because he never missed an opportunity to enter an illegal deal, to make a criminal bargain, to reap a harvest from some unsuspecting victim. And the hue of all these enterprises gave a baleful gleam to his character and to his practice as well.

And that was how he played, and that was how he paid for his success. He worked fourteen hours a day for six days a week. He was clever and experienced ; but he remained in a murky level from which neither money nor any other form of success could lift him. Sometimes, he noticed the disparaging glances of honest accountants. Sometimes, these men spoke to him. He knew that had he applied to them before he had gone into business on his own, there was not one of them who would have refused to give him a senior appointment, for his abilities and personality had already attracted attention. Now it was different. His talents were still remarkable, but they had gone into all sorts of shady directions and were no longer admired.

By the end of a dozen years, he was rich. His fortune always surprised him when he considered it, for what he had envisaged for himself had been something quite different in which wealth was only the concomitant of other rewards. He had wanted friends, success in his profession, a good reputation. Instead, he had only an abundance of money. Almost twenty thousand pounds. Gained from his work, from his dividends on his investments, from the rents of awful little properties, from deals, bribes. A harvest. By then, he was married. But love, too, had lost its influence on him and become nothing but a memory.

A new ambition laid hold of him. He yielded to what had become a lust for money. It surged through his blood and became a devouring passion. He forgot his early principles. He became ruthless, adroit in evil things. He went out for the money and was in nearly every despicable deal, never far away when someone was to be plundered. He remained in the background, a powerful figure to whom rascals went with their plans to invoke his wits and his bully's spirit, his cold resolve and his advice.

Something of the shade, of the solitude in which he worked in his attic suite, remained always upon him. He had the appearance of a lonely animal tucked away in its lair under the slates in the big building which comprised Foss, Brighart and Molloy's premises. His tenancy

79

was always under consideration from the partners. They often decided to give him notice, to rid their place of his presence. Yet, probably because he paid a good rental, and also because he was out of sight in the place, he was allowed to remain.

Sometimes, Collis wondered about himself. He tried to imagine what his end would be. He terribly feared death. But he did not feel any fear of disgrace, exposure, a scandal. He made a will and left everything in trust for his wife and children. He was amused then. He looked furtively at his wife and wondered what that commonplace, illiterate woman with her four children would do with his thousands.

And that question, too, made him ponder about himself. He sat alone in his dusty attic and looked out over the expanse of the city. He heard the roar of life in the streets. He saw the tiny figures far below in the street : minute specks swarming upon the pavements and roadways. But significant specks ! Like himself.

And again he tried to imagine what his end would be. The end of all crooks and rascals ? Or the placid comfort of a rich old man ?

" Funny thing! " he thought. " You can't tell."

XV

This was the man Kelpey had faced. The blow which Kelpey had dealt him soon ceased to pain, but the rebuff which Kelpey's words had given him increased moment by moment with an intensity which pained his wounded pride and his thwarted intentions.

It was all like a hard, contrary gust of wind impeding him. He expected difficulties in such an affair as this. Things seldom went according to plan. There was always a hitch, a setback, something to be smoothed away by threats, more ruses, blandishments. Sometimes, he was able to turn sudden setbacks into good account. Generally, he took enormous risks and worked through to success by a sheer, barefaced impudence which carried him safely along before anyone had time to discover his intentions.

This time, he was completely defeated. Kelpey had failed him, had wriggled away from his influence and spoken to Foss. The result would surely mean exposure and disgrace and a terrible scene with Rennenberg, and much more.

But what troubled him principally was the almost certain loss of two hundred, if not four hundred, promised pounds. To have to suffer the loss of that fine bribe! To see it all pass out of reach after such a wonderful promise of attainment! This first substantial failure! This exasperating sense of defeat and loss!

His greed mourned in him. His cruel spirit sought revenge. The necessity for communicating swiftly with the bogus Rennenberg and for making immediate, fresh plans lay upon his tense mind with a weight which burned him far more than did the heat in the streets through which he plodded. He wondered what to tell Rennenberg, what to do.

" It wouldn't help him now, even if I did tell him," he concluded.

He had lapsed into a state of mind in which his own chances in the enterprise were all that mattered. He wanted his bribe, his share. Had he not fulfilled his part of the bargain ? Had he not been shrewd and helpful and therefore deserving of the stipulated reward ? And was it his concern now if the German was in that terrible danger ? And would it help Rennenberg were he to tell him of his danger ? Or would it further his plans were he to find Smith and Lane and tell them what had happened ? No! Of course not!

He decided that silence was the only alternative left. Silence in all directions. Not a word to anyone. Nothing more to Kelpey. Over the whole project : silence.

His mind accepted that glib solution. So easy it seemed to accomplish, so full of promise for himself. For after all, the duel lay now entirely with Foss and Rennenberg, and if the latter were unimpeded by fears he might be able to play his part in such a way that Foss would be persuaded by him.

Collis sighed with relief and satisfaction. Then the pavements seemed cooler, the streets shorter, the air somehow streaming with gracious currents from a cool, temperate source and caressing his wet brow and his soaked body as he walked towards the city centre.

There the lights shone along the pavements ; and in the cafés and supper bars and milk bars, as well as on the high walls, the neons gleamed, spewing out flashes of colour above which the cloudless night sky domed the world with delicate hues from an afterglow which was to linger on the horizon's edge until dawn itself overtook it. And in that still crowded district, the heat was hard and unyielding, and in no degree diminished from its majestic prowess of noon. It lay heavily everywhere, oozing from the grills along the pavements, flooding out from the open doors of the all-night counters, gushing from the cinemas with the crowds, and streaming with them to the late trams and 'buses.

Collis was very thirsty. The licensed bars were closed and there remained only the soft-drink counters. In the " Nirvana," he found a small table under the edge of the balcony. He sat down and ordered an iced orangeade.

The big place was full. Under the lights, under the fans, on tables which stood packed closely together were hundreds of youths and girls, men like himself, women in little groups, parties. His glance ranged over the scene. His ears caught snatches of conversation and laughter before the words were obliterated by the general clamour. He smelt the heat here. His hot hands rested on the marble surface of the table and found it warm too.

When his glass was set before him, he put his fingers around it. The coolness travelled through his fingers and palms, and he felt it moving deliciously about his wrists. He lifted the glass and drank. The ice-cube touched his lips. In his mouth and throat and stomach, the chill lasted for an instant. The taste of the orange lay thickly on his unaccustomed tongue. Lowering the glass, he continued to hold it between his big hands.

His glance wandered to the crowded balcony which stretched all round the big room. There, too, the tables were thickly packed. He heard laughter and talk from above. Somebody leaned over, directly above him, and withdrew when his glance flashed up. Staring about him, Collis noticed the relapse into indifference and pleasure ; the heedless drift towards a new spirit bred by the fierce heat. The languor of it was in the air. The sensual pulse of it touched his own hot body. He drained his glass and ordered another.

Somebody had worked through the crowds at the door and around the tables thereby, and was taking the empty chair at his table. Collis knew him by sight. Although he had never made his acquaintance, he had seen him frequently in some of the more reputable bars. Had stood beside him in crowds at counters. Knew his name. Knew that he was an adventurer, of sorts. George Jey. A gentleman. A man belonging to a good family whose wealth had evaporated. A man of no especial looks, but whose demeanour expressed the consciousness of certain virtues and ethics. A luckless gentleman.

Their eyes met. Jey had grey, unwavering ones in a small, round head on a neck which was fashioned erectly on a good pair of shoulders. He was forty-seven and of medium height, with a certain flabbiness.

He nodded to Collis. " Mind if I . . ." as he drew out the chair.

" No. Go ahead! " Collis said.

" Thanks. Very warm. Almost tropical. We don't . . ."

Some scuffling in the balcony overhead drew Jey's glance upwards. A loud shout rose above the general noise. Portions of the flimsy balustrade snapped and fell clattering on the tables below. A youth and his girl at an adjoining table shielded their heads with upflung arms. Shouts rose. The slop and rattle of overturned glasses, and a sudden shriek from nearby, ripped the scene wide open for disaster at the instant before Jey's loud warning lifted over all other sounds.

" Look out! "

He was out of his chair and had swung himself and Collis far under the balcony when the heavy, marble-topped table crashed down from above upon the chairs and the iced orangeade and the little table at which he and Collis had been seated. It fell with iron legs whirling, and shattered chairs and glasses and rolled off heavily. A malicious, lethal thing around which a little space of ruin and panic spread to the feet of a horrified crowd.

Collis tottered against a table and sent glasses tumbling. People pressed past him towards the ruin at which he had sat a moment before.

" The balcony . . . table! " he was shouting.

All the exits were suddenly crowded. People pressed in. All over the vast floor, there was movement, surging all ways. There was thudding and shouting overhead. An authoritative but pale figure in evening dress—the manager—was trying to advance through the crowds. Three hysterical women, one of them holding a bruised, torn arm, were the centre of a swarm not far from Jey and Collis. A waitress clutched Jey.

" Are you all right ? My god . . . when I . . ."

She was swept away in a sudden rush of the crowd from outside. Collis trembled. Jey was dragging him backwards towards one of the exits.

" This door . . ."

Someone stopped him. " What was it ? Lucky you got up in time. Lucky . . ."

Jey had an uncomprehending, bland look which conveyed nothing. Only Collis was in distress. Upon him, Jey had a firm, guiding hand.

" Through here . . . come on . . . this way! "

Behind, the noise was that of panic and anger. Arms were raised. Fingers pointed to the balcony.

Jey worked his way through the crowd at the door.

" Just a minute, please! If you please! "

Collis was clinging to him. The two of them came out on a side-street.

" Some fool falling off his chair and cracking the balustrade . . ." he said, when they were free of the crowd.

He straightened his jacket and collar and tie. Removing his hat, he pushed out a dint in it. Collis stood panting beside him.

" Might have killed us, have killed us! " he gasped.

His sweating, terror-stricken face mouthed words.

" . . . might have . . . could easily . . ."

Jey glanced backwards at the mob around the " Nirvana." He laughed tersely.

" I don't like choruses," he said, guiding Collis to the 'bus stage.

" But straight down at us! Another second . . . if you hadn't . . ."

" Yes, near thing," Jey muttered.

" But if you hadn't grabbed hold of me . . ." Collis exclaimed.

He began to laugh hysterically.   Little flutters of breath broke from his stiff lips and became stupidly entangled with his words until Jey interrupted him.

" Which way do you go ? "

" . . . got you to thank, you know.   If you hadn't had the presence of mind . . . I can tell you, I'm grateful. . . ."

Jey pointed to the 'bus which had stopped before them.

" This one ?   This yours ? "

Collis saw the indicator.   " Yes . . . this . . . this'll do."

" Then I'll say good night."

Jey disappeared behind the little crowd pouring on the 'bus.   He was out of sight in a moment, and Collis was swept aboard the vehicle where he stood for an instant peering from the platform, until the passengers and the conductor urged him inside.   He found a seat and flopped down weakly.   He was dazed and frightened.   The clamorous, normal world rattled and chattered gaily about him.   The conductor came to collect the fares.   The 'bus went quickly through the streets. But Collis could not understand how all this could continue so indifferently while death had brushed so closely past him only a few minutes previously.   Death!   That heavy table!   On the very spot where only a moment before he and Jey had been sitting!

When he rose to alight, his limbs trembled and he had to clutch the straps with both hands.   He got off like an old man uncertain of his steps.   He felt sick and horrified.   Standing on the pavement, he waited a little while and then walked the few steps to his house and let himself in.   And as he stood there, trembling violently, with his lips open and his breath rustling through his throat and mouth, Daisy appeared at the end of the hall.

His return was so unlike his usual quick entry and slamming of the door and mumbled greeting before he walked through to his room, that she realized at once that something had happened to frighten him.

" Jack!   What's the matter ? "

Her voice had the apt tone to engage his sudden need of her sympathy.   He hung up his hat and wiped his face with his handkerchief and came unsteadily towards her.   She watched him apprehensively and followed him to the room which he liked to use :   the little room overlooking the yard.   She stood nearby while he lowered his body slowly into the armchair.

" Jack! " she breathed tremulously.   " Jack!   What 'appened ? "

He lifted a solemn glance to her.

" . . . nearly killed . . . a big table . . ." he began.   Then in a rush of words came the rest.

" . . . in the ' Nirvana ' . . . just sat down and had a glass of orangeade and finished it and a chap comes in and sits down at my table, and then it all happened. All of a sudden. Bits of the wood rails from the balcony . . . and then this chap shouts out look out, and jumps up and grabs hold of me and . . . just like that . . . just in time . . . gets us clear . . . and the table comes down . . . heavy table . . . right on top of ours . . . split our skulls open would have . . . would have killed us easy . . . only this chap—chap called Jey . . . another second and we'd have been killed . . . split our heads . . ."

" Jack, 'ow awful! Jack!"

He trembled. " Shook me up . . ."

He began again. " I heard a bit of a row going on in the balcony, but never thought. I saw somebody lean over and look down. Never thought . . . never crossed my mind. Just sat there . . . then the bits of wood came down. There was a scream . . . I remember now somebody screamed. Some woman. Then this fellow . . ."

" What did they do ? " Daisy said.

" Awful row. Everybody jumping up and crowding round. And this fellow Jey . . ."

" But who did it ? Didn't they get 'im ? "

He stared at her in silence. He remembered the big figure leaning over the balcony and withdrawing before he could see the features. But something about the shape . . .

" No, I don't know who did it," he said hastily. " I don't think . . ."

His hands shook. His breath fluttered over his shuddering lips.

" Here, I'll get you something! "

Daisy hurried away and returned with the whisky and a glass.

" You've 'ad a nasty shock. You better take a strong nip."

The whisky helped him to recover from the initial shock. His hands stopped trembling. His pulse decreased. He sat back in the chair and put his feet on the footrest which Daisy placed for them. But later, all his horrified thoughts assembled again, repeating the whole horrible episode for him. He saw again the horrid lethal object whirling down and crashing upon the table. He heard the screams and shouts, saw the running together and breaking apart and the whole tangled confusion of the place. But worse than these memories was the one increasing idea that he had been the target at which the table had been aimed.

His suspicious thoughts grew from a mere trickle of an idea to a roaring heat of terror from suspicion. He swallowed more whisky. He got up and braced himself. But the idea remained, and he connected it with Rennenberg and Smith and Lane.

He imagined that Foss had denounced Rennenberg as an imposter and that Rennenberg had suspected treachery and had tried to revenge himself.

" No . . . no . . ." he said aloud, dismissing it. " Wouldn't do that! Couldn't . . ."

He went to bed. He could not sleep. He yielded to terror which melted before sudden comforting ideas which only made more hideous the ensuing gulf which opened from larger apprehensions. Trying to kill him! Or were they after Jey ?

He was wide awake, a big sweating body enwrapped by the heat and made porous to fear by his evil conscience.

" Perhaps it was Jey," he said to Daisy. " I wish I knew. I wish I could tell. I'll have to find him and ask him. I'll have to see . . ." he kept mumbling.

★

XVI

★

That night, the heat settled more heavily than ever over the city. It possessed all living things, all the streets, the buildings as well. It heaved from the hot pavements and walls and encircled the towers and the roofs. It invaded houses and devoured the air there. Nothing impeded it as it intercepted the hosts of sleep whose advent recumbent man awaited. In the loftiest, most spacious rooms it was as much an intruding presence as it was in the cramped, unhealthy rooms of row upon row of little brick houses clustered in the streets near the River and the gaunt mills. The body could not elude it, nor could the mind ignore it. The coolest sheet absorbed it, and the nude body was its prey. It cunningly awaited mankind in private gardens where he sought to sleep in tents and loggias. It was on the flat roofs where whole families attempted to escape it. It absorbed the water which was sprinkled on terraces. The luscious fountains, sibilant and plashing in the silence of the night in magnificent private gardens, could not lessen it. Throughout the city, water sprinklers plying along the main roads made no impression against it.

The man named George Jey who was a permanent guest at the " Crown " in Derby Street, slept quite successfully because he adopted a ruse of the tropics and clutched to his nude body a bolster which absorbed the heat from his flesh. In fitful moments, he yawned, lay on his back, and wondered when Foss would send word to him to depart for Germany. He had a passport and a visa. He had a bag packed. He had a revolver. Presently, he turned over on his side and slept again, saying aloud to himself at the moment before sleep came to him : " Such things . . . such things don't happen! "

Foss at that moment was wide awake in the bed next to Tilly's. He had discarded all the bedclothes and was lying on his back with knees drawn up and his arms outstretched. Where his body touched the bed there were little sources of heat which he found unbearable. He shifted his position constantly and found fresh attitudes. But after half an hour he knew that he would find no more sleep that night. He sighed and sat up and looked at Tilly.

She was soundly sleeping. One pale, shapely arm lay over the thin sheet which covered her to the waist. The other was folded and curved beside her. Foss watched her in the dim light, seeing her cherished features, her pretty head and its dark hair spilling about the pillow. He enjoyed looking at her in this way, for it was only at such moments that he felt secure in his love for her and certain of her. Awake, she was herself: frivolous by nature, extravagant, wilful, uncertain and sly. But asleep, all her faults were diminished by her beauty. And it was her beauty that he loved. He sighed again, this time loudly. And thinking about her and pondering her wilful nature, his mind filled with a sour little anxiety.

" I wish I could trust her! " he whispered.

He got up and went to the window and stood looking down on the garden. All was hushed there. The trees and bushes stood rigidly in the heat.

" Rolly! " Tilly said softly.

He liked the sensuous, languid way in which she called to him.

" Can't you sleep ? " he said, going towards her.

" It's hellishly hot," she murmured, stirring slowly and flinging off the sheet.

He looked down at her lax body. Slim, white, with the skin softly radiant in the half-darkness of the room, its perfection of shape found grace in all her movements.

" He's rather nice in some ways, isn't he ? " she said.

" Who ? "

" Herr Rennenberg," she said.

" Do you like him ? "

He hardly listened to her answer, for in his opinion she liked the wrong people, chose the wrong sort of friends, never consorted with the wise and honourable.

" . . . but, for all that, he's a rat."

" What ? What's that ? Do you mean Rennenberg ? "

" Yes. I said he's a rat, although I like him in some ways."

He chuckled. " If she knew," he thought, yawning. He seated himself in a chair near the window. " And if she could help me."

Then his thoughts moved out again over their problems.

" That duplicate . . . just in time! And it proves that something has gone wrong in Berlin. Or doesn't it ? Is it a mistake ? And is this fellow genuine ? But the original of that duplicate . . . where is it ? Lost in the post ? Intercepted by the German postal authorities ? I wish . . . I wish I could speak to Von Pless! "

He went back to bed and stretched himself as he lay at full length.

" Why do you think he's a rat ? " he asked Tilly.

" All Nazis are rats! " she said. " That's my opinion of them, after the way they have treated the Czechs."

" I don't know that he is a Nazi."

" I asked him," Tilly said. " And I think he is."

He sat up and looked at her.

" When ? When was this ? "

" When you went to bring the cigars after dinner. I wondered if he was, so I asked him point blank. I said . . ."

" What did he say ? "

" I said : ' Herr Rennenberg, is it indiscreet to ask if you are a Nazi ? ' He was rather nice, in his way. He said : ' Mrs. Foss : if I were to tell you that I am a Nazi, you would despise me. And if I were to tell you that I am not a Nazi, you would not believe me.' "

" So what did you say then ? " Foss asked.

" I asked him to tell me the truth."

" Did he ? "

" He said : ' The success of my business depends on my being a Nazi.' "

" Did he ? " Foss exclaimed. " Is that what he said ? "

" I just smiled. So long as he doesn't ' Heil Hitler ' me or anyone in this household . . ."

" That's right," Foss said, " just smile. But don't ask him any more indiscreet questions."

" That wasn't indiscreet! "

" Still, just smile."

" Why ? " said Tilly, folding her hands under her head and drooping a slim leg over the edge of the bed.

For a moment, Foss was inclined to tell her why a smile and silence were the best retort to their guest's more positive remarks, for she seemed to him to have acquired already some adroitness which might serve his own purpose if he could persuade her how best to use it.

" Because . . ." he began, then he stopped. It would take so long to explain. He could not summon his tired, anxious mind to make the effort ; also he knew that Tilly would have neithei the patience nor the wit to follow him and help him. She was too headstrong to follow him in an affair such as this one. Therefore, he chose silence.

" I'll tell you to-morrow. Remind me . . ." he said, lying back on the bed.

Tilly relaxed. Drawing in her leg she composed her body in another attitude and was silent. How near she had been to one of those troublesome crises when Rolly discovered her in one of her escapades, only she knew. She closed her eyes, and opened them again quickly to glance at Rolly. Did he know? Had he guessed the number of questions she had put to Rennenberg? So you are a Nazi, Herr Rennenberg? Are you a Storm Trooper, or whatever it is? Have you seen Hitler? Do you believe that Nazi Germany is going to conquer the world? All these, and several more. Had Rolly overheard her cunningly overcoming the defences of their guest, and had he discovered what sport she had had and intended to have with this German?

She felt an impulse to giggle.

In the bedroom across the landing, the German was lying naked on his bed. He was troubled, vexed, and uncomfortable. The heat was appalling. But much worse than the heat was the redoubtable character of his hostess who, after dinner, after ices on the terrace, had gathered all the forces of an inquisitive nature and turned them cunningly on him within the space of five minutes! To probe, to ambush him when his mind was unwary, to duel with him, to withdraw only to advance in another direction with another subtle question.

" Foss ? " he thought. " Simple! But this Tilly! "

He was surprised to discover that he was afraid of her. He tried to analyse this fear and its reasons. For years, he had met only the women of the Continent: German women, French women, some Sudeten German women : all of them of a type which he imagined he understood. The German women were good and loyal Germans. Those who were not, suffered for their crimes. And in a way he had often suspected but had never troubled to analyse, he felt that they suffered even when they were loyal to the Party. Now, thinking of Tilly, he knew why they suffered. It was because they were women ; because they were dominated by men ; because men had ordered their lives even in the most personal matters. But here, at last, was a member of the female sex, and she was not afraid of him. She asked him questions and mocked him and opposed him in such a way that she seemed to be fighting him for all the women who were so ruthlessly dominated by the Nazi Party. And he was horrified. She had a freedom which the women of Nazi Germany would never enjoy, and she used it like a weapon against him. He was unaccustomed to it, and was therefore inept and afraid. But he was afraid of himself.

He saw the daring ruse by which he had obtained admittance to this household. The corridors of lies and subterfuges! His assistants who had travelled over to join him in this city! His real purpose in coming here. His identity as a responsible agent of the Geheime Staatspolizei! His mission, and the trail of horrible brutality stretching far back to Berlin and to the pale, blood-spattered figure of Von Pless and dozens of his confederates in a plot which the authorities were convinced extended to the figure of Foss!

Despite his fears, he believed in himself. He was supported in his belief by the confidence which his superiors in Berlin had in him. Also, his knowledge of Foss's affairs, gained during three intense days of perusal of all the agency files in Von Pless's office, as well as by the numerous questions which he had put to Von Pless, bolstered him. He was here to entice from Foss the final knowledge, the last word, the truth which Von Pless would not or could not confess. He knew it was here, in Foss's mind. He believed that, although there was no proof supporting the belief.

But already, he was weakened by what had happened to him in England. The great and thrilling sense of freedom which came to him from all the influences of existence here was like wine which he tasted for the first time. And more potent, and more dangerous, was this enemy, this woman Tilly.

" I must be careful," he told himself.

He had been trained. He was clever, intrepid, and resourceful. In Berlin, he had a great reputation. But this woman had weapons which he lacked. She was not so much one woman : she was all women. The insulted, degraded women of Germany, whose boys were stolen from the influence of home life, whose personal rights were denied, whose bodies were scarcely their own. And she met him with questions, with scorn in her eyes.

He sighed. The heat was intolerable. Sleep had couched itself pleasantly beside him for an hour. Now he was wide awake. He got up and slipped on a dressing-gown and stood at the window. He felt very lonely and far from all the things which supported his beliefs. And in this hot silence, and amidst all the beauty of the world which spread beyond the garden and its fat trees to a sky wherein many stars and planets shone, he felt the intense ideas which had burned for so many years in his mind begin to cool, to become heavy and dull, to melt at last before all the width and quietude of the universe.

He felt an indescribable terror rise in him. His loneliness frightened him. His disloyalty horrified him. Covering his face with his hands, he turned his back to the window, to the stars and planets, to the velvet night, and made an effort.

He recovered himself. But he was still afraid of what had happened to him. Suddenly, he heard voices. Listening, he distinguished Tilly's and then Foss's. He crept to his open door and listened and even went into the passage and stood there. But he could not distinguish the words.

They stopped. Then there was only the slow pulse of the heat and the sound of his own pulse in his ears.

He crept back to his room and tried to sleep.

Part Two

THURSDAY

★

I

★

Thursday dawned brilliantly. For an hour, the liquid light of early day flowed freely over the world. The sky was a soft blue colour. Sunlight sparkled on the river's smooth surface. The glory of summer bloomed in the foliage of trees, in the colour and the freshness of the morning.

By nine o'clock it had staled. The relentless sun dried the dew, poured upon the world a stiff yellow light which consumed colour and the fluid grace of the new day. By ten, the day was already old, yellow, hard behind the haze ; and the temperature was still rising. Ninety-eight, a hundred, a hundred and one! And nothing allayed the heat as it sought a fresh conquest and moved across the shade and burned the air. Of the four great elements, fire was enthroned in might.

Foss drove into town very early.

" I shall see you about eleven," he said to Rennenberg, after an early breakfast. " But don't hurry on my account. It's going to be warmer than yesterday. If you don't come at eleven, I shall know that you prefer to spend the day at home. We can discuss the rest of our business this evening. Don't let Tilly chase you into town! "

" What was it you were going to tell me ? " Tilly asked Foss when they were alone. She was in a lavender dressing-gown. Full-sleeved, flimsy, it was a mere petal about her body, and her small pale hands came out of it like subtle little tendrils, to caress, to entwine, to express her character, to take his secret from him. She yawned.

" You told me to remind you about something," she said.

Foss lifted a bulging brief-bag from the floor.

" Did I ? I can't remember."

" Something about . . ."

She slowly jerked her head in the direction of their guest's room.

91

" Don't you remember ? "

" Oh, yes! Yes, listen, Tilly, my dear."

He rested an arm along her shoulders and lightly kissed her powdered cheek.

" I'll telephone you during the morning. I want you to take care of Herr Rennenberg for me to-day. Keep him nicely entertained. . . ."

" What ? " She bridled, drawing back. " What ? All day ? "

" All day."

" Oh, but I've things to do, Rolly! That's unfair! I must keep some appointments."

" Sorry. Just for to-day."

She fluttered her hands and rose to follow him to the door.

" Rolly! Rolly! "

" Take him with you! " he said. " Show him to your friends! "

He moved on abruptly. The crisp rustle of her garments as she hurried to overtake him seemed to him to express not only her exasperation but all the lively grace of her movements. For an instant, something poignant alighted in his heart. He had an acute sense of her beauty, and was never quite prepared for these moments when some delicate fancy conveyed it to him and strangely afflicted his heart.

" Rolly! It's so unfair! Can't you take him ? " she pleaded.

He tapped her supple buttocks.

" I give him to you! " he said, smiling. " I leave him to your mercy! All to-day, and perhaps to-morrow as well."

" Oh, but you said you'd take me to the Ballet to-morrow! "

" I haven't forgotten. I'll get the tickets to-day. Three."

" Three ? Must we take him ? I don't like Nazis! I don't care for him for breakfast, lunch, and all the rest of the day! "

" Then lose him, lose him! " Foss whispered. " Drown him in the swimming-pool! Hand him over to your friends. But keep him away from me! "

Her frown and silence followed him like a little thread which she would not loosen from him. He waved a hand as soon as he sat in the car.

" To-night, darling! See you about six! Have a lovely day in the shade! "

She pouted, and all at once she put out her tongue at him. He chuckled and let in the clutch and drove off. A moment later, his laughter ceased abruptly and a great flock of heavy thoughts entered his mind.

He drove faster than usual, almost urgently, hurrying in through the leafy suburbs and then by a short cut through the smoky manufacturing district and along the old commercial quarters amongst the dusty gutters and the straw-strewn entrances to yards and the heat and the yellow glare of the sunlight. It was twenty minutes to nine when he alighted and left the car at the rank with the crippled attendant. He crossed the road and turned the corner, smelling the petrol-fumed, stale air off the roads and the hot smell from the pavements. He saw groups of charwomen from his own premises and other buildings coming in one direction against the first swarms of clerks and other workers coming off the 'buses. As he entered the big building, the Commissionaire saluted him. Several junior clerks passed him on their way in. He tried to compose his mind. He had things to remember.

First, the facts about the letter and the duplicate from Berlin. Where was the original letter! And the absurd fashion in which Kelpey had told him about Rennenberg. And what to tell the staff about Rennenberg, if any of them were to ask him. And the tickets for the Ballet.

He saw a pert, junior typist rush past him.

" I want . . ." he began.

The girl turned to him. " Good morning."

" Tell Miss Dewlash . . ."

" Yes, Mr. Foss."

He hurried into his room and tossed his brief-bag on the settee near the wall and hung his hat and gloves on the stand. Settling quickly at his desk, he made notes on the pad, ringing the one about the tickets for the Ballet. He threw down his pencil and rang for Kelpey. There was no response. The room was very warm, with an odour of floor and furniture polish. He got up and started the fan and opened wide the windows.

" Boy! " he called loudly, touching the bell at the same time.

A diminutive youth appeared.

" See that all the fans are started, and open all the windows and doors. All of them! Straight away! "

He waved the boy away. He heard Miss Dewlash enter her room.

" Miss Dewlash! Miss Dewlash! "

She came in drawing off her gloves. She gave him a smile.

" You're very early, Mr. Foss! Couldn't you sleep ? "

" Five to nine ? That too early ? "

She smiled and waited for him to continue.

" Before you start anything, ring up the theatre and get me three good seats for to-morrow night's performance. And after that . . ."

The telephone bell rang.

" . . . three good seats. You know where I like to sit."

He lifted the receiver. Someone began to ask an involved question.

" What ? What's that ? Wait a minute! I must refer to the papers first. Get the papers, and bring them up to me."

A messenger entered and left for him a pile of letters which she placed in the basket marked " IN." She was followed by the chief accountant. He carried a thick folder which he put down on Foss's desk and slowly opened.

" What's this, Matthews ? "

Someone else tapped on the door and came in and stood waiting in the background.

" Shall I ring up the bank, Mr. Foss, or will you ? It's just to make sure that these Berlin transfers have been made."

" But they're not due yet, are they ? "

" They were due the day before yesterday, the twentieth."

" Then they must have gone through safely."

He glanced at Matthews, and knew that his sudden terror was written all over his face.

" Not up to closing-time yesterday," Matthews said.

" That's unusual! That's not like Von Pless."

" I know. I suggest we send a cable."

" What's the total ? The whole sum . . ."

" The total consignments amount to twelve thousand, eight hundred and forty-two pounds. That sum includes our commission."

" Telephone the bank. And let me know."

Matthews gathered his papers.

" I'll get on to them as soon as they open."

Behind him were several juniors standing in a short queue which moved towards Foss's desk. A messenger entered and delivered a small sheaf of letters which Foss pushed to one side as he dragged the telephone towards him.

" Get me my house. I'll hold the line."

He glanced up at the clerk nearest the desk.

" Yes ? "

He watched the commonplace, familiar face as the clerk bent forward and stated his errand. Like all the other faces, it represented something of the business : accounts, contracts, shipping forms, advices, consignment notes, bills of exchange, translations.

" Mr. Templeton says shall we arrange to ship these by the *Cora* or the *Sir Lancelot*, sir ? He wants to know . . ."

" What's in it ? What's the difference ? Why ask me, eh ? "

Foss wasn't sharp. He smiled pleasantly. In the long queue of faces, he saw all the factual knowledge of the business represented by features whose details he had never actually studied until now when, with his thoughts arrested for an instant, he discovered that something of all their personal lives was impressed indelibly on the faces of these employees. Here, a jocund spirit. That one, an impressionable, meditative sort, surely ? Another, independent, humorous. He heard them whispering together, turning and showing one another letters, papers. They smiled, nudged one another. And he liked them like this, in the mass.

" You know as much about these vessels as I do," he said. " You and Mr. Templeton should be able to make your choice. Learn to make a decision! "

The clerk smiled wanly. " The vessels are all right, sir. There isn't much to choose between their rates and their speeds. The whole point is that the *Cora* makes the voyage direct, but the *Sir Lancelot* touches at two Italian ports."

" So what ? " Foss said. He knew that he was being facetious, but he was surprised that nobody smiled and acknowledged his good humour. His glance flashed over the queue, and he saw more clearly than before the reflection of private lives : not in the terms of character, this time, but in the indications of individual thought. He felt rebuffed. He felt a sudden spurt of anger.

" So what ? I said! So what ? " And he frowned.

" We have to consider the possibility of a war, and the entry of Italy as an ally of Germany," the clerk said.

There was utter silence. All the faces were turned solemnly to Foss as though he alone did not appreciate the imminence of warfare. He was struck by a sudden chill dread. He hadn't read the newspapers this morning. Hadn't seen the news. Didn't know what had happened. And his employees knew this and were watching him to see the truth strike him and startle him.

He held himself in readiness for it, and said equably :

" Of course, I'm quite aware of that. I'm glad you came to me first, however. Until you receive specific instructions to the contrary, that is until the possibility becomes fact, continue as usual. Tell Mr. Templeton to advise me what vessel he ships by."

He heard the maid in his house answer the telephone. He said quickly : " Mary, go and ask Mr. Rennenberg to come to the 'phone, please."

The shipping clerk withdrew.

" Yes, Mr. Foss, I'll go and call him," Mary said.

The second figure in the queue stood forward with folded arms. An athletic figure, a square man of thirty-five, assistant to the cashier. As soon as Foss glanced at him, the man held up a cheque between thumbs and forefingers and presented it for Foss to read first.

" For your signature."

He placed the cheque on the blotter and lifted Foss's fountain pen and handed it to him, at the same time running a forefinger firmly along the dotted line.

" What's this for ? What's this ? " Foss said.

He perused it rapidly, murmuring, then he signed it for the firm. The clerk blotted it and nodded his thanks and withdrew. Someone else took his place at the moment when Rennenberg spoke.

" Yes, Mr. Foss ? "

" Ah, Rennenberg! There's a query I want to mention to you. The Berlin agency. Transfers. Some thousands of pounds. Due on the twentieth of this month. . . ."

" Yes ? "

" . . . but not yet received. No notification yet from our bankers. I wonder if you have any information about them."

" A transfer ? "

" Yes. Paid into Von Pless's account. Several thousands of pounds paid into his account, and he, of course, instructs his bankers to transfer the sum to our account over here."

" Oh, yes, yes! Yes, I have some information about that, Mr. Foss. The sum is fifteen thousand pounds, isn't it ? "

Foss heard him distinctly. His heart lurched. He said quickly : " How much did you say ? "

" Fifteen thousand."

It gave Foss a fraction of a second in which to recover himself.

" Not quite as much as that, I think. . . ."

" Oh, yes! Fifteen thousand."

" No, pardon me. The correct sum is twelve thousand, eight hundred and forty-two pounds."

" Ah, yes! Yes, I remember. Yes, I have some information regarding that, Mr. Foss! "

Was it a threat ? Was this the climax after all deceit and subterfuge had been penetrated ?

" Good! " Foss said, with an effort. " Has it gone through ? May we expect the usual notification ? "

" I don't think that we should discuss this very important matter over the telephone," Rennenberg said.

" As you wish. But has this transfer gone through ? That's all I require to know at the moment."

" Mr. Foss, I should prefer to discuss it with you this evening."

" Any hitch ? Anything gone wrong ? " Foss said.

" Oh, my dear sir, you understand the situation, surely ? But as I said, to-night."

" And in the meantime ? "

" You will have time to consider what you have to say to me."

" I don't understand."

" Mr. Foss, you have much to tell me." It was said in a whisper. " I shall rest here all day. It's so pleasant here, and the city is so hot. Best if we defer our discussion until to-night."

" I don't quite understand. Discussion ? "

" Yes. The fifteen thousand, you know."

" Twelve thousand."

" And that, too."

" But meanwhile ? "

"I shall tell you this, Mr. Foss. Everything depends on you, sir! Von Pless, I think, would wish me to stress that."

Foss chuckled. "Well, I suppose so. So, until this evening . . ."

"Yes, good-bye!"

Foss replaced the receiver and put his hands on the edge of his desk.

"Yes, next? What is it?"

He beckoned them forward to let them thrust letters, contracts, queries on paper, reports, at him. When they spoke, he listened attentively and replied from his extensive knowledge of the firm's affairs. His mind was a great mass of factual knowledge which they approached either to increase in tiny degrees or to invoke. Occasionally, he peered along the queue and called forward a certain employee. He puffed and panted in the increasing heat. After half an hour, he got up and removed his jacket. Miss Dewlash came in.

"Just a minute!" he said, halting the queue. "I can't attend to anything more until I've read my post. All come back in twenty minutes."

"Oh, sir! Only this . . ."

Their protests rose in a chorus. He frowned and made an irritable exclamation.

"Very well, very well. Quickly, though. Miss Dewlash! Don't go! Tell Mr. Kelpey to come in. Or listen! Listen! Some of you go and get Mr. Kelpey to settle these matters."

Four of them left the queue. The rest closed up again and waited patiently while he examined papers, called for facts and figures, gave decisions. It was one of those mornings when everything seemed to depend upon his word, his decisions and advice. Deeply in himself, he enjoyed it because it afforded him a sense of power which emphasised all the factors of his own success and that of the firm. But it vexed him. He wanted time in which to disentangle his secret problem from all other minor problems. He wanted to ponder what Rennenberg had said, and who Rennenberg was, and what would happen this evening. The minutes passed and there did not seem to be much likelihood of the queue dwindling or the bells ceasing to ring or the flood of letters subsiding. He set himself a more rapid pace which he imagined would presently release him from the immediate matters. But it didn't.

By eleven, he was immersed in the avalanche. And by then he had submitted to it because he recognized what sort of a day was ahead of him. This morning's activity characterised the life of a firm such as his. Perhaps twice a month things happened this way. The mails were full of letters which necessitated a reply by return. The telephone rang repeatedly. An urgency lay at the root of routine and could not be appeased. It communicated itself from department to department, like a shout which raised an alarm and which echoed across the sultry

D

air. It was that sort of a day, and Foss knew that he would have to tolerate it. And because Brighart and Molloy were on holidays he alone bore the pressure of it and the pace of it. Everything devolved upon him. He took Brighart's calls, and interviewed Molloy's agents. He said yes and no after digging expertly amidst the mass of facts. He answered Brighart's and Molloy's letters.

" Kelpey! " he said, whenever he saw his assistant. " I want to see you ! "

Then somebody telephoned or called, and he and Kelpey were carried off on separate streams of the current across which he shouted, signed cheques, letters, answered queries. Until just after midday, when there came a lull. He dabbed his wet forehead and lifted the telephone receiver.

" Get me my house. I'll hold on here."

When the servant answered he said : " Mary! Listen! Go and ask Mrs. Foss to come to the telephone. But, now listen! Don't tell her who wants her. Be very careful not to say. Just say it's a friend. Understand ? "

He sat back and waited. The chair's hot upholstery burned against his back. He leaned forward over the desk and heard with a cool, delicate sense her approaching footsteps and the rustle of her sleeves. Then came her lilting greeting.

" Tilly Foss here! "

He laughed quickly. " And this is Tilly Foss's husband! "

She was silent. He stopped laughing because he was always careful not to provoke her anger. And already in her silence he suspected the sudden lurch of her thoughts about a subject which angered her.

" Tilly, listen, please! " he said, quietly.

" You listen to me, Rolly ! " she retorted. " Damn you! That's what I want to say to you! Listen to me, you beast! "

" Now what's the matter ? "

" This German is the matter! And I'm worried, and I don't thank you for parking him on me for the day! "

" Worried ? Why ? Have a jolly time with him! "

" Rolly, this fellow stinks! "

" Oh, I say, my dear! That's rather . . ."

" So he does! All Nazis stink! "

" Tilly, you don't know that he is a Nazi."

" I think he is." Her voice dwindled until it became a whisper. " I can tell it. The way he acts. The way he talks. You know I'm clever at finding out things about people."

" Oh. he's nothing like that, Tilly," Foss said.

" I'm digging it out of him."

" Now look here . . ."

" It's all right," Tilly said. " You needn't worry about me. He's just as frightened as I am."

Foss exploded. " Now, listen! Stop talking nonsense! Just be careful. Just have a nice quiet day at home. What are you doing ? "

" We've been in the swimming pool. Now we're sunning ourselves, and we've just had ices, and he's telling me about Germany."

" Remember what I told you, Tilly! "

" I tried to, Rolly, but it's too late."

" What do you mean ? "

" Rolly, he's a brute. I know. I can feel it. And two awful dagoes called to see him, and he's put through at least six calls. If you want my opinion . . ."

" I don't! You're too suspicious-minded! You imagine silly things. You and your nonsense! "

" Well, come and take him away out of this before I grill him! Rolly, I can't help it! You know what I am. You know that I see clean through people. You know what a little bitch I am when people have a secret. I simply must get it out of them, or else die of misery. You know I'm inquisitive."

" Nonsense! Stop behaving like a half-wit! You've got a touch of sunstroke, if you ask me! Now go back and behave like an intelligent person, instead of being a fool! "

" It's your fault! " she shouted. And lowering her voice, she added : " You left him here with me."

" Don't be silly! Oh, don't be so silly! Remember what I said to you. Remember he's a business associate of mine."

" I like that! "

" I must ring off now."

" Rolly! Just a minute! "

" Good-bye! Must go, now! "

" You beast, Rolly! "

He hung up the receiver because someone entered his room at that moment. The avalanche resumed. At ten minutes past one, he got up and rang for his secretary. There was no response. He put on his jacket and hat and hurried out.

Dewlash's room was empty. So was Kelpey's, adjoining it. Over the entire building, a hush had fallen. It was the lunch hour. He saw junior typists and clerks eating sandwiches at their desks and sitting in little groups around tables which had been dragged from their places at walls.

Down in the street, the sunlight flared on him like the tip of a flame. He crossed the road to the shade and stood there, hesitating. To drive home and have lunch with Tilly and the German ? To get the whole business settled one way or another ? To decide it within the next hour ?

The idea bloomed attractively in his mind, offering him a possibility of release from suspense. To terminate the inward struggle between good and evil! To renounce his part in the plot, and to decide for honesty! To close his mind to the attractions of money, and to return to all the reputable pursuits of export!

It was as cool upon his mind as a sudden breeze upon his body. The anticipation of a release from a sense of peril! Next moment, he suffered an equivalent sense of loss. To renounce fifteen thousand pounds!

In the select little café to which he wandered, he sat trying to decide what to do.

" If he isn't Rennenberg," he thought, " then who and what is he ? And how is it that he is so conversant with our business ? Yesterday afternoon. And last night. So sure of himself. Never a mistake. Which proves that he is in Von Pless's confidence. And yet no word about the plot. And I dare not, I simply dare not open the subject. And if he is a fraud, as Kelpey says, and it might be, might just be, then the whole business must have been discovered. Von Pless arrested. And this fellow . . ."

His suspicions about Rennenberg became more fantastic. They held his mind in a vice. They drew awful visions for him. He felt himself to be involved in a counter-plot. He trembled.

But after half an hour during which he had eaten a salad and an iced sweet, he emerged from his thoughts only to discover that he was rooted in the determination not to renounce the fifteen thousand pounds. Why panic ? Why jump to conclusions before he had discovered the truth ? Why assume that Von Pless had been arrested ?

It appalled him. Was he so corrupt ? Was he so stupid as to imagine that he—Roland Foss—could enter that fantastic project and operate it successfully ? So large and so bloody a business! So desperate! Could he continue in it, when the normal, healthy world buzzed and chattered around him, as now ? All the healthy, energetic stir of a normal life in this city, while he harboured that tense, horrid secret!

But was it normal and healthy ? Was it not tense ? Was not this environment in which he lived as subject to the insane repercussions from Hitler's actions as was the rest of Europe ? Was he not a part of that intense scene on the Continent ? Was this suspense normal ?

Foss thought : " A single bullet would end it all. Jey is ready. If I gave him the word now, he would take the next train to the Capital and begin his journey. He is ready. It would end the suspense in which the world has lived for five years. That maniac in Germany! Why not ? Why not destroy him ? Von Pless, myself, all the others, Jey ? Haven't we the right ? Isn't it feasible that we are the chosen men ? Or is there another way ? "

He pushed aside his plate. His hands were damp and trembling. The other way, the longer and perhaps better way. A war. Such a war! Steel and fire and destruction! The longer way, but the sounder way. To achieve the cleanliness. To destroy standards of brutality and aggression rooted in ideas. To kill the idea and not one man who had encouraged it! To destroy his works before his eyes!

And yet, the other way! With its rewards. . . .

He thought slowly : " I can't go on. Von Pless has been arrested. Everything must have broken down over there, and somebody managed to get a letter through to me to warn me."

His resolves collapsed under this presentiment of truth, and he stood at last amidst the patient, unafraid masses of his own countrymen. Patient, calm people, awaiting with a certain tenseness and vexation the final act which would bring them into warfare. Reasonable, kindly people, contemptuous of force, contemptuous of Hitler and the Nazis, but content to wait until a certain hour of a certain day when they would be challenged. And then . . .

He got up and paid his bill and passed out into the hot street. And at once, all the affairs of the firm swarmed again in his mind. And yet beneath them, and despite all his conclusions, there lay the tantalizing, unsolved problem regarding Von Pless and the plot.

He returned to his office, because there remained fifteen minutes in which he might ponder that problem again.

Someone had lowered the blinds in his room. That pleased him. The windows were wide open. Sultry air was static in the room, but the sunlight was excluded. He sat down on the settee against the wall below the enlarged photographic portraits of his father and grandfather. Relaxing, removing his jacket and turning up his sleeves, he jerked off his left shoe with the point of his right shoe. His hot foot was momentarily cool. He sat up and removed the right shoe. The carpet beneath his feet was cool, soft, pliant. It reminded him of the time when he had run barefooted on grass or played on sandy beaches. He walked slowly about the room. The thick pile of the carpet was pleasantly resilient beneath his feet. He felt lighter, cooler, as though he were walking on a plane above all his problems. He felt refreshed.

" I shall have to have it out with that German! " he thought. " I shall have to . . . to . . ."

He wondered rather fearfully what he would say. All at once, a dread word came of its own volition into his mind.

" Gestapo! "

He held his breath. He remembered what Tilly had said. Her suspicions. Her probing suspicions!

He heard Kelpey come in.

" Kelpey! " he shouted. " Are you there, Kelpey ? "

There was no reply. He touched the bell. The assistant appeared. "Yes, Mr. Foss ?"

He had several letters in his hands, and he kept his eyes on them.

"Listen, Kelpey! Never mind what you have there! Leave that."

Kelpey put down the letters on the desk. He had a curious, inimical air of concentration in his gaze. Foss noticed it at once.

"What's the matter with you ? What are these letters ? Show me. . . ."

"Nothing, sir, nothing. Only . . . only this . . . I . . ."

"What is it ?" Foss said.

"I . . . found this . . ."

Foss grabbed the letter. He recognized it. It was the original of the duplicate which Dewlash had shown him yesterday. Slamming it on his blotter and spreading his hands over it, he glared up at Kelpey.

"Oh! Indeed! Found it! Found it, eh ? A nice thing! He finds it at last! My personal assistant finds this letter and brings it to me . . ."

He paused and smiled sardonically.

" . . . when I have already seen the duplicate! "

Foss snorted angrily and suddenly snatched the letter and thrust it into the drawer. He leaned forward and wagged a forefinger.

"And there's something else I want to talk to you about! Yesterday . . . at five o'clock . . . that stupid note you brought . . . that note you brought me in to show me . . ."

"Oh, yes, Mr. Foss! "

Kelpey's voice was tremulous. Foss, too, was trembling.

"Yes, I want to explain about that, sir."

Foss shook his head and closed his eyes. He held up a stiff hand. "I don't want any explanations."

He saw Kelpey's features twitch and then settle into the same constrained expression as before.

"I don't want them. Remember, in future . . ."

"But, sir, he isn't the real Rennenberg! I know that for a fact."

The constraint vanished from Kelpey's face. His expression was transformed.

Foss interrupted quickly : "I said I don't require explanations! In future, make sure that important letters don't wander round the office! "

"I'm not trying to excuse myself, Mr. Foss," Kelpey said. "Only I don't think you quite understand . . ."

Foss sat with his gaze averted. His hands padded amongst the papers on his desk.

"Oh, really! Really ? "

" . . . you don't realize who that man is, sir," Kelpey added.

Foss sat back in his chair and pretended to read a letter. " I know perfectly well who he is. I know everything about him that it is necessary for me to know, so you need not stand there trying to tell me."

He looked up. With surprise, he saw that Kelpey had turned pale.

" He's a crook, sir," Kelpey said.

" Don't be absurd! " Foss retorted.

" I don't know his real name. He calls himself Rennenberg. I met him one evening, and he was sitting with Collis and two other Germans. At least, one of them was German, I think, and the other said he was Dutch."

" Collis ? "

" He rents the attics."

Foss's gaze was riveted upon Kelpey.

" And they were talking about a necklace," Kelpey went on. " I was surprised when I saw him come in here yesterday afternoon, sir. Especially when I knew that Herr Rennenberg was not coming . . . when I saw the duplicate of that letter."

" Were you ? Well, you needn't say more. I have my wits about me, thank you. You seem to imagine that every German is a crook, and that your employer is a fool. You had better give up such foolish fancies. About this letter : as I said before, don't let it happen again. You can go."

" Thank you, sir."

Foss watched him go. Collis . . . Collis.

" Collis, and a necklace, and two other men . . . Germans," he was thinking. " Well, I can soon get to the root of that! "

He got up and padded along the corridor to the narrow, bare flight of stairs leading to the attics. Kelpey heard him pass and knew where he was going.

Foss reached the door at the top of the narrow stairs. He rapped loudly on the panel and waited. The little door shook on its flimsy hinges. There was only silence and the heat. He tried the handle. The door was locked. He rapped again. Up there, the heat was stifling. It penetrated the roofs and walls and poured over the wood-work and diffused an odour of dust and dried paint which the lungs breathed with difficulty.

Kelpey heard him return to his room, and he knew that he had not spoken to Collis, for the latter had been out all day.

" Now it's over," he thought. " He knows. I've told him. He knows who that German is : a crook. He'll deal with him. I've told him everything."

He relapsed into long, contented thoughts, seeing his life with all its pleasant labour and pursuits returned to its normality.

The rest of the staff came back from lunch. Over the premises the heat increased, and the thermometers in the corridors recorded it. A lethargy possessed the mind.   The body flagged.

Dewlash came to Kelpey's room.

" Did I leave three tickets for the Ballet in your basket by mistake ? "

" Three tickets . . ."

His hands began to sort the mass of papers.

" Not here . . ."

" I had them this morning.   I sent the boy to get them, and I put them amongst some papers.   Look again, will you ? "

He found them in a little envelope.

" Are these . . ."

" Thank goodness! " she exclaimed.

" Everybody talks about this Ballet," he said.

" They're a famous company," she said.   " I saw them in London, last year."

" Are you going ? "

" To-morrow night," she said.

" What is a Ballet ? " he asked.   " Music . . . dancing . . . I've never been to one.   What do they do ? "

" Then you ought to go!   Why don't you ?   I think you'd enjoy it."

" What's it all about ?   Is it a play or something, with special music ? "

She came back to his desk and was silent as she looked intently at him.   Her dark eyes seemed to him to probe his ignorance of all the things of culture which composed her personal life.

" Go.   You'll enjoy it," she said, quietly.   " I know you will."

" But I don't know anything about it! "

" Never mind.   Just go and enjoy it. Just watch and listen. That's all you need to do."

" I wouldn't get a seat now, would I ? "

Looking up at her he wondered : " Did she find my silver pencil where I dropped it ?   I must have dropped it in her flat, last night. Has she got it ? "

" You might," she said.   " Ring up now."

As she went out, he lifted the receiver and dialled the theatre.   In the extravagance which so often characterised him, he booked an expensive seat for Friday night's performance.

" I was lucky," he said, sauntering into her room.

When she saw his frank, ingenuous expression, all the irritating, baffling points concerning letters from Berlin, the visit of a German who called himself Rennenberg, and all the shadows of deceits, drifted out of her thoughts.   With them went a sense of frustration which had mocked her natural curiosity.   Nothing seemed very important at that moment except the recollection of Monday's strange little quarrel and the emotion which it had released and the sense of newness and sympathy in their understanding. And, also, there was the interesting fact that she had discovered his pencil in her sitting-room.

" It's dancing, isn't it ? " he asked. " Dancers in white dresses ; and classical music ? "

" Yes," she said, simply. " All the beauty of sound and movement. I'll lend you some books about ballet, if you'd care to read them."

Foss came padding into the room. He glared at Kelpey as though he were surprised to see him there. Then he tapped a letter which he beld in his left hand and which he gave to Dewlash.

" Write to these people . . ."

He saw the theatre tickets. " Are these mine ? "

" Yes, three tickets. Row D."

" Good! Good! "

He turned slowly away.

" What do you want me to say to these people ? " Dewlash said.

He was at the door, yawning.

" Oh . . . say . . ." He broke off and made a gesture with his hand. " Say we agree to their terms," he added, going out.

The messengers were bringing tea. On Foss's desk there was a small, brown earthenware teapot covered with a woollen cosy. Beside it were cup and bowls. Standing against the desk, Foss poured himself some tea and dropped in two cubes of sugar and added milk. He let the tea cool for a few minutes during which he sat on the settee and surrendered mind and body to the languid afternoon. His problems were at a distance. Occasionally, some latent energy of will made imperative a particular detail which, at the moment when his thoughts assembled rapidly about it, collapsed amidst cloudy indifference. The telephones had ceased to ring. The activity in the premises had flagged and found at last a mere drifting pace under the heat.

He got up and sat at his desk and sipped the tea. From adjoining rooms he heard coming the sounds of typewriters. A messenger delivered a neat sheaf of letters for his signature. Lazily, he lifted his pen and wrote his name under the formal : " Yours faithfully."

Five minutes later, he touched the bell for his secretary.

" I want to get away at five sharp. Is there much more for me ? "

He handed her the letters he had signed.

" About half a dozen."

She waited with her hands holding the sheets upright on the desk. " By the way," she said quickly. " That duplicate from Berlin. I haven't come across the original."

He sustained her gaze, thinking : " And now she, too, wants to know . . ."

" I have it," he said, nonchalantly.

" So it turned up ? "

" Yes, it turned up."

" But . . . it said . . . the duplicate said that Herr Rennenberg could not come."

" That's true."

She smiled quickly. " But what about the Herr Rennenberg who arrived yesterday ? "

" What about him ? "

She closed her eyes and tightened her lips for an instant.

" Mr. Foss, is the Rennenberg who arrived yesterday the Rennenberg . . ."

" I think," he interjected slowly, " I think that Von Pless is a little confused. We can take it that Herr Rennenberg has arrived after all."

He looked at her with an expression which almost implored her to close the conversation.

" I can't make head or tail of it," she said. " I understood that Herr Rennenberg was coming yesterday. Then came the duplicate saying that he would not be able to come. I haven't seen the original. It didn't come to me. I don't know who brought it to you . . ."

" Here! " he said, opening the drawer and thrusting the original letter at her. " Here! Take it and put it away in your safe with the duplicate! And let them stay there."

" But I still don't understand! " she protested.

He sat back in his chair and said with a tone of finality : " I hope you never will, Miss Dewlash! "

But even when he had said that, her features still showed some slight reflection of irritability and rebuff which he felt obliged to appease.

" But I can tell you," he whispered, " that neither I nor anyone else here understands just what has happened."

He saw what he imagined was complete realization of his secret begin to reveal itself in her features. He was afraid that she would go on from that realization and delve and evoke words and explanations from him. He held up a firm hand.

" And that's a confidence," he added.

" I understand," she said. And it was as though she had closed a little door forever on the information.

When she had gone. he yawned and got up to put on his shoes.

" And now there's Tilly and that blasted German," he thought. He smiled when he remembered Tilly ; but the idea of returning to the German raised an altogether different response in him.

II

Tilly was twenty-six. She was the third daughter of a chemist whose home was in one of the new villas two miles south of the city. His shop was in East Ward, and prior to the move to the villa, he and his family had occupied four rooms above this shop. In one of them, Tilly had been born.

She was the beauty of the family. She had energy, self-assurance and ambition. When these qualities successfully removed her from the villa, she tried to forget her past; and although she sometimes drove to visit her mother and father, she secretly resented their unexpected visits to her, for this unwelcome lifting of the curtain which screened a past which, with its intolerable economies, semi-poverty, and general constraint had so often appalled her, was an event which mocked her complacency in this later period.

During the five years in which she had been married to Foss, she had discovered a new world for herself. It was her revolt against the old one in which she had lived. It hated poverty. It turned savagely from it. And it delighted her. It was a world of self-indulgence.

Foss was forty-three. He had remained single until his thirty-eighth year because he was conscious of his unprepossessing appearance and also because he lived very comfortably in a large flat which was usually full of his male friends. He was unwilling to trust himself in marriage. He enjoyed his work and believed that there were few eligible and attractive women of his own age. When he met Tilly for the first time, he was impressed by her beauty. The effect it had upon him was sharp, almost disastrous to his peace of mind. He felt that without her presence in his life, everything of his existence was trivial, dull, without purpose. For the first time, he wondered if his wealth was something which might mitigate his short, plump appearance and his lack of good looks. He determined to pursue Tilly.

He had not far to go. The hunt was brief. It was all over within three months during which she had never been very far from him. She seemed to him to be the perfection of beauty, and he had always an acute sense of that beauty. Yet he knew that she was selfish, shallow-minded, vain and wilfully extravagant.

He had not been married six months before he discovered all this. It was not altogether a surprise, for there had been indications of her character long before the marriage. Time merely confirmed what he had suspected : the frivolous heart ; the shallow mind ; the self-indulgent nature. But he had no criticism to make. If she was poor in many ways, she was enriched in others. She preserved for him in his private life the fluid of her youth and beauty of body. She was the young, fresh flower, the fragrance of the young bloom, the colour of the fresh petal.

But he never quite trusted her. He defined limits for her beyond which he forbade her to go. Limits of extravagance, of indulgence and self-expression. When she edged beyond them, he made others to encompass her ; and these, too, she cunningly destroyed. Afterwards, she wept in a storm of simulated repentance which was not contrition at all but only exasperation because he had made bounds for her. He forgave her her whims, petted her, loved her.

But how to reform her ? How to transform her feckless pleasures into the pursuits of a reasonable, intelligent woman ? He tried to discuss politics, commerce, international affairs with her. He discovered that she had a quick mind and an energetic spirit. Yet, no matter how far he drew her towards a serious interest in life, she reverted to a world of limp-minded men and women, of wealthy half-wits, of indolent chatterboxes concerned only with their bodies and their clothes.

He sought for the reason, and found it. He himself had always had a reasonable income, an amount of money which permitted him to live comfortably and without niggling restraints. It was not so with her. He knew that she had known semi-poverty, the depressing rigour of economy. Now she hungered for the sumptuous, the spaciousness which his money could afford her. She was not so much the product of her nature as the product of the half-penury which she had known for so long.

He used to speed home to her after the day's work, to discover in what way she had crudely satisfied her incessant desire to escape her childhood and girlhood. This evening, he sped home because all day she had had to cope with the German. And he appreciated what demands that must have made upon her character and her temperament. Already, she had described what had happened. Now he had an increasing apprehension of the conclusion of certain alarming episodes.

When he approached the porch after turning into the drive, he sounded the horn three times. This was a signal which she answered sometimes by two contralto notes which echoed about the hall at the moment when he entered the house. Often, too, she came running swiftly downstairs to greet him in the hall. To-day, there was only the drone of the summer insects, and the great swathe of heat to meet him as he entered the house through the open doorway.

He halted. The house was very silent, a part of the hushed, tremulous world under the heat. He called softly.

"Tilly! Tilly!"

Then he saw her. Clad in a light summer frock, she stood in the shade near one of the portico's pillars on the other side of the house facing the garden. He caught that glimpse of her and hurried through the hall and dining-room and out to the terrace. She heard him coming and turned slowly to him. He was horrified.

Her eyes were full of defeat and weariness, and her body—as she leaned against the pillar—was in an attitude of exhaustion. In all this, he read the whole tale of her day with the German.

"Tilly!" he cried, running to her.

She shuddered into his arms and clung whimpering to him.

"Tilly, Tilly, my dear!"

She broke away from him and struck her clenched hands together as she poured out her grievances.

"He's beaten me at tennis! He raced me in swimming! He beat me at croquet, and won twelve shillings from me at bezique, and he's so damned good at everything, blast him! A damned superman! A prig! Just a Nazi prig!"

"Sh! Sh! There, never mind!" Foss murmured.

"I hate him! I'm sick of him! The whole day with him! And nothing but his superiority, his Nordic superiority or something! And he let me know it! He didn't stop reminding me about it all day! His beastly race! Take him away! Take him away!"

She threw herself into the nearest chair and sobbed heavily. Foss leaned over her and put his arms around her.

"There, there . . ."

"Rolly!" she said, "Rolly, I'll have to rest for two hours. I'm all out. Take him away, please. He's a rat!"

"Sh! You mustn't say such things! He's our guest!"

She sat back violently. "Guest! I like that! I found a revolver amongst his things! Loaded! I emptied it, just for safety."

"Tilly! Really, you are . . ."

She was sullen but mollified now. "Well, you know how inquisitive I am. You shouldn't have left him with me."

"But, Tilly!"

"Yes, and another thing Rolly : He said he met you in Berlin early in the year, in February. You told me you went to Paris then!"

"Of course! It was Paris. I told you . . ." Foss stammered. "Why, I haven't met him before in my life!"

She made a heedless gesture. "Well, I'm going in to rest now."

"Yes, do! You go in and have a good rest before dinner. That's right. I'll tell him . . ."

As she went in, Foss saw the German in the lush, hazy distance of the garden : a big figure in flannels and a blue shirt, stretched lazily on a long chair.

"Rolly!" Tilly called, coming slowly back to him, "Rolly, what is he here for?"

"Rennenberg?" he asked.

"Yes, what's his business? Two dagoes called to see him. And he kept using the telephone. What is he in England for? I want to know!"

Foss raised his eyebrows. "My dear, he's an associate of our Berlin agent, Von Pless!"

She pouted as she turned away. "He's unpleasant. He's nasty!"

Foss went down the terrace steps and through the wide garden. The German saw him approaching and waved energetically to him. Foss waved back and chose the shade of the trees.

"Here," he thought, "in this garden, now, or later this evening..."

His guest had risen and was strolling towards him. He offered his hand to Foss.

"My dear sir! Happy to see you again! Are you coming to sit down? It's wonderful here, in the shade, and I've had a delightful day! Your wife has been most kind, most kind."

"I've just seen her," Foss said. "She's rather tired and has gone to rest."

"Oh, I'm so sorry!"

"Just a touch of sunstroke."

"I'm very sorry."

The German sat down opposite Foss. His eyes were lustrous. His skin was lightly burned by the sunlight. An immeasurable happiness was reflected in his features when he smiled.

"I think this has been the happiest day in my life," he said, exuberantly.

His candour not only astonished Foss but roused repugnance as well.

"Really!" Foss murmured.

"Shall I tell you why?" the other said. And he leaned forward with his hands on his knees and stared with a peculiar intensity at Foss.

"Do," Foss said.

"It's because I admire England so much, sir! I always have. I admire your achievements, your national characteristics, your great traditions, your habits, everything! I have always wanted to visit England, from the time when I first began to learn English at school. I wanted to come and stay a long time and absorb your customs and your greatness. I wanted to taste England in every way. And to-day, I have done so! In this fine English home, in the company of your gracious lady, in this beautiful weather! To-day, I have possessed a little of your country. Everything has been wonderful, enchanting!"

Foss struggled to find his way from this deluge of emotion.

" I'm so glad," he said, simply.

" England! " continued the German, ecstatically.   He extended his arms wide and sighed.   Suddenly, he burst into loud laughter.

" But poor England!   So . . . so completely . . ."

Foss watched him and smiled.   He was uneasy.   He felt the German's presence as something charged with threat and very ominous.

" So completely what ? " he ventured to ask.

His guest threw up his hands and exclaimed on a high note of laughter :   " So completely stupid!   So stupidly free! "

Foss stopped smiling.   The German's laughter ceased, but his big, healthy face remained brimming with a smile which faded slowly into a peculiar, concentrated expression.

" And so vulnerable! " he added, earnestly.

" To what ? " Foss asked.   " Vulnerable to what ? "

He did not wait for an answer.   Instead, he went on :

" You said you loved England, didn't you ?   Shall I tell you why you do ?   It's because you are like a child who sees another child's toy.   And instead of being content with your own playthings and improving them and getting the best fun out of them, you want to take the other child's things and make them like your own.   It's a habit of childhood.   It's sheer envy, that's all.   I know we have a good history, on certain pages.   But it's the future, and not the past, which should be looked to.   We're a rich country, and we belong to a rich Commonwealth of nations.   And we're free.   You don't understand freedom. You haven't got it yourselves, over in Germany.   And you envy it in others and want to take it from others.   You say it's a weakness and that we're vulnerable.   Vulnerable to thieves, like you!   That's all! "

" Vulnerable to all the benefits of freedom! " retorted the German, pleasantly.   " You are like people who have eaten so well for centuries that you are suffering from a surfeit of freedom, of this kind of food! "

" Never mind! " Foss said.   " If you admire us, why not have some freedom yourselves ?   Why suffer so much regimentation ? "

" We are wise," the other said.

" Are you ? " Foss retorted.   " Wise ? "   Then he lost his temper. " You call it wise to suffer a tyrant to rule you ?   You think it wise to ignore your own national traditions of learning, of science, of art and so on, and revert to the bloody habits of a mob of savages ?   The way you have all stood by without a word of protest and seen the Jews amongst you tortured, insulted, dispersed and killed!   Is that good, or wise, or even humane ?   Is that greatness ?   And then your attitude to your weak neighbours!   Why, sir, you are a nation of plunderers!   You are bullies! "

The German grinned.   " You have a wonderful record in that direction yourselves," he said.

" Perhaps! In the past. Not now . . ."

" Even now! You dominate . . ."

" But we have a system of government which permits all of us to criticise. With you, the restraint of criticism is ruthlessly exterminated! Is that progress, sir ? Is that civilization ? Of course not! It's savagery and madness! "

Foss snorted. The German smiled at him again.

" You are angry with me," he said, mildly.

" Not with you, but with Hitler and the Nazis and with the German people for tolerating what they all know is an evil. Your ideas are silly. . . ."

" For an Englishman, you are very frank, Mr. Foss."

" Don't you like it ? " Foss said. " Does it hurt you ? It should convince you."

The German dropped his arms and let them hang limply over the sides of the chair. A ripple of uneasiness passed over his body as he settled himself deeply into the chair. His smile faded, and rancour seemed to take substance from his flesh. He looked at Foss with a tight, tense stare.

" Here it comes! " thought Foss. " Now he'll begin! "

And the ignominy of having to sit there and wait while this German chose the moment and assembled all his redoubtable wit and cunning angered Foss. This inquisitor who had doubtlessly lounged thus before the hapless Von Pless! This fanatic with his silly ideas!

Foss rose slowly. " Will you excuse me, Rennenberg ? I have had a hard day. I must go in and change and bath."

The other glared sullenly at him.

" Perhaps," Foss went on, " perhaps you would like to come in and rest before . . ."

The German made a wide motion with his left arm.

" Sit down," he said curtly.

" Surely you'd prefer to come to the house and change," Foss said, calmly. But he was angry and afraid of his anger.

" It has started," he told himself. " We are alone, and he is beginning his mission. This is the moment which he anticipated when he left Berlin."

" I prefer to stay here," Rennenberg said. His voice was flat and it rasped. An arrogance puffed itself into his mood. " I want to speak to you," he added.

" Forgive me," Foss said. " After dinner . . ."

He indicated the house with his hand and turned slowly, inviting his guest to accompany him. Rennenberg stretched out a hand and caught him in a hard grip and swung him backwards. Foss stumbled. When he recovered himself, he saw the German grinning at him and cuddling between his hands a little revolver.

112

" So sorry! " the guest said. " I hope I didn't hurt you. Now sit down and talk with me. After that, we shall enjoy the evening . . ."

" Put that thing away! " Foss said.

" Sit down! Sit down! " Rennenberg said, pointing the weapon at him.

Foss moved towards him and thrust an angry forefinger at him.

" Rennenberg," he said, remembering that Tilly had told him that she had emptied the revolver. " If you don't put that revolver away, I shall have to take it from you."

" I said ' sit down ' ! " the German shouted.

He turned the weapon towards the nearest rose-bed and pulled the trigger. A trivial click was all that the weapon emitted. Foss laughed loudly as he watched him. Their eyes met for an instant, then the German jumped from his chair and rattled away at the bushes with his revolver until he had turned the chamber and realized that the weapon was empty.

Foss sat down and chuckled loudly.

" You must have forgotten to load it! " he said.

Rennenberg gave a rapid glance at the revolver and smiled shame-facedly as he stuffed the weapon away in his hip pocket and sat down again.

" So sorry! Did I frighten you ? "

" No," Foss said, emphatically. " You didn't. You insulted me."

" I'm sorry. I only threatened your roses."

" You pointed the revolver at me! "

" It wasn't loaded."

Foss rose and beckoned the German to come with him.

" Why did you bring it out ? Was it to defend yourself against me ? Did you require it to help you in your conversation with me ? "

" I was merely proving your courage," Rennenberg whispered, taking Foss gently by the arm and shaking him.

" You had something to tell me, hadn't you ? " Foss said.

" Not exactly, but you had something to tell me, surely! "

" I wanted to ask you about that transfer."

" Quite! That was it. I thought we could get it over before dinner. I was rather impatient. . . ."

" And murderous! " Foss said.

" Oh, please! I merely wanted to test . . ."

" I know! Don't explain," Foss said. Then he looked squarely at the man who called himself Rennenberg.

" You made a mistake," he said, vigorously. " You made a very great mistake. Now I don't think we need say more about it."

In silence they reached the terrace and parted to go to their rooms.

" That's that," Foss thought. " He's bogus. He isn't the real Rennenberg. They must have arrested Von Pless and sent this fellow over to get information out of me. Thank God someone in Von Pless's confidence was able to send that letter and the duplicate!"

He stood near the window in his dressing-room and looked out at the fat elms and chestnuts at the far end of the garden. Their full foliage was as still as the leaves in a picture. Only the sounds from the surrounding land made them real and gave them life in the scene : the lowing of cattle on the pastures half a mile away ; the rattle of a reaping machine ; the shouts of labourers in a distant field. Around the trees, the air had a soft, green haze through which beams of sunlight shone in all the glory of summer, of life.

But what Foss saw was an office in which five men were seated around a table. Suddenly, the door burst open and crashed back against the wall. Armed men poured in and surrounded the five startled, half-risen confederates at the table. Weapons encompassed those five men. Shouts sounded. Orders were given. Chairs overturned. Von Pless and his friends were made to stand against a wall with their hands above their heads. Big Gestapo men tore open the drawers of the table, broke open the filing cabinets, poured out papers which were removed in baskets. Throughout the building, Gestapo agents, armed, were ordering the staff from the rooms. In the street, there were vans into which the plunder was thrown, and into which the staff were taken. Von Pless and his friends were pale and silent. They saw and heard what was happening. But their eyes were empty except for the large terror which was reflected in them.

Foss wondered what Von Pless and the others had confessed. Things had been done to them. The body had been made the hostage of the mind ; and the mind's secret had been divulged because the body had been probed. What had they said ? A mumbled word, his own name ? And on that word a series of orders had been given. A mission had been entrusted to this man who called himself Rennenberg and who had come to England and put himself in touch with Collis. Perhaps to gain entry, as he had done. Perhaps to watch the building and to listen, and to find Jey.

" And now," thought Foss, " there is only myself. Nobody but myself and Jey know. Brighart and Molloy are away. So now it is just myself and this German."

He turned aside from the window and began to undress.

" He'll fight for it," he thought. " He'll work hard to discover what I know and what I intend to do."

Apprehension touched him. " These fellows are experts. They're trained . . ."

He wondered if he should telephone to Jey and renounce everything, Or give the word for Jey to leave for Germany. To support Von Pless, even at this emergency. To continue, to go through with it all. . . .

114

" Why not ? " he thought. " Perhaps, in Berlin, there are men waiting for Jey to arrive, to give him instructions. To go ahead, even now . . ."

" Rolly! "

It was Tilly calling sleepily to him from their room. He put on a dressing-gown and went in.

" Rolly! "

At that moment, they heard the single note from the telephone as someone lifted the receiver. They looked at each other, Tilly from her recumbent position on the bed, Foss from his place near the door. Then they heard Rennenberg. An authoritative, sharp voice.

" Hullo, hullo! "

A door was closed noiselessly on the conversation.

" All day . . . in and out to the telephone! " Tilly said, sitting up.

" He's a busy man," Foss said.

" Rolly, come and sit down here. I want to tell you something."

" Rest, darling, just have a good sleep and come down to dinner all nice and bright."

" Here . . ."

She patted the edge of the bed. " And listen . . ."

Grudgingly, he obeyed her. " Well, what have you to tell me ? "

" Rolly, you told me that you went to Paris! "

He closed his lips and frowned and swayed slightly.

" Now, I told you . . ."

" Rennenberg said you were in Berlin in February! You told me you were in Paris! " she said.

" You know perfectly well . . ."

Suddenly she stiffened. " Look here, Rolly! What is all this business ? Tell me ! I want to know everything. Who is this fellow ? What has he come to England for ? Why does he carry a revolver ? Who are these men who came here to see him ? I want to know! I must . . . I must . . . I can't bear to be kept out of a secret! "

" He's the associate of our Berlin agent. I told you," Foss said, equably.

She was silent. Her gaze was fastened on him, and she broke it only to get off the bed and close the door. Then she came back and faced him.

" Now then, Rolly! " she said. " Tell me the truth. I'm determined to know it."

" She's worse than Rennenberg," he thought, gazing at her with a sullen look.

III

" I'm waiting! " she said, flatly.

Foss sighed. " I've told you . . ."

" You haven't! There's more to it than that. I want to know what's going on! I have a right to know! "

He attempted to rise from the bed. " Tilly, why do you . . ."

She pushed him back. " Sit down! "

He made another attempt and contrived to remain on his feet and stand facing her.

" Now look here, Tilly, you're being very unreasonable! I always confide in you . . ."

" Good! Do so now! "

" . . . I never conceal anything from you."

" Don't try to now, then! Tell me why this Nazi has come from Berlin, and why he's armed, and why he hangs over the telephone half the day. Everything! "

Foss sighed with exasperation. " You are . . ." he muttered, wandering to the window and then turning to face Tilly.

" Very well," he said. " Since you compel me! I'll tell you again. His name is Kurt Rennenberg. . . ."

" Lie number one! " Tilly said. " You know very well that that isn't his name! "

" It's the name he uses! "

He frowned. He knew that he had made a slip. Tilly, too, knew it, for she came slowly towards him, arms folded, hips swaying, a smile of triumph on her face.

" Uses ? What's his real name ? "

" Oh, you and your blasted suspicions! Your everlasting suspicions! Your mind is full of gibberish and intrigue! " he shouted.

She pouted at him and turned slowly and sat down.

" Rolly," she said, in a tone of such calm and enticement that the sudden change startled him, " what is the mystery about him ? "

He flung round to explode on her again, but this time her glance swerved away from his ; and although she tried to conceal that sudden weakness, it was too late. He saw in that wavering of her eyes all the evidence of intrigue.

He went slowly towards her and leaned over her, putting his hands on the arms of the little chair and moving his face relentlessly towards hers.

" Now, Mrs. Foss! Now you can tell me the truth! Speak out! What's the nasty, sneaky little game, Tilly ? "

He looked into her large, dark eyes. He saw them flicker once and recover their flawless, innocent loveliness. They were frank and clear. He smiled, and resting his cheek against her perfumed skin, he kissed the pearly lobe of her ear and whispered : " Come on! Out with it! "

She gently pushed him away. Her glance rested pensively on the point of her slippers.

" I'm waiting," Foss said, patiently.

She looked up at him. " Rolly, I've got a splitting head. Bring me some aspirins, please! "

" First of all, you can tell me what he said to you."

" Oh, Rolly! My head! "

He rested his hands gently around her chin and held her head while he peered into her eyes.

" How can you do it ? " he exclaimed in a whisper. " How can you sit there, with your eyes as clear as crystal, and that innocent look on your sweet face, while an inch or two behind your eyes there are all those wicked thoughts! You little bitch! "

He thrust her gently away from him and went to the window.

" As if I can't see the game you are playing, Tilly! " he said, laughing. Looking over his shoulder, he saw again the large, lustrous eyes.

" Do you take me for a fool, Tilly ? Do you ? "

He turned and stood facing her with folded arms.

" Because I'm indulgent to you, Tilly, you think I am a fool! Because I don't ask you questions, you take it for granted that I don't notice things. But I see plenty. I know when you have done something you shouldn't have done. I know when some fellow has written you a nice letter and you have had lunch with him. I know when you are scheming a bit of extravagance. And I know that you and Rennenberg are up to mischief. You love intrigue, don't you ? I know."

Tilly lowered her head and dabbed her nose with a tiny handkerchief. Foss chuckled. He went over and stood beside her chair.

" Fancy you doing a thing like that! Fancy you, Tilly! I thought I could really trust you not to do something very foolish and mean! "

She pouted, and without moving her head she gave him a rapid glance. Tears glistened in her eyes.

" You miserable little bitch! " he whispered.

She burst into loud sobs. Flinging herself back in the chair and burying her head in her arms, she cried :

" My head is splitting! Bring me some aspirins! "

" I wish," he said, laughing, " I wish it would split wide open and spill the truth! "

On her dressing-table amidst an untidy assortment of brushes, combs, cosmetics and jewellery, he found a bottle of aspirins.

"I'll bring some water," he said, hurrying into the bathroom adjoining the bedroom.

"It's your own fault," he told her, when he brought the glass. "You've tangled yourself in a lot of suspicions. You're up to the neck in one of your favourite games, aren't you ? "

She swallowed two tablets and sipped the water.

"Rolly, I forgot to tell you that a man called to see you, this afternoon," she said.

"Who was he ? What did he want ? "

"He asked to see you. He said it was urgent."

"Why didn't you telephone me ? Why didn't you tell him to come to my office ? "

"I did. I told him . . ."

"What was his name ? "

She wrinkled her forehead.

"It was . . . I'm trying to think. It's on the tip of my tongue."

"Describe him."

"Something beginning with ' S ' or . . . no, it was . . . oh . . . anyway, he was about thirty-five, at least he looked that age, or perhaps a bit older. Not tall, rather nice manners."

She glanced up at him and said : "He said it was very important."

"Can't you remember his name ? " Foss said.

"I'm trying to remember."

"Was it Jey ? " he ventured, although he knew that Jey would not have called.

"That's it! Yes, Jey! A rather nice man, very polite. Not what you would call good-looking. . . ."

"Yes, that's Jey," he said. He was worried. "He wants a job. I suppose he thought I might have come home for lunch. What did he say ? Did he leave a message ? "

"He asked for you. I told him you were in town, and he said he'd call on you. I didn't quite catch his name. It might have been Kay or May . . ."

Foss said again : "He wants a job in the office."

"Does he ? He said you wanted to arrange some business with him."

"You know very well that nobody called, don't you ? " Foss said.

"Rolly! "

He turned away. "I don't know when to believe you. You had better lie down and sleep a bit."

"If you knew what sort of a day I have had," she moaned, covering her face with her hands.

"Oh, I can guess, I can guess! " he exclaimed.

"You can't, otherwise you wouldn't stand there and insult me and laugh at me."

118

" Oh, yes, I can, Tilly," he insisted. " I know what you have been doing. Asking questions, ferreting for facts, intriguing! "

He went to the bathroom and turned on the taps. " I've no sympathy for you," he said, emphatically. " You get yourself in a tangle, and when everything is beyond you and you have a bad headache, you lie there and moan."

" Well, anyway, Rolly, I emptied his revolver and hid all the ammunition, didn't I ? " she said.

" Oh! Revolvers, ammunition! " he exclaimed. " Your head is chock full of rubbish! You've been reading a thriller, or else you've got a touch of sunstroke. You'd better stay in bed! "

He closed the bathroom door and untied the girdle of his dressing-gown. He began to whistle softly He got into the bath and lay at full length in the tepid water. He folded his arms and rested his gaze on the white tiles and thought :

" He probably went down like a nine-pin after half an hour with her. She put a dozen questions in the way she does, and probably got everything out of him. After that, he must have persuaded her to turn her attentions to me."

He sighed with anxiety and exasperation.

" She can't be trusted. She's too fond of indulging her suspicions."

He wondered about her. All at once, he roused himself from his thoughts and got noiselessly from the bath. He opened the door cautiously and peeped into the bedroom. Tilly was not there.

" Treacherous little cat! " he muttered.

★

IV

★

Tilly was in Rennenberg's room. Rennenberg was seated in a little armchair near the open window. Tilly was standing.

" When you told him about the revolver, wasn't he surprised ? " he said.

Tilly looked at her reflection in the mirror of the dressing-table. She pushed a strand of her hair into place.

" A bit, I think," she said. " But I don't think he believed me."

Rennenberg laughed. " Didn't believe you ? "

" He never believes me when I tell him things that surprise him. He never trusts me . . . ."

" Really ? "

" He's lost the habit," she said, turning and facing her guest. " He's very jealous of me. If I want fun, and if I meet my friend, he sends detectives to watch me. I have to be frightfully careful. I can hardly turn round without him suspecting me of something. He's the most jealous man I've ever met. And tight-fisted, too. I hate him. I do, really. It's abominable."

" You aren't very truthful, are you ? " Rennenberg said.

" That's a very indiscreet remark to make to me," she retorted.

" Are you ashamed of yourself ? " he said, chuckling.

Tilly lifted her eyebrows and pouted. " I am as truthful as most people."

" You're awfully amusing, Mrs. Foss," Rennenberg said. " You're so frank, too! "

" I'm rather tired," Tilly said, sinking gracefully into a chair. " I've had such a tough time with Rolly."

" Didn't he divulge anything to you ? "

She shook her head and sighed. " No. I did just what you told me to. Then he made me angry and that made me cry, but that didn't make much difference."

Rennenberg said : " That's just what Von Pless and the others told me. They said he was stubborn and that he was determined to force them on to take action. All the way through, ever since the first word of the plot, he has taken the lead and driven them . . ."

" Of course, I'll say this for my husband, Herr Rennenberg. He's very clever. He's got enormous drive."

" Yes, but too much of it, Mrs Foss! Too much! He doesn't appreciate the danger . . ."

" I know. Rolly doesn't! He's got terrific courage."

" Von Pless warned me. He said I would have a difficult task in persuading Mr. Foss to delay everything for a month or two."

" Is Rolly really mixed up in this business ? " Tilly said. " Is he really ? I can't believe it. Really, I can't."

" I swear most solemnly to you, my dear Mrs. Foss, that your husband is one of the ringleaders in this plot," the German said. As he spoke, he leaned forward and emphasized his statement with his hands and the solemn expression of his face. Then he added : " I have been sent expressly by Von Pless to beg him to postpone everything. I am a close friend of Von Pless. He and I have spent many long hours together discussing every detail of this plot. And he begs me, and all the others who are concerned in the matter have implored me, to try to persuade your husband not to go forward just yet."

" Tell me this," Tilly said. " Are you a Nazi ? "

" Mrs. Foss, you asked me that once before, and I told you. It is, if I may say so, an indiscreet question. I must tell you. For the sake of my business, for my own personal welfare and that of my friends, I am a member of the Party. It is just a matter of discretion on my part. . . ."

" And you are in this plot, too ? "

" I am as much concerned in it as your husband, Von Pless, and the others. I think about it day and night. I see only the figure of Adolf Hitler! "

" Rolly has never breathed a word to me about the thing," Tilly said. " He never mentioned it to me, not in half a word."

" Oh, he probably gave his word of honour. . . ."

" He's so clever," she said. " He knows how to hold his tongue."

" If only you could have induced him to speak. Then you could have persuaded him to postpone everything. You could have discovered the names of his confederates here, and I could have gone to them and begged them to wait," Rennenberg said.

" He's so close . . ."

" No! I shall tell you what it is, Mrs. Foss! " the German said. " He has cleverness. He is much too clever for you! "

" Yes, I'm afraid he is," Tilly said.

" You can't do anything to help him, can you ? " the German said.

" I'm not thinking of Rolly at all! " she exclaimed. " Why should I do anything to save him ? Let him run into trouble! Let the Gestapo or whatever it is get him when he goes to Berlin again! I don't mind! I'm not thinking and racking my brains to help Rolly . . ."

" Aren't you ? " Rennenberg said. " Perhaps that is why you took the cartridges from my revolver and hid them! "

" I don't like revolvers and guns," she said. " They might go off. Then there's trouble."

" Then he would be out of the way. And you would be free! "

" Don't be silly! I don't think like that. I have plenty of freedom. When I said I would help you to try to persuade him and to find out just what his plans are, I did it because you said you would reward me," Tilly declared.

" You haven't been very successful, have you ? "

" No. I have to be inspired."

Rennenberg smiled. " Well, hurry up and become inspired, because if anything went wrong in Berlin and Von Pless were betrayed, I can tell you there would be trouble for your husband and perhaps for the rest of us too! "

Tilly jumped from her chair. She stood before him and clenched her hands. " Oh, you keep on saying that! That only frightens me! Let me think! Oh, let me think! Don't keep on threatening me! Give me time to get an idea. I've told you I want the reward. But you must give me time to think! "

She flung round and walked away from him.

"You are mean! You asked me to help you, and I promised to do my best if you promised to give me that pendant. . . ."

"Afterwards!" said Rennenberg, flatly. "After you have done your part," he reminded her.

"Yes, I know, I know! But you don't help me! You just tell me what the Gestapo will do to Rolly. If you had any sense, you'd give me that gorgeous diamond and platinum thing now, and then I'd feel inspired to help you."

"I told you, Mrs. Foss, that it will be yours when you find just what his intentions are in this matter," Rennenberg said.

With a great flourish of her long gown, Tilly got up and went to the door.

"You're so silly! You're so stupid!" she declared. "You can't do it yourself, so you ask me to try. And instead of helping me to put my best foot forward, you only frighten me with threats about what the Gestapo will do to Rolly when he goes to Berlin. What do I care what they'll do? All I care about is my reward! If you won't help me, I can't help you!"

She was at the door when Rennenberg called to her.

"Look!"

The case lay open in his big hand, and Tilly could see the diamonds lying like brilliant drops of ice on the plush lining.

"I've seen it already," she said, frowning at him. "What's the sense in dangling that thing in front of me, like a carrot before a donkey? If you're going to give it to me, let me have it now. Then I shall have to work for it!"

Rennenberg held it towards her. "Take it, Mrs. Foss! Please have it."

As she came forward, he rose and took the pendant from the case. Tilly's face was radiant. She delicately parted the neck of her gown, and Rennenberg deftly fastened the piece about that warm, white column which the gown had revealed.

"So!" he said, softly, stepping back and bowing. "Very charming!"

She gave him her hand and he raised it slowly to his lips and then released it. Tilly went to the mirror of the dressing-table and looked critically at her reflection. Her features gleamed. Her hands came up swiftly in a childlike gesture of excitement. She saw the little pendant lying on her breast and flashing the facets of its stones at her.

"May I really have it?" she asked, glancing at the German. "Is it mine now?"

"For a price," he said.

"Naturally! You didn't think I was cadging it from you?"

"Cadging? Please."

"Begging for it."

122

"Oh, no! But the price is high, Mrs. Foss."

"You've said that before, and I promised to pay it," Tilly retorted.

Rennenberg stood against the wall with his arms folded. He laughed.

"You don't trouble to ask the amount, Mrs. Foss."

"Of course not! I know it'll be more than sixpence."

"But as a matter of fact, the price cannot be reckoned in terms of money."

He became solemn. Coming away from the wall and standing near her, he watched her with a serious, pensive gaze.

"I hope you're not going to drive a hard bargain," Tilly said.

"No," he said, shaking his head. "No. I think you know my terms. But now I wish to be quite sincere with you, Mrs. Foss. It's time you and I ceased to be frivolous. Let us sit down and discuss everything."

He offered Tilly a chair and waited until she was seated before he sat down opposite her.

"I hope you won't be tedious, Herr Rennenberg," she said. "If you don't mind me saying so, you Germans are awfully long-winded sometimes. A friend of mine had a German gentleman staying with him once, and we all had to listen while that guest led us through all the caverns of his mind. Dreadfully tiresome!"

"I shall be brief," Rennenberg said.

"Yes, do, please. Rolly won't be long in his bath. I'll have to skip back to the bedroom soon."

Rennenberg said : "The price of the pendant is truthfulness."

Tilly was silent. Her big, lustrous eyes regarded him as though he had made a grotesque stipulation. She blinked several times.

"It's very simple, after all," Rennenberg explained. "All you have to do is to tell me the truth."

"Very well," Tilly said.

"I want you to be quite honest and frank with me, Mrs. Foss. I appeal to those qualities in you. Von Pless has sent me over here to persuade your husband to defer his plans. I am in the closest contact with Von Pless, both in business and in this important affair. Your husband knows that. But he will not discuss the plot with me. He has told me nothing. I am in the dark. Meanwhile, dangers increase both in Berlin and over here. Von Pless and all his friends are in grave peril. Any action now on the part of your husband would only increase that danger. I swear most solemnly to you, Mrs. Foss, that that is the truth. Your husband is so determined to continue that he won't divulge anything to me. I suppose he is afraid that I shall interfere. But that is what we must do. I must find his associates here and have a word with them. That is where I want you to help me. I implore you to help me in this, and incidentally to save Von Pless."

Tilly sighed. " I'll do all I can," she said.

There was a pause. " Well ? " Rennenberg said.

" I said . . ."

" Listen, Mrs. Foss, please ! Surely your husband has confided in you. Surely you know the names of his confederates here ! "

" Rolly never confides in me," Tilly said, sadly. " He doesn't trust me. I think he is going to divorce me soon."

Rennenberg got up and stood before her.

" You are not speaking the truth, are you ? You love your husband. He isn't going to divorce you. He trusts you very much, because he's fond of you. Isn't that the truth ? "

Tilly shook her head ruefully. " No, really ! " And lifting her clear eyes to him, she added : " He hasn't breathed a word to me about this affair. It surprised me awfully when you told me about it."

There was a little frown beginning on her brow. Her hands twined restlessly together.

" You keep asking me to tell you the truth, but when I do you won't believe me."

" It seems so incredible to me," he said, reflectively, " that your husband has made these journeys and has never told you what is happening."

" You don't believe me, but I'm speaking the truth."

" I believe you," he said.

" I want to help you," Tilly declared. She stood up. Coming face to face with him, she continued : " But I must know more about everything. You don't trust me, any more than Rolly does, do you ? "

" I have told you everything, everything ! " he exclaimed.

" Except one thing," she said.

" And what is that ? "

She lowered her head and glanced obliquely at him.

" You didn't tell me that the bottom has fallen out of this plot because Von Pless and all the others have been arrested. And you didn't tell me that you are one of the Gestapo agents, and that you've been sent over here to find out what Rolly is doing."

" What nonsense ! " he exclaimed, laughing tersely. " Oh, what nonsense ! I told you all about myself ! "

Tilly smiled as though she had been discovered in something mischievous. She fondled the pendant.

" May I keep it ? " she asked, holding it between her fingers.

" Certainly ! But don't forget the price ! And don't let your husband see you wearing it, yet ! "

He gave her the case. Their hands met. He took her hand in his and carried it to his lips and bowed formally.

" I must go back now," she whispered.

When she was gone, he took a coloured handkerchief from his pocket and wiped his face and neck. For several minutes he stood pondering his conversation with her.

" What a woman! " he thought. " What a woman! "

He had confided in her, bribed her. But she was still herself : uncertain, sly, unpredictable. His sense of failure increased.

★

V

★

Tilly returned noiselessly to the bedroom. She lay on the bed and removed the pendant. Holding it in her hands, she admired it for a while before folding it in the case. A few minutes later Foss came into the room from the bathroom. Tilly appeared to be fast asleep. Her eyes were closed. One arm was outflung limply with the hand upturned and the fingers like slender petals opening. The other lay along the line of her body which was slightly turned so that Foss saw the graceful curve of her hip.

He stood at the foot of the bed and looked down at her recumbent form. A supple body ; a dainty woman ; her dark hair framing her face. He leaned over the back of a chair and watched her ; and he smiled. He knew her features so well in all their expressions. He had studied them, as now, many times, and knew their reflections of mood as well as all the inflections which slumber or her thoughts rendered to them. In sleep, they cast off all the influences of mood and tempera-ment so that he saw then only the natural beauty of their shape and texture. A sense of calm and contentment entered his heart at such times.

He was smiling now because he knew that she was pretending to be asleep. Her features had not the deep relaxation and submittance to some natural composure which sleep would have afforded them. She was shamming.

Creeping forward, he tickled the sole of her left foot. At once, a little tremor agitated her slim leg and the curve of her thigh and travelled over her body to break into expression in a tight smile on her face. Then her eyes opened.

When from sleep her body stirred thus and her magnificent eyes opened, his insensitive spirit was often excited by the power of her beauty. In the mornings of countless days when he saw her emerge from sleep to a new day, a kind of personal dawn came subtly to him at the instant when her gaze rested upon him. Then there rose in his spirit a curious, forlorn emotion which he could never conquer. Her beauty afflicted him for an instant. She was his, and yet he could never truly possess her inconstant soul which, no matter how he encompassed it with love and indulgences, remained at a little distance behind all the barriers of her temperament and character.

" You weren't asleep! " he exclaimed.

She stirred and sighed. " It's so hot! "

" It's your conscience," he said. " You've got a wicked heart, Tilly."

He shook his head at her and turned towards the dressing-room. She called him back.

" Rolly, you know the value of things like this. Is this genuine or a fake ? "

She was holding at arm's length in her small hand a pendant of diamonds whose stones were set simply in platinum.

" Where did you get this ? " Foss said, taking it. " Who gave you this ? "

" It isn't mine," she explained. " Eileen showed it to me, and I said it was a fake. She thinks it's worth a thousand, at least. So I said I would ask you to value it, if she left it with me."

He knew that she was lying to him. He was accustomed to her falsehoods. He hardly considered them at this moment, for his memory had stirred and he had recollected what Kelpey had told him this afternoon. Rennenberg and Collis. " . . . and they were talking about a necklace, sir."

Without a word, he went to the dressing-room and found a small magnifying glass in the waistcoat of one of his suits. He came back to Tilly. She was lying on her back with her arms folded behind her head and her feet crossed.

" Is it genuine, Rolly ? "

He examined the stones. " No . . . it's . . ."

Crossing to the window, he stood there and turned the stones under the magnifying glass.

" Collis, and this German, and Kelpey . . . about a necklace," he was thinking.

He saw serious flaws in the setting. An inferior thing. And none of the diamonds was genuine. He tried to price the whole thing. The platinum, perhaps . . .

Then he turned and went to the head of the bed and tossed the thing towards Tilly's outstretched hand.

" A fake ? " she exclaimed.

" No good. Imitation," he said. " And badly set, too. The platinum is worth a trifle. The whole thing . . ." He pursed his lips, and added : " Twenty quid, at most. At the outside."

He saw the edge of the case protruding from beneath the pillow. Coming slowly round the bed, he leaned down and stretched over Tilly's body.

126

When his hand came up holding the case, a startled look filled Tilly's face. She made a single swift movement to snatch the case from him ; but her attempt was ineffectual and weak compared to Foss's smooth, successful action. She checked herself abruptly, and only a little frown remaining on her face betrayed her chagrin and guilt. Next moment, she recovered herself.

"Oh, that's the case! Put them back, Rolly. I'll tell Eileen."

On the lining, he saw the name and address :

"WERTHEIM. LEIPZIGER PLATZ.
BERLIN."

"Who gave you this ? "

Tilly was staring at the ceiling.

"It's Eileen's. I'll have to tell her . . ."

He was waiting for her to turn to him. His silence had an implacable, terrible compulsion which she resisted for fully a minute and which drained her courage and cunning.

He broke the spell. His anger deluged her.

"You got it from Rennenberg, didn't you ? Look ! Here's the address in the case. I know this store. A big place, full of stuff like this ! "

He flung the case and its contents on the bed.

"I know all about it ! " he continued. "I'm not a fool. I know what he's here for ! I know that he gave you this as a bribe ! Well . . ." He broke off and snorted contemptuously. "Well, he set a nice price on you, didn't he ? A trumpery bit of junk ! That's what he thinks of you ! "

He looked at her and met her calm, frank stare.

"You little fool ! To let him win you like that ! To persuade you to spy on me ! "

"It's a present," Tilly said.

"What for ? " he demanded.

Tilly sat up. "Shall I tell you, Rolly ? "

She put her feet on the floor and leaned backwards on her arms.

"Shall I ? "

He was waiting for her to speak. He was waiting to hear what Rennenberg had told her.

"He said I could have it if I promised to find out what you intend to do about this business with Von Pless."

When he heard her say that, an immeasurable relief touched his heart. He could not prevent himself from uttering the thoughts which opened in his mind.

"Now I know ! " he said. "Now I know for certain who he is and what he's here for ! "

He came and sat down beside Tilly. He put his arm about her.

" He wouldn't tell me, of course!   He was too cunning to mention a word of it to me! " he continued.

" I've had a dreadful day with him, Rolly," Tilly said.

" Yes, good lord, yes, you must have had! "

Her eyes were never more lovely than now, he thought.   He took her hands and drew her towards him.

" Rolly," she said, " I'm not such a mean little bitch, after all. Am I ?   I did my best to dig his secret out of him.   I was awfully afraid, all day.   I did my best, though."

Foss wiped his forehead and sighed.   " Yes, you're clever, Tilly. You have courage. . . ."

" But, Rolly, you haven't been very open with me, have you ? "

" Forget it," he whispered.

" You can tell me everything now, can't you ?   You were awfully close, really, you were!   All these months, ever since February, and you never breathed a word to me about it.   Rennenberg wouldn't believe me when I said I knew nothing about it."

" Don't talk about it, Tilly," he whispered.   " It's finished . . ."

" Is it ?   Why ?   Won't you go on with it ? "

He interrupted her with a tragic glance.

" They must have arrested Von Pless and the others," he said. " They were probably questioned, and you know what that means. Our guest was there, watching and listening."

" Oh, Rolly!   Horrible . . ."

He stood up.   " Tilly, say nothing, nothing at all.   Just keep silent.   Silence as thick as this heat."

" Yes, very well."

" Because he's in England to get the last word which will close the indictment against Von Pless."

" All right, Rolly."

" I trust you, Tilly," he said.

" Well, then tell me everything, Rolly.   Tell me now, everything."

He got up and stood at the window and looked at the great chestnuts and elms and beeches all bathed in the evening sunlight.

" It doesn't seem . . . even possible . . ." he murmured.

He felt returned to the normality of which the verdant scene in the spacious garden was a part.   Fat, somnolent trees brimming with fertility and colour ; heat and light ; the glare from the still waters of the swimming pool ; the neat lawns ; and the clatter of crockery and the chatter of the servants' voices from the kitchen.   Summer, freedom, peace.   But in Berlin, an empty suite of offices which had been sacked by the Gestapo and ransacked as the bodies of Von Pless and his confederates had been for one nerve from whose writhing tip the truth would emerge.   And in the rest of Berlin—in the Government offices—

the brutal determination to make war. And here, in England, and not a dozen yards from this window, the agent of the Gestapo.

" Tilly, we shall have to be careful! "

" That rat! " she exclaimed in a whisper. " The common brute! Where's his piece of rubbish ? "

Foss was faintly amused.

" On the raw! " he said.

" As if I were a tart! "

" But listen, Tilly," he said. " Be careful. Now you know what he is. And don't return that thing to him yet. Not yet."

" The gangster! "

Foss said : " That's just what they are, all of them! "

" Rolly! " she said, earnestly, " I hope we go to war against them! I do really. I know it sounds a terrible thing to say, but I hope . . . oh, I hope we declare war on them and get at their throats and finish them! "

Foss sighed. " Don't worry! It's going to happen. That's what is going to happen."

★

VI

★

" Siesta," thought Jey as he lay unclothed on the bed in his room, " siesta is a very sensible habit."

The room was on the upper back floor of " The Crown " in Derby Street. It was cheap. It was between a room occupied by two waiters and another in which slept the junior porter. It was light and airy, with a window which faced east. Pride—the vestiges of an inordinate social consciousness from a recent past when his family had been wealthy and privileged—had secretly lamented and had cavilled at this refuge which was all that the hotel management could contrive for him upon the terms of permanency. At first, the room was the constant reminder of his drab fate. He saw nothing but the faded festoons on the wallpaper, and hated their colourless innocence. He heard nothing except the interminable mumbling of the two waiters on the left and the disharmonious whistling of the junior porter on the right. He stayed out of it all day and bolstered his heart with the illusions of comfort in the fashionable bars and lounges, and came home very late with an apprehension and distaste which was somehow never realised. The room encompassed him gently. It was high ; and when he looked out of the window, he saw the far, eastern horizons, and felt himself to be above the city and on a level with the clouds.

" Risen in the bloody world! "

With a sneaking feeling of sentimentality, he bought two prints. Vermeer's " Head of a Girl," and a Peter Scott. He got out his few books and arranged them in a little case which he bought at an auction. After that, he had a dim sense of being at home. The place was mute, cleanly. In the early hours of spring and summer days, it was filled with a flowing, pearly light, so fresh, so joyous, that the hush and wonder of it made promises to him. And in the dusk, he saw from it the first evening star trembling with a precious light. After that, he cherished the room. He swept it, tidied it. It pleased him. He felt restored.

To what, he hardly knew. To patience, to innate virtues, after twenty-two years of fruitless faith in a garment of privilege which was as threadbare as his intelligence ? To the recognition of the fact that he had been educated more by a belief in the family wealth and the niceties of social behaviour than by schoolmasters, life, experience ? To sanity, to commonsense after years of puffy pride and inordinate belief in class ?

He was forty-seven, strong, a solid dapper man with the lines, the attitudes, the scars of experience inscribed on a geniality which embraced pretty well anyone nowadays. He had no good looks to commend him. But he had the family chin, square and determined and softened by a dimple. Above, his face with its podgy nose and heavy lips and prominent brow over grey eyes was flowing with amiability. There it was : a commonplace face, but good-humoured. He thought it was all that he could show to the world in these days when his pockets were empty except for the hundred and fifty per annum from the tumbled fortunes of the family. But unknown to himself, there was a poise of distinction in all his movements ; and the least observant eye could detect it and appraise it as being quality. But whither was he moving ?

He hardly knew. Didn't ask himself. Dared not. Hope had been squandered so frequently in the past that he dared not dip into his heart for more. Frustration and failure were his lot whenever he ventured, for he had worked. At twenty-five, he had gone to Malaya with some thousands of pounds which he had lost in bad seasons, bad markets, bad company. At thirty-two, he had tried again. Farming. An insolent scheme, all on paper, plus a bit of cheap land and three thousand loaned by an aunt and eight thousand gathered from gullible investors. Apples and pears. He believed more in luck than in himself, for he had neither knowledge nor experience. He contrived to pay out twenty shillings in the pound two years later. But there was nothing left for himself, except some saddles, his car, and the remainder of a ten-year lease on a nice cottage.

He took a correspondence course with a college of journalism. He wrote, and lived on bread and cheese and beer in the local. He came back to town and got into a crowd who were always about to get him a job in an uncle's office.

He took inferior posts in offices where everybody seemed old and evil and cynical. He felt cold in his heart, chilled by this vision of a world in which all was a blowing dust of cynicism. He fled from it. It was like a bad dream. Trying for something else, he joined queues and felt a mournful sense of the inadequacy of his experience, his temperament, his character for the job which hundreds of more apt men needed. But he got the job. Something in his character leaned out and took it from beneath the ready, anxious fingers of the rest.

Within a month, it was obvious that he was out of his depth, past the time when he could learn, remember, identify his cheerful, oblique character with the spirit of the place. A good fellow, a gentleman, but useless, quite useless.

And between times, he was invited to week-end house parties. He was a good shot, a good rider. He filled a gap. He liked to rest on the delusion that he was still in the swim amongst his own people. He loved comfort, and self-indulgence, and the talk. But he was startled out of himself when he was approached with odd requests for his services. Then he knew that he had lost an indescribable attribute which, because he could not name it, he could not recover.

He had unwittingly gained the reputation of an adventurer. He travelled to Paris, to bring back a headstrong, romantic youth—the son of an old friend. He took an elderly lady to Biarritz and parked her there for the winter, to keep her out of earshot of a raging family scandal. He flew as passenger and ballast in a 'plane piloted by a famous pilot competing in a reckless, continental air race. He took risks. He sold out his personal safety, but kept intact his honour.

There was unemployment and the ripple of crisis after crisis. The wind was blowing across the Continent and increasing to a gale. Soon, it would become a hurricane.

" Then I'll be wanted," Jey thought. " Then we shan't have to ask for a job. We'll be ordered into one. They'll need everyone! "

In the heat, he lay on his back and pondered his fate as he took siesta.

" I'm a symptom of the age," he thought. " Although I did a couple of years in the artillery in the last show, I'm a part of the economic sickness, the pig-headed misunderstanding, the mistrust. There's going to be a terrific war to cure it all. Then off we go again! "

Then he guffawed so loudly that the echoes rattled and rebounded from the festooned walls. He had remembered the day when Foss had come to this room.

Foss sat on the little cane-bottomed chair near the foot of the bed. Although he was small and rather quiet and composed as he spoke, his repute and integrity as the senior partner in a big business seemed to inflate about him and render everything in the room ridiculously small and shabby. He glanced at the top row of books on the shelves. A guide to Paris leaned against a tattered volume of O. Henry's tales. His small plump hand righted a modern copy of Shakespeare's plays. He said slowly and without looking at Jey.

" I've got a mission I should like you to undertake for me, Jey."

His hand came away from the bookshelf and joined his other hand, and he sat like a solemn little solicitor perhaps, or a doctor. His own repute in the city, his own integrity which had swollen about him a moment before, rebounded on him and made him appear small and insignificant.

" Have you ? " Jey had said. " What is it ? "

" I want you to go to Berlin, Jey."

" Anywhere, anytime," Jey said.

" And from Berlin to Munich."

" I'll go on one condition, Foss," Jey said, facetiously. " I'll go only on the condition that I don't have to hob-nob with the English aristocracy's balmy nephews looking for the angelic light in Hitler's eyes! "

" You don't seem to think much of Hitler," Foss said.

" I can't stomach him. I never could."

" Some people admire him," Foss said. " A great many of our own people . . ."

" Then they ought to be shot! " Jey said, flopping back in his chair. " And Hitler with them."

" Shot! "

" I'd like to shoot the swine, Foss! He's human rubbish. Gosh, in America when a gangster gets out of hand, the Federal blokes just aim to kill! That's the way! "

Foss smiled. His eyes came up to Jey's and stayed in a fixed, odd stare.

" Is it ? " he said slowly, and the two words echoed about the room and became oddly and terribly accentuated by his smile, and fantastically amplified by the silence which he maintained and which he seemed purposely to control so that Jey would realize . . .

Jey sat forward quickly.

" What ? I say . . ."

" You said you'd like to, didn't you ? " Foss said very quietly.

" I said . . ." Jey began. He stopped. He felt as though he had been enticed cunningly into a tight little web.

Foss stopped smiling. " Jey, I should like your word as a gentleman that you won't divulge what I tell you. May I have it ? "

" Yes. I give you my word on that," Jey said.

" Thank you. You know the rest," Foss said.

" What ? "

" That's all there is to it, at present," Foss told him.

" I can't quite . . . I don't quite . . ."

" First to Berlin, where you'll meet certain people. Then to Munich, where you'll meet others."

Jey said : " You're not serious! "

" You said you would like to shoot him," Foss said, solemnly.

" You're not serious! "

" I came to ask you," Foss said. " We're willing to offer you three thousand pounds, plus expenses. The plans are made, and I can tell you that they're thorough. Our German associates have seen to that."

Jey stood up and stuck his hands into his pockets. He saw the books on the top shelf of the bookcase, and he thought how like one of O. Henry's extreme episodes was this mission. An incident between the covers of a book, to be read as fiction and not as truth. But fiction, as he knew, was melted into the reality of life in these years, so that the commonplace reality was assuming more and more the incident and hue of romantic fiction. The barriers were dissolved. Anything went. A deal with two ghastly gangsters at Munich. A blind eye to shocking crimes against weak nations. The bow and smile of diplomacy. The equation was not so much solved as no longer stated.

" Good Lord, Foss! Me ? " he exclaimed.

" Let me explain," Foss said.

As he spoke, the picture filled up. It took colour, form, substance. It filled with figures. Von Pless and others.

" I thought all opposition was ended," Jey said. " I thought the Gestapo knew its job."

" So did I. But they're organized. Von Pless has explained everything to me. They have funds."

" You're quite sure this isn't some dirty stunt of the Gestapo to fan up a crisis and declare war on England ? "

Foss laughed. " Von Pless is my commercial agent in Berlin. I know him very well."

" It licks me," Jey said. Then he chuckled.

" I've often said I'd like to shoot the fellow. But it's a horse of a different colour . . ." He broke off and shook his head. " I just can't see myself . . ."

" All the better," Foss said. " You keep your nerve for the moment when you squeeze the trigger."

Jey sat down again. " It's no good, Foss. I just can't see myself in this. The trouble is that I can't . . . can't sort of imagine myself doing it. I don't see the thing in relation to me or to things in general. It's just like an absurd story."

" Don't try to," Foss said. " Just say yes, and then listen while I explain everything to you."

" The trouble is that it all sounds so damned unreal. I know you

133

are asking me to do this thing. But what makes me shy off it is the fact that I don't think it will ever come off. We're due for a war, Foss. It's coming."

"Not if someone fires a shot."

"Don't you believe it!" Jey said. "It's on the cards, this war. We're nearly there. Shot or no shot, the show is due to start."

"Not if someone fires that shot," Foss said. "You don't understand what it is like in Germany at this time. He's the pivot of everything. Remove him—and my German friends say this—and the nation throws off restraint and dictates to the Generals. And the majority of Germans don't want to go to war."

Jey was silent. Foss leaned forward and said : "Say yes, and let's get down to the details."

Jey laughed slowly. "It sort of gives me a destiny, doesn't it ?"

"I won't deny that it does," Foss said, solemnly.

Jey pondered it all for several minutes. Foss rose and lifted his hat from the top of the bookshelf and his overcoat from the chair.

"Tell me yes or no, in the meantime."

"Well, I'll say yes," Jey said. He added quickly : "But I want to be honest, Foss, and tell you that although I'll do what you ask me to in the affair, I still don't believe for an instant that the thing will come off."

"You don't put much confidence in yourself, do you ?" Foss said.

"Oh, that! I'm not thinking of my part in it," Jey said. "I'm thinking about things at the other end, in Berlin and Munich. I don't think your friends in those cities will ever escape the Gestapo. The way the Gestapo works is not like a detective force looking for a murderer. They don't wait until the crime is committed. They assume that the crime is about to be committed, and they keep eyes and ears open and suspect everybody. I bet you they'll get your fellow Von Pless long before I get to Berlin."

"I told Von Pless I would do my best for him," Foss said.

"It's dangerous. It's a pretty big risk to run."

"I'm willing to take it. I believe in this business," Foss said.

Jey regarded him intently. "Do you ? Do you, really ?"

"Absolutely."

Jey had an uncomfortable feeling that Foss was not speaking the truth.

"What do I do ?" Jey said.

"Come to my office to-morrow, and I'll outline everything for you."

Jey went. He was shown a map and asked to memorize it. He was given the names and descriptions of people, and signals which he would exchange with them. He was asked to renew his passport and to obtain a visa. He was given an alibi. Finally, Foss told him to wait.

Jey waited. He waited throughout the spring. Then Foss told him to be prepared day and night. Jey packed a suitcase and was never out of reach of messengers. Once, in May, Jey spent a week-end out of town. When he returned, he stood for a while in the silence of his little room. The tiny place knew him. His few cherished possessions knew him. They were the mute presences who saw and heard him and who understood his secret despairs and contentments. They watched him brush and furbish and repair his few suits. They saw him count his money at the end of the day. When he sat down to read or write letters or ponder, they watched him. He felt their serene approval of all the ways and means of his life. But when he considered the preposterous mission which Foss had offered him, he felt the whole room liven in mockery. Then he laughed.

" It won't happen. The Gestapo . . ."

Nevertheless, something which momentarily frightened him and seemed to connect him at last with the plot, happened one night in the " Nirvana."

" A thing like this," Jey said to himself that night as he let himself into his room, " doesn't happen for no reason at all. That fellow Collis . . . I know that fellow has rooms in Foss's place. Is he in this business, too ? Was the table thrown down at him, or at me ? "

He had little imagination with which to pursue the incident deeply. Nor were his nerves so much on the surface that they were afflicted by the affair. He slept soundly.

But the whole incident rose to the surface of his mind as he lay taking siesta.

" Foss said ' stand by, now,' and I am. But if I'm nothing but a mark for tables. . . ."

Footsteps sounded outside his room. And voices. Somebody rapped loudly on the door.

" . . . or worse . . ."

And he was on his feet and standing in an attitude of terror, real sweating terror from a mind full of absurd ideas of flight and pursuit. His flight, and the pursuit of him! He stood like that for an instant, and then relaxed and was astonished and ashamed.

" Mr. Jey! You there, Mr. Jey ? "

One of the staff. Jey called back cheerfully : " Come in! " and snatched his patched dressing-gown and got into it at the moment when the door opened. He saw the waiter behind a sallow, sombre figure.

" This gent wants to see you, Mr. Jey."

Jey recognized the unhappy figure of the " Nirvana " incident.

" Hullo! Come in! "

He shoved a chair forward for Collis and sat down on the edge of the bed.

" We've met before, haven't we ? " Jey said.

Collis tried to smile. He let himself down slowly into the chair and sighed.

" How are you ? " Jey said, swinging his legs and folding his hands between his thighs. " After the bit of excitement, last night ? "

★

VII

★

" That's just what I've called about," Collis said. He took the little wicker chair heavily, stirring in it so that it creaked as it settled under his weight. He lifted his moist face to Jey.

" My God! " he panted. " That was awful! "

" Yes, I've thought since," Jey said. " A pretty near thing."

" Near! Awful! I can't forget it," Collis said. His splayed nose shone. His upper lip had a heavy dew of perspiration. His unhealthy skin glistened. All over him, the figure which he usually cut was cracked and its attitudes were dissolved. His poise was gone, melted by fear ; and all that was left was his obvious distress. For the first time, Jey noticed his clothes. Distress of mind had become in Collis almost an attitude of the body ; and the body had a dirty collar and a creased tie, cuffs which were grimy, and a suit which was stained and dusty.

" An accident," Jey said.

" No! "

Collis was shaking his head. " Couldn't have been. I've thought it out. It's been on my mind ever since. I stayed home this morning and puzzled it all out."

" I still think it might have been a pure accident," Jey said. He nursed an ankle and waited for Collis to speak.

" Couldn't have been," Collis repeated : then he said in an altogether different tone : " Tell me just what you thought about it."

Jey swayed back a little and grinned. " I thought it was damned careless of the management to let those drunks in."

" Drunks ? "

" A bunch of them on the balcony. I heard them."

" But didn't you think . . ."

" I thought we had a lucky escape! "

" I know. I owe my life to you."

" Don't think about it."

Collis shook his head mournfully. " I can't get the affair off my mind. I'm a busy man. I've got a big business of my own . . ."

" Excuse me," Jey said. " Your name is Collis, isn't it ? "

" That's right. Collis. Accountant. As I was saying : I've got a big business. But to tell you the truth, I was afraid to leave the house to-day."

" Were you ? Were you, really ? Why ? "

Jey said that and slowly put his feet to the floor and folded his arms.

" Because of what happened."

" Three or four drunks! "

Collis shook his head vehemently. " It was done deliberately."

" I'll admit they were rather far gone."

" They were as sober as I was! They did it deliberately! "

His mood had changed. It was sullen, truculent. He was trying, Jey thought, to insist an idea from all his nervousness.

" Might have done," Jey said. " Although . . . a pretty murderous sort of thing to do."

" Yes! Murderous! "

" It never occurred to me . . ."

" Didn't it ? You mean to say it never struck you that it was done on purpose ? "

" Good Lord, no! "

Collis looked hard at him. His distress was clothed now, armoured with resolve above its weakness.

" Do you mind if I ask you a question, Mr. Jey ? "

" Go ahead! "

" Have you been out to-day ? "

" Not yet. I slept late . . ."

" So you haven't been out at all ? "

The tone was offensive. Jey answered it curtly.

" No."

Collis sat back. He had an air of relief and triumph. His manner was impudent, coarse, suddenly self-assured.

" Why not ? "

" What the hell! " Jey exclaimed. " I've told you! "

" You don't usually stay in all day, do you ? "

" You don't think that you're being just a little too inquisitive about me ? " Jey said.

Collis flung out an angry, vibrating hand.

" Look at it from my point of view, can't you ? " he whined.

" Where's your office ? " Jey said.

" You know."

" I'm asking you. . . ."

" I've seen you on the stairs, two or three times. I've seen you going to Foss's place . . ."

" And you have the rooms above their place, haven't you ? "

" Yes."

" Then if I were you," Jey said, " I'd get back there and look after your business."

" Let's come to the point," Collis panted. " I'll be blunt."

" You are! "

" I apologize. I never meant to be. The fact is, I've had very little sleep, and I admit I'm scared."

" No need to be."

" But look at it from my point of view. Those fellows push a table over a balcony. What for ? What for ? That's what I want to ask you! That's what I'm asking! It was for you, wasn't it ? They meant it for you, didn't they ? "

Jey stood up. He felt better on his feet.

" How do I know ? "

He leaned against the wall and folded his arms over his agitated heart.

" You do know! " Collis said. " You know they meant it for you, don't you ? Why don't you admit it ? "

Jey grinned. " Is that why you couldn't sleep, Collis ? Is it ? Is that why you stayed home all day ? Is that why you came here ? You're frightened, aren't you ? But you're not frightened on my account, are you ? "

Jey was surprised at himself. He had never bullied anyone before. And certainly he had never let his tongue race off against a poor-spirited, trembling fool. He stopped quickly, and was glad when Collis answered him with some spirit.

" It was meant for you! And you know it! " Collis shouted.

His anger was from fear. Perspiration dripped from his upper lip to the curve of his chin, giving him a sorrowful aspect. His nose shone. His forehead had glistening drops of perspiration that ran together as though from the heat of his thoughts.

" Why don't you speak the truth and out with it ? " he raged. " They were after you! You know they were! You had your eye on them, because before the thing had time to touch us, you were out of your chair. It proves . . ."

" It proves," said Jey, " that you want to believe they were after me and not after you, doesn't it ? "

Collis shook his head. " I'm worried. I've got no enemies. I can't make out . . ."

" Why! " Jey exploded, " you've got more enemies than you could ever count in a month of Sundays! "

He felt an extraordinary exhilaration, as though in one moment he had seen peril bearing down upon him and in the next had safely avoided it.

" Haven't you ? Why, you must know it! "

And while the little room echoed with his words, and Collis

floundered to deny them, Jey thought : he'll take it! He'll confess, in a few minutes. If I hold on like this . . . he'll give in and tell me. That table was aimed at him, and not at me. It couldn't have been intended for me. . . .

Collis's eyes stabbed their gaze at him and then swivelled towards the floor.

" I've got no enemies . . ."

" Look at me, Collis! Look up! "

Collis complied. His head lifted slowly, and his eyes brought their gaze up as though head and eyes were weighted with an immense guilt.

" Why don't you go to the police ? " Jey said. " If you're so afraid."

" What's the sense in that ? What could they do ? "

" Protect you."

Collis looked down again at the floor.

" Why don't you tell me the truth, Mr. Jey ? " he whined. " You could trust me. I know they were after you. And you know it."

" I've never set eyes on them before or since," Jey said.

" They meant it for you. They're after you, and that's why you stayed in all day."

Jey said : " And so did you, didn't you ? Now confess! "

It was deadlock. Collis got up slowly and stood looking mournfully through the window. For a moment, his body was lax. Then he grinned. His thick breath rushing in and out over his teeth was a snigger of fear and exasperation as well.

" We're both hiding something, Mr. Jey, aren't we ? "

" What a conscience you've got! " Jey said.

" Same as yours, probably," Collis said. He tapped Jey on the arm. " We're in it together. You know it was for you, don't you ? I know you do! But you want me to believe it was meant for me."

" You know what my answer to that is," Jey said.

Collis was still grinning. " Don't you feel scared ? "

" I wasn't, and I'm not now," Jey said.

Collis sat down again and wiped his cuff across his forehead and sighed. " It's so hot . . ." he murmured. And looking at Jey, he said : " I can't go, Mr. Jey. I'm afraid of them."

" You can't stay here," Jey said.

He stooped down and drew from under the bed his shoes and socks. Pulling on the socks, he glanced up at Collis.

" You're up to some dirty work, I suppose."

" No, no, I told you, I'm in business . . ."

But the lie was inscribed on Collis's broken poise and in his dull, wavering gaze and his irresolute air.

" Pull yourself together," Jey said, tying the shoe laces with a firm movement, " and go to your office."

" I'm afraid to go out."

" You came here safely, didn't you ? " Jey said, reaching for his garments.

" I ordered a taxi."

" Order another."

Collis was silent. Jey drew on his vest.

" What are you frightened of, Collis ? "

Collis took some time to answer. He sighed. " I've led an honest life," he mumbled.

" Then fear not! " Jey said, from under his shirt. " Go and do some work."

" Look," said Collis. " Couldn't I wait outside and then go out with you ? "

Jey turned his back on him and drew on his trousers.

" I'm not going out," he said. " I'm going down to the lounge for some tea."

Collis's whole face twitched. His upper lip flicked up and bared his teeth.

" No, you wouldn't go out, would you ? Oh, no! You're too careful to do that! "

" Not until the sun leaves the streets," Jey said.

Collis rose quickly. " So you won't tell me ? " he said, angrily.

" Tell you what ? "

Collis mumbled in chagrin. For an instant, his thick body had a brutal stance and he looked what he was : mean, greedy, a bully. His courage flamed momentarily in him and expired in the next instant. His body lost its truculent line. He stumbled past the little bookcase like a sick man weak on his legs.

" You'll be all right," Jey said, standing at the door.

Collis put on his hat and looked along the passage and then at Jey.

" You're not going out until later on ? "

" Not until it's cooler. If it ever gets cooler."

It seemed to satisfy Collis. He nodded. A thin smile passed over his face.

" That proves . . ."

He went off in the direction of the stairs. Jey closed the door and stood quite still near the bed.

An infection was left in the room as insidiously as the exhalation of germs. He felt symptoms begin already in him. Fear grew and twirled about his mind. He remembered what Collis had said. " That proves . . ."

And although it did not seem feasible, it proved something to him. His thoughts began to impact as they mounted and flowed. He felt

140

the perspiration pour out in a prickly fever on his body under the sudden hot pulse of fear. And it seemed to him then that for a long time he had been foolish. He had told Foss that he would undertake that mission, and he had visited Foss frequently and been given instructions. He had renewed his passport, obtained a visa, packed a suitcase, vowed to Foss that he would not divulge his errand. But he had allowed himself to become enmeshed in something which was taking size and substance around him while he walked heedlessly amidst it. He did not know the extent of it or the ebb and flow of it. But he realized now that it had become large. Already, it was filling with figures. There were men in a balcony of a restaurant : bold, determined men who did not hesitate to send a table hurtling down. Upon him ? Upon Collis ? And was Collis a party to this plot ?

He sat on the bed as miserably as Collis had sat in the chair. His head drummed with fearful thoughts. His hands were damp.

" Now I'm in it," he thought. " This is what I'll be like when I get my marching orders, and when I arrive in Berlin. Now I'm in it. This is the feeling . . ."

But all at once he stood up and finished his dressing.

" It won't happen," he told himself. " There won't be any marching orders. Foss won't give me the signal. Von Pless will be arrested, and everything will crack up."

He stood still for an instant.

" It won't happen," he thought, " because already . . . already the State Police in Germany . . ."

He felt cold in his loins as he remembered the table crashing down.

" At me . . . Collis was right . . . it was for me! "

He finished dressing and tidied his room. Five minutes later he went down to the lounge and ordered tea. While he was waiting, he read the afternoon edition of the local paper. Seven deaths from the heat. Many minor casualties. Reports from the country. Scenes in the city.

He turned the pages. News from the European capitals. Threats, taunts, tension. Fear. On the other side of the page, the racing news, the cricket news. The waitress brought his tea, and he lowered the newspaper and poured himself a cup.

" There's the weather of the air," he thought, " and there's a sort of weather amongst human beings."

The lounge was stuffy. A single fan droned from a high place on the rear wall. The open windows admitted the sound of the traffic. But the desired wind, the cool gust for which mankind waited, did not come. The motionless brown curtains hung listlessly in their folds like sulky things disinclined to signal a change. In the chairs, Jey and the other guests sat drowsily. Two commercials were totting up the day's orders. An elderly woman, permanent like Jey, leaned towards them.

" I don't know how you manage in this weather! "

It was an opening gambit which they declined. Two grins, and then the plunge back into the order books. She cast around for someone else. Jey got behind his newspaper. He heard someone snoring, and envied him. Two swarthy men came in and took a little table near the door. One of them flicked away a wasp which buzzed about an empty cup on the tray. The other spoke in an earnest, murmurous tone to which the other answered with swift, assenting nods.

Jey finished his tea, yawned. Boredom touched him. And behind boredom were all the incessantly attentive moods of impatience, despair, hope and desire, all awaiting the moment when boredom would admit them. He put aside the newspaper and stood up.

In a way which attracted his attention, the two swarthy men rose too, and passed into the hall ahead of him.

" About seven ? " one said. And Jey fancied he detected something of a guttural flavour in the speech.

" Eight," the other remarked, clipping the vowels. " Make it eight."

Jey stopped at the desk. The Receptionist had gone to tea, and the porter who had taken her place for fifteen minutes shook his head.

" No letters, sir! "

One of the swarthy men had halted nearby.

" No letters, Mr. Jey," the porter added.

Jey saw the swarthy man glance quickly at him. A significant glance. Jey put on his hat and strolled out. He did not see the two men leave. He did not want to. They were behind him, but he had lost the habit of looking over his shoulder, of casting a glance backwards. There was only regret, despair, and ignominy for him when he did that. He preferred the present and the future.

He chose the shady side of the street and made for the heart of the city, stopping only at the theatre where he booked a seat for himself for to-morrow night's performance of the Ballet. After that, he had nowhere particular to go, and nothing particular to do. He looked in windows and saw the new season's goods, and his own dim reflection.

" SMART. LATEST DESIGNS."

He hurried away. Designs on his life. Designs of Foss's, extending preposterously. . . . He stopped at Cellingworth's and looked at the pipes and tobaccos, and saw again his own podgy reflection with the hat at its jaunty angle, and the little tuft of greying hair rising from under the brim near his left ear. Not bad, really not so bad for forty-seven, but a war . . . a war would give him a place in something . . . some army depot or something . . . or factory . . .

He saw the reflection of the two men who had been in the lounge.

" I thought I heard them saying good-bye to each other," he thought. He spun round quickly. But they were trained for such eventualities. They were already shaking hands when he faced them, and there was nothing, positively nothing, which he could do next except walk on. In freedom, with absolute freedom.

And that was the fretting, monstrous fact about him, as he strolled with one hand in his jacket pocket and the other swinging freely. His shadows watched him walk amidst the crowds along the pavements. And the fact that he was free to move thus, to go where he liked when he liked, and not to suffer restraint, roused their lust.

For they had to remember that this was England. Here, no matter how hard, how dark and implacable were his resolves, he was protected by the traditions of freedom. Authority did not concern itself with what the mind held. But in Germany . . .

They followed him, one a short distance behind him, the other on the opposite side of the road in case he were to cross. And their thoughts were identical. In Germany : the tap on the arm or shoulder, and the muttered request to halt, to come quietly to a certain place. And then : then the extraction of the secret from the substance of the brain.

Their hands jerked in their pockets. To lay hands at last upon him! To probe him. For they knew that he, too, was involved. They had not known it until this afternoon, although they had suspected it last night when they had seen Collis enter the " Nirvana " and sit waiting there. Waiting for someone ? Surely ? And looking over the balcony in all the attitudes of drunken men, they had seen Jey take a seat opposite Collis. And had seen Jey swing Collis and himself out of danger when they themselves had thrust over the table. And this afternoon : that terrified figure coming from the taxi and passing rapidly through the hall of the " Crown " to make for Jey's room. Which proved . . .

The evening exodus from the commercial districts was at its peak, and it was difficult to follow Jey amidst the packed pavement-crowds. A jaunty hat, with a greying tuft of hair above the ear ; that was all the eye had to cling to. And it was soon lost, and soon fortuitously found again. But a long walk . . . far across the teeming district . . . a mile, but such a mile on this sweltering day!

And then they lost him. They went through a rapid routine then. They quartered the busy street, moving on and then stopping, walking parallel to each other, and finally stopping and giving it up. One crossed the road to the other. They felt foolish, mocked, defeated. It would not have happened in Berlin!

Jey was watching them from the steps of the Prudential Buildings fifty yards behind them. He had hurried on through the crowds and then swung on to the packed platform of a 'bus going in the opposite direction. From the step of the 'bus, he had seen one of his shadows peering to find him. Jey dropped off some distance behind and came cautiously up on them. The Prudential steps were good cover, and the shadows didn't think of looking there. A stream of clerks and typists poured down the steps, and Jey's head amongst them hardly showed as he stood there and watched the visible discomfiture of those two.

"They're on to me," he thought. "They're definitely on my tracks."

He decided to get right out of town for the evening. A ride out to the country, and then a walk ? But he was not so fond of solitude as to seek it as a means of escape. He loitered on the steps, keeping his eye on the pair, and made up his mind to get over to Pelham's and spend the evening there.

He came down the steps and moved with the crowds to the 'bus stage. A firm hand fell on his shoulder. He winced and jerked round, staggering back and then recovering himself.

A large man, a very large man, in a grey flannel suit and a grey trilby, with grey gloves and a rosebud in his buttonhole was shaking his limp hand.

"Jey! Have we or have we not met before ? " A large, resonant voice from an immense face, red and packed with good humour.

"Harry! How are you, old man ? "

"Thirsty and hungry and glad to see you, George! "

He took Jey by the arm.

"You're coming with me, George! "

"Oh, but Harry! As a matter of fact, old man . . ."

He hung back for a moment, really afraid, quite afraid of that pair now that Collis had proved to him that they would stop at nothing.

"An appointment . . ."

"Come on! I'm thirsty, and I bet you are, too, George! "

Harry kept hold of his arm and together they walked on towards the "Lion."

"We've just got back, George. Had a very nice day. Lovely weather. Warm, of course. But oh! Sweet to see the Course and the colours! Nice to get out for a day like that."

Jey said yes, did you good, and what were the starters like and how had Harry made out on the day. But he did not listen to what Harry said in reply. He saw the pair cross the road and he knew that they had seen him, for he and Harry had not been two minutes in the lounge before both of them came in and took a table near the door. And at once they put between them a little mass of documents which they leaned over and discussed as though nothing else in the world mattered.

"I'm asking you," Harry boomed, prodding Jey with a fleshy hand, "what you'd like to drink!"

"Sorry! Sorry, Harry! Something long, thanks. A Bass."

When Harry had given the order, he offered Jey a cigarette and said : "Anything wrong?"

Jey wanted to say no, no, just the heat ; but instead he winked at Harry and gave a slight jerk of his head towards the pair at the far side. It was twenty past six and the evening sojourners were dribbling in and settling over a preliminary ale prior to steady guzzling.

"Which one?" Harry whispered, and because he knew what sometimes happened to gentlemen of limited means, he imagined that he knew what Jey's trouble was at this moment.

"Couple of dagoes near the door," Jey said.

Harry looked slowly all round the lounge and then back at the Bass which the waiter brought. He chuckled softly.

"Very much?" he asked.

"This time, they want my blood," Jey said.

Harry nodded and pursed his lips. "They spoil a nice evening," he said. "I thought we'd have a couple here and then get along to the 'Emperor' and have dinner."

"Not unless I can shake off that pair," Jey said.

Harry drained half the contents of his glass. "You leave it to me, George."

"They've been at my heels since five," Jey said.

Harry winked. "We'll take our time, and then we'll slip them."

He was a nurseryman in a large way of business, and when he said 'slip them,' Jey had a fantastic notion that he intended to separate them from each other. He laughed quickly and then spoke to Harry.

"How?"

"When we're ready, we'll sail out of here and take a taxi. I'll go by the main door, and you can slip out through the side door out of the cloakroom. I'll meet you in Alfred Street with the taxi. How's that?"

"Good enough," Jey said.

"Easy!"

Presently, when Jey beckoned the waiter to give the second order, Harry said : "And order me a taxi for seven sharp, will you?"

"Now," said Harry, a little later, "I get up and then you get up, too, and we just saunter out to the hall where you nip along to the cloakroom, while I take the taxi round to Alfred Street."

He stood up slowly, lifting his huge bulk from the chair and passing through the lounge beside Jey. The pair at the table near the door gave no sign that they saw them.

"Off you go!" Harry said, in the hall.

Jey turned off to the cloakroom. An attendant was leaning over the little counter and reading *Film Weekly*. Behind him on the racks and in the lockers were a few hats and a single raincoat. As Jey came in, he straightened up and said good evening. Jey crossed over to the basins and turned back his sleeves.

It was at that moment that the bell rang over the counter. After that, everything happened with a curious suddenness which frightened Jey as he stood leaning over the basin with his wrists under the water from the " Cold " tap.

The attendant stiffened as the bell rang ; and coming from behind the counter, he opened the door leading to the hall and peered along the passage. A waiter approached.

" Ringin'! " the attendant complained. " You know I can't leave the desk! "

" Not for you," the waiter said. " He pressed all the bells! Hit six or seven before he got the right one. It's someone in the lounge. Collapsed . . ."

They were joined by a page. Jey saw for an instant his baby face full of an expression of cynical knowledge, and heard his childish treble.

" . . . flopped off 'is chair! They want a wet towel."

" Towel . . . face towel . . . wet! " exclaimed a porter, running towards them.

Then a reassuring voice sounded along the passage.

" It's all right! Leave it! "

But attendant, waiter, and page went quickly towards the lounge. Jey took his hands from under the tap and flicked the water off them before he turned to towel them in the clean white roller beside the mirror. He saw his reflection in the glass and thought for an instant that for middle-age it was not bad, still preserved, still good enough to label as thirty-eight if ever the time came for him to enlist.

" As it will," he thought, looking at his finger-nails, and turning half-round.

He heard the door swing open and plunge back on its heavy hinges, and he thought it was the attendant returning. But there was no sound of footsteps, and presently he turned to see who had come in and why that person stayed near the door.

There was nobody there. Someone, he thought, just putting his head in. He drew down his sleeves and put on his hat. For a moment as he turned to go out by the little exit near the toilets, he wondered what had happened to the customer who had collapsed.

Briskly, because he knew that by this time the genial Harry would be waiting for him in Alfred Street, he swung open the rear door. There was a little flap window confronting him. It opened on a yard ⸗ some sort, some kind of yard or space contrived amidst the high walls and the silence of those rear premises. And the whole aperture was filled by a face whose eyes peered at him.

He recognized the face. That of one of the pair : a swarthy countenance. He had a sudden impulse to step over and bang down the flap, and he would have acted upon it but for the appearance of a hand in the little opening beside the face. A hand holding a revolver. Face and hand making a compact threat. The eyes riveted upon him, and the weapon's snout showing like the awful, blank eye of death itself.

" And I'm standing here . . ."

The thought drove down through his mind, and in fear he hesitated and knew that he was the target and that if he did not move he would never move alive again. He dived towards the tiled floor.

" Like a backfire . . ." he thought, when the report came. And with the report was the stinging crack of the bullet against the white tiles behind him. He crouched, huddled against the wall, face up-turned, realizing that if the hand only poked itself in a few inches and deflected the weapon and took a blind shot, or five blind shots, he would . . .

And he saw it come in, as though his thought had touched that murderous brain with the suggestion.

" Lord . . . Lord . . ." he gasped.

He jerked his sweating body to his feet and seized with both clawing hands the warm wrist and clung on with all his weight. The weapon tipped at once from the strong fingers. Under the ringing echoes of the report and the crack of the bullet against the wall, he heard a sharp cry. The wrist went slack in his grip. He clung on for an instant. He thought of calling for help. He foresaw in that instant all the excitement : the staff, the revolver, the police ; the questions, the facts, the truth. And he let go.

The hand withdrew and he was left only with the echoes stinging still in his ears, and the revolver lying on the floor. He heard rapid footsteps outside, followed by the slamming of a wooden door. Then silence.

He shut the flap and locked it.

" If anyone . . ."

He lifted the revolver. A warm, heavy thing, making a deadly weight in his hand. A thing still warm about the butt, odious, with its recent purpose indescribably reflected in its shape. He glanced at the wall and saw the tiny sore upon the tiles, high up on the opposite side, with the cracks spreading an inch or two all round the hole. On the floor, a fine film of dust was spreading, with here and there a flake of tiling and plaster.

He scooped the flakes together quickly and gathered them and dropped them into a basin nearby. Then he tried the door. It was locked. He turned the big key and stepped out quickly into the yard. It was then that he was conscious of the huge bulge which the revolver made in the pocket of his jacket.

He saw the wooden door leading to an alley, and he hesitated. In the yard, the heat lay thickly. Above, high on the wall, the sunlight struck the bricks. The roar of the city's traffic echoed hereabouts and flowed down the walls. Looking up, he saw a waitress wiping a plate at a window. Somebody was whistling melodiously near another window, and the sound came out with all the stark indifference of normal life to the individual tragedy. Jey went across to the door and lifted the latch with one hand and kept the other hand on the revolver.

" If he's waiting for me, and if the other one is there with him, I'm ready," he thought. But his heart was thudding heavily as he stepped into the wide alley. He knew that the waitress high above was watching him. The whistler was still whistling. Life was active, incessant. But his fear boiled in him and dragged at his feet and raced his pulse. He let the door bang close behind him, and one hand rested for a moment on its hot wood before he moved off.

He saw a handcart with a commercial's baskets piled on it, and a tired porter sitting on one of the thick shafts. Beyond, near the side door of a neighbouring hotel, was a waiter with a white cloth hanging to his knees. He was talking to a youth in an overfashioned plum suit.

" . . . by eleven."

" That'll do, because me and Doris won't be gone until then."

" I'll tell Iris . . ."

Jey hurried past. He could see at the far end, the pavements and cobbles of Alfred Street. The taxi would be there, and he would be there soon. If his thudding pulse didn't load his body more than this, and if one of the pair didn't come at him. And this heavy thing in his pocket! And what to do with it ? And how to sit in the " Emperor " with Harry, with this lump of mischief in his pocket ?

He went on. When he reached the end of the alley, he came out slowly, hand on revolver, ready.

But there was only the usual line of parked cars, and a late horse-drawn cart at the far end, and the heat and straw and figures clustered about the entrance to a store-yard. And Harry sitting like a nabob in a taxi standing a few yards inside the street.

" I thought," said Harry, lugubriously, as he moved along the seat, " quite thought you'd lost your way." He winked at Jey as the latter got in and sat back.

" D'you make it all right, George ? No followers ? " he whispered. Jey nodded. " You haven't been here long, have you ? "

"No, no," Harry said. " Matter of fact, only this minute."

" Then you wouldn't have seen . . ."

The taxi trundled slowly over the cobbles and out into the main road.

" Seen what ? "

Jey stooped low over his shoes to tie slowly the laces, for the taxi was going past the " Lion " entrance and he thought it would be wise to keep out of sight. He dawdled over the laces, and suddenly drew off the left shoe and pretended to shake out a piece of gravel. By the time he had replaced the shoe and tied it, the taxi was so far past the " Lion " that he felt it was safe to sit upright.

" Sorry, Harry! You were saying . . ."

" George, you've got something on your mind, haven't you ? "

Jey grimaced. " That pair."

" No," said Harry, shaking his majestic head. " No! That wouldn't worry you. And if it did, you know your old pal Harry wouldn't let them serve any writs or whatnots on you."

" You're too kind, old boy."

" No. You've got a worry." And he glanced sideways at Jey and added : " Personal ? Anything two blokes could do about it instead of one bloke ? Be a privilege, old boy. . . ."

Jey smiled. " Thanks, Harry! Thanks. A matter for one bloke, I think."

Harry loosened his grey hat. " You know best."

But he was wondering why Jey carried a revolver, and he could not remember having seen it bulging so prominently and lying so carelessly in that pocket when he had first met Jey this evening. Both were silent until he glanced slowly at Jey and saw the thin shadow of a problem lying upon those familiar, amiable features under the tilted hat and the gay tuft of grey hair.

" You know what happened, of course ? " Jey said, meeting Harry's huge gaze.

" You mean to your friends back there ? "

" They put up a show, I think," Jey said. " And when I went to get out by the back way, one of them was waiting for me."

" Go on! "

" A near thing," Jey said.

Harry chuckled. His fat arm nudged Jey.

" A writ, or something ? "

Jey laughed swiftly. " Nearly a writ, Harry."

The taxi drew up outside the " Emperor." Jey got out ; and before Harry had heaved his great bulk to the pavement, Jey had paid the fare and was waiting. Harry frowned. " You should have let me . . ." he mumbled. But he was thinking : " If we toddle into this place with that murderous bloody thing shining in Jey's pocket. . . ."

Once in the hall, he took Jey by the arm. A porter greeted Harry. A couple resplendent in full evening dress passed towards the restaurant. The door opened, and as Jey moved forward he caught one glimpse of his pair reflected in the clear glass of the door as they strolled in. They were less than twelve feet away.

Then Harry saw them. And he might have been nonplussed at that moment had not Jey breezily moved off with him towards the Cocktail Bar at the far end of the hall where, around a semi-circular counter beyond which a dapper, white-coated figure was agitating a polished shaker, a few smartish youngsters were already gathered.

" You see, Harry, they cling, don't they ? "

" What do we do ? " Harry moaned.

" Try again."

" Would have been nice here, George. No, no thanks, I never touch spirits."

Jey had a Paradise while Harry squatted near the imitation stained-glass window and waited. Harry could see the big object still bulging in Jey's jacket pocket, but now the pocket lapel was drawn out.

" If he doesn't park that thing," Harry thought, " some smarty will spot the shape of it for what it is. I'd a good mind to tell him."

Jey came over to him. " Shall I look out the land ? "

" Yes. Take a look round. Perhaps they're gone."

Before Jey could turn away, they came in. They stood not more than six feet away and ordered a couple which the barman served quickly. Harry got up. Without a word, he and Jey moved out down the hall and through to the street.

They walked. Harry was annoyed. Why doesn't George out with it, he thought, and tell me ? Lugging round that gun!

" In here ? " Jey suggested, outside the " Cranborne."

" It's just a question of your limpets," Harry said. " But in we go ! " And without halting, the two of them swung in, the door opening for them with the porter's salute to Jey.

" I think we've slipped them," Jey said.

The hall with its thick carpet and its air of cool comfort was curiously quiet after the noisy street where the heat held all sound within a tiny, hard compass. Here, the murmured voice was as pleasant as the suggestion of the tranquil mind which it afforded the ear. Here, the sedate company, attended by all the tradition of the place, represented Church, the Law, and the circle of substance that liked to identify itself with the virtues, the opinions, and the security of the professions. A large matron with a pretty daughter-in-law glided towards the dining-room.

" . . . been out of touch for years . . ." she said.

" He loves it," the daughter-in-law said.

The matron was silent. Jey thought : she'd sulk proudly for a month over nothing. I know them! Like Aunt Lily.

He and Harry left hats and gloves in the cloakroom and washed. And while Harry was bent over the basin of cold water, Jey let memory unscroll its panorama of family life : Aunt Lily, Aunt Laura, Vincent and his incessant warble : " We spent ourselves in that war, but the oncoming generation frittled away the victory! " They were all creatures cast upon single notes, single idiosyncrasies.

" And I was pretty much the same," Jey thought. " I ran to clothes."

He remembered how he had always kept up a good appearance. The best clothes, always. Until now, when it was the personality which counted. He saw his reflection in the tall glass near the roller towel.

" This big revolver . . ." he thought, anxiously.

He went to the counter. " Have you a biggish piece of brown paper ? "

The attendant produced a strong sheet. It had a trade label on one side and was a little crumpled from use.

" That's fine! "

Jey put it on the floor against the counter and deftly removed the weapon from his pocket and wrapped it while Harry was waddling hands and face in water and the attendant had his back turned.

" And a strong piece of string, please ? "

Jey tied it on the counter. It looked like a wrapped tool.

" Going to leave it, sir ? "

" I'll keep it," Jey said.

In the dining-room, he carried it like something very precious which he had just bought, but when he and Harry were seated, and when Harry was engrossed in the wine list, he dropped it silently to the floor between his feet. And thereafter, throughout the courses, he held it between his shoes and under his shoes, and finally edged it right back against the wall. And forgot it, together with the fact that somebody had tried to murder him.

Harry, after the light conversation of dinner, had settled back to elaborate an idea.

" You say, George, that society is mistrustful of its members, and maybe it is. But that is only one bit of the trouble. Society will always have that peculiarity. It'll always be like that : a bit suspicious, and so on. But our trouble nowadays is in our lust for speed. Sometimes, I like to read a bit of history. I like to read about the reign of Queen Victoria. Now look at that shrewd woman! George, that old Queen had a relative on pretty nearly every throne in Europe. There was international mistrust and crisis then, just as there is now. There was plenty of national aspiration then, just like now. But she held it all within bounds. It seems to me that that old lady had an idea, George, and if she'd had another fifty years of life she'd have succeeded with it."

" England bossing the whole of Europe! "

" Not a bit of it! A united states of Europe. If she'd have had her way. Her son had the same idea, with his Entente. But it wasn't enough. By then, the idea was halted."

" It couldn't work," Jey said.

" George," Harry said. " Man likes to get together in a mass, no matter how nationalistic he is. He likes unity. History reveals it. He likes to bring everybody under the umbrella. Read history and discover it! Old Victoria wanted a united states of Europe—whether she knew it or not. Pity they didn't carry on her tradition and bring it about. But Science is destroying the idea."

" You're a reactionary! " Jey said.

" Am I ? I'm for a sedate life! I don't like speed. We're at the mercy of the radio, the telegram, the telephone, and the things of speed, George. They rule us, and they drive us to the edge of the pit. They make us live right on the edge of decisions, and they don't give us time to deliberate. The international crisis boils up and the world knows of it in five minutes or less. And instead of the interval which the old forms of communication granted us to allow us to apply thought and commonsense to problems, we're hurried to give a reply in a matter of minutes. The people get hold of a few facts and they boil up and run together. The panic spreads, and panic isn't reasonable. We live at the end of radios and telephones, and we're sort of extended into space to catch every sound. That isn't peace! It isn't even natural! It compels us to act without thinking first."

" It's what we're accustomed to," Jey said.

" George," Harry said, in his slow, dignified way, " we're not machines. We're works of Nature. We're animals, and we're a part of natural things like air and earth, fire and water. We live on the earth, by the earth, and the good Lord has given us a divine example to follow. I'm a horticulturist. I see the seed go into the soil, and days afterwards I see the little shoot which grows in the course of months to the plant. Weeks later comes the bud which blooms. And I know that that seed wants earth and air and warmth, and that the plant wants light and rain, and sunlight for warmth. But gradually. In a way which will allow it to imbibe it all in proportion. Not speedily. Not like we live. Not faster than light, or as quick as sound or something else! Nature is wise. If we deny that wisdom we perish in wars. If we go on accelerating the speed of modern life, ᵕᵕᵕ ught to ask ourselves first of all why we do it, and if the purpose ᵕᵕᵕ But there isn't an engineer in the whole world who could ᵕᵕᵕ v he wants more revolutions per minute from his machine.

He'd say because he thinks he can get them, and because that's progress. He's right. But to what purpose is he going to apply the extra revolutions ? He doesn't know! He simply doesn't ask himself, or care, so long as he gets them. But the awful thing is that when a war comes, the extra revolutions give the enemy speed, and your engineer has to set to work to better his own efforts! "

" There's a limit," Jey said, " and when we've touched it we'll sit back and relax! "

" You mean it's just curiosity ? " Harry asked.

" I think so. And when we've satisfied our curiosity we'll be reasonable."

Harry laughed. " No! Then we try something else."

" We've gone under the sea, under and over the earth, and soon we'll be in the stratosphere. What then ? Then we'll have to come back to earth! "

" No, George, on we go! I said we're a creation of Nature, but we're wonderful and fantastic. And I'm not quite sure that we haven't the power to make all our dreams come true."

" How ? "

Harry wrinkled his big forehead. " We say we discover this or that. But I'm wondering if it isn't just a matter of inventing. We dream, and the next thing we do is to bring the dream into reality."

Jey smiled. " You're dreaming! "

" Let's go," Harry said.

It was not until they were in a taxi on the way to Harry's house that Harry noticed the absence of the bulge in Jey's pocket.

" Left it on the floor! " he thought. " And a nice thing if they open it! "

He thought for a moment of asking Jey what he had done with it. He was worried, deep in his big heart.

" Jey," he said, " we've not seen your pair for quite a time now! " And he chuckled.

" Keep your fingers crossed," Jey said, looking about in the dusk.

" You think they're still on your tracks ? " Harry said.

Jey nodded. " They mean business."

And as he reminded himself of what had happened in the " Lion " he felt a quick, sickening sensation of fear. It was the recoil in himself of his rash promise to Foss. His life was balanced upon that promise, and around him the forces were gathering and he could not discern them or assess them except in terms of revolvers and bullets and murder. Looking up, he saw the soft night sky already sprinkled with silver stars. Something in his spirit expanded joyously but was cruelly circumscribed by the sharp recollection of a hand thrusting itself through a little window and aiming a gun at him.

" They'll try again," he could not help thinking.

Without warning, the taxi swerved and mounted the pavement and crashed into a small tobacconist's lock-up. A big saloon had swung out as though to cross in front of it, but had turned quickly. The crash of glass, the jolting of the vehicle, the shout of the driver, rattled in Jey's ears. It was all like the extension and realization of thought, and he sat quite still in the awkward attitude into which he had been thrown, and he was quite calm, quite unafraid, for he knew that they had tried again without success.

A crowd surged round in a matter of seconds.

" That big saloon! " Harry was saying loudly. " That fellow was at fault! "

Jey climbed to his feet and looked above the heads of the crowd. He heard the driver shout.

" . . . right over on me! I 'ad to turn . . ."

Two policemen appeared. Jey saw the saloon. It had stopped twenty yards away, on its right side.

" That saloon! " he shouted to the policemen.

But there was such a crowd around the taxi, such a screen, that Jey knew at once what had happened. He went quickly with the constables and found the saloon empty and unattended. A newsboy said : " I seen 'em! They got out quick and went that way! " He pointed in the opposite direction where the evening crowds thronged the pavements.

" Hired! " one of the constables said. " That's from Smith and Hanlet's garage! "

One of them noted the number in his book and stayed. The other returned with Jey to the smashed shop-front and the taxi. The driver said : " Come straight at me! Must 'ave been drunk! On'y thing I could do was turn quick! "

Harry looked at Jey. But Jey was remote in his own thoughts.

" Lucky," he told himself, " lucky I left that parcel on the floor under the table! "

" You gents hurt ? " the constable asked.

" Hurt ? " Harry said. " I'm insulted! "

" I'll take your version . . ." the constable said, edging the crowd back from his elbows.

It took twenty minutes. Jey and Harry left together and hailed another taxi. Harry was taciturn. Lying at the root of all his thoughts was an irritating conviction that Jey was in serious trouble.

" Why doesn't he say so, instead of nursing the thing to himself ? "

" Jey," he said, " you must be fond of adventure! "

Jey grimaced. Their eyes met. Harry tapped his arm.

" Those two," he said, quietly. " They're not duns, Jey! They're a couple of thugs! They're dangerous! "

" I'm beginning to think so," Jey said.

" I know it already! " Harry remarked.   " I don't feel comfortable. I don't mind confessing that I'll be glad when we get home! "

★

VIII

★

Jey felt safer in Harry's garden. It was in the suburbs south-west of the city, far out in a quiet locality through which the taxi had brought them speedily. Coming out from town Jey had sat erect with his gaze ahead. He saw Harry glance apprehensively back along the road.

" Let's hope we aren't being followed this time," Harry said.

Jey thought : " If they're coming, looking back won't stop them." And he disdained to glance back, although he was more afraid than Harry.

" You nip in quickly," Harry said, when the taxi stopped.   " You don't want to be seen."

It was quiet in the house. Harry's wife was away on holidays, and only the servants and Harry were there. The radio which had been blaring loudly from the kitchen softened to a mere purr of sound when Harry and Jey entered. A maid appeared.

" Make some sandwiches, please, Ella.   And bring them out to us."

The garden was secluded. It lay on the fringe of larger gardens whose trees and tall hedgerows and walls screened it. Appointed with a large lawn beyond which were beds of choice roses and banks of innumerable blooms, it lay under the night like a lush, perfumed thing, living, vital. Its scents filled the warm air. In the dim light only the pale blooms were visible ; but all of them—the deep red roses of varying shades, as well as the white and orange ones—were fragrant.

" You can breathe them," Jey said, quietly, settling himself in a garden chair.

" They love life," Harry said.   " Colour and scent . . ." he said, pensively, stretching out his thick limbs.

The maid brought cucumber and lettuce sandwiches, and a tray with glasses and a bottle.

" If I didn't know you, George," Harry said, filling Jey's glass, " I'd say you were up to your neck in trouble."

Jey took the glass and fingered its slim stem and its cool, fine shape.

" I'm puzzled," Jey said.

" You know that pair don't like you ? "

" I've never seen them before this evening."

"The more I think about it, the less I like it," Harry said. "This is a peaceful country."

"I've got no enemies," Jey said; and he had at that moment a vision of Collis, earthy, fearful, evil, saying the same.

"Worries me," Harry said. "To think . . ."

He offered Jey a cigar.

"I won't, thanks," Jey said, for he was thinking: two points of red light.

He wondered why Harry didn't smoke, and supposed that it was for a similar reason.

"I've spoiled your evening, Harry. I'm sorry," he said.

"If it had been twenty years ago, I'd have enjoyed it," Harry said, offering the sandwiches.

"I can't tell him," Jey thought. "I'm pledged to silence. What's more, he wouldn't believe me."

"I wish I'd been born poor," Jey said, seeking for reasons, threading his way back from this moment of fear and anxiety.

"You think you'd have been . . . sort of . . ."

"Not different, really," Jey said. "Same things would have come out. But other things with them. I'd have had to fend for myself. I'd have had a place. Small one, perhaps, but a place."

"I don't know," Harry said. "I suppose it does mean something to have a place."

Jey laughed. "It means a lot when you feel you haven't one!"

"But that's the material side of things. I think it's more important to be able to think reasonably. The person who thinks reasonably gets the best out of existence."

"You can't exist on thought."

"It isn't so much thought," Harry said, "as what faith and a calm mind can do for you."

The maid came to call him to the telephone.

"Who wants me, at this time o' night?" he exclaimed to Jey.

Jey sat waiting in the darkness and heat.

"He's treated me to a dinner, and paid the taxis," he thought. "But I've left him with a puzzle he'll never work out!"

Harry came back laughing. "George, you left a parcel in the 'Cranborne.' They've just found it and told me. They said they'll send it out by messenger, straight away."

"My parcel!" Jey softly exclaimed. He got up and looked at his wrist-watch.

"Getting late, Harry!"

They walked slowly through the garden to the house.

"Listen," said Harry, at the sideboard of the dining-room, "before you go, my lad, you have a stiff one. Take my advice."

He took out the whisky and poured Jey a portion. Jey splashed in the soda. The doorbell rang. Harry answered it and brought in the parcel.

"Take it, George, but remove the paper before you leave this house. Shall I ring for a taxi?"

"I'll walk, thanks."

"You're walking into danger, old boy. Would you like to stay the night?"

"No, thanks all the same. I'll be safe."

"I'll 'phone you to-morrow, George, just to . . . sort of . . ."

". . . verify my existence?" Jey said, laughing.

"I'm worried," Harry confessed.

Jey put on his hat. The familiar, jaunty angle with the wisp of grey hair under the brim.

"Take care of yourself, George!"

"I'm well looked after," Jey said. "Thanks for the evening, old boy!"

In the darkness near the porch, he unwrapped his parcel and gave Harry the brown paper. Then he said good night.

It was nearly midnight when he reached the "Crown." He had made a detour, coming through the south of the city, by unfamiliar streets, and then in from the east. It had taken forty minutes. Frequently, he had looked to right and left with an apprehensive glance, but he had not stopped or looked back. Under the heat, the city was restless. He saw many late pedestrians still lounging outside the closed cinemas and the early restaurants. Passing the ends of streets leading towards the city's heart, he caught glimpses of the colourful neons and the great pools of light along the shopping thoroughfares where the windows were still ablaze. It looked gay, somehow enchanting, and he would have strolled that way had not his wary thoughts counselled him to remain in the narrow roads where the half-darkness shrouded him.

Once inside the hotel, he felt safer. The old night porter was in his crib near the door, with the great board of numbered keys beside him. A bottle of Guinness stood empty beside a tumbler on which four rims of brown froth showed evenly down the inside. Some crumbs lay on a plate near the glass, and a few were sprinkled down his waistcoat. The evening newspaper was spread wide over the desk, and the old pensioner lounged and gaped and snoozed over its print.

"'night, John! Any messages for me?"

John sat back in his high chair.

"Hullo, Mr. Jey!"

He was in no hurry. He liked company at this time, and he was in the mood for any of the gossip of the town.

"Any letters?"

The old man got slowly off his chair and turned to the big grill. Mumbling, and with slow hands, he went through the partitions.

"No . . . James, Jackson . . . nothing for Jey . . . no. No, sir!"

"Good!"

"Very warm still, Mr. Jey."

"Very."

Jey yawned and sighed. "Anybody called for me?"

It was a casual question which the old man answered at some length, wandering round it and threading upon it all the aimless substance of his words.

"You ask me, sir . . . and as far as I know, nobody was in . . . although there was two big parties . . ."

"Two? Two fellows?"

" . . . no, parties . . . from the north. Thirty, forty strong each . . . stayin' the night on the way to France and Belgium. Busy. Very busy evening, Mr. Jey. But they're all tucked in snug now. Hungry, thirsty, all talkin' at once and asking for time-tables and labels and francs and change and I don't know what. Full up! We're full up to-night. Them two rooms either side of you . . . we put Ted and Charlie and Bill out. They're sleepin' on the roof. Said they'd sooner sleep out there than in the storeroom. And we put two gents in the room on the left and a married couple the other side. . . ."

He rambled on until Jey yawned again and bade him good night.

"Two gents," Jey thought. He went along the passage on tiptoe and stood for an instant outside his room. He could hear them, next door. He listened. He left his door and crept to the next one and listened. He stooped down to the tiny aperture of light showing at the keyhole and listened.

They were murmuring to each other in German. It was all he wanted to know. He went to his own door and put the key in the lock and entered. The murmuring from next door ceased immediately. He switched on the light and looked round. He knew his room as intimately as he might have known the cherished features of a wife. He knew it so thoroughly that the least disturbance of its customary aspect was apparent to him. Now he stopped, for he knew that it had been entered. The top drawer of the little wardrobe was not quite closed. A scrap of paper was on the threadbare carpet. A book was out of place. The chair was not as he had left it near the end of the bed.

His heart was thudding swiftly as he stooped and drew from behind the wardrobe the locked suitcase which was in readiness for his journey. He unlocked it and was relieved. It had not been touched.

But everything else had been combed, gone over. It irritated him. It gave him a sharp feeling of discomfort. His room had been invaded. More, his personal life had been violated.

It was like a little wave beginning to lap about him; and as he sat down and loosened his shoes, he felt the tide which impelled that little wave, and knew that he was not only in grave peril but at the end of a long phase of his life.

He put away the revolver and took out the one from his suitcase and slipped it under his pillow.

★

IX

★

When Collis left Jey's hotel that afternoon, he stood like a man on the edge of a precipice. The city encompassed his body, but his own thoughts opened like gulfs before which he swayed. For years, he had ranged furtively in the city and had often wondered what his end would be like. Now he believed that the end was very near.

His thoughts worked in a swift fashion, throwing up awful fears, sudden flashes of recollection, curious suspicions. He remembered what Kelpey had told him: "I didn't tell that German a word about our agency. He knew almost as much about it as I do!" And he wondered how Rennenberg had reached that knowledge. He suspected all manner of deceits and subterfuges. He felt that he had been tricked and mocked. And it occurred to him that he had blundered into something that lay around him in huge skeins of intrigue which his slow wits had failed to notice until this moment when it was too late for him to break through. He was nothing but a dull instrument, a pawn which would be swept aside.

The idea terrified him. Swept aside! Destroyed! Murdered! His breath tore from his lungs.

Suddenly, out of all the mist and murk of his life, the thought of home came with all the old associations of comfort and solitude. The comfort of eating what he liked, of drinking, of tasting the silence after the racket of the city. The solitude wherein Daisy awaited him. And if it was all long-since staled, the delusion remained. Home, for years, had been nothing but the place wherein he slept, wherein Daisy and the four children lived, wherein he kept things. But his terrified spirit knew no other haven.

He cut out to the taxi-rank in the centre of the roadway.

". . . home," he mumbled stupidly to the driver near the leading vehicle.

The man stared at him with a dull, heat-drained gaze. A cigarette butt, dead and stained, hung from the corner of his lips. His clothes emitted a stench of petrol and hot cloth.

" Duke Square," Collis added, struggling with the door.

The man jerked it open for him, and as Collis scrambled in he asked him : " Duke Square ? What number ? "

" Never mind the number! Hurry! " Collis said.

For an instant, the man moved with an attempt at alacrity, but by the time he reached his seat at the wheel his body had relapsed once more into its indifferent line. All day, he had suffered the heat and the fumes of the city until something of himself had surrendered and he no longer cared.

" For goodness sake . . ."

He heard the excitable fare muttering at him and banging the panel. He turned out carefully and took what he thought was the best route. The panel rattled. Glancing at the mirror he saw a furious face and hands. The face mouthed words which he heard faintly through the panel.

" Left, you fool! To the left! "

He exploded in one obscene word which he repeated like echoes until his rage was cold, hard. Then he drew up at the pavement and flung himself round. When he shot the panel back, Collis's panting stream of terror hissed out.

" Shut up, or get out! Who's drivin' this cab ? Me or you ? Think I don't . . ." the driver retorted.

" It's to the left, left . . ." Collis whined.

" . . . think I don't know where ? Seventeen years in this city! I know it now. I know the best quick way. Let me do my job prop'ly, can't you, can't you ? "

He slammed back the panel and turned the taxi out. Collis huddled back against the worn upholstery. He saw the greasy arm-straps, the patches on the cushions, the frayed and grimy rug, the brimming ash-tray. These things were the mute witnesses of modern adventure, modern romance : the quick run to the theatre, to the hotel, to the station, or back. The moment before or after journeys, appointments, pleasure. And they were frayed, sordid, cynical from so much experience. And the back of the driver's head seemed to Collis to be like them : indifferent to romance, tragedy, the peril of others.

" Hurry, hurry! " he whined.

The traffic signals thwarted him at one crossing, but were open further on. But at the junction where the wide artery from the commercial district intersected the narrow vein from the east, there was congestion. The taxi halted in a block of drays, cars, other taxis.

Collis glanced about fearfully. Behind was a taxi in which three men were seated. They were watching him. One of them pointed excitably at him, whereupon the others began to wave and laugh. At once, Collis huddled down out of sight. He remembered Rennenberg and Smith and Lane : three Germans who had hinted at their criminal pursuits, their association with men who worked the Bremen-New York ocean route, the long continental express routes, the world-famous hotels. He remembered Jey, and the episode in the " Nirvana." He tasted fear as though it were something floating thickly in the air. His belly spewed it into his mouth. His spittle was hard and thick with it. Death . . . the end . . .

But it couldn't happen! Not in broad daylight in this taxi, in this city where he had lived for so long! Not in this sunny street on a June afternoon. Not death. Death was only between the pages of a thriller. That was mystery and crime-fiction. Only fiction. A puzzle. Not real . . . not likely to happen in actuality.

But would it ? Hadn't the table crashed down ? Wasn't Jey keeping to his room ?

Fear travelled over his limbs like a deadly caress. He gibbered in terror at the touch of it. The authentic mumble of abject terror.

The congestion opened. The taxi moved on. Abreast of it, the taxi with the three men kept pace for half a mile, the three passengers gesticulating at Collis whenever he peeped up at them from the cushions. He saw menace in their grins. He heard for an instant their concerted shout, and it was like a threat.

At the entry to Duke Square, his taxi was twenty yards ahead of the other and about the same distance from his home.

" On, on a bit! " he shouted, when the vehicle stopped.

Then he saw that the other taxi had stopped. The men had alighted.
" No, stop! "

He intended to get out and make a run for it. But already one of the men was approaching. Collis tried to raise the window. He thought of the strong glass, perhaps bullet-proof. The driver was standing with hands on hips, frowning at him.

" Tell him . . . don't let him! " Collis cried.

The window was stiff. Collis's hot hands slid along the strap and then came away in a hopeless little flutter of terror as the big head was thrust in. A big, pasty face, stiff with truculence.

" Digby, isn't it ? Bob Digby ? "

Collis huddled back and shook his head.

" No ? Not Bob Digby ? Used to be at Miller's ? "

Collis was speechless. But fear was peeling off at last and anger was beginning.

" I could 'ave sworn . . . we was saying . . . we was sure . . ."

" No! I'm not! I said . . ." Collis shouted.

The pasty face was washed by a smile. " Sorry, sorry, ol' man! I could 'ave sworn . . . Bob Digby . . . sorry! "

It disappeared from the window. Collis swallowed hard spittle and alighted. The driver watched him in astonishment and saw his trembling hands and limbs.

" You all right ? What number . . ."

" Yes, yes! Here! "

But the trembling hands spilled the coins and the fearful mind could not calculate. The driver gathered the money and took his fare. Collis stumbled off.

On the other side of the Square, a tall man was lounging in the shade. When Collis saw him, the man stood away from the wall and walked swiftly across the roadway. Collis tried to run. He reached number seventeen and thrust in the key and opened the door at the moment when the stranger reached the foot of the worn steps.

" I say! Mr. Collis! "

He was a tout of some sort who had waited an hour ; but his drifting, persuasive voice was the sly sound of doom trying to waylay Collis. It was cut short by the slamming of the heavy door. Then all the familiar odours and things of the hall caught Collis's senses, and for the first time in years he was sensible of them. Tears of relief gushed into his eyes ; and the advent of Daisy from the kitchen was sufficient to release them in a dribble which was mingled with his smile and the soft suspiration of words which were lost under the clamour of childish voices in the yard.

But if she was strangely and sweetly welcome to him at that moment, he too appeared in a new light which startled her. She saw in his fearful expression a positive appeal.

" Oh, Jack! Jack! What's happened ? Aren't you well ? "

He had no words. A sense of deep safety cuddled his heart and rendered words unnecessary. He sighed and went to the dark little room which he used as office, lounge, and dining-room. Outside, the starkly yellow afternoon curved high above the shabby yard and the whitewashed walls on which old zinc baths and the paraphernalia of household laundry was hung between the rancid water-butt and the coal house. The window was lowered, and the lively shouts of his children at play rattled into the room. He sat down and wiped his face with a dirty handkerchief.

" Jack! What is it ? "

Daisy stood over him in an attitude of thin devotion.

" It's all right, all right," he said. " Just the heat . . . the heat . . ."

Daisy was not yet dressed for the hours of evening leisure. With her dirty apron, her old clothes, old shoes, and with her face unwashed and her hair untidy, she would have exasperated him had she met him thus on a normal day. Now her slatternly appearance was transformed by her air of distress which seemed to him to reveal a love which he had imagined to be long since extinct. But love was not all. It was the sympathy and readiness to safeguard him which love expressed that mattered so much to him at this moment.

" Have something, Jack," she suggested. " 'ave a cup of tea. Drink a nice cup . . ."

" Some whisky," he said.

" You 'ad the last, this morning."

" Get's another bottle, Daisy. Skip round to Fred's, but be quick. . . ."

He gave her a pound note. " And shut the front door."

When she returned, she saw that he had removed his jacket and collar and tie. He had taken off his shoes and put up his feet on a chair. A glass stood on the table at his elbow, and he reached out eagerly for the bottle while she shouted through the window at the children.

" Stop that noise! Your father says you got to shut up! "

He uncorked the bottle. " Let 'em play," he mumbled, filling his glass.

" Don't you want no soda-water ? "

He did not answer her. He swallowed almost half the contents of the glass and ran his tongue over his pale lips.

" You're run down," Daisy said. " You're prop'ly run down, that's what it is. And when you're like that, the least thing knocks you out. You've 'ad a nasty shock. What you want is a good rest, Jack."

Looking at him as he lay panting and shuddering in the chair, she began to question him. He seldom confided in her, and even when he did his remarks hardly conveyed anything to her upon which she might fashion a solid idea of his life in the city. Her idea of his work and the men with whom he consorted in the evenings was scant, fragmentary, and gained only by the few facts which he gave off during moments of anger or excessive good humour. But she had another picture of his life, and this one referred to the few hard facts which were true of him. In a detached way, she suspected him of all manner of criminal enterprises. She had no knowledge of them. They did not shape into any definite form for her ; nevertheless, from her intimate knowledge of his character, she believed that she knew what engrossed him. And of his life in that murky region, she had a thin, persistent curiosity which she satisfied in her own way.

He answered her tersely at first ; but later, when he had consumed more whisky, he became surprisingly communicative. He was drunk, yet he spoke vigorously. Names were repeated loudly. Kelpey, Foss, someone called Renberg, others called Smith, Lane, and Jey. And against all of them he poured his fury in all the purpose of revenge for some kind of insult or wrong which they appeared to have done him.

163

It hurt her to listen. It was a vision of a world of brutal pursuits of evil, of rewards and revenges. Her interest waned, because she herself feared violence and evil. Yet, as she watched him and listened, she had a sudden desire to lift it all from him and appreciate the full extent of his ambitions and purposes.

" I can't make it out, Jack," she said, timidly. " Is it about a deal ? Is it something important ? I'm on'y asking so as to help you, see ? "

The question only ignited afresh all his rage. He thumped the arm of his chair and shouted incoherently, his sluggish tongue tripping over the words. Then the house echoed to the thump of the door's knocker, and he was instantly silent.

" Don't go ! Sit down ! Don't go ! "

He was trembling again with terror. The knocking began again, and this time a thin call sounded through the letter-box.

" It's Ada," Daisy said.

Collis subsided. He poured himself more whisky. By the time Daisy and her sister, Ada, entered the room, he was singing and shouting, flourishing aloft his arms and laughing.

" Well, that beats . . ." Ada began, then she drew back. " He's enjoying himself, I must say ! "

" Don't say nothing," Daisy whispered, taking her by the arm. " Leave him alone."

They went to sit in the stuffy front room amidst the bamboo pieces and the photographic reproductions of a younger Collis and Daisy.

" Don't say nothing, but there's some awful trouble, I think," Daisy said.

" What about ? " Ada said.

" Wait a bit," Daisy said. She disappeared and came back with the remains of the whisky and two glasses.

" He was nearly killed last night," she began, pouring whisky into the glasses. Ada studied her attentively. She could not understand her mood with its flashes of curious excitement about what seemed to be only sordid and even tragic. She herself had of a different texture to Daisy. She had style and knowledge of the world and purpose ; and she knew the kind of life which Collis led.

" What's this ? "

" Nearly killed. Sittin' in the ' Nirvana ' and all of a sudden a table comes crashing down on where he and some chap called Jey was sitting, and on'y for Jey shoving 'im back or something they'd 'ave been killed. He was in an awful state."

" That shows you ! That shows you at last what some people think of him," Ada said.

" And last evening, a chap calls to see him. . . ."

" I know, I know, he's always in some dirt, Jack is ! I told you . . .

I used to warn you from the start . . . I used to say ' Jack's in every dirty game,' but you wouldn't believe me."

" Well, I never interfere with him. I let him go his own way."

" Doesn't do. You got a right. . . . However, what happened after that, after the table ? "

Daisy chose her own words and her own time. But to Ada, the affair had a sombre aspect and a quickening movement which seemed to her to denote the knitting threads of Collis's fate.

★

X

★

Although formidable in many degrees of character, Collis—like many other men of so-called strong temperament—was afflicted by an absurd weakness. It was the fear of death. Disgrace, imprisonment, poverty, were perils which threatened him without terrifying him. He believed that they were predictable and that he could successfully counter them. But to die by some untimely circumstance long before a ripe age which he envisaged for himself, seemed to him to be a possibility which he could not avoid. He believed that it would come from one of the trivial indispositions to which he was subject : colds, slight fevers, bilious attacks. To die in middle-age, without having tasted the solid joys of retirement! To be cheated thus! To work for years, to accept hazards, to incur enmity and spite and to be heedless of it all, only to lose the fruits! To die!

He took the greatest care of himself in the cold months, in the rainy seasons, in the proud months of early spring when the breezes made draughts in his office and his home. He went to bed and stayed there until his colds were gone, his aches soothed. And although he had never disclosed his fear of death to Daisy, she was dimly conscious of it in him.

She realized that he feared to die and that he saw death awaiting him in every trivial pain or fever. And this fear which subjected him was the complement to the single, abiding obsession which her shallow mind harboured. What he feared, she awaited with an anticipation which was so different from his that she hardly dared to examine it. His death! His passage out of her life! Her freedom, at last! And her enrichment!

It stirred her imagination. It was the only idea upon which she had ever truly exercised her imagination to any depth or at any length. It was a whole chapter which she had read surreptitiously by slyly lifting the pages before fate had turned them for her. And on those pages she saw recorded the extent of Collis's capital. The investments; the properties ; the cash at bank. They made a total which staggered her thoughts. Whenever he was sick and stayed at home in bed, her dream became clearer and more profound. To come into the possession of that wealth! To be able to live in the country ; to stay in bed every morning for as long as she liked ; to do no work ; to eat fine food ; to have fine clothes ; to spend money in the big shops ; to ride in her own car ; and to go to theatres, to London, to Blackpool!

Daisy was not intelligent, but she had instincts which she trusted implicitly. And they were apt to guide her towards certain goals. She lived by them. When she first met Collis, she was flattered by his love for her. It was a sensual, possessive love, and she soon knew this. He had a lust for possession. Her body, her life, as well as money, houses, and the possessions of other men. He wanted to fashion a world for himself in which he was absolute master ; and because this idea was apparent to her and intrigued her, she submitted to him. She bore his children, yielded all to him, believed what he believed, not because she was weak willed, but because the spectacle of this man with his devouring lust for possession made the most amazing drama which life could offer her. He believed that she loved him and that he was master in all things ; but her incredible secret was that she never had and never would or could truly love him, and that at any time she could move a mere fraction of space from him and leave him without some kind of defence which her presence made for him. And then . . .

And now it seemed to her that her dream was about to come true. He gibbered in terror and bursts of bravado in one room while she and Ada chattered in another. They heard him shouting names. Smith, Lane, Kelpey, Jey, Renberg.

" Who are they ? "

" I told you . . . I don't know. I seen Kelpey, a young chap. Jack never tells me much. I never ask."

They could hear Collis shouting in the adjoining room.

" . . . you said two hundred each! Let's see some of the colour of your money! It's due! "

Ada sniggered. Daisy sipped her glass and shook her head.

" Don't listen, don't listen! He'll go on like that for hours,"

" Who's this fellow Renberg, or whatever he calls him ? "

" Must be a new one," Daisy said, lighting a cigarette and blowing out a noxious cloud of smoke. " I've never 'eard him speak about that one before."

" Sounds bad," Ada said.

" Oh, I can't bother about it," Daisy said.

Ada said flatly : " Then you ought to! "

"I never ask. I don't care. And I don't want to care," Daisy said, perkily.

Ada crossed her trim legs. "That's one way of looking at it. There's another, though. You ought to know how you stand. If anything happened to him . . ."

The two of them glanced significantly at each other. Daisy's manner became solemn.

"I know 'ow I stand," she said, quietly. "I'm not such a fool."

"You don't want to get let in for a load of trouble if anything happens to Jack," Ada said.

In appearance, she was fair, pretty in a pale way which she warmed and coloured. Unlike Daisy, who never gave more than a few minutes at a time to her looks and dress, she lavished whole hours upon herself, achieving a style which gave her the illusion of beauty, of personality. But in reality, she looked what she was : a reflection in some minute degree of current, commonplace ideas of beauty and style, worth, and ideas. She believed in herself, in her ideas, her ambitions, her progress. But she was complacent, all the time. She worked in a factory, and earned good money. She went about. She knew the names and talents of most of the film stars. She believed that she knew what life was and how to live it. How to get her way. How to love, hate, deride. But her life was circumscribed by her belief in herself, and she never as much as put her head beyond the prison of her few ideas to discover the world outside. Didn't know. Didn't want to. Didn't want to marry. Wanted only to be near Daisy so that if anything happened she would be there to share a wonderful life with her.

It was a wild dream, and half of her purpose in life was to entice Daisy towards it. She was always nearby when there was trouble, a quarrel or danger. She was never far away when Collis was ill.

"You've got your future to think of," she said.

She represented much to Daisy who trusted her emphatic ideas about the world. Ada was bold, was optimistic, was courageous ; and Daisy confided in her.

"You watch yourself," Ada said. "I see trouble. What's this you were saying about somebody trying to murder him ?"

Daisy related the incident in considerable detail.

"See ?" Ada remarked. "I've told you before, haven't I ? No good shedding tears after he's gone if you don't take good care that he's left you provided for."

"Well, I've took good care," Daisy said.

"You haven't! I know. It's not in you to."

"There's a good policy," Daisy whispered.

"What's the good of that ? You wouldn't be able to live on that, would you ?"

" No," Daisy admitted.

" That's what I'm trying to tell you! "

Their eyes met over the rims of the whisky glasses.

" Look," Daisy said, " don't say anything, will you ? Don't let out what I tell you."

" Then don't tell me if you're afraid I'll blab! Did I ask you to tell me ? "

" I've seen the will," Daisy whispered.

Ada lit a cigarette. " Have you ? " she said, indifferently.

" I found the copy."

" That's nothing."

" There's nineteen 'ouses in Essex Street, and seven in Devonshire Row, and some in Lancaster Parade. And there's some shares in a brewery, and things. I went through his papers, not long ago."

Ada shook her head. " Doesn't mean anything," she said, pensively.

" Course it does! All that! "

" Not unless it comes to you through his will."

" Well, it does. I saw it. It said in the will."

Ada looked at her and laughed. " He's not dead yet! "

Daisy smiled her pale smile. Ada dropped ash into the ash-tray.

" You know as well as I do he'll live to ninety. And you'll slave yourself here with him and the kids and never get a glimpse of heaven or what you deserve. You'll be all in all to him, and you'll die of it! "

Again their eyes met. This time an incredible, terrible idea passed from Ada to Daisy, and from Daisy to Ada, at an identical moment. Both were speechless. Both were afraid for an instant, and then emboldened.

" You fuss over him! " Ada said in a whisper, touching Daisy's knee. " You nurse him! You give him the best years of your life! What for ? What for ? "

Daisy looked away. A hard, determined expression grew in her little features.

" You're giving him your life! " Ada went on, still in a whisper. " Why ? "

The expression was blooming in all its baleful light upon Daisy's face.

" Let him take the consequences for what he does! " Ada went on. " Don't fuss over him! Let fate work! "

It was the support and encouragement for which Daisy had long waited. It was the sound of life coming nearer to her and enticing her. And she was ready to listen and to go.

" If he was my man, I'd know what to do," Ada said.

After that, she was silent. They smoked. They filled their glasses from the bottle and drank.

168

" I'll put the kids to bed," Daisy whispered. " Don't go. I won't be long. I'll be down in a tick."

As she passed the room in which Collis sat, she heard him mumbling.

" . . . afraid, Jey! You're afraid! You're in this! Why didn't he tell me ? I got him in! I did everything! "

She brought the children in from the yard and drove them upstairs and then stopped at the foot of the stairs and listened to Collis.

He stopped mumbling and appeared at the door of the room. She passed rapidly up the stairs and leaned over the top banisters and watched him as he went to the telephone in a dark recess of the hall. When she heard the single note as he lifted the receiver, she crept down the stairs and listened.

" Hullo! " he bawled. " I want to speak to Mr. Rennenberg. Tell him. Tell him it's Mr. Collis."

There was a pause. A hawker went past in the Square, calling his stock : apples, oranges, ripe tomatoes.

" Hullo! Hullo! " Collis shouted, impatiently.

Upstairs, the children were shouting at play. Daisy darted up and burst in upon them.

" Shut up! Your father can't 'ear on the 'phone! Get to bed! Start undressin'! "

She shook them rapidly in turn and then hurried out and crept down the stairs.

" Rennenberg! " Collis shouted. " That you ? Collis! Jack Collis. Listen! I want to see you, quick! I've got to! I tell you . . ."

He paused. Anger and truculence waned to a loud whine of complaint. " No, it isn't! That's not playing fair. And another thing : that table. Oh, yes you do! It was someone you know. Smith or Lane. It's . . . No, look here! Look! "

The complaint in his tone waned as his anger had done a minute previously. Listening, Daisy heard it. She knew what was happening in him and to him. It was the end of a phase of his life. He had touched a height, reached a climax, and now he was on the downgrade.

" I tell you, I know it was you or one o' your chaps! What 'ave you got against me ? Listen! What have I done to deserve that from you ? And why . . ."

It was an abject moan. It was supplication. For his life, perhaps. She could hear him panting, almost sobbing.

" I did my level best for you, and you can't deny it! No. No, but . . . but why try to . . . to wipe me off like that ? Yes, you did, Rennenberg! And what about what Smith and Lane promised me ? What about my share ? It isn't fair. I trusted you . . ."

It was as though he knew his doom, or had a vivid presentiment of it and was begging for mercy.

" Why don't you treat me fairly ?   I only ask . . ."

There was a pause.   A moment later such a shout filled the hall and rolled in dreadful echoes about the house that she knew this was the end.   It was a yell of agony and terror and anger and all the rest of his emotions.   Such a cry as might ring only once through an old house in all the years of its life.

" It was you!   I know it!   You and Smith and Lane!   Devils! Damned . . . damned devils! "

Then a silence more awful than any yet assembled in the heat and stillness of the house.   The children stopped their play and opened the door of the room.   Scampering up to them, Daisy admonished them in whispers and shut the door before creeping downstairs.   From her place on the landing, she saw Collis leaning against the wall near the telephone.   She checked an impulse to go down to him.

She stood there, holding back, wilfully standing apart from him in this moment of extreme peril.   Next moment, he lurched heavily out of sight along the hall.   Then the door slammed as he passed from the house.

From the window of the front bedroom she watched him go unsteadily down the steps and along the pavement.   He was wearing an old hat and the grey jacket which he kept for use at home.   He looked desperate, odd, as he passed out of sight.

She ran downstairs and rushed in to Ada.

" Here! " she gasped.   " He's gone out! "

Ada was pale.   Her hands holding cigarette and tumbler were shaking.   But she had a nonchalant, indifferent air.

" I heard," she said, sipping at the glass.

" But . . . he's gone!   Somebody called Rennenberg.   It's somebody called Rennenberg," Daisy said.   And she sat down and clasped her hands together as though the first act in a climax which was as significant for her as it was for him had rung up at last.

She breathed quickly.   Her tight little lips had to sentinel her throbbing heart and all the wild joys which danced and sought to burst into sound and smile from it.   But her hands were leaping together and her dull eyes were alight for the first time in years.   She turned to Ada and met a strong look of approval.   Neither of them spoke for a while.   They smoked.   They drained the last of the whisky.

" He's gone to see them," Daisy said.

Ada gave her a long, level look.

" They'll kill him," she said.   " Now they'll kill him! "

Upstairs, the children were running about and shouting.   It was long past their bedtime, but Daisy did not trouble to go up to them.

XI

Although Collis had swallowed a considerable quantity of whisky during the two hours in which he had been at home, as soon as he reached the locality in which Smith and Lane had their office he found himself in need of further sustenance of that kind.

He entered the first public house he saw. It was empty except for four customers and a barmaid. The heat and odour of the district poured in through the open door and challenged the smell of beer and the pervasive stench of the casks. The brass handles gleamed in the evening sunlight which fell athwart the lines of gin and rum and whisky bottles. The glass tumbler in the barmaid's hands flashed once. A dog toddled in and sniffed along the spittoons near the counter and coursed to the feet of a young man seated behind a newspaper. A man in a cap and a brown suit lifted a pint glass of mild and said to nobody in particular :

" Can't get much worse."

" Sun spot," the barmaid said, taking another glass in the polishing towel. " They say it's because of a spot on the sun. A gent was saying . . ."

Two little men at the far end of the counter laughed softly.

" Ever 'eard about the spot . . ."

She inclined head and body towards Collis, smiling perhaps at him, perhaps at what she had not heard about the spot.

" Double," Collis said.

He took it and sat down on the bench near the wall. He was not in a hurry. He knew that no matter how late he called at Smith and Lane's office, they would be there or would return shortly. Drinking slowly, he let the liquor bolster his nerve. Something accumulated in him : anger, a sense of injustice, a passion for revenge, a lust for money. His just bribe. He let the force gather in him.

It filled him pleasantly. He tested it against his grievance. He let it move out to challenge that grievance and disperse it. He drained his glass and got up for another.

" Same," he said, curtly.

He saw the barmaid's big eyes assess him. She smiled pleasantly, whereat he knew that he had found appraisal in good terms from her. That pleased him. He went back to the bench and sipped the whisky. It made him perspire. But it renewed the force within him. It brought it to boiling point. His body became erect, and he threw himself back against the wall with a sudden mutter which drew eyes to him.

He saw the barmaid flash a glance at him. The man behind the newspaper peered swiftly at him over the top of the sheet. The two little men at the far side stared at him. Licking his lips, the man in the cap watched him from under shaggy brows.

Collis drained his glass and went to the counter.

" Same again," he said.

" Another double, sir ? "

He did not answer. He looked sullenly at the girl and waited for her to serve him.

She put the glass before him and he paid, reaching for the drink at the same time and tossing it down before his change came. Then he left.

He walked quickly through the hot streets until he reached the main road to the city. He waited for the traffic to clear before he crossed towards the old, decayed district in which Smith and Lane had their place. At the corner of Great South Street, he stopped and looked at his jacket.

He saw with annoyance that he had come out in the frayed, dirty grey jacket which he kept for wear at home. It looked odd against his blue trousers. Moreover, except for a piece of string, a button and a cork, its pockets were empty. His wallet, his keys, his pipe and tobacco pouch, his handkerchief and his letters and paper money were in the jacket hanging behind the door in the room at home. He stood frowning, wondering whether to return home and change. Presently, he continued his journey.

He had known Smith and Lane for a fortnight. Had he been acquainted with them for ten years, his association with them would have been no deeper in spirit and mood than at present. It was rooted impersonally in the conditions of criminal enterprise, and that was all he wanted. That, and the virtue of crooks to crooks. The terms : the offer and acceptance. And the good faith. He understood them, and they understood him. The rest—their German nationality ; their aliases ; their own lives—was not his business.

He could not recall the exact moment or circumstance which had brought him into contact with them. In a noisy bar amidst a company of men like himself. But although he could remember that, he did not trouble to recall the exact moment when intention had united them. Out of the noise and jostling, words had flowed. The mind had considered them. More words had passed. Later, he met them again. And again, with others, with Rennenberg. More words. Then handshakes. A bargain. And he believed that through his quick wit and enterprise, the project had flourished. He had that pride in himself. But it was spoiled by mistrust and fear.

Mistrust was founded on what Kelpey had told him of Rennenberg. That the German was well acquainted with the agency affairs of Foss, Brighart and Molloy. Tendrils of suspicion spread rapidly through his mind and became rooted in mistrust. He felt deceived, made small by these men whose secret motive lay shadow-like about them without disclosing its nature to him. Where was he ? What real part had been given him ? Was he in the lead, or a mere dupe who would be discarded, extinguished for fear of evidence remaining ?

His imagination worked at a furious, fearful speed. But he was no longer afraid. Fear was submerged beneath the fumes of whisky. A long time would elapse before it came to the surface in his mind.

Anger, hatred, a sense of enormous injustice impelled him. And with these all swirling in his mind, he arrived shortly before nine at the shabby old house where Smith and Lane's office was located. Like its neighbours along the street, the house was a relic of a fashionable district. Now its large and small rooms were let to petty tenants, and its wide hall that had formerly welcomed a world of fashion, dignity and wealth, was open day and night to a wider world of crumby trade. Struggling agents ; shifty dealers ; the dust and rubbish from the fringes of reputable commerce, alighted here, sojourned for a while, and were blown to a higher or lower plane by the winds of fortune. And here, on the topmost floor, Smith and Lane had an office.

An arm painted upon the wall of the hall and terminating in a small hand with extended forefinger proclaimed that a dozen tenants were on the second and third floors. Collis climbed slowly the dusty stairs. There, the heat was as thick as the silence and the age-old dust and murk of the place. He paused to draw breath on each landing. His face was wet, and he wiped it with a trembling hand.

At the top landing, he halted. He tried to recover his breath and compose himself. Only a few steps separated him from Smith and Lane. He glanced along the passage to the frosted glass of their door. A large bill had been pasted across the glass.

OFFICE TO LET

It was like a blow in the face. It confirmed so many of his suspicions. Hurrying to the door, he grasped the handle. His rage exploded. He kicked the door and shouted. Standing back, he panted.

A furtive sound came from inside the room : a chair scraping softly across the bare boards. He held his breath and listened. Silence enveloped him. He put his face to the glass and tried to see inside the room.

" Smith ! " he shouted ; and he imagined that he saw the shadow of that big figure in the room. " Smith ! Open the door ! It's Collis ! " he shouted, angrily.

He waited. The silence resumed. Then once more he seized the handle and shook the door. Nothing happened. He stood away at last, baffled, angry, mocked.

It was then that the door opened slowly and Smith appeared before him. So sinister, so menacing was the way in which that large figure had opened the door and shown himself that Collis was taken unawares by it. His anger was frozen into fear. His words dried on his tongue. His body went slack.

Never before had Smith appeared so foreign, so evil. All the features of his character which had commended themselves to Collis in the first days were now stripped of their original essence of fidelity to a project ; and he stood there in all the true terms of his character.

" Oh, come in, come in! " he murmured. His manner was pensive, but it seemed to Collis to express all the menace of some secret purpose.

Smith's voice had momentarily lost its competency with the language. He spoke with a guttural inflection, almost carelessly, quite without heed. And this, too, presented him in a malicious light.

Collis went in. He could not speak. His heart was beating at such a rate that its pulse filled the arteries and veins of his neck and constricted his throat so that he could scarcely breathe. Nevertheless, he approached Smith and tapped him on the shoulder with an accusing forefinger.

" You said . . ." he contrived to remark, " you said . . . as soon as Rennenberg got to the house . . . you said . . ."

" Sit down," Smith said, closing the door and pointing to a chair.

" . . . you said you'd give me my commission," Collis said, following Smith about the room.

Smith stared pensively at him but did not speak.

" Now didn't you ? " Collis said, and already there was a fresh note in his voice. Placating, persuasive, weak, it was the sound of fear.

" Sit down, please," Smith said.

The office was bare. It had nothing but a small table—much stained and scarred—three small chairs, and a large, old-fashioned hat-stand.

" Didn't you ? " Collis said, taking the chair and then looking round at Smith who stood behind him. His weakness occurred to him. It was so unlike the mood and force which he had induced in himself in the public house that he rose quickly and confronted Smith. He wondered what the latter had been doing here. The table was bare, and except for a hat on the stand and some illustrated magazines there was nothing to indicate the tenancy of the place.

" That's what you said, Smith," Collis declared, and now his tone was emphatic. An edge of anger sounded in his words as he continued : " And look here, why are you clearing out ? And another thing . . ."

He had much to say. It was all assembling hotly in his mind. But Smith's detached mood baulked it and offered only the same menace as before.

" Let's have everything straight! " Collis exclaimed. His fury whirled from his tongue at last. " What sort of a game are you playing ? I help you : I do everything for you! But what do you do, eh ? I know. I'll tell you! You try to get rid of me, don't you ? I know, I know! "

" What ? " Smith exclaimed. His features livened. Their shadow—all the threat and cruelty lurking in them—was obscured by a smile. But the smile itself was full of evil.

" Yes! " Collis panted. " In the 'Nirvana.' I know. That table . . ."

" Please, I don't understand," Smith said.

The foreign intonation, as well as his vivid eyes, made an innocent impression which Collis felt for an instant until he remembered that Smith was thoroughly criminal.

" It was you, or one of your crowd," Collis persisted. " A dirty, treacherous thing to do! Might have killed me! You and Lane are in something pretty big, aren't you ? I know. You won't let me into it, will you ? Oh, no! No! You only try to kill me! You . . ."

The words spurted from his livid lips and became at last nothing but the expression of his fears. The fine, bold surge of them which he had wanted did not happen. They had a drunken inadequacy to express his anger and grievance. They were weak, like himself at this moment. And Smith, watching him, knew it, and had nothing to say. The whole of that outburst with all its reflections of fear, anger, complaint, rolled by his ears without exciting him in the least.

He patted Collis on the shoulder and gently impelled him to sit down.

" Listen, Collis! " he said, " everything is going so nicely. Now I have to go and meet Lane, and then we come back. You will wait ? You wait here for us, please. Half an hour. When we come back, we settle everything."

He put on his hat. He gave Collis the illustrated magazines.

" You wait . . ."

" No! " Collis said, furiously. " I won't. I'll come with you! I'll see fair play! "

" Please! " Smith said. A warm, placating hand rested on Collis's shoulder. " Please wait! "

He inclined his head and smiled.

" I want a fair deal! " Collis shouted, thrusting away the hand.

"Yes, yes, of course," Smith said, assenting, nodding his head. "Yes. In half an hour, we come back. I promise."

Collis was sullen. He sat on the table and stared at Smith.

"Look at the pictures, then we come back," Smith said, moving towards the door.

"But look here, old man . . ."

"Please. I have to go now. In half an hour . . ."

It was all so plausible, so comforting, that Collis wavered.

"Well . . ."

Smith was at the door. "Not long . . ."

"Well, be quick, won't you?"

Smith made a cheerful gesture with his hand and went out. The door slammed loudly after him. Collis took a chair and began to turn the pages of the magazines.

He examined the illustrations. For several minutes, they engrossed him. Then from the silence and heat, and from all the horizons of his mind as well, something large advanced like an enveloping mass which frightened him.

He got up. He tried to open the grimy window. It was stuck fast. Through its filmed glass he saw an ugly sea of roofs and chimneys stretching to a row of smoke stacks. Above, the evening sky was yellow. Below, far below in the drab yards, there were only dirt-bins, refuse, the leaning doors of old sheds. He was panting. Little spurts of panic were driving like tiny flames from a huge furnace of fear at the back of his mind.

He went to the door, determined to wait no longer. He turned the handle. The door was locked from the outside. He stood there, his hand slack for an instant about the knob. Then the hot flame of panic travelled down his arm and through his wrist, and he began to wrench the handle and cry out in a whimper of alarm.

The heat was suddenly monstrous. But worse than the heat was his terror from the conviction that he was the victim rather than the accomplice of Smith and Lane. The silence of the little room proclaimed it to him. Its door was firmly locked from the outside. The rest of the building was deserted. Nobody would enter until to-morrow. He was alone, a prisoner, condemned . . .

His fingers slipped from the door handle and he tottered back towards the chair. Before he could reach it, he fainted. His thick body swayed. His outstretched hands groped towards the chair and then swung round and touched the wall. He slid down slowly and lay crumpled against the wainscot.

XII

Smith met Lane at a corner fifty yards along the street. They met without greeting, like two evil currents flowing from opposite directions and joining rapidly to sweep onwards towards a common outlet. They walked rapidly to the nearest 'bus stage. They were the only persons waiting there, and presently they began to talk in undertones.

" Did you see him ? " Smith said.

Lane nodded. " He gave me final instructions," he said.

" Well ? "

Smith waited for them with some apprehension. All day, ever since the TO LET notice had been affixed to the office door, he had known what Rennenberg's final orders would be.

" We are to close down," Lane said. " Then our part of the mission is ended. We take the midnight express to London."

Smith looked away to the hazy distance of the street. Something of his inner calm and resolve seemed to waver for the first time. He glanced at Lane and met only a look of intense happiness.

" . . . going home! " Lane whispered.

" To close down ? Close down ? " Smith said, sadly.

Lane looked steadily at him, perhaps to encourage him, perhaps to reprove him, or to find the answer to certain questions which occurred to himself at that instant. Smith writhed under that hard stare. Breaking away from it, he said testily : " He has a good time! He doesn't move from Foss's house. Tea on the lawn in the shade! Swimming in the pool! Ices on the terrace! And when he can't extract anything from Foss, he tells us to close down! He orders us to kill! "

" That's enough! " Lane said, imperatively.

" But we are not in Germany now! " Smith retorted. " Here, it is a capital offence . . ."

He was becoming louder and more demonstrative. His hands started to gesticulate. Lane nudged him.

" You fool! Stop talking! Not another word! "

Smith sighed. " Very well! Now it's all right. I know. Only I don't . . ." He struggled with the language, as he always did when he was excited. " . . . only I don't can like . . . I do not . . ."

" Stop talking! " Lane said.

A 'bus appeared at the far end of the street and came swiftly towards them.

" I don't like the killing," Smith murmured. " Things went wrong in the ' Nirvana.' If it goes wrong now . . ."

" It won't! " Lane said.

They boarded the 'bus and were carried swiftly towards Sheraton Road where Kelpey lived. Neither of them spoke. They sat inside the vehicle, with their hats on their knees. At this time of the evening, there were few passengers, and the conductor had time to study Smith and Lane as they sat side by side, erect, not talking, their eyes looking straight ahead. They had an unmistakable suggestion of the foreign, the unfamiliar, about them. The indescribable mode of behaviour and the slight difference of cut and texture of their clothes made it obvious. Who were they ? What was their errand ?

A little later, they alighted. As they passed the conductor, he had a better opportunity in which to study them. He noticed that they had an expression of sullen concentration. He signalled the 'bus to proceed, then he leaned out and watched them. They went towards Sheraton Road, in step, erect, like men marching. Then, almost as though by design, they broke step, opened their jackets and lounged slowly along. It was like an act of deception, to allay suspicion. But their progress was heavy with purpose. Too heavy! Where . . . in what particular place . . . had he seen them before ? He remembered them. He would continue to remember them.

Smith and Lane entered Sheraton Road and walked towards Kelpey's home. They knew the house. They were only a few yards from it when Smith put a hand on Lane's arm and tried to stop him.

" It won't help," he said. " It's murder. Here, it's murder. Then their police come. They go to all the roads and the railway stations and watch! "

" Be quiet! " Lane whispered.

" What are you going to do ? " Smith whispered, and he hung back as though he were about to run away.

" Don't be a fool! " Lane said, sharply, walking on and taking Smith by the arm. " There are all sorts of ways . . ."

" But the police . . ."

" There are accidents."

" But . . . but . . ."

Lane ran quickly up the steps of the house and rang the bell. Smith followed him slowly.

An elderly woman stood before them.

" Good evening."

" Good evening," Lane said, raising his hat. " Is Mr. Kelpey at home ? He's expecting us."

The woman was small, tart. Everything about her was sparse and acid.

" He's out," she said. " Went out about ten minutes ago."

" Yes, I know," Lane said. " He told us he might have to run out for a few minutes. He told us to wait for him."

" Never said a word to me about it," the woman remarked.

" As a matter of fact," Lane said, " we weren't sure that we could come. The train was a bit late."

The woman's tone became more civil. She imagined that the visitors were Kelpey's relatives—cousins, uncles—or that they might be here on some business relating to her boarder's position with Foss, Brighart and Molloy. She dared not stand in their way, for she saw circumstances personal to Kelpey and important to him.

" Perhaps you'd like to wait upstairs in his room ? "

She invited them in. " It's this way."

Going up the stairs, Smith said to her : " Terribly warm, isn't it ? "

" Oh, my word, yes! "

She held open the door and they walked in.

" I'll tell him as soon as he comes home."

When the door closed behind her, Lane suddenly seized Smith's big, warmly damp hand and shook it. He murmured something in German. They looked at each other and began an examination of the room.

It was a large room, sombre with its old-fashioned furniture, solid with it. Little in it denoted the character of its occupant, except the modern bookcase, the desk, and a small chair. But against the bluff, big things of the room, those few modern pieces made little impression. They did not predominate. They were like Kelpey's simple character in its contact with the world of affairs.

Within a few minutes, the visitors had opened the desk and worked expertly through the few personal papers locked there. Letters. A few pages of a diary which had languished after a fortnight. Three short poems which Kelpey had attempted. Some addresses noted on a slip of paper. And some photographs. Except for his stationery, that was all. In the bookcase there were many books. Cheap sets, and a few odd novels much thumbed. And a little pile of magazines. There was absolutely nothing to incriminate him.

Smith whispered : " It's a waste of time."

Lane did not answer. He crossed to the table in the centre of the room. Three new books lay wrapped in the paper with the book-seller's label upon it. One was a good copy of Flaubert's " Madame Bovary " in the original French text. The others were an English translation of that work, and a French Grammar for Beginners.

" Learning French," Lane whispered.

Smith looked at the books rapidly. He was restless and afraid.

" We can't stay here," he whispered. " There's Collis . . ."

" We must wait," Lane said. He sat down at the table.

Smith stood watching him. Presently, he took the chair opposite Lane.

" What are you going to do ? " he said.

" There are ways . . . plenty of ways . . ."

" It's murder! They'll arrest us! This woman here has seen us. She'd tell the police . . ."

Lane frowned at him. " Oh! Murder, police, arrest! You talk like a schoolboy! Do you think I would do it here, in this room ? Do you ? "

He made an abrupt gesture and leaned forward.

" I told you. It will be an accident. I shall invite him into town. . . ."

" But suppose he won't come with us ? "

" I said I shall invite him into town, and in the traffic . . ."

He made a quick movement of his elbow. His dark face had a hard, concentrated expression.

" . . . a fatal accident," he said, flatly.

Smith was silent. He lowered his gaze to the surface of the mahogany table. During the past fortnight, he had lived under a constant peril which had been accentuated by all the wonderful delights of freedom. He had taken risks. Now the end was in sight. Within two hours, he and Lane would be travelling to London on the first stage of the journey home. His whole spirit anticipated that journey. He feared the least thing which might prevent it. And most of all he feared this murder which he and Lane had been instructed to commit. Not so much the murder as the consequences.

" They're thorough," he whispered, in German. " They act quickly. . . ."

A clock in a neighbouring church tower struck ten.

" You frighten yourself," Lane said. He offered Smith a cigarette and took one himself and lit it.

" Ten! " Smith said. " And we have to see Collis, too! "

" There's time," Lane said.

Then Smith exploded. In a swift outburst in German, he exclaimed in a taut whisper, leaning over Lane : " But he's harmless! A boy! An innocent young fool! Why run such a risk for the sake of . . . for . . ."

He broke off, stammering, and seized his hat and clapped it on. Near the door, he turned. He waited. Slowly, Lane rose from the table and, taking his hat, came towards him. Without a word, the two of them went out and passed down the stairs.

" He's probably waiting for us at the station," Lane told the landlady. " We might meet him along the road."

" I'll tell him you called," she said, opening the big door for them.

Ten minutes later, Kelpey returned. That morning, he had advertised in one of the local papers.

> " Young man, intelligent, in executive position, desires private
> lessons in French. State terms to Box number."

" Foreigners ? " he said, when Mrs. Larkin told him about the visitors.

" Yes, now you mention it . . . yes, I'd say they were."

He did not doubt that they had called in answer to his advertisement. He hurried to his room, expecting to find a card or note of some kind from them. The only evidence of their visit was an aroma of cigarette smoke and the open books on the table.

But he was not disappointed. He had gone out shortly before their arrival in answer to a telephone call from a young Frenchman who had seen the notice in the newspaper and who had contrived to find his name and address. He had offered his expert services, and Kelpey had called at his home and made suitable arrangements with him. They had discussed a course of tuition, books, and had arranged for two lessons a week of an hour each.

Kelpey forgot about the two men who had waited to see him. Taking the books from the table and turning their pages, he remembered the books which he had seen in Dewlash's room. He remembered, also, that he had dropped his silver pencil in her flat. What pleased him most of all was the fact that she had not yet returned it to him.

He was very happy. He had forgotten about Collis and Rennenberg. His personal life had developed in this interesting manner, and he was completely absorbed in it.

*

XIII

*

It was almost eleven when Smith and Lane entered the house on whose top floor they had rented an office. The night was very warm ; and, instead of abating, the heat seemed to have increased since dusk when the magnificent oriflamme of sunset had unfolded over the land like a great conflagration of the skies. Now it was withdrawn below the western horizon ; but in that distance all the brightness of day still shone, and over the night scene a thin wash of light remained.

Going up the stairs, Smith and Lane approached their office noiselessly. In the half-darkness, they could see the bill pasted across the glass and proclaiming the termination of their tenancy. Standing for a few seconds outside the room, they listened for some sign of Collis's presence inside. The light was not showing, and there were neither sounds nor movements coming from their prisoner.

They glanced at each other. Smith shrugged his big shoulders and noiselessly inserted a key in the lock and turned the handle. Without haste or nervousness, he returned the key to his pocket and pushed open the door.

He went in ahead of Lane and switched on the light. Collis was sitting on one of the hard little chairs near the awful window. The room was foul. The air was stale and the heat seemed concentrated in the small space. Collis seemed to have become a part of the silence and the foul atmosphere and the gloom. His big body was collapsed in the chair. He was pale and dazed and obviously ill. His breathing was audible from a distance, and at a glance it was plain that his terror and thirst had reduced him to a state of coma. Lane left the door wide open, while Smith advanced slowly and gently patted Collis on the shoulder.

" There," he said, softly, " we have come back, Collis."

Lane stood a little way inside the room and watched. He could hardly breathe in the fetid atmosphere.

" He is drunk," he said, facetiously, sniffing the odour from Collis.

Smith turned round. " Shut the door," he said.

Lane slammed it and came over to him.

" What are we to do with him ? "

Smith was speaking to Collis. " We weren't long, were we ? I said we would come back in half an hour, didn't I ? "

He was trying to beckon Collis to full consciousness, to a sense of his surroundings. But Collis met him with a blurred, uncomprehending look and an incoherent mumble.

Smith grimaced and looked at Lane.

" Come on," Lane said, tersely. " Leave him. Lock the door and let him . . . let him die! "

The last word seemed to travel deeply into Collis's mind, for he stirred at once. He moved stiffly and got to his feet, still weak, and yet with some purpose in all his movements.

" Don't be a fool! " Smith whispered to Lane. " Leave him here ? Wouldn't the police know that we locked him in ? No! Outside, on the stairs."

Collis seemed to revive now that he was on his feet. Like a tide retreating from him, his coma left him. The air which had come from the passage was like wine to him. He breathed it. His body took a stance. His eyes recovered light and power. His stature seemed to increase. Suddenly, he rushed towards the door. His movement was like an explosion in him. He seized a chair as he swept past his captors, and he stood there, confronting them, challenging them, his back to the door, his left hand groping for and finding the handle and turning it. He saw Smith and Lane glance rapidly at each other. Then he saw Lane bring out a revolver.

At once, Smith made a movement to take the weapon from Lane.

" No! No! Not here. . . ."

His voice was loud, almost a shout. Lane hesitated. The weapon was lowered. At that instant, Collis threw himself at them. His right arm whirled the chair. He thrust the table before him, hemming the others in a corner near the window. He was like a giant, brutish, panting. He heard Smith shout in German, and saw Lane leap aside and dart towards the door. Collis brought the chair crashing towards Smith.

It was impeded by the electric globe and the wire. The globe exploded and sent down a tinkling shower of glass. The wire tripped the chair. Collis stumbled. Then chair and body lurched sideways, making a great noise. In the next instant, all was a confusion of thudding feet, heavy bodies, shouts. Smith huddled fearfully behind the table, crouched, hands up in defence, waiting. Collis ran round the table. His huge hands reached for Smith at the moment when Lane ran across.

Lane held his revolver by the barrel. His right arm flashed up and then fell. Collis's body went slack. The head flopped loosely to the left shoulder, while the groping hands made ridiculous movements and the body slithered slightly and finally crashed headlong.

Except for the sound of Smith's panting, there was silence in the room. Lane bent over Collis's body, and in the gloom Smith saw him point the revolver at the chest.

" No! " he shouted. " No! Leave him! Don't kill him! "

Lane looked up at him. " Our orders were to . . ."

But Smith rushed at him and snatched away the weapon and began to tidy the room.

" We are not in Germany! " He indicated with his head the prone shape on the floor. " He won't get over that blow quickly! You have fractured his skull! "

Lane stooped down and turned the head. There was a big swelling where the butt had struck the back of the skull.

" No harm . . ." he whispered. Then he saw Collis's left foot. It was twisted in such a way that Lane knew it was broken.

" His ankle is fractured," he said, rising.

Smith pushed the chairs back into place under the table. He gave a cursory glance at Collis.

" Help me to lift him outside," he said.

" Leave him."

" Help me . . ." Smith said, leaning over the body.

Lane walked to the door and opened it and waited there. He had a sullen, detached air which Smith noticed when he looked towards him. For a moment, Smith hesitated. He glanced at the body of Collis and then at Lane. He stood back as though he were loth to leave Collis there.

Lane was waiting patiently with his back to the room, and at last Smith took up his hat and came towards him. They went into the passage. Smith closed the door behind him and locked it and put the key into his pocket. He and Lane went noiselessly down the stairs.

" Finished! " Smith said, when they were in the street. He glanced at Lane and nudged him. " Finished! " he added, and there was an exuberant tone in the word.

" We have not fulfilled our duty," Lane said, glumly.

" But it is all finished! " Smith exclaimed, excitedly. " Now it's all done! Now we take the train . . ." and he broke off, panting from excitement and anticipation while Lane, who was of a different texture of temperament, smiled wanly and shook his head.

" Not as we were instructed," he said.

Smith laid a persuasive hand on his arm as they walked through the warm night.

" But all the same . . . wisely, better for Herr Rennenberg who might have to remain another day or two yet. Much better for him. Now he has a clear field, and no police to watch him. Much better! "

He broke into a high-pitched burst of laughter.

" Now we can go home, Ludwig! "

" Sh! Be careful! " Lane said, laughing.

" Yes, yes, of course," Smith said, whispering. But his body was trembling with excitement, and he could not prevent himself from sudden little bursts of laughter in which Lane joined.

" Home! " Smith whispered.

Rennenberg had given them that order with the others. If his drastic instructions regarding other matters had not been fulfilled with the perfection which marked his own methods, certain reasonable excuses could be offered and would be accepted, for Smith and Lane expected to meet him again at a place and time in the near future when the mission would be accomplished successfully. Their destination was Berlin, at a certain headquarters where they would await Rennenberg. And his meeting with them there would denote the successful accomplishment of all their efforts. Imperfections would be forgotten then. And if he failed to return . . .

It did not occur to Smith and Lane that he might fail. Nothing occurred to them as they hurried towards the railway terminus except the single, thrilling fact that they were on their way home. Only later, when the express drew out of the station and they saw the long, low line of lights marking the great highway which skirted the city, did they feel a definite curiosity regarding the outcome of Rennenberg's task.

It would have been interesting to wait and discover what action he was determined upon.

XIV

A positive and urgent clarity defined all Rennenberg's thoughts that evening when, after an excellent dinner, Foss led him to the terrace overlooking the garden. A final conception of his task loomed in his mind, and he felt alone and very anxious. So little remained to be done, but that little was so much. He had given orders, and he believed that they had been obeyed except in the case of Jey. So there remained only Foss and Jey. And Jey was the sword—so Rennenberg believed—while Foss was the will which would guide its stroke.

Rennenberg was tired. The weather was still very warm ; and although he had had opportunities in which to relax his body, his mind was wearied by all the efforts he had made to decide a course for himself and his assistants. His nerves were taut. The heat upset him, and he could not escape the incessant thought which reminded him that he had reached the climax of his errand.

He sat between Foss and Tilly, his body recumbent in a long chair, his hands lightly coiled about the cool glass in his hands. He saw the thick trees in the near and distant prospect of the garden, and the clear heavens above them. The sun was setting, and all things seemed to him to be suspiring after the immoderate heat of the day. Exquisite colours had their moments at this hour of sunset and dusk ; and in the long, level shafts of sunlight which fell across the world in a gentle, limpid light, the shadows of trees, plants, shrubs, and walls, lengthened in one direction and gave to those immobile shapes some strange and lovely appearance of motion.

His thoughts were waylaid for a time by that subtle mood of the scene. But in a little while something beckoned them forward again with a persistent urgency. Time was passing. He had been Foss's guest for more than a day, yet he had accomplished so little. Foss was as uncommunicative as ever.

Rennenberg felt this pressure of his mission lying with an intolerable weight upon him. It made him more nervous. The languor of the evening had descended upon his host and hostess, and although he too appeared to share it, he was tense beneath his air of relaxation. His talents could not pierce Foss's reserve and caution. All his powers of observation and penetration met only an emptiness and a bland stare. He had been forthright, blunt, domineering. He had cajoled. He had lost his temper and threatened Foss with a revolver. He had declared himself in that positive way. Also, he had withdrawn in order to entice Foss into a mood of confidence. And he had enlisted Tilly's aid and was waiting for results which he knew would not satisfy him. Two hours ago, he had given her that pendant, and she had returned to her husband. What had she done in that time ? What word had she for him ?

He glanced swiftly at Foss, and then at Tilly. Of the two, Tilly appeared to be the more pensive. Her hands rested on the arms of her chair. Her gaze was upon the distant prospect of the garden ; but her thoughts were of him, for her glance came slowly to him and into her face a look of quick recognition mounted as though from the juncture of her thoughts with the reality of his presence. He smiled meaningly ; and slowly in reply her smile came, and it was full of rebuff and contempt for him.

She sat upright, and looking about her as though she had emerged from long thoughts and were seeing the garden for the first time since dinner, she rose slowly.

Rennenberg and Foss stood up.

" Going in ? " Foss said.

" For a little while," she said, " Please excuse me."

When she had gone, Foss pointed to the chairs.

" Sit down," he murmured. He went on quietly : " By the way, I mentioned to you this morning about a transfer due from Berlin. Twelve thousand, eight hundred odd. Due on the twentieth. Up to three this afternoon, we had had no word of it from our bankers. I'm rather worried about it. You told me that you had been advised about it."

" Yes," Rennenberg said. " Yes, I remember."

In a tight voice, Foss said : " Von Pless has never yet been late with his quarterly transfer."

" No ? "

" Never," Foss said.

" Perhaps there is a very good reason."

" Such as ? "

Rennenberg settled himself in his chair and turned to Foss.

" Perhaps he has gone on a holiday."

" In that case, he would have instructed one of his staff to make the settlement."

" Perhaps the staff as well have all gone on holiday."

It was the statement of a fact, the rending of a veil.

" Have they ? You think . . ." Foss began. " Surely, not all of them! "

" Yes, perhaps all of them," Rennenberg said.

" But . . . that's a very serious matter! Why didn't you tell me this before ? Why didn't you say so when you arrived yesterday afternoon ? "

" Tell you what ? " Rennenberg said.

" Why, that Von Pless and all his staff . . ." Foss began, then he stopped.

" What about Von Pless and all his staff ? "

" That . . . that . . . that they have . . . perhaps . . ."

" Have what ? "

" Oh, gone away on holidays! " Foss said, angrily. " Whatever that means! "

" I said that perhaps they had gone," Rennenberg rejoined. " It was the only explanation I could think of."

Foss got up and walked to the edge of the terrace and remained there for several minutes. When he came back, he stood looking down at the recumbent German and said :

" Will you answer me one question ? "

Rennenberg inclined his head. " Certainly! "

" Have Von Pless and his staff gone away ? "

Rennenberg looked up at him with a frank expression on his face.

" It is the only explanation I am able to offer," he said.

Foss sat down and faced him. " I should like to ask you several important questions."

" Please do so," Rennenberg said.

" Has Von Pless been arrested ? " Foss asked.

The German's hands were resting on his knees. He raised his fingers and extended them to their length and spread them. Then he relaxed them and let them fall back to his knees, saying at the same time : " It seems to me to be very probable that he has."

" That's a very serious thing," Foss said, quietly.

" It is," Rennenberg said.

" But upon what grounds . . . why ? He is a member of an ancient, influential family! He is . . ."

" Perhaps," said Rennenberg, sitting upright in the chair and turning to Foss, " perhaps he has been indiscreet."

" But he loved Germany! "

" Then his safety is assured."

Foss regarded him in silence for several seconds.

" As a friend and close business associate of his, sir, you don't seem very perturbed about him," he remarked.

" But I am! If it has happened, I regret it profoundly! " Rennenberg declared. He sat back in his chair. " But it is rather a common occurrence in Germany. The Reich does not tolerate treachery."

"But our friend . . . why, he loved Germany! He was not at all . . ."

"Not at all what ? "

Foss made an expostulatory gesture. "Not a traitor."

"Are you sure ? " Rennenberg said, leaning forward and lowering his voice to a whisper. "Are you quite sure about that, Mr. Foss ? "

Foss was silent. He looked puzzled and dismayed.

"Shall I tell you something I heard about him ? " the other said, still in a whisper. "I think it would interest you very much. In fact, I very nearly told you about it yesterday when I arrived, only I thought it would distress you."

"What is it ? " Foss said.

"Shorly before I left Berlin," said the German, "I was told on very good authority that our friend was involved in a very dangerous enterprise. Sometimes, of course, one hears such things about prominent people in Germany, and there is no truth in them. Especially at the present time. . . ."

"Of course, there is no truth in that! " Foss interjected. "Von Pless is eminent in commerce! He is a loyal German! "

" . . . and sometimes," said Rennenberg, suavely, "there is truth in them and they are confirmed by facts."

"Not in this case! Von Pless is loyal! " Foss said.

Rennenberg laughed. He put a hand on Foss's arm and let it rest there while he said : "When I heard this, I went to our friend and asked him. Shall I tell you what he replied ? I know it would interest you. I swear by all that is most solemn that this is the truth, sir. Von Pless confessed to me that he was involved in this conspiracy. He gave me all the details."

"I don't believe it! " Foss said. "I can't believe it! "

"I am speaking the truth, Mr. Foss! "

"But . . . but . . . are you sure that Von Pless . . ."

"Positive! " Rennenberg said. "In his own words, he told me everything, everything! You see ? I know all about it! That's why I am here! That's why he sent me! "

He chuckled and stood up, and offering his hand to Foss, he leaned down and spoke seriously.

"In such an affair, one has to be most discreet. I admire your great discretion. Mr. Foss. I admire your loyalty to Von Pless and his friends in this enterprise. And I give you my solemn word that he disclosed everything to me before I left. He said that it would be best for you not to send your man over until you hear again from Berlin."

Foss did not accept Rennenberg's hand. Instead, he stared at the German with a look of incredulity.

" I don't understand ! "

Rennenberg smiled. His hand remained outstretched.

" Some time ago, Von Pless advised you that I would come."

" Well . . . yes . . . he did."

" You see ? You can trust me. Now you can trust me, Mr. Foss. I have been associated with Von Pless in the later stages, but I swear to you most solemnly that I am very near to him in this business. He told me everything, except one detail."

Rennenberg waited for Foss to speak, but Foss remained as before : cautious, mistrustful.

" I really . . . really, I don't understand ! "

" Just one fact which he did not impart. The name of your man. Von Pless said that he would leave you to introduce me to him."

Foss shook his head. He looked completely bewildered.

" You may trust me implicitly," Rennenberg urged.

" But I have ! " Foss declared. " I have discussed everything with you. What else is there ? "

" Yes, what else ? " whispered Rennenberg.

" There's nothing else, really . . . there's nothing . . ."

Rennenberg withdrew his hand and sat down.

" You are admirably cautious," he exclaimed.

Foss leaned forward. " Do you think Von Pless and his staff have been arrested ? "

" It does seem likely, considering that you have not yet received advices about the transfer."

" Listen," said Foss. " You say you are his associate. Now that he has been arrested, will you venture to return to Germany ? If you do, surely you too will be arrested ! "

" I must take the risk."

Foss sighed. " We shall have to appoint another agent, now that Von Pless has gone," he said.

" I shall be happy to do anything for you in that direction," said Rennenberg.

" And suppose you, too, are sent away . . . on holiday ? "

" Then it will be a very difficult situation for you and your partners. You will have to appoint a trustee—your bankers—for the time being, until you find another agent."

Foss pondered the remark. " It's an unhappy business. I had no idea that Von Pless was implicated in such matters."

Rennenberg chuckled. " You knew all along, from the outset ! " he declared. " Von Pless told me so. You were in Berlin last February, and several times since, helping him in the affair ! "

Foss shook his head. " I am a partner in a firm of export agents, Herr Rennenberg. That is my occupation."

Rennenberg frowned and made an impatient gesture.

" Then explain the fee of fifteen thousand pounds which is to be transferred through a bank in Geneva! Is that in connection with legitimate trade ? "

" Certainly! " Foss said. " But I wouldn't term it a fee. Commission is the word. Our usual commission . . ."

" But it doesn't appear in the accounts, does it ? "

" Surely Von Pless mentioned it to you ? "

" Of course! He said it was your fee."

" Commission," Foss insisted. " It covers a considerable consignment of glass and chinaware. . . ."

" Nonsense! " Rennenberg declared. " Nonsense! "

But doubt was reflected in his expression. He had not heard before of this fact which Foss insisted. He looked intently at his host and struggled to maintain a belief that the fifteen thousand pounds represented a fee.

" If you care to come to my office to-morrow," Foss was saying, " I'll show you the relevant accounts. We agreed to accept the consignment as a favour to Von Pless. They are imports to us. I admit that we don't usually engage in import, but the whole point of my several visits to Berlin was to examine, primarily, this business. In the end, I and my partners decided to appoint a special agent of our own to work in co-operation with Von Pless in this business."

" But why were the financial arrangements to be made through the bank in Geneva, instead of by the usual channels ? " Rennenberg asked.

" I'm surprised that Von Pless didn't inform you," Foss remarked. " The whole business rather troubled him. You see, the consignor happens to be a Jew. Von Pless felt that to trade with him might be . . . well, might be frowned upon by the authorities in Germany. That's all. There is no mystery about that, is there ? "

Foss was very red and angry. He had risen and was standing beside Rennenberg who looked up at him with the air of an inquisitor confronted with an astonishing piece of truth.

" I'm surprised that when Von Pless took you into his confidence he did not tell you that," Foss added. Then he turned away, still with an angry expression on his face, and went to the edge of the terrace.

Rennenberg watched him. The explanation was so plausible in every way that he could not dismiss it as a falsehood. It had a flavour of veracity which would not yield to the pressure of his suspicions.

In imagination, he saw Von Pless's pale face under the glaring lights. The eyes were melted by that fierce light, and by the hours of protracted examination, to two hard points which were like the reflection of a final core of reason. The rest of the face was a haggard, reduced substance across which brutal weals showed. And the voice which sounded from the bruised, distorted lips was similar to the voices of hundreds of other victims who had confessed to other crimes against the State. They all confessed in the end. But whether it was the truth which dribbled out at last, few could determine. Truth and falsehood were tangled, and what issued was only in answer to the suggestions of the officials.

Rennenberg knew that mistakes were made often by himself and his colleagues. They would continue to be made. It happened. It was certain to happen. The innocent sometimes suffered with the guilty. And it was deplorable that under prolonged examination the innocent frequently confessed to crimes which they had never committed. Perhaps this had happened in the case of Von Pless.

Rennenberg could not reject Foss's version. It found an edge of belief in his mind where its cogency humbled his self-assurance and halted every feature of his belief in himself.

It had a salutary effect upon him. He had lived for so long upon a single, strident motif that his consciousness had become inept to appreciate what was outside the narrow, cruel line which his existence determined. Truth was as he saw it. Duty was as he interpreted it. Good and evil as he saw them. Life was as the Leader told them it was and must be. And he and his colleagues compelled others to accept these beliefs. They were the shepherds folding the flock. And they were the watchdogs, as well.

But vigilance had distorted reason. It had penetrated too deeply into the mind of man. It was so hungry to see, to hear, that it had gone too close to man and suffered a distortion of vision. It saw ridiculous things and paid much attention to them. It heard absurd rumours which it examined sedulously. It was so concerned with the inner volume of trivialism that it became nervous and apprehensive. Finally, it grew vicious, horrible, a little insane.

Perhaps it was sweet for Rennenberg to experience a little drench of sanity. As he stared at Foss's sullen little figure, he felt within himself a cool, refreshing conviction that there were two worlds : the tense one in which he had existed for seven years, and another—an easy one, badly regulated, full of a curious confusion of good and evil, justice and injustice, poverty and wealth, misery and happiness—which represented mankind. It was the large, normal world, and it had some rich potentiality which gave it hope. The other—his own—was insane.

His heart trembled. He felt as though he had been struck violently by this idea of two worlds. He realized that no matter how he and his comrades imposed an order upon their countrymen, the latter would continue to live a secret, personal life which was influenced by the rest of mankind. Man belonged not so much to himself as to the cosmos. Man was life, a part of the whole universe, and he would never be supreme, and nothing could make him supreme. He was subject to laws which were older than his most ancient philosophy.

Rennenberg was shocked by his lack of faith. He was suddenly revolted by what he and his comrades had done to Von Pless. An error ? Under a false warrant ? In horrible cruelty upon an innocent man ? A man who had foolishly tried to deal with a Jew and who had resorted to suspicious expedients in order to conceal his actions. Was that true ? Was that the whole story ? He jumped from his chair and went to Foss.

" Let's walk a little."

His voice had a new quality. There was a forlorn note in it : humble, unhappy, nervous.

" I hope you're satisfied," Foss said, sullenly, going down the steps towards the lawns.

Rennenberg was silent. Again, in imagination, he saw the tortured face of Von Pless, and he realized with horror that he had torn open a human mind and ravaged it irretrievably without discovering what he had sought. Instead, he had found only the evidence of fear, pain, and the inner life of man. He had heard certain statements, but now Foss had been able to explain them credibly to him. He had seen the reflection of fear, but that too was explicable. But what he had discovered of the inner life of man was like an act of enormous sacrilege which he had committed and which, from this distance, appalled him.

" The things we have done ! " he thought. And he was silent.

Foss was speaking. " I thought you were a very different person from what I have discovered you to be," he said.

The reproach in his words only increased the German's nervousness.

" I imagined you were Von Pless's associate," Foss said, " sent by him to discuss business and to arrange the final details of this import. I had faith in you. I treated you as a person of good faith. I have opened my home to you. But what are you ? "

" We will say no more about that, if you please," the other begged him.

Foss glanced rapidly at him. " At last, we understand each other perfectly ! "

Rennenberg bowed slightly and was silent. But it was a sign of candid acknowledgement ; and Foss could not resist a comment.

" You have arrested my good friend, Von Pless, and closed his agency and interfered with much profitable trade. For what ? For mere stupid suspicion ? "

" Don't let us discuss it any more, please! " Rennenberg said.

" But what steps will you take to restore my agency ? That is what I am anxious to know! Why don't you release Von Pless ? What about the quarterly settlement ? And what am I to do about this large consignment of goods from Prague ? "

Rennenberg made a little gesture. " The agency will be restored. Apologies will be made. I don't know what will be decided about the Jew in Prague."

" I feel very strongly about it," Foss said. " I rather supposed that you would frown on the Prague business. But as regards my agency in Berlin. . . I feel that a grave insult has . . ."

" Quite, quite," Rennenberg said. " But everything will be restored."

They walked in silence. Twilight had passed to night, and night drew from the soil and the plants and their blooms rich odours which the air diffused. The huge trees stood patiently in the heat. Insects droned in the air. A long way off, a train was whistling. The stars were reflected in the still surface of the swimming pool beside which Foss and his guest were seated.

Foss was elated by his triumph, but at the same time he felt that there was some necessity for him to establish that triumph more definitely. How to do so, how to win from the bogus Rennenberg an acknowledgement of defeat, he did not know. He felt that perhaps the best way to achieve the full sense of success and to impress the German with it was to say nothing more at all of himself or Von Pless, and to pass on to other conversations as though the first were conclusively terminated.

" What is happening to you, over there in Germany ? " he said. He shook his head. " You are a fantastic lot," he added.

Rennenberg had many rejoinders ready. He had been trained to give them. They were in the nature of factual monologues relating to the history of Germany since the rise of Bismarck. They were an exposition of events seen through the distorted vision of a lunatic ; and he felt curiously ashamed of them at this moment.

" We have suffered," he said briefly.

" Only because you enjoy suffering," Foss told him. " You inflict it on your own people, and on your neighbours. I have never studied history. . . ."

" That's obvious," Rennenberg said, with a smile.

" I'm a man of commerce," Foss said. " I understand my job and everything relating to it. No man can know everything. I have studied what applies to my work, and I know the way of the world in which I live. I leave the rest alone, in the same way in which I trust my dentist, my doctor . . ."

" That's typically British," Rennenberg interjected.

Foss laughed. " Nothing is typically this or that. You Germans have the habit of imputing all sorts of ridiculous habits on us. This is typical of us! That is typical of us! You watch us like a cat watches a mouse! You are obsessed with us! If you are the proud master race which is going to rule the world, what a trivial, narrow idea you have of other people! If we are so small, so absurd in our habits, why do you bother to notice us ? "

" You aren't very polite," Rennenberg murmured.

Foss was silent for several minutes.

" I don't understand it at all," he said, presently. " The way you regiment yourselves. The cruelty you do to men, women and children. The awful blind stupidity of your attitude to Germans who are Jews. The ideas about German blood . . ."

" One must be a German to understand them," Rennenberg said.

" Nonsense! You know it is nonsense! Sheer nonsense which no reasonable, intelligent mind would ever accept! "

Foss used a coarse word, then he laughed. " The idea that blood can be anything but what medical science tells us it is! Blood is blood, and it will never be anything else but that! It's a fluid which sustains life in the human body. If you were to cut open a German body you would not find that the blood was of an especial quality! You know that as well as I do! And it's a great pity that some of the clever men of the world haven't pointed that out to you and your Hitler before! "

" Blood is consciousness," said Rennenberg.

Foss laughed loudly. " That isn't sense to me! It's just three words of nonsense, that's all! But I suppose that if I were a German, I should have to believe it or keep on saying it, under orders from a Leader, until I believed the damned phrase to be something glorious! What a crowd! "

" But you English have a blood consciousness! " the German said.

Foss sighed. " What a fallacy! There you go again! You English! Why the devil can't you forget us! You have this sick obsession! Do you think you can rule the world with such ideas ? Do you think you can do anything for yourselves with such idiotic notions ? Never! Not even for a day! "

Rennenberg had many arguments with which to counter Foss's ideas, but in himself he was subdued and could not use them. He had a sense of failure. He felt himself to be a traitor, for he had allowed himself to see all his ideas in relation to wider and more reasonable ones than those that had supported him for so long. All the influences of freedom enticed his spirit and his intellect. And he yielded momentarily to them.

" Never for a moment! Never, not even for a single day! " Foss repeated. And he added: " You get all these ideas from sick old philosophers who have a grudge against humanity, or from damned old bullies with nothing better to do than to brew wars! "

" Exactly! " said Rennenberg. " That's just what you British have always done! "

" Perhaps. But we aren't doing it now! "

" Quite! Why not ? "

" Because we have learned that there is nothing to be gained . . ."

" Certainly! Nothing for you. Because you have so much! "

" Oh, Lord! " Foss groaned. " Oh, Lord! "

Then he tapped his guest's arm. " Our Empire, as you call it, is no longer the kind of empire about which you fellows dream! It consists of . . ."

" I know what you are going to tell me."

" It isn't so much territory which we possess and govern! "

Rennenberg laughed. " How simple is your outlook, Mr. Foss! " he declared. " Your mind reduces everything to such simple terms! Either you are very ingenuous or else you are very subtle."

" It's time we stopped the high phrases," Foss said. " It's time we used a plain language and took the philosopher's frills from words and used simpler ones when we have something to say! Then we can see the mind and the heart of things! Don't forget this: if your Hitler is going to make war across the world for the sake of all the insane ideas of your damned philosophers of the blood-creed, it'll be the ordinary man in Germany and all the other ordinary men all over the world who'll do the fighting. And the ordinary man won't tolerate his ideas being wrapped up in pompous language. He's plain and straightforward himself, and he has no need to speak like a two-faced diplomat. If a war comes, that dirty game will stop, and so will all the cynical language of it. We're all half sick of it already. We know what it is. And that's why I prefer plain language. Render down three-quarters of your stirring phrases, put them into simple language, and they show up for what they are: tripe! "

" But your simplicity conceals cunning," Rennenberg said.

" You're too suspicious," Foss said. " You complain about the wilful insularity of the British, but you Germans have segregated yourselves in all sorts of hideous ideas for three generations. What's that but insularity ? Why don't you come out of it ? You left the League . . ."

" We shall," Rennenberg said.

" You mean that you are going to make war ? "

" Yes."

Both were silent. They drank iced beer and ate sandwiches which a servant brought out to them.

"Pity, isn't it?" Foss said at last. "Of course, you want it, you love warfare, and we know it. We know we shall have to fight you. But it's like standing on a beach, on the edge of the sea. It's like saying to yourself that we shall have to cross that sea and try to reach an unknown land. Miles away. Years ahead in time. God knows how many years. And such a sea! Awful storms, and terrible currents. That's what a war in Europe will be like. That's what it seems to me it will be like."

"Does it?" the German said, and it was plain from the way in which he spoke that he did not envisage war in that way.

"You don't see it like that, do you?" Foss said. "You don't think of the war itself. You only anticipate the victory which you think you'll have. Whether the victory will be yours or ours, nobody can tell. What matters is this: whoever wins the war will have to rebuild the world, not on any blood-superiority idea, but on something stated in simple terms, something which the ordinary man can understand and believe in. Not some blasted cynical election phrase, not something out of an old humbug's volume of philosophy, either! No! This war is going to be different, and the victory too! You'll find that out, if you win. You'll discover that a few millions of fanatical Nazis won't be able to rule thousands of millions of other men. Guns and idiotic ideas won't give you peace. To rule well, you'll have to give men freedom. The kind of freedom you despise. Even to run a business successfully, one has to give employees a chance to be individuals."

Rennenberg did not reply. He pondered what Foss had said, while the night with its immense quietude and its stars gathered about them like a huge, attentive presence.

"Suppose it rested with you," Foss said, presently. "Would you begin it? Would you start the war?"

Rennenberg smiled as he turned to answer. "You are such a simple spirit, Mr. Foss!" he exclaimed. "Don't you know that a war is not started by one man, by the signing of a declaration or the decision of one man. It is decided by the impulse of the blood of . . ."

Foss groaned. "There you go again!"

"Well, let me state it simply for you," Rennenberg said. "Let me put it like this and say that it is a demonstrative reflection of certain innate instincts which compel movement of masses towards the expression of certain theories which are favoured by circumstances produced . . ."

Foss shook his head. He could not listen to it. "You're incurable!" he murmured.

He got up and wandered slowly around the swimming pool. The water was cool and enticing, and when he rejoined Rennenberg he suggested that they should bathe.

They undressed in the cabins beside the pool. Later, after the swim, after they had loitered talking in the garden, and had said good night to each other after returning to the house, Foss remembered principally the body of the German. Big, finely proportioned in robust lines, it expressed to him a proud cruelty which had aroused his anger. He remembered the strutting gait, the obvious vanity of the German in his flesh and bones. Then he was glad of his triumph over him. He was no longer ashamed of his lies and deceits. Instead, he was pleased by what he had done.

"At least, I have tried to save one German from another," he thought.

But his pleasure in his triumph was all mingled with anger and with hatred of Rennenberg's cruelty.

" We shall have to fight them," he thought. " They have this idea of their superiority, and it has gone into their bodies. They have translated everything into blood and flesh, and they have this desire to kill. There will be a war! "

Tilly stirred in her bed as he entered the room.

" Rolly," she whispered in the silence and stillness ; and her voice seemed redolent of all the kindlier things of the world after the clipped, hard tones of the German.

He closed the door and came over to her.

" What happened ? " she said.

" Oh, it's all finished," he said, and he was surprised to discover that he had made the decision without any difficult process of thought. He had renounced everything, left it all far behind.

" We settled everything quite satisfactorily," he said.

" But what happened, what happened ? " Tilly said, sitting up. " Tell me."

He glanced at his wrist-watch. It was three o'clock.

" Oh, it appeared that the authorities in Berlin suspected Von Pless of being concerned in some ridiculous plot. They have arrested him and his staff. This fellow is some kind of official, I think, sent over to ferret out some facts. Fortunately, I was able to convince him that the plot was nothing more than a transaction with a Jewish merchant in Prague. The insane suspicions of these Nazis! The way they think and behave! Their brute minds! "

" So there isn't a plot ? " Tilly said.

" Of course not! You listened to Rennenberg . . ."

" I thought there was! "

" Von Pless was arranging to buy the whole stock-in-trade of the Jewish merchant. Almost a quarter of a million sterling, in value. I was to sell it over here . . ."

"Rolly, you know that isn't the truth!" Tilly said.

Foss was silent. He frowned. He yawned and passed his hands over his face. His lies recurred to him.

"Oh well . . . oh, well, anyway, it convinced our guest, and that's all that mattered. I had to think of Von Pless."

"Are you sure it convinced him?"

"I believe so."

"Don't be so sure," Tilly said, lying back again on the pillows.

Part Three

★

I

★

A huge mass of towering cumuli floated above the western horizon on the dawn of that new day. The early sunlight striking it with long, rosy beams, tinted its topmost edges and its rotund lower surfaces so that it shone with a shy, pink hue that contrasted sharply with the pale blue of the sky. But by nine, that proud mass had risen higher in the firmament, and it drew upon itself the whole glory of the morning sunlight. It was dazzling in its flashing whiteness. Behind it, in ranks, were other masses of cloud, pressed together like figures in an allegorical procession. Their bulging curves gleamed in the sunlight, but their folds were sombre, dark, delicately fashioned by their own weight one upon the other. And the whole line hung far off in the summer's distance above the horizon, with a warm, desultory wind blowing from it in single gusts that did not abate the heat.

The weather was changing. There was moisture in the air, and a promise of storm. The heat had melted in its dry core ; and everywhere its persistent drip poured in a hot torrent. Occasionally, from an indefinable distance, thunder sounded.

Foss slept late that morning. When he awoke, he felt at once the change in the atmosphere. The heat was no longer rigid. There was a kind of movement in it. He saw the window curtains swaying. He felt his own moods assembling and resuming after sleep. Something of them was amended, gone for ever.

He sat up and stretched his arms. He felt refreshed. His mind was light, even joyous, because its burden was removed. Joining his hands on his knees, he pondered his long conversation with the German.

"Von Pless must have confessed," he thought. "But not everything, not all the plans."

199

He felt regret for what he himself had undertaken. He tried to dissociate himself from his part, from all the lies which he had told Rennenberg.

" At least, I have served Von Pless well," he concluded.

He saw Tilly stir in her bed, and he watched her awaken. When he saw her eyes open and noticed their magnificent, living light come to him, he felt for an instant the old, indefinable emotion. It was quickly transformed. Now it seemed to him that he understood her at last. Her beauty, with all the frailties and virtues of her character, represented in some degree life itself: unpredictable, beyond rules, subtle.

" Rolly," she said, sleepily, " what are you going to do about Rennenberg ? "

" It isn't what I am going to do," he said. " It's what he is going to do that matters."

He got out of bed and went to the bathroom and turned on the taps. He saw Rennenberg, fully dressed, strolling in the garden.

" He's up and dressed, already! " he told Tilly.

He hurried over his bath and dressing and sped down to his guest. They met and gave each other the civilities. Rennenberg offered his hand.

" Hope you slept well," Foss said.

They sat down to breakfast without waiting for Tilly. Some buoyancy had returned to Rennenberg's mood ; but with it there was all his former resolve expressed in the erect lines of his body and the concentrated look on his face.

" I must say good-bye to you to-night," he said. " I shall have my luggage sent to the station this morning, and to-night I shall begin my journey."

" I hope you'll be able to come with us to the Ballet," Foss reminded him.

" Thank you, yes."

" You'll have ample time to catch the express to London."

Rennenberg accepted the coffee which Foss passed to him, then he folded his arms on the table and leaned forward.

" There was something which I wanted to ask you," he began.

Foss raised his glance to him and waited. Rennenberg smiled.

" Do you intend to continue your negotiations . . . with the Jewish merchant in Prague ? " he said.

Foss slowly raised his head.

" No ? " said Rennenberg. " No ? " And he broke into laughter which was full of all the elation of his spirit.

Foss said solemnly: " It seems to have excited the suspicions of your people in Berlin and to have got Von Pless into trouble. I am

not anxious to continue. Also, I have heard no more from him.
Nor have I received advices about the forwarding of the goods."

" And you don't intend to send your agent over to continue the
negotiations ? " Rennenberg asked.

" No."

Rennenberg fastened a sharp gaze on him. Foss said:

" If you can contrive to see Von Pless when you reach Berlin,
perhaps you'll tell him."

" I shall see him as soon as I get back."

" Do you think," Foss said, " that you'll be able to settle everything
quite . . . quite . . ."

" Everything," Rennenberg said, suavely. " Quite satisfactorily."

" I'm glad," Foss said.

He rose to depart. He asked Rennenberg to excuse him.

" I shall see you here, at dinner, this evening."

" Thank you, yes."

A little later, Tilly entered the breakfast-room. She greeted Rennenberg with apologies.

" I'm so sorry," she said. " I'm not as energetic as you
are! "

She took her place opposite him. " What a pity you have to leave
us to-night! The weather is going to change. It's going to be cooler.
Couldn't you stay ? "

" I must return to Berlin," Rennenberg said.

" I believe you are glad," she exclaimed.

He looked down at his plate and considered the remark.

" Yes," he said, looking up at her, " I am glad."

Tilly laughed. " You're awfully candid! "

" Best to speak the truth," he said, lowering his eyes again.

" Look," Tilly said. And she held out to him the case with the
pendant.

" Oh, I had almost forgotten . . ."

She interrupted him. " Herr Rennenberg, I'm afraid I can't accept
it. I haven't . . . I don't think I could pay the price."

" No ? " he said, pleasantly.

" I'm afraid I haven't been much help to you."

" None at all," he said, taking the case.

" And another thing," Tilly said. " It's a fake."

Her eyes met his. She had a high, scornful expression.

" Imitation," she added.

Rennenberg nodded. Nothing seemed to upset him.

" Yes, imitation," he admitted.

" A cheap piece of junk from a department store! " she declared.
She laughed derisively. " Your silly stories about my husband and
his agent, Von Pless! "

He seemed momentarily discomfited.   His glance wavered as he put away the case and resumed his meal.

" May I give you some more coffee ? " Tilly said.

" Thank you."

He handed his cup to her.   Again, their eyes met.

" Is it true ? " Tilly asked, lowering her voice and pouring coffee for him.

" Is what true ? "

She did not continue at once.   She rested her elbows on the table and sipped her coffee.

" Are you a member of the German State Police ? " she said.

Rennenberg smiled.   He looked across the table at her.   His smile increased, and he began to laugh.   It swelled to an enormous sound which cracked across the quiet, morning air and made ripples which echoed about Tilly's ears.   She lowered her head and blushed in confusion.

" Please!   Excuse me! " Rennenberg exclaimed.   And he broke into a louder outburst during which he kept trying to stop and beg her pardon.

" Did it sound awfully silly ? " Tilly said, when he had recovered his breath.

" Oh, I must tell them about it when I get back to Berlin! " he exclaimed.   " I beg your pardon, Mrs. Foss.   But, really, it was so . . . so, really so . . ."

She put down her cup and joined her hands under her chin and fastened her splendid eyes in a level gaze on him.

" Now tell me the truth," she said, imperatively.

And this time he could not escape behind a deluge of laughter.   He was conscious of her probing eyes and her determination to have the truth from him.   There was nothing he could say, except to speak candidly.

" A member of the German State Police ? " he said.

" The Gestapo," she said, waiting for his answer.

" Yes," he said quietly, sustaining her gaze, " yes, I am."

It did not appear to have made as much impression on her as he had imagined it would.   Her eyes remained on him and there was no change in the expression of her features.

" Not a very clever one," she said.

It was like a question which she expected him to answer.

" Cleverness . . ." he murmured, pensively.

His tone seemed to her to designate cleverness as a quality which was no longer important now that other and more subtle qualities were demanded of people like himself.

" Who is clever ? " he asked, politely.   " Really clever ?   It is such an overrated gift."

" Perhaps you excel in another way," Tilly said.

" Such as ? "

" Perhaps you are very cruel," she said.

There was silence. They continued the meal. Presently, Tilly looked across at him with an air of grievance.

" The exasperating thing is that nobody would believe me if I told them who you were, who you really were. One of the Gestapo," she exclaimed.

Rennenberg grinned. " Quite! " he said. " Quite! "

★

II

★

By eleven, Rennenberg had packed his cases and been driven into town by Tilly. The coupé stopped outside the main railway terminus and Tilly waited patiently at the wheel while Rennenberg called a porter and left his cases in the Luggage Office. When he returned to the car, Tilly said pleasantly: " Where to, now ? "

" Thank you. I think I shall take a 'bus from here."

" I've plenty of time," Tilly said. " Let me drive you."

" You're very kind, but I won't trouble you."

He raised his hat.

" Well, this evening," Tilly said. " About five. At the central 'bus terminus. Until then . . ."

" Opposite Surrey Street," he said.

" I suppose," she thought, as she watched him board a number four 'bus, " I suppose he knows this city as well as I do." She wondered why he had refused her offer. She saw him disappear inside the 'bus, then she let in the clutch and drove steadily after the big vehicle.

It was not easy to keep pace with it in the streams of traffic weaving along that main road. Nor was it easy for her to watch the alighting passengers. Often, the 'bus travelled at a speed which outstripped her careful progress and which left her far behind with the traffic signals against her. She sped on and overtook it. Then it dawdled from corner to corner, only to sweep ahead round a bend. Passengers swarmed off it when she was at a distance. Others alighted as it travelled slowly around corners. Tilly's eyes ached with the effort she made. Her nerves were tired. She saw the 'bus stop at last at its destination in the city's centre.

It was empty. The driver came down from his cab and joined the conductor amongst a crowd of other 'busmen.

Tilly grimaced. Cleverness was not all. To be effective, it had to equate with certain factors. To pursue a 'bus across a city and to follow the movements of a certain passenger necessitated a little more than vigilance. Luck was what she had needed.

Rennenberg had got out with other passengers shortly before the end of the run. There he had waited on the pavement before crossing to the opposite side of the road. He saw Tilly in her car and watched her draw up at the terminus and look towards the 'bus. Then he knew that she had followed him. He waited until she drove off again before he crossed the road and joined two of his assistants. They were swarthy men.

All three walked slowly along the pavement with Rennenberg in the centre.

" Well ? " he said.

The others were silent. Rennenberg looked sharply from one to the other.

" Well ? "

" He is twenty steps behind us," one of them mumbled.

Rennenberg smiled sardonically. " I understand," he said, bitterly. " You have brought him to me to attend to."

" This one is very clever. We had no luck . . ."

Rennenberg cut short his explanation. " You have had time and opportunity. Plenty. You had all day yesterday, all last night, this morning. And yet he is still alive! "

One of the men murmured: " We made two attempts. No luck . . ."

" But he's behind us now, you say! " Rennenberg said. " Shoot him! In the traffic here . . ."

" It would be dangerous . . ."

" You are afraid! " Rennenberg said, scornfully.

" To-night, he goes to the theatre. We thought . . . in the crowds, afterwards . . ."

" You are afraid," Rennenberg repeated. " You think only of your own lives! You forget to whom your lives are dedicated."

" It's difficult . . . here . . ."

They were despondent and silent after that. Rennenberg said: " You have become infected with . . . with the English air."

They walked on a little way until he saw the clock above Jackson's, the tobacconist.

" Twenty past eleven," he said, halting.

He looked quickly and intently at his companions. He felt a sudden pity for them.

" Travel by the eleven-forty," he said, coldly. " You'll have plenty of time to get to the station."

When he said that, he saw their dark, apprehensive eyes fill rapidly with the reflection of relief and joy. Then again he felt pity for them. He remembered what Tilly had said. " Perhaps you are very cruel." He had a fierce, momentary grievance against her for that. Cruel ? When he could feel this gentle sympathy for men who had failed in their duty, failed in themselves, failed to help him. Men who had left in his hands a final responsibility.

" You are certain he goes to the theatre this evening ? " he said.

They told him the name of the theatre. He smiled.

" You had no luck," he said. " You and the others missed him when he met Collis in the ' Nirvana.' You have missed him since. You had better go. Go home now."

He knew that they hankered to return to Germany, and he believed that he understood why they did. They were sick for home. This alien scene, with its loose freedom, its plenty, its enticements, mocked their ideas and bewildered them. It made a dreadful comparison which confused the mind. It tortured the heart until the spirit craved a return to the familiar environment which had sustained it for so long.

" If I do not return," he said, " tell them that it is my firm conviction that Von Pless and all the others are guilty."

They hesitated. " But Herr Rennenberg . . . you'll come back . . ."

" It's time you went," he said, glancing at the clock.

" If you're convinced about Von Pless," one of them said, " there is no need for you to wait. Come with us! "

" And Foss's man ? " Rennenberg said. " That assassin! "

He looked sternly at them. The moment of parting had come. He took farewell of them crisply, saying it—the fantastic shibboleth, the pantomime.

" Heil Hitler! " in an undertone.

They echoed it in the same way, men, adults, sapient man in the twentieth century of a Christian era!

" Heil Hitler! "

A moment later, he was alone. He stood on that corner in the heart of the city, and he felt a loneliness of such dimensions and profundity that it encompassed his soul. He knew that it was the lot of all human beings to be alone in themselves, to be for ever separate, one soul in one body. But there was love, friendship, comradeship to mitigate the loneliness. There was work and pleasure which enabled the soul to extend itself towards other souls. There was hope. Yet, as he stood there, he felt stripped of those conditions, exposed to the truth of himself, awfully alone. And longing for home.

He envied his assistants who were on their journey to Germany.

He thought sadly of the Fatherland, as though it were suffering. And he pitied himself as he stood so many miles from it and from all the things which had formulated his character and bred a creed in him. It seemed to him that by travelling so far from Germany, as well as by staying here for a fortnight, he had unwittingly broken bonds which could never be repaired. A feeling of hopelessness began in him. He looked about him.

He saw, heard, felt, tasted, and smelt the scene. It was typical of any English city. This was the normal pulse of English life, and his senses detected its character and its strength and weakness. His critical mind began to examine it. He experienced a vague contempt. He lifted his head proudly.

" We shall conquer them," he told himself.

A terrible thing happened. The words were mocked and obliterated by the scene around him. He struggled to find again their sound and his belief in them. He closed his eyes to extinguish the scene about him and to escape all its influence. But he heard still the incessant, lusty clamour of it, and he detected then all the lusty individuality which the voices expressed.

In his own country, the voices were different. They were in unison. They all said the same thing, making a single note. Here, there were thousands of notes. And he knew then that to defeat these people it would be necessary not only to defeat armed forces but the millions of individual voices of the souls of these people as well. A task beyond human effort!

His own spirit collapsed at that moment. An innate essence of its foundation failed. He moved off then, aimlessly, walking only because his body found relief in movement. He wandered far out across the city to a small park in the fashionable western ward. He sat down on one of the seats in the shade. Sometimes, when the seat became full of elderly men and women, he got up and chose another. He was a bewildered soul, sundered from the hysterical vortex which had sustained it. Around him, he saw nursemaids with young children, smart women, prim old men. The air was warm. Perfumes rose from the flower-beds. In the sky, immense white clouds towered. The children sometimes approached him, smiled shyly and spoke to him. The nursemaids addressed him. The old men spoke to him about the weather, about places they had lived in where the climate was very warm. He listened, nodded, smiled, but could not speak, for in his mind there was only a turmoil and thunder of collapsing ideas.

There was thunder in the air, but he did not hear it as such. It seemed to him to come from his immeasurable dejection and his broken hopes. It was like a pulse, and presently it frightened him.

Shortly after three, he left the park and returned quickly to the city,

He boarded a tram and went upstairs. The passage of the air about his bare head soothed his mind. He remembered his vows.

He clung to them, and presently something resumed from them. He remembered his mission. He recalled the falsehoods which Foss had told, and he remembered Jey. When he alighted from the tram, he walked the short distance to the great main thoroughfare of the city and entered the nearest restaurant. He was very thirsty. He ordered tea and sat heavily in the chair and waited.

Then he saw Jey come in.

Jey chose a table opposite him and sat down facing him. There was nothing in Jey's behaviour to indicate what he was thinking or that he had recognized the man who called himself Kurt Rennenberg. He ordered tea and sat waiting patiently for it.

But he was thinking: " He's the chief! They reported to him. And he's sick. Sick with his own dreams! "

He had followed Rennenberg all day, from the moment when the two assistants had left their chief standing alone. Now he was tired and very thirsty and hungry.

Rennenberg watched him furtively. Once, the German's big hand moved under the edge of his jacket towards the hip pocket where he kept his revolver.

" Now! " his pounding thoughts urged him. His leaping heart awaited the moment. " Now! At this short range! Eight feet! Now! Point blank . . . nothing between us! Now! I could not miss him! In less than a minute it would all be over! Five bullets . . . point blank! "

His hand moved towards the accessible pocket, then it stopped. His arm trembled and became limp. The waitress brought the tray and spread the crockery. His thoughts swung back from the impulse and beat like gigantic wings about him. He bowed his head as though in failure and shame.

When the waitress left him, he glanced at Jey. Again their eyes met. He knew that a last chance still awaited him even were he to fail now. But he saw the challenge in Jey's resolute expression; and he brought his hand up to the table and poured himself a cup of tea.

At a few minutes before five he got up and left the restaurant. Jey followed him ten seconds later and saw him a few yards ahead. He stood watching him.

Rennenberg crossed the road and waited near the 'bus terminus until ten minutes past five. A smart coupé drew up near him. A fashionable young woman was driving. Jey recognized her. It was Tilly.

Rennenberg raised his hat and got into the car and was driven off.

Jey puffed and panted. "What a day!" he grumbled, aloud. "He was in a funk! What a funk! I gave him a chance! I waited for him! I wonder why he wouldn't take it."

The heat was very oppressive. It was moist, and the sound of distant thunder was in the air. Hot, slow gushes of wind flowed through the streets, and already the whole western sky was dark with cloud.

Jey went slowly back to the "Crown" in Derby Street to pass the two hours before the Ballet.

★

III

★

Towards four that afternoon, Kelpey left his office and went to Dewlash's room. The messengers had brought tea to the staff not long ago, and Dewlash had pushed aside her papers and was sitting with her arms folded on the desk. When she glanced up at Kelpey, his presence did not seem to alter the flow of her thoughts. She looked at him as though he were the focus of all those thoughts.

"I've lost my silver pencil," he said.

"Have you?"

She stirred her cup.

"The day before yesterday," Kelpey said.

"Why don't you advertise for it?"

"I know where I lost it," he said.

Their eyes met. "In your room," he added.

"Here?"

"No. In your flat."

He added quickly: "I called about nine, the night before last. You remember . . . I said . . ."

"Yes, I remember."

"I said I would call."

She sipped the tea and then lowered the cup and said:

"You were late."

"Did you wait?" he asked.

"Yes, I did. Until nearly nine."

"I was there just after."

"But you said you'd come about eight," she reminded him.

"I'm sorry," he said. "I'm sorry."

"So was I. I would have enjoyed a run in your car."

She looked up at him. Her features broke into a smile. Then she laughed softly and leaning forward, she rested her hand for an instant on his. "Next time, don't be late!" she said.

" No. Of course not. But when . . . when can I . . ."

She opened the drawer of her desk and took out her handbag.

" Is this it ? " she said, holding up the pencil.

She offered it to him. " Take it now," she said.

He heard footsteps in the corridor outside and recognized them. Those of the Commissionaire and a visitor. They stopped outside his room, and he heard the Commissionaire knock on the door.

" When ? " Kelpey said, quickly. " To-night ? After the theatre ? If I bring the car, can I drive you home ? "

She seemed to consider it. She put aside the little tray of tea things and slipped a fresh piece of paper into her typewriter.

" To-night ? " he asked. " After . . ."

" But I'm going with a friend," she said. She glanced up at him and added: " She lives quite near me."

His face brightened. " All right. I could drive you both home."

He heard the Commissionaire enter his room.

" I'll see you . . ." he said, quietly. " I'll look out for you . . . afterwards, with the car. Shall I ? "

Then the Commissionaire tapped on Dewlash's door and came in.

" Shall I ? " Kelpey said.

She glanced up at him with a smile and nodded quickly.

" Oh, Mr. Kelpey," said the Commissionaire, " Mrs. Collis here wants to see you."

Kelpey saw her behind him. Clothed neatly and simply, she was no longer the slatternly person he had encountered at the house. Nor was she possessed by the same cautious spirit as then. She was quite different. Distress was in her mood, and although she tried to control it, it glimmered in her and flashed into momentary expression with a verbosity which changed almost at once to her customary timidity.

" It's about him," she exclaimed as soon as Kelpey brought her to his room. " See ? I thought I'd come and ask you because you know 'im, and you called, and so . . ."

" Sit down, please," Kelpey said.

She took the chair and seated herself on the edge of it. Watching her, he could not help comparing her to her husband. Her character in its swift manifestations was furtive, not fearful, but sly and reduced to these attempts to create little channels for itself before she would trust herself to words.

" What's happened ? " Kelpey said.

She was no longer the rejoicing spirit dreaming of wealth or ready to let Collis disappear along the murky road of his fate. Fear tapped her. Remorse agitated her. Her courage had dwindled, and something which she had not suspected in herself now commanded her. A dim sense of duty. But the ruins of dreams were in her moist, troubled eyes, and contrition was eloquent in her tearful tone. Anxiety stirred her cracked little hands in a writhing, tiny storm.

" I haven't seen 'im since las' night," she said, sniffing back the tears. " He went out 'bout eight or nine, and he never come back, not all night."

Kelpey heard it and was afraid. " Rennenberg, and Smith and Lane," he thought.

" Perhaps he's had to go out of town," he suggested.

" No. I would 'ave known. No, see ? He went off quick. He was wearin' the old grey jacket, the one what he keeps for wearin' in the 'ouse."

" Didn't you ask him ? " Kelpey said.

" No. I never asked 'im. He went out quick."

" He'll come back. If I were you, I wouldn't worry."

She put a sodden handkerchief to her nose. Her body shook.

" But all his things is in the jacket at 'ome. Keys and money and everything."

" Perhaps he's upstairs," Kelpey said. " I'll run up and see."

He knew that he was not there. He knew that Collis had not been in all day. Still, he thought he would make sure.

" I'll see," he said.

Foss met him in the corridor at the foot of the bare stairs leading to the attics.

" Run up and ask that fellow Collis to come down to my office," he said. " I want to speak to him."

" I don't think he's there, sir. His wife says she hasn't seen him since last night."

Foss made an irritable little gesture. " Run up and see. Make sure. If he isn't there, leave a note for him to see me to-morrow."

He passed quickly towards his own room while Kelpey ran up the narrow flight. At the top, Kelpey listened for an instant before rapping on the door with his knuckles.

" Collis ! " he called.

He tried the handle. The door was locked.

" Collis ! Are you there ? "

There was no reply. He waited a little longer and then returned to his room.

" He's not there."

" I know," Daisy said. " Something must 'ave happened to 'im."

" I wouldn't worry," Kelpey said. " He's all right."

" I'm afraid," she confessed.

"There's nothing to be afraid of," he said, as though he and she faced the same danger. "Is there?" he added.

It came slowly off her tongue. "Yes, there is."

"What?" he said.

In a little gasp of terror which seemed to escape from the restraint of her fractured caution, she told him.

"There's somebody called Rennenberg."

Her pale glance flicked towards him. She saw his own look of alarm. At once, all her fears were confirmed, and in the next minute she told him everything. The table crashing down at the "Nirvanna": the awful day which Collis had spent yesterday; his telephone conversation with Rennenberg.

". . . and there's this Jey . . . somebody called Jey."

It opened everything with a baleful expansion. It was as much his concern as it was hers. He had to listen and try to help.

"Have you told the police? Have you looked . . ."

She bent her head and wept loudly. "She just sits there and cries," he thought, angrily.

"Hadn't you better tell the police," he said. And he thought desperately: "Let them come into it! Let's clear it up before . . . before . . ."

"No. See? My sister said that we better wait, so I thought . . ." she began, then she stopped and sniffed loudly.

She remembered her secret treachery, her dreams. Remorse admonished her, and she cowered and wept before it.

"I'm frightened something's 'appened to him."

The telephone rang. Kelpey sat down to answer it. Messengers left letters for him to sign and took away others. The forlorn, crumpled little figure on the edge of the chair sat like centuries of pauper-consciousness waiting for anyone—for Kelpey, for authority—to help her.

"Look," Kelpey said, when he replaced the receiver. "Wait downstairs in the Commissionaire's room. Don't say anything to anyone. Just wait there, and when I've finished up here I'll come down."

"Yes, all right."

He repeated his advice and led her to the stairs. Half an hour later, when he had finished his work and when Foss and the staff had gone, he sat down at the telephonist's table and made a call to one of the hospitals.

It took several minutes. Speaking at last to the porter in the Casualty Department, he enquired for Collis, somebody called Collis, perhaps a casualty. He was asked to wait. He heard voices in the distance, footsteps, a voice at the far end, this time a young, peremptory, female voice.

" Yes! What is it ? "

He stated his enquiry again.

" Hold the line ! "

He waited. The receiver irked his ear. His thoughts were confused. He heard a door slam in the hospital. " Slow, so slow they are," he thought, " not organized, not like the American hospitals in films." Then a loud, rude male voice:

" What's this you want ? Somebody . . ."

Kelpey went over his request again.

" No. Nobody brought in here that name."

He tried another hospital. The porter said: " What ? In a grey jacket, blue serge trousers . . ."

" Collis. Jack Collis . . ."

" . . . this morning, about half-past nine, man with a fractured ankle. Man about forty-five, about. Loss of memory, and shock. Nothing to identify. . . ."

Kelpey described Collis. The porter said briskly: " Yes, that's the chap. Sounds very like. Could you come over ? "

" I'll come now. I'll bring his wife."

He went down to Daisy. " I 'phoned to the hospital. They think . . ."

She started to cry. Leaning against the wall and dabbing at her nose, she broke into a long outburst of remorse interspersed with sobs.

" I told her . . . I said it would all come back on me . . . and that what you take you 'ave to pay for . . . I said . . ."

" He's got a fractured ankle, and he's suffering from loss of memory. I said we'd come over straight away."

He led her out to the 'bus stage. The crowds from the big offices swarmed past her, brushed her aside as though she were a leaf against their lusty gale. She stood almost helplessly, bewildered by the vigorous healthy pulse of the streaming crowds, unable to scramble, afraid in her timid heart. Kelpey drew her back to the wall.

" I don't know . . ." he murmured.

He turned to her. " Look! Wait here. Don't go. I'm going to bring my car, and we'll drive over quickly. I'll be back in ten minutes. Don't move from here."

He hurried away and swung on to a 'bus. Within ten minutes he was back, beckoning to her from the curb. He leaned over and opened the door for her.

" Jump in! "

She got in awkwardly, tripping, then suddenly stepping back to the pavement.

" I'm not used to cars."

He got out and helped her in. He thought of Collis: surely a rich

212

man; a man who made money, who owned property. What for ? And to what use did he put it ? The rancid, stifling house, with its dead furniture, dead air ! For what purpose . . . so much money, so much work and criminal scheming ? Money ! And no other purpose. I'm not used to cars !

He drove quickly. Time, too, seemed to Kelpey to race ahead of them. It was swifter. It had broken from some curious control which all his plans for the evening seemed to have had upon it until this fearful little woman had come to him. It fled forward. He saw it measured in masses of minutes on the clocks. Twenty to six. Ten to.

They reached the hospital shortly before six. Kelpey led Daisy through the doors to the hall of the Casualty Department. The porter at the desk was waiting for them.

" Oh, about . . . you've come about that casualty."

He led them to one of the numerous little surgeries around the big waiting-hall. Kelpey saw a few patient figures on the benches. Dull, inquisitive eyes watched him. A young child was scrambling over the back of the bench. Whispered voices sounded. The child spoke aloud.

" Ma ! She's crying ! "

A blowsy woman gripped the child angrily. The long, tiresome hours swept through her hands as she shook the boy.

" Di'n't I tell you ! " In an awed whisper. " Now you sit down ! "

Patience, the supplication to all the authority of relief, of something for nothing, of hallowed medical skill ; the tradition which made them approach nurse, doctor, porter with the cringe of extreme humility ; all this was upon them. They whispered. They waited patiently. Patients. They would wait for hours. They would have to. They had a card in dirty fists. A doctor—almighty being!—had told them to come. A porter told them to wait. They had done it for generations. And nobody ever came to tell them that they need not whisper, need not be intimidated by nurse, doctor, the air of the place. And Daisy was one of them. Whispering, sir-ing the porter in the white jacket.

" Wait here," the porter said. " I'll tell Sister."

The little room had a large, ugly couch, two chairs, and a smell of carbolic and ether. Sickness, disease, suffering. It dripped in the air. Not even the gay laugh of two nurses off-duty in the grim garden outside the window could dispel it. Laughter in the face of incessant sickness and pain and casualty.

" What was that you said about someone called Rennenberg ? " Kelpey said.

Daisy looked at him behind a veil of anxiety.

"You said your husband telephoned to him last night," he added.

Something like a ripple moved across her face; and out of the pale skin and the little lines and the wan, blinking eyes, he saw emerge the cunning and caution which he had encountered on his first meeting with her. Her gaze wavered from his.

"Did I? I can't remember sayin' . . ."

"But you told me! You said that he 'phoned to Rennenberg, and that there was some trouble!"

Her hands clasped quickly and she made a plausible expression to accompany her words.

"Oh, yes, that's right, yes! I sort of . . . well, he di'n't say exactly . . . I mean, I might 'ave took it wrong, because he never says much about business to me, see?"

"You said . . ."

Her fear of truth in the form of words was the one positive thing in her character; and to avoid anything which circumscribed her timid soul with a statement of fact, her sly nature had given her wits the speed of the hare, the little bird, the rabbit.

"I don't know 'is business! He never tells me . . ."

"Like a rabbit!" Kelpey thought. He was angry. When he spoke, his voice was loud.

"But didn't you come to my room not long ago and sit there and tell me the whole story? About how . . ."

The door opened noiselessly and a young house surgeon entered the room. His hands were in his pockets. He lightly kicked back the door with his slippered foot and stood before Daisy and Kelpey, saying pleasantly: "I hope you're not going to be disappointed!"

The stethoscope dangling from the outer breast pocket of his jacket swung with his movements. His hand pushed it back; and as Daisy spoke, he turned away and then gazed sideways at her with an intent look.

"Yes, sir, my 'usband went out las' night. . . ."

In a pleasant voice, without rudeness, he cut her short.

"What is your name, please?"

"Collis, sir. Daisy Collis."

"Can you remember what your husband was wearing when he left home last night?"

"Oh, yes, sir! The grey jacket and his blue trousers belonging to 'is blue suit."

He grinned. "That's it! And a biggish man, round head, hair on his hands?"

"Yes, you could say . . ."

A Sister entered the room. Small and practical in a quick way, she took charge of Daisy.

" You've come to find your husband ? "

They all smiled. The house surgeon opened the door and as the Sister and Daisy went ahead, he followed with Kelpey. They went through the Casualty waiting-hall and through the outer hall to a corridor leading to the wards.

" Are you a relative ? " the house surgeon asked.

" No. Her husband has a suite of rooms above our place. I know him. She came to my office about two hours ago. . . ."

" You say you know him ? "

Before Kelpey could answer, they were joined by a thin, middle-aged woman in a dark uniform.

" Matron! " the young doctor said. " His wife has come! "

She walked with them to the ward, past the doors of other wards, past little rooms in which probationers were sorting medical stores. A Sister drew her aside once.

" Matron, Mr. Hutchinson can't operate until eight."

" Oh, what a nuisance! But . . . I'll 'phone to him."

" This chap has a fractured ankle, and the police . . ." began the house surgeon, addressing Kelpey. Then the Matron joined them.

" Mr. Hutchinson has been detained. I hope he won't be later than eight! "

The three of them turned into the ward. A nurse opened the red screens around a bed not far from the door, and as doctor and Matron and Sister went forward with Daisy, Kelpey had a glimpse of Collis's big body under the bedclothes and the surgical cage over his foot. Voices mingled quietly: that of the Sister and house surgeon speaking to Collis, then Daisy's tremulous remarks ; and the Matron saying to the Sister :

" . . . a matter of minutes, or perhaps weeks . . . in such cases."

Kelpey was at the fringe with the young ward nurse. He craned his neck and edged forward inquisitively. Collis was staring at Daisy with heavy, uncomprehending eyes in a face whose earthy hue was darkened by the stubble of his beard.

" Jack! Jack! Don't you know me ? I'm Daisy! "

It was a thin, timid sound, yet resolute to find him, to entice him from all the mists and chaos of his life and to bring him to a kind of safety. It was like a thin little line which she hurled towards him and which reached him but which he could not grip.

" Collis! " the young doctor said, bending over the patient. " Jack Collis! That's your name, isn't it ? Jack Collis. Here's Daisy . . . your wife, Daisy . . . come to see you."

Collis spoke then. " What's it all about ? Where am I ? Who are all these . . ."

His voice was from fear and regions of confusion from which he was unable to detach himself. And suddenly, as though from the impact on his senses of the sounds and faces, he closed his eyes and put out his hands to shield himself. His words came in a loud dribble. He was gasping.

"Don't look at me! Let me alone! Let me alone!"

The Sister standing back beside the Matron shook her head. The austere Matron, standing with folded hands, said:

"Let her sit down. . . ."

"A chair, please!" the Sister whispered to the nurse.

". . . and when he becomes quiet he might recognise her."

The doctor was saying softly: "That's all right, Collis. You're in hospital. Everything's all right. And here's Daisy. Here's your wife, Daisy!"

"Jack! It's me!"

The Matron whispered something to the Sister to which the latter replied with a significant glance and a nod of her head.

"Let me know," the Matron said. "The Inspector asked that we should inform him at once."

Kelpey heard her with alarm. Inspector! Inform him! He wondered what ramifications the affair would have, and how deeply it would penetrate his own life. He glanced at the clock on the wall above the door. Ten past seven. And he wondered if he could get away in time for the Ballet.

Waiting, he heard Daisy's wisp of words. The Sister was murmuring to the house surgeon. From the ward itself, the sounds of a curiously active world lifted on the warm air: the light rattle of surgical instruments on a rubber-wheeled trolley; the healthy call of a young patient to another on the opposite side: "Pawn to Rook's fourth!"; the slight sound of music from a portable gramophone; the dragging cry of pain from behind the red screens around another bed; and laughter and quick voices from a little group of patients in chairs. It was a whole world, detached from the outside world.

"Daisy! Hullo, Daisy!"

Collis spoke. His voice was loud, full of surprise. Recognition was in it. He started to laugh softly.

"Daisy! What's the time? Where . . ."

The threads were resuming in him, running together again, with the familiar, constant presence of Daisy rushing into them beside him.

"There!" said the Sister, briskly, laying a hand on Daisy's shoulder. "Now you're happy!"

The doctor came away from the bed.

"I think I'll go now," Kelpey said. "She'll want to stay."

"Yes, she had better stay with him for a while," the Sister said.

Kelpey edged back out of sight of Collis. He did not want Collis to see him. He wanted to get away, to stand apart from what had happened, for there was an Inspector who was waiting to be informed. There was foul play, somewhere, and he was anxious to remain at a distance from Collis and Rennenberg.

The house surgeon walked down the ward with him and out along the corridor.

" You know him ? " he asked Kelpey.

" He has offices above the place where I work."

" Where's that ? "

Kelpey told him.

" Oh, he was found in another part of the city. The police brought him in. He was found on the stairs. They think he'd been locked in a room at the top and had broken his way out."

" A nasty affair! "

" You don't know anyone who could give information to the police about . . ."

He stopped and looked quickly at Kelpey.

" I know very little about him. I just see him now and then at work."

" Well, thanks for bringing his wife along. It's helped us."

It was a quarter to eight when Kelpey reached his apartments. He was in a hurry. He hardly noticed the storm gathering over the city. He saw vicious violet light stab from sky to earth, and heard the crack of thunder. A few heavy drops of rain fell, and the air was momentarily filled with a sweet, fresh odour ; then the heat and stillness resumed until long gusts of hot wind stirred the accumulated dust of the gutters and pavements into swift movement under the sombre light of the sky. But he gave no heed to it. He was hungry and thirsty, and late. He drank tea and crammed some lettuce and ham into his mouth and hurried into his bedroom.

Scrambling out of his clothes and reaching for his evening suit, he thought despairingly : " I'm late! It's started by now."

Eight struck from the neighbouring church tower. His hands fell in dejection, and the dinner jacket which he had held fell from his fingers to the bed.

" It's no use," he said, unhappily. " I've missed it."

He knew why he was late. It was not because he had taken Daisy to the hospital and been detained there ; instead, it was because he had taken a letter to Collis and asked him to translate it. And from that one foolish action so much had happened that he wondered if its consequences would ever cease to echo in his life.

He pondered it all for a long time, seeing Collis's plight as the first stroke following the advent of the bogus Rennenberg. Others would surely follow. From all the silence and obscurity which covered the German, events would begin. And then ? He puzzled himself until his mind was confused. At last, merely to escape all these persistent, revolving ideas and the presentiments which they bred in him, he finished dressing.

He left the house at a quarter to nine and drove to the theatre. He had never before seen the sky so dark in daylight. The sullen face of storm leaned over the city and darkened the streets, hovering in masses of grey cloud in which lightning trembled and from which heavy drops of rain fell in brief showers. The heat was as relentless as ever ; but the brief, thin showers filled the air with a moisture which was sweet and refreshing to the parched lungs. Thunder pulsated across the sky, and from the laden clouds more heavy drops of rain were loosened. Some leaves from the trees opposite the theatre were whirled loose by a gust of warm wind and sent in a rustling scatter across the roadway. And all these signs of the imminent storm gave a welcome sense of movement and release to Kelpey's mind as he entered the theatre.

It was sustained by the chatter and activity of the audience returning from the foyers and bars after the last interval. The orchestra had come back, and already the instruments were sounding in prolonged, repeated notes and little runs and rushes. Throughout the theatre, there was an air of anticipation which matched Kelpey's feeling of relief. He found his seat and sat down and looked about for Dewlash. He saw Foss and his wife and Rennenberg, but he failed to notice Dewlash and her companion a short distance to his right ; although had he turned in that direction he would have seen Dewlash lean forward slowly and glance at him and then settle herself perhaps more happily than before. Perhaps because she had seen him at last. Perhaps because word that the storm had broken had reached the audience during the last moments of the interval and she was anxious about some conveyance home. But he did not see her. He anticipated the end of the performance, and felt that curious sense of relief in himself as he settled himself and saw the lights expire and the curtain rise.

But he felt at once that he had missed something which was essential to complete understanding and enjoyment of the Ballet. He referred to the programme only to find it as unintelligible as before. He had arrived too late. Something had happened: the theme had been stated already in all the delicate terms of music and movement, and what he saw was only the flowing, exuberant climax of it ; and what he heard was only the full flood of sound from all the variations of the theme as they were beckoned into this last act. Nevertheless, he was entranced. It was new to his experience. It was sound expressed in the subtlety of movement. It was movement made delicately exquisite by the bodies of the dancers. Austere and formal one moment, it became frivolous the next. It was comedy, and then tragedy. There were figures which, presently, he recognized in their rôles, so that there grew gradually in his mind some perception of the theme. But it passed to conclusion long before he could find the full measure of appreciation in himself. It delighted him but ended when he had tasted only half its power to satisfy the very senses which it had rendered to him.

Yet those new senses in him seemed to him to open a fresh phase of life ; and as he rose from his seat and made his way towards Dewlash, he saw her as someone who, like himself, would remember this evening for its significant beginning of a new period in her life and his own.

He mentioned that he had been detained and had not arrived until the last act. She introduced him to her companion, and the three of them walked slowly with the rest of the audience going towards the main exits. The foyer and stairs were crowded, and after a few minutes the audience was halted. Word came back along the stairs and gangways that the storm had broken, that the street was flooded, that traffic was disorganized.

Kelpey saw people beginning to move towards the side-exits leading to the narrow street flanking the theatre. His own car was parked there, and he guided his two companions rapidly towards those doors.

" This way," he said. " If we're quick . . ."

He explained: " My car is opposite the door. It only means crossing the pavement."

They took his arms gratefully and entered the pit and hurried along the rows towards the passage. A little crowd was gathered, hesitating, and the door opening on the street. There, a gust of warm, rain-drenched air met them.

" Right opposite the door," he said to Dewlash, pointing to his car.

It was no more than a dozen feet away, but it was separated from them by a curtain of torrential rain which drummed and hissed upon the pavement and made a flood. Lightning stood almost solidly in a vivid, violet trunk from earth to sky as he moved out in an impetuous rush and opened the car's door. Dim behind the downpour, he stood and beckoned to them, hand outstretched, rain already saturating his raincoat. The skies seemed to crack with an enormous single sound which roared away through space and loosened rain in a heavier torrent. Hesitating for an instant, Dewlash and her friend shook their heads, beckoning him to come back. The rain almost hid him from sight. But he was beside them in the next moment, his young hands firmly gripping their arms, guiding them out to the car and quickly helping them in. He closed the door on them and sped round through rain which stung him, which poured heavily upon him, and through water which was swirling across the roadway in ripples which lapped his ankles. Again, the great wrist of lightning threw out its vicious fingers. The thunder was muffled when he got into the car and closed the door.

A moment later, he drove off carefully, moving out cautiously through the little floods and the puddles of the side street to the wide main road where a wild mist of rain cut down upon the vehicle.

" Can you get through ? " Dewlash asked, leaning forward. " Will it be all right ? "

Her hand rested lightly on his shoulder. He turned slightly, very quickly, and nodded.

" I can manage," he said.

She did not remove her hand. It rested on his shoulder as though to help and encourage him.

Through the windscreen, he saw in the semi-circle swept by the wiper on the glass a distorted scene, grey, shot with startling, gigantic stems of lightning, flooded in the road by sweeping torrents that thundered on the car's roof and spilled across the bonnet. It was almost impossible to see in that wild downpour. Pavements and gutters were no longer visible, for rising floods coveted them ; and the rain splashing there raised a low fringe which the wind agitated until the entire scene seemed swept by steam. The lightning momentarily blinded him. Yet he was conscious all the time of some indefinable, delicious progress of his life from the past three days of tension, heat, anxiety, to this storm, and onwards towards a future in which the hand that rested lightly and a little nervously and yet gratefully upon him during this difficult journey would swing fondly in his own.

★

IV

★

Only a small part of the audience left the theatre. The rest remained on the stairs and along the corridors and in the foyer. The management left open the premises for shelter, and in the little lounges coffee and sandwiches were served. Occasionally, to these cheerful people in the lounges someone would come from amongst the crowds lining the stairs and relate pessimistic details of the storm: traffic suspended ; roads and pavements flooded ; the tempest unabated. And in a desultory way those who had finished their coffee would saunter towards the stairs and stand amidst the crowds there to watch the rain and the lightning.

Foss and Tilly and Rennenberg were at the foot of the main stairway, near the gilded doors.

" My car is in the car park, fifty yards away," Foss said to Rennenberg. " I really don't know how I could reach it through this. Have you plenty of time ? "

" Two hours," Rennenberg said. " My suitcases are at the station. I have only to follow them."

He smiled slowly and rather pessimistically.

" I should think an hour would see the worst over," Foss said. " I could try then. Have to. You won't get a taxi or 'bus on a night like this."

" Plenty of time yet," Rennenberg murmured.

Standing against the wall, they watched the scene and talked in desultory snatches.

On the opposite side of the road, in the doorways of large shops, many of the audience were sheltering. They had got that far and then given up. Now they were watching apprehensively the rising flood which moment by moment edged towards them over the gutter and across the pavement. Bolder ones amongst them stepped out quickly and splashed their way to shelter in safer places a little distance along the road. Around them, stiff streaks of lightning seemed to play; and those who remained in the doorways saw their companions of a moment before surrounded by the reflected strokes and the thick torrents of the rain.

Amongst those who remained was Jey. He watched the rain and the lightning. It was like a portent. All day, he had waited for a call from Foss ; and when he returned to the " Crown " shortly after five, he expected to find awaiting him the message which would send him on his journey. If it was to come at all, it would have to come now—within the next hour—for the midnight express was the last train by which he could travel to-day. And to-day was the last one on which he must travel in order to reach his destination by the stipulated time. His cases were packed, and in himself he was prepared.

But he knew that Foss would not give him the signal. He had a presentiment of disaster: he felt that plans had failed, and that he would not be given the signal to depart.

" It won't happen," he told himself. " There's going to be a war."

He saw the hard needles of the rain striking the pools in the road and making floods all around. The lightning illuminated it all in a baleful brilliance and was reflected in sudden, blinding shocks from the running water on the road and pavement. The thunder reminded him of gunfire ; and as he smelled the fresh, cold, steely odour of the saturated air, he thought: " Steel . . . smells like cold steel . . . metal . . . in the air! "

And it was like a portent. " This," he thought, "this is what it will be like! A storm of metal! They've told us that."

The storm after a long period of tension and uncertainty. He mused about it, and saw the water approaching his feet. He glanced at his wrist-watch. Nearly eleven.

"The 'buses will be full," he thought. "I'll have to walk, or else wait for hours here. The storm will last all night, and I'm fairly caught in it!"

He decided to cross to the theatre before the flood caught him. And he knew that someone in the crowd there would surely offer him a lift. Foss, perhaps. It was his only chance now that the water was only a foot away from him.

He chose his course, seeing a gap a little to the left. He saw the crowd near the theatre's portico, and he noticed Foss and Tilly.

"He'll give me a lift," he thought. "And he'll tell me about my journey. He'll say no."

He drew the collar of his raincoat higher about his neck and jammed down his hat about his ears before he poised himself to cut across.

Rennenberg had seen him and was watching him.

"Now," thought the German, his mind pounding from the pulse of his desperate heart. "Now! Before he comes across! Before Foss is able to tell him! Before he sets out! Now!"

His right hand unbuttoned his coat and moved quickly to the weapon in his hip pocket. He saw Jey poised to run. He saw him settle again the collar of his raincoat and jam down his hat. He edged his way to the front steps, and then burst through towards the pavement at the instant when Jey began to run towards the theatre.

Foss saw him. He saw Jey, too. He had been watching Jey and hoping that he would not cross and speak to him.

He called loudly: "Rennenberg! I say! Don't go . . ."

He knew what was going to happen. He was struck by an awful fear. His words dried up as he gasped. He saw people turn and stare at him, and heard a little ripple of excitement begin with a murmur and swell quickly, as his own fear was swelling.

Rennenberg had drawn his revolver. Jey was nimbly jumping the puddles and coming over. Foss tried to signal to him. And Rennenberg—turning for an instant and seeing Foss make that sign, and hearing the shouts from the crowd—rushed into the roadway.

A big saloon car emerged from the side street and came splashing swiftly along the road. Rennenberg, with arm raised and revolver aimed, was in its path. Lightning swathed the scene for an instant: the shining, rain-shrouded saloon ; Jey running ; the German stanced a yard from the car. The klaxon sounded wildly. Foss ran out. His shout was smothered by the thunder, by the furious note of the klaxon and the screams from the crowd.

Foss saw Jey dart to one side. He saw the German stumble to avoid the car and become an ungainly, slipping form that fell sprawling before the wheels. A shot sounded, and a window high above the opposite pavement cracked and opened to send down a tinkling cascade of glass at the instant before the big saloon lumbered slowly over the prone body and came to rest across the road's camber.

A strangled cry sounded. The man who had called himself Kurt Rennenberg was lying on his back amidst the rippling pools and the beating rain. His arms were outflung and the revolver lay a few feet from his hand. His right leg was horribly bent under him. He rolled over, muddy water saturating him, blood pooling for an instant and then merging with the flood which jerked his hat and pulped it. His bare head showed palely for a moment before the muddy water discoloured it.

Men ran out, Foss amongst them, Jey beside him. A caped constable strode towards them and leaned over that saturated form.

" What now ? " Foss thought frantically. " And now what ? What now ? "

" Dead ! " somebody said.

Hearing that, and pushing his way forward, Foss refused to believe it ; but looking down he saw that it was true.